Charles smiled. His ice-blue eyes pierced her heart, as did his words. Tears she fought to control filled her eyes, her throat throbbed with pain, she couldn't swallow.

Beth turned away—desperately wanting to run, to be far from this man she'd so foolishly come to love with all her heart. Was she forever destined to fall in love with the wrong man?

Charles took her in his arms, searching the depths of the tears she tried to deny. "Beth," he began, "I've waited too long for just the right moment to tell you. . . . "

I can't bear it, she thought. *I don't want to hear. . . .*

The Secrets of the Roses

A NOVEL

Lila Peiffer

THOMAS NELSON PUBLISHERS
Nashville • Atlanta • London • Vancouver

Published in Nashville, Tennessee, by Thomas Nelson, Inc., Publishers, and distributed in Canada by Word Communications, Ltd., Richmond, British Columbia, and in the United Kingdom by Word (UK), Ltd., Milton Keynes, England.

Unless otherwise noted, Scripture quotations are from The Holy Bible, KING JAMES VERSION.

Scripture quotations noted NASB are from THE NEW AMERICAN STANDARD BIBLE, Copyright © 1960, 1962, 1963, 1968, 1971, 1972, 1973, 1975, 1977 by The Lockman Foundation and are used by permission.

Library of Congress Cataloging-in-Publication Data

Peiffer, Lila.
  The secrets of the roses : a novel / Lila Peiffer.
    p. cm.
  ISBN 0-7852-8192-4 (pb)
  1. Upper classes—California, Northern—Fiction. 2. Family—California, Northern—Fiction. I. Title.
PS3566.E335S4   1994
813'.54—dc20   93-42076
                                                CIP

Printed in the United States of America
1 2 3 4 5 6 7 8 — 99 98 97 96 95 94

To my precious family,
who are also my best friends:

To Rick,
my husband and forever sweetheart

To our children,
Terry, Eileen, Tim, Sally,
their loving spouses,
and our eight grandchildren

The gentle glow of dawn filtered across the rose garden. Each new ray of sunlight added another brush stroke to the picture Elizabeth Townsend indelibly painted on the canvas of her mind. From her bedroom alcove high above, she savored each detail with the discriminating eye of an artist who might never pass that way again.

Roses of endless variety captured her eye, each with its own message and memory. The pinks and reds blended casually with the phlox, blue lobelia and white alyssum that spilled along low borders of the taller masses of color. The masterpiece below had the exquisite composition of a still life, but nothing in her life was standing still. Tomorrow would attest to that.

Other dawns would have found her down among the roses, tending and talking as softly to them as to the two beloved children she could never call her own. The roses shared secrets, known only to her and God. But now from above, before the full light of day, she began gathering a bouquet of memories that spanned a quarter of a century and beyond. . . .

Charles had designed and built Rosehaven for her when she was a young bride, and its magnificence still bloomed fresh every morning. She studied the tapestry of romantically evocative fountains, pools and pathways among the typically English gardens. It was the perfect setting for the half-timbered Tudoresque mansion which appeared to have been mined from a distant past. Rather than being nestled in this quiet, affluent community just twenty-five miles south of San Francisco, the estate seemed more like the English countryside where she had spent half her childhood. And slowly, lovingly, she began to let it go. She had come to the end of an era.

Her heart felt no sadness, but an inseparable blend of bittersweet nostalgia. She wondered if she would have the courage to go back and live it again—to endure the burden of the secrets that had protected those she loved.

Her years at Rosehaven had been exquisitely rich with the brush strokes of beauty and joy, yet she realized that the companions of purpose and pain had given the scene its deeper, more meaningful hues.

She knew the ache of pruning away those tender areas of her life that cut low and deep. But along the way she discovered heartache turned to joy in the hands of God, a revelation she yearned for her sophisticated San Francisco friends to understand. They probably never would, and they'd certainly never understand what they would read in tomorrow's newspapers . . .

ELIZABETH TOWNSEND, WIDOW OF WEALTHY ARCHITECT/ENTREPRENEUR, CHARLES TOWNSEND, GRANTS ROSEHAVEN TO PHILANTHROPIC FOUNDATION

The ring of the phone interrupted Beth's thoughts. She decided to ignore this unwelcome intrusion, but then reconsidered. It must be something important since it was now only 7:00 A.M.

"Good mornin', hon. It's Merribelle—Ah jus' knew you'd be up, darlin'. Ah'm going over our reservations for the Art League luncheon at the Mark Hopkins today and Ah didn't see your lil' name, but of course *you* don't need a reservation, and you are coming, aren't you?"

Those syrupy Southern tones had wooed her into so many commitments through the years—but not today. "No, Merribelle, I won't be there."

"But sweetie, that's impossible! You know this is our recognition luncheon. You just have to be there. It'll ruin everything if you're not." The usually saccharine voice turned to exasperation.

Beth understood her friend's frustration. Merribelle's pleading hinted that for the fourth consecutive year Beth would receive what amounted to the League's Outstanding Woman of the Year award. She felt like saying, "Frankly, my dear, I don't give a darn," but of course she didn't.

She wasn't being rude, or arrogant, or ungrateful of appreciation. She simply had become weary of being the belle of the ball. Her life was linked with more people than it could hold, and their demands were more than she could carry. The new challenge she had created for herself would consume her total energy. The very thought of it stimulated her to fresh vitality.

Beth's voice was sympathetic. "I'm so sorry, Merribelle, but it's just not possible for me to get away today. I have some very important things to take care of. That's why I didn't make a reservation." She braced herself for the explosion.

"What could be more important than our most prestigious luncheon of the year? Surely you know what's happening, and Ah'd think you all could change your lil' ol' plans."

"I just can't, dear."

"Well, what in the world are you doing that's such a big deal? Ah haven't wanted to say anything, deah, but you're just so different since . . . well, since, you know, since . . . Charles has been gone. He was a wonderful man. Ah believe you really loved him and 'spected you'd just fall apart in grief, you two were so close. You didn't at all. You just carried on with your usual faith and strength. Ah'd be a basket case if Ah lost Henry. Ah hate to say this, but either you didn't love Charles as much as we thought, or you have a bigger God than Ah'll ever understand. Beth, what are you up to?"

A choking lump swelled in Beth's throat. Tears cascaded down her cheeks in a sudden torrent from the sting of those words that had broken her quiet reverie. Her voice strained to utter, "You'll find out tomorrow."

Oblivious to her own insensitivity, Merribelle's curiosity demanded, "Darlin', you can tell me. Hon, what is it? You're not ill or anything terrible, are you? Or is there another man?"

The stabbing hurt turned to instant anger. *Lord, You take control of my tongue and my temper,* Beth whispered under her breath. "I said you'll find out tomorrow, Merribelle, and that's all I can say now. Goodbye—hope the luncheon goes well."

Beth felt numb, immobilized. She replaced the ivory and gold French phone in its cradle on the delicately carved writing desk and stared blankly through the lace curtains. For sure, she had a bigger God than Merribelle would ever understand, and praise God for the Christian friends who gave her comfort rather than such unexpected condemnation.

Tears splashed her cheeks. How could anyone doubt her love for Charles, or how deeply she missed him? A double grief engulfed her. When Henry or any of these other men were taken, their wives would have no consolation—no hope, no promise of heaven's gates and spending eternity together. Only nothingness.

Beth thought about all the years that she and Charles had poured out their love to the social and cultural elite of San Francisco's wealthiest and most prestigious families. Charles had been an outrageously brilliant man, but he had given God the credit for his considerable wealth. The more they gave away, the greater was God's supply. Through the years, Beth prayed these wealthy friends would want to know more about the love of God, and the grief that invaded her morning was the reminder that they were spiritually deaf, dumb and blind.

Literally millions of dollars had been raised in charity balls, home tours, auctions, concerts and rose shows at Rosehaven. The mansion and grounds had been written up in rosarian, architectural and design magazines as "a virtual museum, containing the most significant private collection of fine art and antiques in this country."

Charles had been delighted with the quality of the photographs and articles, but he had also believed, as he often said, "A museum, or any facsimile, should inspire creativity and beauty that reproduces itself. It should be for the enjoyment of many and not just a few." So, at certain times of the year, they had opened the grounds and galleries to an appreciative public.

The greater their generosity, the higher the pedestal they had been put upon. Beth had lived her whole life on a pedestal. But the heights became dizzying. Woe to her if she fell off. Merribelle had made that quite clear, and often referred to Charles and her as the "Lord and Lady of Rosehaven" with great vicarious pride. In Merribelle's mind, friendship with the Townsends had been the ultimate status symbol.

That made Beth increasingly uneasy, and caused her to do some serious soul-searching, not at all sure what she would find. God's plan for her life had to be wider and deeper than living as a sequestered dowager queen in a vacuous kingdom. She had lost her identity—not feeling like a real person anymore, just a continuance of her peers' unalterable expectations.

Merribelle's disruptive phone call confirmed beyond a doubt how horrified her affluent friends were going to be when they learned what she was about to do. And she couldn't have been more excited!

Beth answered the soft rap at the door. Tillie held her breakfast tray, spread with a snowy antique linen napkin, a fragrant rose, freshly squeezed orange juice, croissants, her homemade English marmalade and, of course, a steaming pot of breakfast tea with milk.

"I thought you'd be hungry, Miss Beth. It's not like you to be in your room at eight o'clock in the morning." Tillie set the tray down on the floral-skirted round table by the bay window and looked with concern at her mistress. "Are you feeling well? Seems to me you'd be worn out, spending all those months working on building plans, and then with the contractors, county commissions and your plans for helping people."

Beth enfolded Tillie's bony shoulders in a warm hug. "Oh, you're a dear. What would I ever do without you to look after me?" Tillie had been her nanny, closest confidante, housekeeper and dearest friend. Tears filled Beth's eyes as she held her faithful servant close.

Tillie stepped back, adjusting her stiffly starched white apron, embarrassed, as always, at a show of the affection she cherished. She eyed her mistress solicitously. "Are you well, Miss Beth?"

"Of course, I feel wonderful. The good Lord takes care of me, just like you do. This is my get-it-all-together day. I need to sort out my thoughts and personal things, make sure my head's on straight while I dawdle in memories. We've had some precious ones, haven't we, Tillie?"

"Yes, and some no one but you and me and the Lord knew about, that I thought would be the death of us." Tears filled her gray eyes. "I don't know how you do it, Miss Beth, but you always come out smiling and just being your loving self. Like you said, it must be the Lord."

"You've got that right. Say, I thought you were taking the day off; you're going to be almost as busy as I am, you know."

"Yes, ma'am, but since you didn't come down as usual, I thought you might need me, and everyone else is off today."

"Tillie, I promise you, I'm fine. You go."

Beth savored each flaky crumb of the warm croissants dripping with marmalade, just as she savored moving slowly into this day set aside to tuck away the past, as though it were delicate crystal. Life is fragile, she reminded herself, and there are times when we must slow it down, not be too harsh on ourselves, nor too abrupt. The present and future will keep. There are times to search within ourselves, rediscover who we are, where we've been, where we're going, and listen to God. This was that special day.

Beth slid long, trim dancer's legs into her most comfortable jeans and tossed on a favorite violet sweater, the same color as her eyes. She grabbed a matching ribbon and, after running a brush through silky black hair sprinkled with wisps of silver, tied it in a pony tail. Her coloring reflected one of the few traces of her father's Irish mother amidst a predominantly English ancestry. A closer look revealed a few more tiny wrinkles in her creamy porcelain-smooth skin. She asked herself, *What can you expect when you're almost fifty?*

It was good the staff was gone today. Beth wanted this day to herself, alone and uninhibited. *Where do I begin?* she wondered. She flooded the rooms with the waltzes and nocturnes of Chopin and the wonderful piano artistry of Arthur Rubenstein—melodies she had first come to love in her little pink tights at the ballet barre.

The dancing child within demanded to come out today. She leapt into well-executed jumps across the expanse of the second-floor landing, gracefully ending the outburst with a lighthearted arabesque and sweeping bow. Although breathless, her body was still lithe and agile.

Stimulated by the exercise, Beth reminded herself it was time to do something productive. She'd begin by storing her personal things, since the furnishings were being left as they'd always been. Her eyes were drawn to the immense pink satin box on the dresser, covered with lace, swags of pearls, and satin roses. Charles had given it to her "to keep your most precious treasures in," he said. Beth remembered replying, "But darling, you won't fit in there."

Gently, as though cradling a baby, she carried the box of memorabilia, the collection of a lifetime, to the top of the ornately carved staircase, then abandoned her intentions of heading down with it. She was captivated by the brilliance of the opposite wall. The sun glorified the rich colors in the enormous stained-glass window of roses she had designed so many years ago.

Beth stood for several fragile moments. The waltzes swirled through the air with a kaleidoscope of colors, an imagery of laughter, of music and voices and a house filled with happiness. She felt lightheaded, and sank to the top step with the box in her lap.

Tears welled in her eyes. "Lord," she said aloud, "You've blessed me with enough joy to last a lifetime, and enough heartache to savor its sweetness. Thank You."

Sitting there, she looked at the beautiful box and thought, *Do I really have the courage to open it? To take the lid off all that's hidden there?* Her hand hovered in debate. *Coward, of course you do,* she told herself. *You can't just move it from one place to another without dealing with what's inside.*

She imagined the contents of the box, with its pictures and mementos, like a mass of memories boiling within. They demanded her attention and dared her to lift the lid and risk a deeper look at her yesterdays. Cautiously, carefully, almost reverently, Beth raised the lid. She thought, *I wish I'd been as organized in storing these prized photographs and souvenirs as I've been in the rest of my life.*

Gently, she lifted out the bundles of faded photographs tied with ribbon, old love letters, newspaper clippings crisp with age, a pressed rose, sweet cards and notes too precious to part with. There were childish trinkets, tendrils of baby-fine black hair, bits and snatches of memories from far-off places, a program from the ballet *A Midsummer Night's Dream*. Priceless treasure and worthless trash to any other beholder sifted through her fingers.

The pale blue ribbon which had faithfully held the archaic black and white photos unloosed itself at Beth's touch. The pictures laid passively in her lap, as though inviting her to pick them up. She could not resist the invitation.

Cautiously, as one would avoid stirring up still waters, Beth sorted through the decades of memories. In a moment, she was catapulted back into a rare and cherished childhood.

Her parents had poured a genteel quality into her life that contrasted even then with her own generation. It was worlds apart from the ones that followed—the ones she now so desperately wanted to save. And she wondered whatever happened to that worthy cliché she'd built her life around: Anything worth doing is worth doing well.

Beth drifted back to growing up in San Francisco in the shadow of World War II. She pictured those little vignettes of life that formed and molded her into the woman she had become. . . .

*   *   *

"Mummy, Mummy, do I get to be a bumblebee? I can do it—please?" Beth pranced around on her little legs, with all the feminine wiles a three-year-old in a pink tutu could present to a mother who is also her ballet teacher.

"Students," Miss Margaret explained with a wink toward her daughter, "each of you will have a part in the spring recital, based on your skills. The three- to five-year-olds will be the bumblebees in the opening scene in the park." Giggles and hand claps interrupted the announcement.

"Ahem," she continued with dignity, "the intermediate and advanced students will perform in *Gisele.*" She suppressed the oohs and aahs to add, "You must never forget—you are dancers. To perform with excellence in this well-loved classic, you must attend all classes and rehearsals. There will be no excuses."

The students were in awe of the exquisite Margaret Sheridan, and danced beyond their ability to win her glance of praise. "Perform with excellence" continually rang in Beth's ears, setting a pattern of discipline, an intense desire for approval.

The Ballet Conservatory of San Francisco was more than Margaret's business. Dancing and teaching were her life; her husband and child were her diversions, and each was content with the arrangement.

It was September 1945.

"Isn't it time, Daddy? It's almost dark." Beth's Shirley Temple curls bounced as she squeezed her parents' hands and jumped up and down in anticipation.

"I'd say about another minute." Her father swept her up in his arms at the moment the crowd at the top of the Mark Hopkins Hotel let out a gasp and a cheer.

From the heights of Nob Hill they saw the whole city suddenly come alive with lights. A trillion sparkling diamonds lit up Market Street and all the steep streets leading down to the Embarcadero. They twinkled in the night sky across the San Francisco-Oakland Bay Bridge to the other side until only a milky glow faded into the distant hills.

"Oh, Daddy, it's the most wonderfulest thing I've seen in my whole life!" Beth shouted with her arms circled around his neck. "Mummy, isn't it bee-u-tiful?"

"Yes, darling, it's the most beautiful sight I've ever seen." Her mother, always so elegantly put together with every eyelash in place, stood with tears streaming down her cheeks. Her father's eyes were wet too. Everyone cried and hugged while the music played the refrain from the song that had become so popular during the war—"When the Lights Come on Again All Over the World." Down on the streets they could see the crowds going wild.

"Look," Beth shouted when she noticed lights in the windows of the houses. She had only been one year old at the time Japan attacked Pearl Harbor and didn't know cities ever had lights at night. "Don't we have to keep the black shades down anymore, Daddy?"

"No, my love, you don't have to grow up in the dark from now on. The war and the blackouts are over."

"Daddy, will the lights ever have to go out again?"

"I hope not, pet. Let's trust that in our lifetimes there will be no more wars."

The depth of Sean and Margaret Sheridan's tears were beyond their five-year-old's comprehension. War was just a word to her, not a reality.

"But a long time ago you said the war was over, Daddy."

"That was last May, pet, when the war in Europe ended. There were lots of countries at war, but now it's all over."

The tears were a blend of joy and sorrow. Germany's air raids on their native London had begun just months after they arrived in San Francisco in April of 1940. Their sentiments constantly shifted from guilty to grateful as they watched the newsreels, safe in America. London had been spared total destruction from the Nazi bombings, but many of their friends had been killed. Their flat was demolished, like more than 75 percent of the homes in the city.

Their joy came from Great Britain's surviving as a victorious nation and from the fact that the London branch of Sheridan & Co., Importers of

Fine Art & Antiques, still stood on Bond Street. All the staff had survived, but not without great hardship. It took the atomic bomb's powerful destruction to do it, but World War II was finally over. The lights *were* on again all over the world.

Men in uniform mingled among the civilians, receiving hugs and handshakes and pats on the back and offers to buy them a drink. The whole city turned to a roaring time of celebration. Every night that first week, the Sheridans drove up Lombard Street to Coit Tower, or over to Mount Tamalpais, or wandered around China Town or down by the wharf to get a different perspective of the lights.

The people were lighthearted too. Wherever they went, folks had something nice and friendly to say, as if each soul felt the relief of the pain and darkness lifted from the world. Beth became forever enchanted with the glitter of the city at night.

*   *   *

Memories of Saturdays with her father bloomed fresh forever.

"Daddy, this is my most favorite day."

"I know, love, you tell me that every week. Does that mean you like Saturdays better than school, more than your ballet and art classes? Even more than cotillion?" On Friday afternoons he watched with no small amusement while awkward little boys and shy, beruffled girls were exposed to the fine art of dancing gracefully with one another.

"Yes, Daddy—I like being with you most of all."

He always looked so distinguished in his impeccably tailored English suits. She'd typically be dressed in a fashionable sweater, swing skirt and penny loafers from their shopping excursions at I. Magnins. Hand-in-hand they would take the cable car or walk downtown from their burgundy-trimmed, gray Victorian "gingerbread" house to Sheridan & Co. on Sutter Street.

The sales staff would greet them with "Good morning, Mr. Sheridan. Good morning, Miss Elizabeth," as they entered the leaded glass and oak doors. Her father meticulously assessed every detail of the store's showroom with a practiced eye for the slightest defect in arrangement or presentation.

Beth imitated her father's discriminating manner. She scrutinized the exquisite antiques on display until she discovered the brocade or tapestry settee with the prettiest silver or china tea service beside it. Touching, of course, was forbidden.

She fancied herself entertaining the queen when no one was looking. "One lump of sugar or two, your Highness?" she would ask her mythical guest. "I'll pour." A vivid imagination carried her through the ritual of graciously serving English tea just like her mother.

Sheridan's galleries bulged with a maze of paintings that invited Beth to enter wide-eyed into fantasyland. She wandered through misty forests, brilliant landscapes and ethereal cities she'd never seen. Deep within the canvases were places only the mind of an artist could go. Beth knew she belonged there. Someday, her own signature would appear on beautiful paintings. . . .

Father's voice called her out of her daydreams. "I say, where's my date? I'm positively famished for lunch."

"I'm here, Daddy!" She would come running.

"Cheerio," he'd call out to the staff as he whisked Beth away for their Saturday afternoon adventure.

"What mood are you in today, love?"

"I'm a princess."

"Very well then, it's the Garden Court at the Palace Hotel for you."

Often she said, "I'm a shrimp-eating traveler."

"Jolly good, we're off to the wharf. And yes, you can buy your friend Hope a shell for her collection. For a little girl, you have capital ideas, love."

Sean Sheridan delighted in whatever his daughter wanted to do. He'd waited a long time for a child, being nearly forty when she was born.

Sean loved to give detailed explanations, and Beth absorbed grown-up information like a sponge. She knew every corner of the DeYoung Museum, Golden Gate Park, and the names of the flower cart vendors where her father bought her violets.

Gradually, Beth noticed that a strange atmosphere had crept into their household. A shroud of secrecy began to invade table conversation. From the darkness of her room, phrases like "economy," "progress," "rebuilding after the war" and, very frequently, "home" were whispered, then hushed. Her parents were hiding something from her.

One Friday night her father announced that their Saturday plans would have to wait—he had to leave for London the next day.

Beth was scared. Everything seemed topsy-turvy and Daddy wasn't explaining anything anymore. She heard him and Mum arguing that night and horror struck her heart.

"Sean, don't be ridiculous. She'll have a superb academic education and the Royal Ballet School offers the finest classical training in the world. Living there, she can give her full concentration to ballet. You'll have her on weekends. She's the perfect age, size, disposition and feet turnout to be a splendid ballerina. It's a marvelous opportunity. I know she'll qualify, and certainly not just because I'll be a teacher there."

"Meg, ballet may be your whole life, but I'm not convinced it's hers." Her father's voice was strained. "You'll smother her with your own ambitions. I appreciate your dedication to your art, and your talent. But a ballerina is only a ballerina—there's no room to be anything else. I've no objection to her training there, but our daughter will live where I live."

They were arguing about her. Beth's world rocked. Some of her friends' parents were getting divorced. Could that be what the secrecy, the guarded tones, the hostile glances they exchanged were about? Were they dividing her between them?

Her mother pressed on. "At the school she'll be protected from the street talk. If it's anything like here, the young people think about nothing but acts of immorality. I'll not have my daughter exposed to that."

"You can't keep her in a cage, Meg. You don't know anything about the street anyway, only life inside the theater or dance studio. Furthermore . . . "

Beth pulled the covers over her head. She'd never heard them argue before. She hated it. When her father had left before on buying trips to Europe, it had never been like this. She didn't know much about God, but she prayed, "Please bring my daddy back."

He did come back, ten days later, chipper as usual, and all thoughts of her parents divorcing were swept from her mind.

"Come here, Beth, I have some marvelous news!"

Beth snuggled on his lap as he announced, "We're going home—to London."

Beth was horrified. "But this is home! I don't want to go to London!" She ran sobbing to her room and slammed the door.

It had never occurred to Beth that her life would ever change. She loved San Francisco, the Bay, the wharf, the flowers, parks and museums. She didn't want to go to some old city that had been bombed. And she didn't want to leave Hope, her dearest friend in all the world.

"Muffy!" she cried aloud, running out of her room and head-on into her father. "Daddy, I can take Muffy, can't I?"

"I'm afraid Muffy is much too tiny to do well on the long flight. Kittens don't like to be moved about."

"Neither do I," she sobbed into his warm, soft chest. "I don't want to go, Daddy. Do we have to?"

"Yes, sweet, we do. And you'll love it, I promise."

On the Saturday before her tenth birthday, Beth and her father walked one last time to Sheridan's, and then to the Palace for lunch.

"Surprise!" On the other side of a huge palm, ten of her best friends leaped from the elegant table and ran to hug her, jumping up and down with excited squeals. There were presents, lunch, ice cream and cake, laughter . . . and then it was over. She faced the dreaded moment of saying goodbye to her very best friend of all.

"Hope, I'll never see you again," the tears began to trickle down her face.

"Don't be silly, of course you will," Hope promised bravely. Then she too cried. "But I'll miss you."

"You're the only person in the whole world I'd give Muffy to. You'll love her and rub her tummy, won't you?"

Father intervened. "I'll bring Muffy to you tomorrow, while Beth finishes packing. It's time to go now, Hope. Your mum is here."

The two girls clung to each other, and Beth was certain she would die from the pain of parting.

"Write to me," Beth pleaded.

"I will," Hope promised. "I'll always be here for you."

Hope's mother walked over to Beth and gave her a hug. "I have a gift for you, dear." She handed Beth a pretty package. It was a pearl-white Bible with her name on it in gold letters. She said, "Remember, Beth, wherever you are, whatever you do, God is always with you."

Those words made her feel better than anything she'd heard for a long time.

2

The roar of the engines of the BOAC airliner thundered while they sat on the ground at the San Francisco Airport, waiting for takeoff.

"I'm scared," Beth admitted.

"That's all right, dear," her mother assured her, "I always feel that way too before we get airborne." She turned to her husband. "Sean," she tenderly brushed his hand, "wasn't it wonderful when we came to the States on the Queen Mary?"

"What's the Queen Mary?" Beth asked, puzzled.

"A big beautiful ocean liner—an elegant city on the seas." Her mother's eyes looked dreamy, lost in the indulgence of her rarest luxury—a time of sheer romance, of silk chiffon gowns, sipping champagne and dancing in the arms of her husband until dawn. Beth had never seen that look before, and then it faded away.

"Why didn't we go that way now?" Beth asked.

"During the war, it was converted to a troop ship to take soldiers to fight in Europe," her father explained.

"Did it get bombed, too?"

"No, the old girl's just put to rest in dry dock somewhere, but she's not dead yet."

Sean Sheridan was the most enthusiastic man on the plane, always prepared for the next thing at hand. His carry-on bag neatly held packets of pictures and maps to accompany a cache of stories to share with Beth on the long flight. He also knew his wife. For the rest of the trip, her enthusiasm turned immediately to letters, papers and teaching schedules from the prestigious Royal Ballet School.

London's Heathrow Airport teemed with travelers of every nationality. If the San Francisco Airport was crowded, this was insane. Beth gawked in all directions, so entranced with the elegantly dressed cosmopolitan people that she almost got separated from her parents.

"Edward, old chap, over here!" her father waved and shouted.

A tired-looking man, with the kindest blue eyes she'd ever seen, approached them.

"Hello, there. How was the flight?"

"Uneventful, just the way we like it."

"Long," said Margaret.

"Fun," Beth volunteered.

"Edward, how are you?" Sean asked as they headed for the baggage claim. There was a tone of concern in his voice as he noticed the sagging lines on the face of his old friend and manager of the shop.

"Frightfully worn, Sean. I've just been hanging on until you came."

"What is it, old man?"

"This is no conversation to greet you with." He looked embarrassed. "It's super to have you back. Business is splendid, Londoners are putting their lives together again, times are prosperous." Beth noticed tears come to his eyes. He looked down at her, and then at Sean apologetically. "Sorry about letting go the stiff upper lip—I've just never put myself back together, six years after the war. And then there's Tillie."

Beth just heard the end of the conversation. She wondered, *Who's Tillie?*

London on maps and pictures and London alive were like two different worlds to Beth. The romanticism in her soul breathed knights on white chargers round its historical buildings, the artist within her gasped at its grandeur, but the child in her switched excitedly from window to window of the big sedan.

The moment Edward crossed Westminster Bridge, Big Ben's bell in the Clock Tower of the Houses of Parliament boomed four o'clock.

"My wife, Anne, will scold us for being late for tea," Edward warned with a smile. He sped faster up Victoria Street, past Buckingham Palace up to the corner of Hyde Park, down Park Lane, past the Marble Arch, and pulled up sharply in front of their flat.

"There now, not too bad." He jumped out, opened their door and extended a hand to Margaret and Beth. "One thing you must get accustomed to in London, Beth, is that the world comes to a halt before anything interferes with four o'clock tea." He chuckled warmly and they all smiled.

"Anne, this is Margaret Sheridan, and here we have Beth. She's ten years old already!"

Anne's brown hair was neatly formed into a chignon at the nape of her neck. She wore a Shetland sweater, classic English tweed skirt, sensible shoes, a friendly smile and proper manners.

Fragrant scones had just come out of the oven. Beth eyed a bowl of thick cream and strawberries and several kinds of luscious-looking jam. Her mouth watered.

"What a perfectly lovely welcome, Anne. How dear of you," Sean hugged her.

Around the corner, Beth noticed a plain, pitifully thin young woman who glanced furtively into the room, then darted into a door at the back of the kitchen when she saw them. The woman had the look of a wounded doe. Beth wondered who she was and why she wore such a tragic expression.

Edward sat shaking his head, with a concerned nod to his wife.

"Well, well, how perfectly lovely to be here," Sean remarked to fill the awkward silence.

"Tea is ready." Anne poured the steaming hot water into the already heated tea pot. She motioned them to sit down in the dining room.

In a few minutes the same girl slipped back through the kitchen, now more curious than shy. Beth was curious too.

"This is our daughter, Tillie. Please come and have tea with us, dear," her mother coaxed gently.

Slowly, Tillie made her way to the table without looking into their faces, and acknowledged introductions with only a slight nod, except when it came to Beth. Their eyes met, and Tillie's searched the little newcomer's as though looking for something lost.

They devoured the scones, and Beth felt delightfully satisfied. She looked at the empty napkin on the silver tray. "Those were yummy, thank you."

"Tillie is our scone-maker—she's an excellent cook, even if she is English," Edward laughed.

"Would you teach me how to make them?" Beth asked.

"I'm afraid you won't have time to spend baking," her mother cut in. The tone in her voice intimated her daughter was above such menial tasks.

Sean made a quick recovery. He quipped, "You can live without music, you can live without books, but show me the one who can live without cooks." They all laughed, and Tillie sent him a shy, appreciative glance.

"Well, old chap," Sean turned to Edward, "if you'll be so kind as to pop us over to The Dukes, we'll be much obliged."

"We're going to stay with a duke?" Beth blinked in surprise.

"It's a marvelous little hotel, darling, tucked away in St. James Place. Feels just like home, and practically around the corner from our shop on Bond Street. I pointed it out on the map."

En route, Sean turned to his friend. "Edward, Tillie does seem, ah, quite shy. Is she well?"

"Our Tillie had a bad time of it during the war. She was engaged to Reginald, her childhood sweetheart who was in the Navy and home on leave. During an air raid, they didn't make it to the shelter in time. Reg was hit, but shouted to her to keep running. All hell broke loose. She was hit by flying bricks too, but she thought he was right behind her. When she reached the shelter, Reginald wasn't with her. He died in the street. For years after the war, she'd wake up screaming with nightmares, reliving those terrible times.

"She's hardly gone out of the flat since then," Edward's tone had grown sad, "doesn't even want to look at the city. She lives in the house, spends her time cooking and cleaning, then re-doing what she's already done. She wants to be busy all the time—blank out her mind, I imagine. It tears me apart when I look at her. She's only twenty-five, yet she's dead inside. And no one can bring her out. What she needs is to get completely out of London, but I don't know how to get her to do that either. She's terrified of being alone, and this is where Anne's and my work is, so she's rather stuck here." Edward shifted uncomfortably in the driver's seat.

"You were bloody fortunate to have missed the war. My parents and sister and her family were killed too. . . . " Edward paused for a moment, lost in his grief. "Now seeing Tillie dead inside constantly reminds me of all that."

"I'm so sorry, Edward. You've done a splendid job in spite of all this," Sean was stunned at Edward's display of emotion. "Now that we've come home, I can at least take some of the load off you at the store."

"Thanks, old man, you know what we British always say, 'Pip, pip, carry on—you can't keep a good man down' and all that. . . . Ahh—here's your little hotel."

Sean turned to Margaret. "In the morning, Edward will drive the Bentley back to the shop and we'll walk over. Then we'll drive about to choose our new home."

"I trust, Sean, that you're being practical, and my options are here in London, close to the school . . . and the shop, of course."

"Wait until tomorrow, and you'll jolly well see your options," he grinned at her.

Where they lived didn't seem as important to Margaret Sheridan as the expediency of getting on with this promising new facet of her career. She would agree to whatever was most convenient.

"I adore it. It's simply perfect, Sean. Kensington is a marvelous location. I even like the name of the street—Sumner Place, with its white pillars and porticoes. And it's close to everything."

"Don't make up your mind too quickly, my love." He wheeled out Oxford Street until it blended into route AI. The road sign read, TO HAMPSTEAD.

"Why are we heading for Hampstead?" Margaret frowned. "It's a million miles from London. Really now, Sean. Please just turn around. The place in Kensington is perfectly suitable."

"It's only fifteen miles," Sean swung around a curve in the shady, winding road.

"Sean," Margaret's voice was sharp, "you know I'm a Londoner at heart. Why are you doing this? It's ridiculous, I'm—" Beth closed her ears to the shrill arguments of her mother that seemed to go on and on.

Beth's eyes shot worriedly at her father. His set jaw announced that turning around was out of the question. She'd never heard her parents argue before they began planning to come "home." Would their new life be filled with bickering and bitterness?

Icy silence filled the big black Bentley. Maybe they were going to get a divorce after all. She wanted to go home to San Francisco and Hope and Muffy. She wanted everything to be like it used to be.

On the plane she'd been thinking what a lucky little girl she was. There were a few other children on the flight, but their daddies weren't showing them pictures and telling them about kings and towers. The trip hadn't been so scary after all—in fact, she now loved to fly. And London exceeded all of her daddy's descriptions. She told herself she'd come to love it just as much as San Francisco. And poor Tillie. She felt a terrible sadness for how the awful war had made her so strange and afraid.

Mostly she felt lucky to have been born Elizabeth Sheridan. One day she would be a ballerina as beautiful as her mother and know as much about art as her father. People would think she was a special person, like they did her parents.

The awful silence had to be broken. She hated the tormented tension. "It's beautiful out here, Daddy."

The fresh springtime foliage on the trees looked like layers upon layers of fluffy green lace to Beth. "The woods and the houses are just like pictures in fairy tales. Oh, look at that wonderful park!"

"Hampstead is rich in old cottages and delightful eighteenth- and nineteenth-century Gothic detail," her father said.

"Look at that big place—it says Jack Straw's Castle. It doesn't look like a castle," Beth commented.

"No, it doesn't. It's a pub. Some very famous people used to gather in the pubs here. I'll show you where the poet John Keats once lived. That 'park' is a cemetery where many of England's greatest poets, writers and artists are buried. They've lived here for hundreds of years among the aristocracy and middle-class professionals." Sean spoke as if only to Beth in the backseat while Margaret sat beside him in brooding silence.

Mr. Sheridan brought the Bentley to a halt on the cobblestone drive of a vine-covered stone house. Beveled diamond shapes sparkled in the windows and roses framed the heavy old arched door.

The English garden surrounding the house offered up a mixed bouquet of heady fragrance blended with lilacs, while vines of honeysuckle, awaiting their season, dripped from a weathered trellis. A palette of color vibrated amid a sea of tulips, primroses and violets.

"I say, do you think you could call this home?" Her father looked very pleased with himself. Inside, the rooms had a cozy charm that invited them to stay forever.

Margaret Sheridan mellowed. "But it's such a distance from the city and the school," she objected mildly.

"This is still considered Central London. We'll soon learn to be commuters. The Tube station is in the center of the village, but you and Beth can take the automobile if you like. The Northern Line will take me to the city in ten minutes."

Margaret frowned. "Sean, where will we find a cook and a house-keeper?"

His eyes lit up. "What about Tillie? The girl's simply got to get out of London to forget the past. She should feel safe here. I'll speak to Edward. In fact, I'll ring him up right now." He went to the telephone.

While they were still leisurely exploring the house, Edward rang back. "Anne agrees, and she's talked to Tillie. It's a splendid break for our girl. Thanks, old boy."

Beth searched her parents' faces. The traces of anger and tension so uncharacteristic of their marriage had been melted away by the warmth of this place. She started to cry with relief.

"What is it, pet?" Her father knelt beside her.

"You and Mummy are through fighting, aren't you?"

"Yes, darling," her mother assured her. "Sean, you've found us a lovely home, thank you. I was rather beastly, wasn't I? Rather caught up in myself, I'm afraid."

"We're not going to be a divorced family?" Beth looked to her father with bright eyes.

"Mercy, no. Put such a thought out of your head. We'll live happily ever after right here, my pet."

Tillie became more than a cook and housekeeper to Beth. Together, they read books like *The Secret Garden* and *Wind in the Willows* in Beth's free moments from the intense demands of her lessons. Beth's sketchbook was always with her to capture the changing patterns as they walked in the woods or sat quietly to listen for the cuckoo bird's amusing trill.

Though Tillie's childhood had died of fright while the bombs screamed overhead, it came alive vicariously while sharing Beth's. Day by day, the shattered pieces of her being began to resemble a whole person. In a few weeks, color blossomed in her cheeks and the frightened look began to leave her eyes.

Beth needed Tillie, too. She shared not only her innermost feelings captured in drawings, but also she had someone in whom she could confide the secrets and dreams she once shared with Hope.

Beth and her mother were unique among the students and teachers of the Royal Ballet School—no other teacher had a child-student. Students came from all over the Commonwealth, and most of them boarded at the school on Talgarth Road. Beth was happy she didn't have to exchange the beauty of their Hampstead home for the austerity of living in the dorms. It was enough to dance on the bare floors and look at the bare walls of the classrooms all day.

The exacting standards of excellence required by the Royal Ballet's Sadler's Wells school demanded even more discipline from teachers than from students. And beyond teaching, Margaret Sheridan performed with the famed ballet company's limited European tours. Whatever she may have lacked as wife and mother, as a ballerina her grace and elegance on stage or in the studio were perfection. And that was enough for her husband and child. Beth worked hard to master the discipline and excellence her mother personified, even though such fame was still beyond her comprehension.

The business consumed more of her father's time than ever before. Edward needed relief from some of his managerial duties, and Sean had to watch the bottom line, plus handle the European buying trips for both stores and the selection of furnishings for their home.

Beth and Tillie's relationship became not that of mistress and servant, but an endearing friendship that grew out of a common need for companionship. Yet out of her conservative upbringing, Tillie always called her "Miss Beth."

Tillie hated the memories of London and vowed never to set foot there again, but Beth reveled in the museums, parks, theaters and galleries. She wore her first pair of nylon stockings to a musical at the Palladium and felt thoroughly grown-up.

At fifteen, Beth still cherished Saturdays.

"Daddy, I never thought anything could be better than our Saturdays in San Francisco, but I love the London store. I think your collection of art is better than the museums'."

"I respect your opinion, love. I needed that. You have an eye for good art. Things have been rather hectic lately, haven't they? Not only with me. You never have an extra minute either. Your life is so full with schoolwork and dancing. I'm pleased with your excellent grades, by the way."

Those ten minutes on the commuter train afforded father and daughter an exchange of insight. On weekdays, he was like every other commuter with a bowler hat and black umbrella. Usually he had to stand, hanging on to the strap while he read the *Times'* pink *Financial*. On Saturdays, the blossoming young woman beside him was the pride of his life.

"Your expertise in art and antiques shows a promising head for business, young lady. Most dancers don't have a pragmatic bone in their well-trained bodies."

She read the newspaper too and became aware of how sheltered she'd been from real life. The practical training and exposure to the business community added to her grown-up feeling. The priceless antiques intrigued her. The world of art was capturing her soul, even though she and her parents had always assumed she would be a ballerina.

"You're sure you want to spend your Saturday in the shop, dusting?" Sean asked as Beth helped with a new shipment.

"The antiques business is fascinating . . . it's where the richness and romance of the past come together with the future." Beth smiled, pleased with her adult statement. "Besides, it's a nice change for my brain and body."

She turned quickly. "Take this eighteenth-century vase for example." The movement was too abrupt. She brushed the Meissen with her sleeve. Horror of horrors, it fell to the floor and shattered.

"Oh, no!" Beth gasped. One of the jagged pieces had the price on it. "One hundred pounds! Oh, Daddy! How expensive. I'll work every Saturday until I've earned enough to pay for it." Her eyes were red and puffy the rest of the day.

The actual retail price of the vase was one hundred thousand pounds—three digits were missing—but he never told her. The vase had been extremely rare and he'd spent two years negotiating to acquire it, yet he placed an even higher value on his daughter's already crushed feelings. At the same time, he knew the importance of fostering her sense of responsibility. He let her work it out.

After several months, he came to her, smiling. "Here are your time cards, Beth. Your debt is paid. Now you know how much work it requires to earn the respectable sum of one hundred pounds. We must celebrate your accomplishment. I'll call The Dukes and ask old George to do something special for luncheon."

"You're hardly a typical schoolgirl, you know, love," her father commented over dessert. "In San Francisco, the sixteen-year-olds are probably dating, drinking and raising you-know-what. They are here too, I suppose. We're just out of touch. But, then, you've never been typical."

"Don't tell anyone I'm sweet sixteen and have never been kissed," Beth laughed. "I don't even know a boy, except the ones in my *pas de deux* class, and I've never had the urge to kiss one of them!"

"Someday, my love, someday, you just might think of something other than ballet. Do you realize every move you make turns into a subconscious arabesque or pirouette? Walking around a corner, getting out of the car . . . are you quite aware of that?"

"Some people sing in the shower—I just move that way, as you say, subconsciously. Just as I have to put whatever I see on paper or canvas."

And somewhere in her subconscious, she knew her desire to express her feelings on canvas was being stifled. She had to draw and paint as surely as she had to breathe. Wherever she went she had her sketchbook and drew all she saw as naturally as a bird sings. She visited neighboring art galleries on Bond Street whose proprietors welcomed her to bring her work in and encouraged her that it had promise.

At eighteen, Beth reached a point of frustration. Applaud the ballerina, deny the painter. Please her mother, deny her inner feelings. A long time ago, she'd gotten the message from her mother—an unspoken edict that feelings only got in the way of ambition.

"Tillie," Beth asked her friend one day, "I wish I knew what I should do. Continue to study ballet, or follow my heart and paint."

"Not everyone has such a choice, Miss Beth. If it 'twas me, I'd follow my heart, but there's never been anything I wanted to do."

Beth completed her upper school academic studies with honors and special recognition for mathematic achievements, which delighted her father. A few years before, the junior part of the Royal Ballet School had been transferred to an elegant eighteenth-century Royal residence: White Lodge, in Richmond Park. Beth danced in the advanced classes, still on Talgarth Road, and taught some of the younger students at White Lodge. Queen Elizabeth had bestowed her Royal Charter on both Company and School, which had thrilled them all.

Edward seemed on the edge of a nervous breakdown, so in every free moment Beth helped her father at Sheridan's. He'd been letting her list new merchandise in their inventory files and mark prices. Her assistance contributed something of value. She felt good about that, and the new treasures they received always excited her imagination. On the surface she was an amazingly accomplished young woman, a promising ballerina. But her heart told her, *You're an artist.*

Occasionally she would pick up the pearl-white Bible. The need to come to a decision, the need to focus on her direction, gnawed at her relentlessly—and much of it had to do with the fear of her mother's reaction. One Bible verse especially impressed her: "Trust in the Lord with all thine heart; and lean not unto thine own understanding." *That would be a relief . . . and it says if I look to Him, He'll show me the way to go. Oh, Lord, wherever You are . . . what should I do?*

Beth decided to face it head-on. "Daddy, what would you say if I told you I wanted to study art instead of ballet?"

Her father regarded her for several moments. "You must have given this a lot of thought, love. Is that what you want?"

"I'm sure of it. But what do you think Mum will say?"

"Let's find out."

Nervously, Beth procrastinated. She heard the anger, the bitter tones of years ago, the lashing out at her father. Would Mum blame him for her decision? Would she turn it into a personal rejection of her lifelong passion for ballet? Would her disappointment be beyond reconciliation?

After three days Beth's anguish became so intense that she couldn't sleep, she couldn't eat, she couldn't dance. So she finally said, "Yes—let's find out."

Margaret appeared less stunned than expected. "You have something within you that's rare, Beth," she quietly said. "It's more than the way you dance—it's your whole being. To be a truly fine ballerina is like any other discipline: You must give it your whole heart, or your audience will only see your movements and never your very soul. Only you and God know what you are meant to be."

Beth flung her arms around her. "Oh, Mum, I love you." Her mother had probably never spoken of God before, and the reference seemed to be an affirmation that He had shown her the way.

Tenderness shone in her father's eyes. Clearly, he hadn't expected such a gracious and understanding response from his wife. "Where do you think you'd like to study art, Beth?"

"In Paris."

"Where?"

"At the *École des Beaux Arts*. I've already sent my portfolio and application and received an acceptance."

Emotions played across both her parents' faces, a mixture of astonishment and pride. "Well, well—you certainly aren't afraid to reach for the top. There's no finer art school in the world. Bravo!" Her father went to the Waterford decanter on the sideboard. "Let's have a toast of sherry. Come, Tillie, join us."

"I'm glad for you, Miss," Tillie hugged her with tear-filled eyes. She struggled for something else to say. "I'll always be here for you."

"That's what Hope said when I was ten years old and leaving for London. Thank you, Tillie. That means the world to me."

"I think you have a letter from Hope, Miss Beth. It has a San Francisco postmark."

"Maybe it's a thank-you note for her birthday present. I can't believe she just turned twenty." Beth tore open the pink envelope and read. "Mummy, Daddy, Hope's engaged!" she shouted. "To a wonderful-sounding man, Josh Sterling. He's twenty-five and flies an airplane for a missions organization." Then she stopped in shock. "Oh, no . . . Mum, the wedding is the same time I'm understudying for Tatania in *A Midsummer Night's Dream.*"

Beth sat on the floor beside her mother and reread the letter with a mixture of joy and despair. "I want to be a bridesmaid for my friend's wedding, but I can't."

"I know, love," her mother tried to comfort her, "but there's a very good chance you won't be merely an understudy. It would be lovely for you to do Tatania in the Royal Ballet before you 'retire' from dancing."

"I think Hope will understand," Beth commented softly.

Beth made both her debut and exit on the Royal stage as Tatania before a highly appreciative audience. The applause would forever ring in her ears.

"Today is not only Saturday," her father announced one unusually sunny morning, "but a very important person's nineteenth birthday. Let's pop over to Harrod's. You'll need a new wardrobe, luggage and linens for your dorm."

"Oh Daddy, you are a love. I'd adore it."

A violet cashmere Chanel sweater and skirt were perfectly designed for her svelte young body and long dancer's legs. The color invariably transmuted her eyes into sparkling amethysts in daylight and sapphires at night.

"Smashing! Positively stunning. Don't bother to bag it," Sean Sheridan told the clerk. "My daughter's going to wear it to lunch."

They'd driven the Bentley in to transport the anticipated carload of purchases and the huge backseat bulged with packages.

"It looks as though we just broke the bank at Monte Carlo," Beth giggled.

"It's no laughing matter—we just broke my bank account." Her father was closer to the truth than his pride would ever admit. He stopped the car along the Thames. "Be a good girl. Hop out and stand right there. I must have a picture of you in all your splendor today."

Beth clowned in an exaggerated cheesecake pose, a ballet position and the classic model's stance.

"Do I look like Suzy Parker? I'll be on all the American magazine covers, just like she is, right?"

"Get serious, pet. Just stand there and look beautiful."

"*Oui, oui, Monsieur,* anything to oblige, *Monsieur,*" she laughed.

"Don't say that to anyone but me," he winced. "I demand that you learn to say *no* in six languages."

At that moment, his heart felt like jelly. They had prepared her in everything she needed to know at nineteen—academics, grace, manners, culture. Everything but the facts of life. She had never had time for boys and knew nothing of the ways of men. It was Tillie who'd explained the phenomenon of menstruation to her. Sean hoped she'd included how babies were made. He and Margaret had dodged that part of her education completely. How had she so soon become a woman? Had he not seen her growing up?

Heaven help her, he groaned inwardly. *And protect her from the Frenchmen.*

3

Bonjour, *Mademoiselle. C'est une belle femme.* Your father described you perfectly. You are most beau-ti-ful woman. . . . "

A rotund man in a black suit overwhelmed Beth the moment she came through the landing gates at Orly Airport. Sweeping his beret from his bald head, he had her gloved hand in his before she realized that he was peeling back the supple leather to kiss her skin ceremoniously.

Instinctively, she withdrew her hand, shaken by this flamboyant welcome. Were all Frenchmen this assertive? Englishmen were courteous, but this man embarrassed her. Then she thought, *Well, he is a friend of my father's.*

Olive black eyes looked up to see the startled expression on her face. "Ahh, *excusez moi, ma chérie,* Eliz-a-beth, you have become most *magnifique* young wo-man. I am François Laugier, you remember me, *oui?*"

Beth regained her composure and laughed, "Of course, François. I was hoping it was you."

"*Enchanté,* oh, hoho, every man in Paree will be at your feet. But because I am an old friend of your father, I must look after you, at least for now, *oui?* He described you perfectly."

"Thank you for coming to meet me. I'm sure I'd get lost in this airport. I've never been to Paris by myself, and things do change."

"*Oui,* change yes, but Parisians, besides finding something to quarrel about, resist change, *Mademoiselle.* The more things change, the more we resist. It is our way. You must still fall in love in Paris. It is impossible not to do it."

François gestured with flourishes while he drove her into the city, waving extravagantly at the wonders of Paris, narrowly missing pedestrians, swerving around taxis.

Beth's heart leaped in terror. He barely missed an old man who shook his fist in their direction. She wanted to scream, "Let me out, I'm too young to die," but bit her lip instead. Obviously her father had never driven with François.

"Paree is a beautiful woman, like you, with flowers in her hair. You remember, of course, the Champs Elysees, most lovely of avenues in the world," he pointed out proudly, "and her gorgeous parks running along its sides, *oui?* My art gallery is around the corner, but another time, perhaps you will visit it."

Beth had always seen the chestnut trees wearing their pink blossoms that looked like ice-cream cones. Now their broad leaves had the first hint of autumn color.

The blast of a horn jarred her momentary tranquility as François abruptly spun the wheel to avoid a collision. She knew that the French drove like madmen, using the horn rather than brakes to avoid smashing into each other, but she'd never experienced it before. *Please, God, just let him get me to my apartment in one piece. . . .*

"See the Arch de Triumphe de l'Étoile," François announced as he swung in a wide right turn down one of the broad avenues. Its hub became spokes in twelve directions. "The Place de Concorde where Louis XVI and Marie Antoinette lost their heads during the Revolution."

He gestured at the Louvre, Notre Dame, the Louvre Palace and the river Seine. As he crossed a bridge, the Pont Neuf, Beth gasped at the dazzling golden statues whose proud figures seemed so eternally sure of themselves. She felt anything but serene at the moment. Her temples throbbed with a fierce headache.

"Ahh, Miss Eliz-a-beth, I present to you the Quartier Latin, the Left Bank of the city, where you will live and study at the greatest school in the world for the arts, *oui?* I can tell, you will become a most wonderful painter, and perhaps, perhaps, you will fall in love."

Are all Frenchmen so preoccupied with falling in love? she wondered. *I'm not here to fall in love. I'm here to learn to paint and study art. I hope everyone realizes that,* she told herself resolutely.

François arrived with a jolt at the apartment buildings where many of the students lived. "Your father, my old friend, did not tell me, *Mademoiselle,* that you were bringing your entire household belongings with you," he puffed as he unloaded footlockers and suitcases and began to carry them in for her.

"*Scusa, Signore, Signorina*—let me help you, *per favore.*" Beth looked up into the most fascinating deep brown eyes she had ever seen in a man.

Those eyes swept appreciatively over her face and figure and back again. She felt her cheeks turn the color of the hot pink suit she wore. *Who is this audaciously handsome Italian?* she wondered. Certainly his elegant creamy cashmere jacket and perfectly tailored slacks were not those of house staff, or even a student. Beth guessed he was in his late twenties.

"Let me introduce myself. I am Roberto Cabriollini."

François interceded, straightening his jacket and setting his beret straight with a jealously critical eye of the younger Italian. "*Monsieur,* I am François Laugier, and this is my charge, *Mademoiselle* Sheridan, and I am quite capable of handling her luggage, *merci.*"

"*Non capisco.* You are huffing and puffing and there is much to carry. I am young and strong, willing and able, and quite harmless, *Signore.* I am at your service."

Beth had to turn her face away so her two knights errant wouldn't see her amusement.

François melted under Roberto's persuasion, unable to argue against the case he presented. In turn, he sullenly snarled at the impatient and uncooperative French apartment manager to whom Beth was showing her rental agreement and receipt. The two men managed to get the pile of baggage up to her second-floor room.

Perspiration poured from François' forehead, causing him to continually adjust the beret, apparently one size too small, from slipping over his eyes. Beth could stand it no longer. She hurriedly excused herself into the bathroom and, behind the locked door, broke into muffled laughter.

Her composure regained, Beth located the frazzled François on the curb and relieved him of the last small valise. He looked spent, his beret now perched uncertainly over his left ear. He glanced about, in desperate search of a graceful escape.

"Dear François, how can I ever thank you? You've been so very kind. You must be exhausted. I do appreciate all you've done."

"*Oui, Mademoiselle,* but what else could I do for the charming daughter of my old friend? It is nothing. . . . "

His weary expression said otherwise. "I am at your service," he puffed, his beret over his heart, searching for a sign that he had done his duty and was dismissed.

"You're an angel, François. Please tell your family hello for me. *Au revoir.*"

"*Oui,* but of course." He kissed her hand hurriedly and backed his way to the little Peugeot, bumping into its side almost without notice in his haste to escape. "*Au revoir, Ma Petit.*" He waved and screeched out of sight.

Beth turned away with a laugh at this comical but sweet man. She caught her breath when she realized the dark, fascinating eyes of Roberto had been watching the scene with great amusement.

"He is nice man, for a Frenchman, *si?*"

Startled, Beth replied, "Yes, yes he is. François is very devoted to my father and I'm grateful for his help."

"*Si*, and I too am your servant, *Signorina*. Allow me to help you, and then you will have dinner with me, *si?*"

"No, thank you, Mr. Cabriollini, I'm very tired and must get my things unpacked."

"Please, call me Roberto. You will be in Paris for some time, *si?*"

"I'm a new student at the *École des Beaux Arts*," she beamed. "Thank you again for your help, Roberto."

His eyes flashed. "I also am a student there—forever a student of the arts."

"Perhaps I'll see you at the school sometime."

"You may be certain, *Bella Rosa Mia.*" He nodded.

Beth was captivated by the knowing look of those smoldering eyes that once again swept over her from head to toe. She shivered, denying to herself the unfamiliar sensation that came over her. *"Bella Rosa Mia,"* he had called her—his beautiful rose. Italians must like hot pink.

"Bouno serra, Signorina," and Roberto strode across the narrow street, whistling as he rounded the corner. Casual, confident, suave and truly unnerving.

Beth's acceptance to the *École des Beaux Arts* had come late, barely in time for the beginning of new classes. She'd asked the school to put her in touch with an English or American girl for a roommate, but they'd already been assigned. In many ways, she felt relieved. She had never shared a room with anyone. The girls who lived at the Royal Ballet School usually disappeared into their dorms after the exhausting classes, to shower, rest or study. She was left to go home or study in the library while waiting for her mother.

Now she felt terribly alone. Yet the excitement of being in Paris, this dream come true, overwhelmed her. There wasn't time to think about loneliness. Art classes started the next day.

Thoughts of Roberto and the way he looked at her circled through her mind. She wasn't sure she liked it. She suspected she shouldn't.

Inside the stone wall of austere iron-barred arches and the huge heavy door, Beth stood in the statue-lined courtyard. She found herself in awe of the ancient classrooms where for hundreds of years students had come from the world over. They had sat in these same seats to learn the secrets of the ages in that delicate and powerful form known as fine art. She was so excited she could hardly breathe.

Alone in her room at the end of that first day, twinges of insecurity crept in. The other students appeared so blasé and self-sufficient. Three French girls seemed intentionally rude or they ignored her. The American girls were friendly enough, but rather a giddy clique, totally intrigued with the gaiety of the Bohemian lifestyle and the Latin Quarter. With the exception of Roberto, who apparently let the other men know he already had his claim on her, only one person offered friendship that first week.

"Hello, I'm Ruth Jerome," a sweet-faced woman of about thirty-five extended a well-manicured hand. "Please let me know how I can help you. New surroundings can make one feel very alone."

"You don't know how I appreciate that," Beth answered. "How long have you attended the *Beaux Arts*?"

"I'm a graduate student, on an extended sabbatical of sorts from staff at the Metropolitan Museum in New York. I'm here working on another master's degree."

Beth looked puzzled. "How is it you're in one of my classes then?"

"Henri, our instructor, is an old friend, and an absolute genius in theory. Many students come back to him from time to time, as Roberto does. I've noticed he's zeroed in on you. I've watched you paint—you have great style, but you look dreadfully lonely sometimes. Just wanted you to know I'm here for you."

Beth remembered Hope and Tillie had said that too. It put Ruth in a special category. "You're sweet to notice."

The instructors fascinated Beth. She listened with her heart as well as her mind as they spoke of color, composition and theory. She experienced the exhilaration and drama of bringing sketches to life on canvas. Beth's zeal enveloped an almost spiritual quality in the extraordinary power of light to create a mood. It appeared in misty mornings, the intensity of midday, the blush of a sunset, or the delicacy of Degas's transparency in his dancers' skirts.

The days, weeks and months merged into a blur. A year passed in the blink of an eye. The other girls had a new romance every week, but Beth's passionate love affair was with art. She perceived all of creation in new dimensions, fervently striving to capture its wonder on canvas.

Her studies pushed almost all else into the background, except a constant contact with her parents and her deepening friendship with Ruth.

Ruth became her safe harbor and mentor, a kindred soul, and one who knew when to whisk her away to a quiet little cafe for dinner. Ruth was brilliant, yet uncomplicated. They could talk for hours or sit in silence with equal ease.

Over café au lait one afternoon, Ruth said, "Beth, I'm truly impressed with your talent. You're the most conscientious of the newer students, and the professors certainly are encouraging. You should be flattered to have your work used as an example."

"Thanks," Beth laughed, "I needed that. My female peers don't seem too impressed."

"You're more mature than they are. They're probably jealous and not quite as serious about their art. They spend too much time thinking about men. It doesn't help that most of them have their caps set for Roberto. Don't think I haven't observed how they all have their eyes on you when he walks you to class and pulls his easel up to yours on field trips. He's quite the dashing Romeo, but you've probably discovered that."

"Well, yes and no."

"Surely you've gone out with him?" Ruth asked, surprised.

"Sort of. We do have coffee here often. This is one of our favorite sidewalk cafes. And we've had lovely walks along the Seine, marvelous times sketching in Montmarte and up at Sacre Coeur. Just casual things like that, but not a real date. I almost went out to dinner with him last month just before I went home to England on Christmas break. But then the study load became too heavy."

Ruth glanced at her watch.

"I know you've got to dash," Beth said hurriedly. "I just want you to know I really appreciate you. Thanks for listening."

*   *   *

A mosaic of Christmas at Hampstead filtered into Beth's mind. Holiday memories blended the pungent deliciousness of velvet-ribboned cedar garlands with Tillie's plum pudding. She again saw the glow of firelight shimmering on mellowed walls. Cherished hours were shared discussing the vivid details of her newfound knowledge with her father. Only his pale, weary face and fragile frame clouded an exquisite vision of home.

Her reluctance in leaving had fought with a desire to return to art classes. And buried down deep, perhaps Roberto had something to do with her longing to get back to Paris.

Strangely, she thought, it was in painting with him that she did her best work. Roberto had incredible talent. He employed bold strokes of color, strong lines that compelled the eye to the heart of his passion for life, which he fearlessly conveyed on canvas. It was magic to watch his gusto in action. His paintings exploded with the brilliance of color at high noon. She perceived and painted the same scene in deep, rich, pastel hues. Her works expressed a sentimentality that made one want to pause and linger, as one wants to cling to the last fading moments of dusk on a never-to-be-forgotten day. They could compliment or critique one another's work with equal admiration and sincerity.

A mutual respect for the other's abilities formed a growing bond between them. Beth was ever aware of Roberto's admiring eyes devouring her every move, and her own racing pulse at the nearness of him. While he persisted, she declined, but she began to wonder how many more times he'd invite her to dinner. How long would this impulsive Italian, who flirted with every pretty woman who crossed his path, be interested in her?

The inherent disciplines learned in ballet, years of placing goals first and other pleasures second, were strong and not easily set aside. She wanted to prove to her mother that she had the ability to be a fine painter. That her father be pleased with her was equally important.

But if she kept turning Roberto down, there were a dozen other women who wouldn't. His talent, charm and elegance drew her to him like a magnet, more than she dared to admit. Her mind swirled with conflicting emotions. She reminded herself, *I've come to Paris to learn to paint, not to fall in love.*

"Look at this!" Beth laughed with Ruth over coffee. She was reading the paper sprawled across the table about fads of the 1960 college kids in the United States. "It isn't their academic achievements that captured the eye of the international press. They've made headlines with twenty-two of them packing into a phone booth, and forty into a little Volkswagen Bug!"

"That's our wild and crazy young Americans. I can't imagine that they're your age, Beth. At your present rate, you're going to be a little old lady with blue-tinted hair before you even have a date," Ruth teased.

"Oh, I've had a date or two, friends of the family. But I've always been so wrapped up in ballet and art I've hardly thought about men. Roberto is the only really interesting man I've ever met. But that could get complicated, and right now, my first love is painting. I guess I sound pretty dull and boring."

"No, just refreshingly different. But I hope you don't make the same mistakes I did. Woman does not live by art alone. Roberto is obviously crazy about you, and he's as elegant a man as you'll ever find. Why don't you go out with him?"

"All right, the next time he asks, I'll say yes."

*   *   *

"You honor me, *Bella Rosa Mia.*" Roberto's dark eyes flashed in appreciation as Beth came downstairs. "You must always wear the color of violets—*magnifico!*"

"And you, Roberto, look like a movie star. You are so handsome." She recognized the exquisite quality of his Georgio Armani suit and custom-made shoes.

"We will go out and—how do you say—*wow* all of gay Paree." He laughed.

Over candlelight at an exquisite little restaurant, Beth smiled happily. "You are a love, Roberto. I've never met a man like you."

"Oh, ho, *Cara Mia,* what about you?" His eyes flashed, with a mixture of anger and hurt. "The other girls, they are looking for a lover, they follow me around. 'Roberto this, Roberto that.' They are silly gooses. You are a beautiful woman, but you have a brain. They would have me in bed a long time ago. But we, we have been talking and painting, painting and talking forever—and you call me a 'love,' " he scoffed. "You English . . . where's your *amore?* Inside your beautiful body, behind your eyes bluer than the sapphires on your finger, is there not a real woman?"

Roberto's fingers played over her smooth white hands, turning the ring to catch the reflections of the candlelight.

The sting of his terse question struck and quivered like an arrow. Yet Beth let it fall without flinching, her eyes fixed on the flame. She had no intention of raising an eyebrow at his suggestive remark.

If he or the others wanted to tease her old-fashioned morality, she'd simply have to endure it. She still hadn't read enough of her Bible to understand it all, but she had decided some time ago that going against God's rules was even more unthinkable than disappointing her parents.

Roberto's sigh drew her back to the moment. "You wish to make a fool of me, *si?*" His voice dripped with sadness and self-pity.

"Oh no, Roberto, no. I am very fond of you. I like you very much—as a friend, as a magnificent painter and . . . as a man. You're a beautiful man." The unfamiliar intimacy of the moment made her pulse pound. "I've had no time in my life for *amore.* My studies have been my love." She was almost getting bored with repeating this truest of statements, even to herself. "Falling in love at the wrong time complicates one's life."

Roberto's eyes caressed her. He leaned across the table and shaped his lips in a kiss. "Loving and 'falling in love'—there is a difference. Love should not be too serious. One does not plan *amore,* it just happens."

Beth took back her hand and looked away from his handsome face. The English and Italians had two distinctly different viewpoints of love. Perhaps the English were too systematic. In a marriage, they looked for a best friend first, romance second. *Amore* was the invention of Italians.

"Come, let us dance," he coaxed. On the dance floor, he swept her into his arms and glided in whirling, graceful steps as the orchestra played "Love Makes the World Go 'Round."

Beth feared Roberto would feel the beat of her heart. His masculine nearness electrified her senses as she floated in his arms. Since cotillion days, she'd seldom danced with a man, except her father or someone his age. Roberto was a wonderful dancer. She was breathless, but not from dancing.

"We make beautiful music together, *Cara Mia.*" He blew in her ear, brushed a kiss across her cheek, and drew her indecently close.

"You take my breath away," she said honestly. "Let's go back to the table."

Roberto's magnificent brown eyes smoldered with adoration. He motioned to the waiter for more champagne.

"You have been to Lake Como, *si?*"

"No, but I've been to Florence and Venice with my father on buying trips."

"Ahh, they are fascinating for the arts, but nothing compared to the glorious beauty of Como. You must come there with me to the Villa Cabriollini." At the shock in her face he quickly added, "To meet my family."

Roberto looked as though he had even stunned himself, and she suspected he'd never invited a woman to meet his family, even casually. It could be misunderstood, too committal. She wondered if he was a man who could be committed to any woman.

"Tell me about your family," she asked. That surely would be safer ground for conversation.

He leaned back, reminding her of a peacock regally displaying his splendor. "My father is Baron Carlo Umberto Cabriollini. The villa was built by a Prussian prince in the eighteenth century on the shore of Lake Como. It has been in our family for three generations. My father and his father before him have been collecting priceless art for only seventy years, and yet it is said by many that in terms of quality, it stands alone as the finest private art collection in the world. Perhaps you have seen some of it shown in the United States—San Francisco, New York or in Europe? The vastness of it can best be *apprezzare,* uh, appreciated, in its own setting, which is rare in itself. You would, but of course, adore it."

Beth watched Roberto's eyes glow with pride. "So you come by your love for art naturally. And you, are you going to carry on the family tradition of connoisseur-collector?"

"But of course. Yet I not only wish to collect magnificent works of art, I must also create them. I am *obligato,* how you say . . . obliged to carry on the work of my grandfather and father. That is what he expects me to do. I am getting ready. But my father, he is so charming, a delightful raconteur with hundreds of stories about the treasures. He opens the villa's gallery to the public, with thousands of visitors during the year. The staff arranges that, but it is one of his personal accomplishments. That, I do not know if I can do so well."

"If charm is a prerequisite, you'll be smashing," Beth assured him. He had the bearing of an aristocrat, but she kept seeing him as a dazzling movie star with teeth that sparkled. Was this man genuine or only a suave Don Juan?

"Come, let me show you Maxims. We must do the town. We have only just begun."

They knew Roberto by name at Maxims and the exclusive club, Les Bains, where a black singer sizzled a torch song.

With Roberto, Paris seemed so much more alive. It was as though she had never before seen the glory of the City of Light at night. Its glittering brilliance rivaled the thrill of the first time she'd seen San Francisco's millions of diamonds sparkling in the night sky after the war.

In the distance, a clock struck three. Roberto walked her up the steps of her apartment as she tried to think how to tell him what a spectacular night it had been. Suddenly he seized her in his arms, clutching her body to his in a flurry of passionate kisses. Beth always imagined love's kiss would be sweetly sentimental and tender, with bells softly ringing somewhere, the fragrance of lilacs wafting through the air. What she heard was her heart, pounding like thunder. She gently but firmly pushed him away.

"Roberto, it's been truly spectacular. I had a wonderful time. Thank you for a beautiful night," she stood trembling.

The darkness hid the disappointment on his face. "Tomorrow," he responded, "tomorrow, we go to the Champagne country, and we sketch its unspoiled little villages all day, *si?* I will arrange it."

Beth walked in a daze to her tiny room and fell back on the bed, staring at the shifting shadows on the ceiling. She felt giddy, not from wine, but the swirling acceleration of her racing pulse. Never in her life had she felt so deliciously confused. Should she or shouldn't she have held Roberto at a distance these past two years? What feelings would tomorrow's date bring? Right now, she had to get some sleep. She had classes tomorrow. In her dreams, she and Roberto danced through Paris until dawn.

Concentration on the instructor's early morning lecture required effort. It was difficult, even though Beth was intrigued with the technique Degas used to achieve the wonderful iridescent airiness in his ballerinas' tutus. Visions of Roberto in the country persisted in crowding the instructor out of her mind.

The three French girls were standing by the front door when Roberto wheeled up in his black Massaratti. "Has he shown you his etchings yet?" one of them asked with a snide smile.

"Etchings? No, we're going out to the country to sketch."

The fabled vineyards where families had grown their grapes and made wines for more than 400 years looked all dressed up for spring, the brown vines bursting with bright new leaves. Roberto quickly set up their easels while the light was right, and they sketched and painted silently for hours. Beth shot frequent sideways glances at Roberto at work—so sure and competent, so deliberate in his bold yet sensitive strokes. It made her feel warm inside to watch him. She was amazed at her own feelings . . . feelings she had never known before.

Truly, he brought out the best in her own work. It was the artist-to-artist relationship that drew her to him, she told herself.

The shadows crept across Roberto's canvas. "That is it. Enough for today." He spread out a checkered cloth under the oaks and brought out a picnic basket he'd had the *ristorante* prepare. "A banquet fit for a queen, *Bella Rosa Mia.*" With a flourish, he arranged the paté de foi gras, cold chicken, bread, fruit and wine.

At times like this when Roberto's mind was absorbed in the romance of art, he talked quietly, with near reverence, of the beauty of God's creation, and the philosophy of the meaning of life. He was a rich-hearted man, a man of many facets.

A heavy gold cross gleamed on his chest under the open collar of his shirt. This pensive mood, his thoughtfulness and incredible attractiveness moved Beth to wonder if she was falling in love. His alluring eyes, set deep beside his sculptured Roman nose, enchanted her. Open admiration shone from her face—she felt irresistibly drawn to this man. Does one have to fall in love with the whole person? Maybe Roberto was right—one doesn't plan when and with whom to fall in love. Maybe it just happens, beyond one's control, with the heart ruling the head. Deep down, she questioned if it was just plain and simple sex appeal. Whatever, the sensation was totally new and undeniably wonderful. Something within her had been asleep, and now, vibrantly awakened.

Idiot, Beth told herself, *these are ridiculous notions. Don't be too serious,* Roberto had warned.

The glow in Beth's eyes had not escaped Roberto. "Come, it is time to go back to Paris." He lifted her up and circled her in his arms in one motion, and his lips were upon hers as he drew her close. Too close.

Gently pulling away, Beth whispered, "You're right, it is time to go."

That look of chagrin and perplexity swept over his face.

He ushered her into the Massaratti and spun silently past the splendid ruins of ancient cathedrals toward Paris.

What does he expect of me? she wondered. Had she offended him? It had been a day of sheer delight and she couldn't believe it had flown so quickly.

"Thank you for a lovely day, Roberto. I truly wish it didn't have to end." She placed her hand on his.

His eyes lit up. "Would you like to come to my apartment to see my etchings?"

The girls had asked her about it. Was it the expected thing to do? She adored his artwork.

"I'd love to."

Roberto stepped on the accelerator with a huge smile on his handsome face.

Roberto's apartment along the banks of the Seine was a startling contrast to the buildings that housed the students. Its opulent interior exceeded anything she could have imagined. But then, one might expect it of the son of a baron—one who would someday oversee perhaps the world's most prominent art collections.

"You like?" he grinned.

"It's *magnifico,*" Beth gasped. Deep white carpet melted into the rich cream of bleached linen walls where Impressionist and Post-impressionist paintings hung in ornate gold frames. Bronze sculptures sat upon black marble pedestals among a collection of furnishings that blended contemporary with antique tapestries in perfect harmony.

Beth gasped again at the gold baroque moldings and black accents in the luxurious all-white bedroom. Her look of adulation at Roberto was returned with a flash of his eyes.

In a burst of passion he had her in his arms, fervently kissing her.

"No, no," she cried, struggling to free herself.

Her resistance excited Roberto as she pummelled his chest. His eyes ignited. "What do you mean, no? You are a little coquette—you have been teasing me, inviting me to make love to you all the day. You are woman, I am man . . . what do you expect?"

He pulled her onto the bed, lavishing her with kisses. Her attempts to push him away excited him all the more. Her protests were halted by his mouth on hers, until she surrendered. And then, nothing else mattered, nothing else existed beyond the arms of Roberto.

"I love you," she whispered in the darkness of the room.

"Little fool," he gasped, suddenly angry, "you are precious to my heart, but Roberto is a lover. He does not 'fall in love.' What is love?"

Hot stinging tears spilled down Beth's cheeks. "I . . . I thought what you felt for me was love. . . . "

Sitting up on the bed, he demanded, "What have you done to me? You break my heart—how could I know you have never had a man before? Roberto thought your naiveté was little game you play. You turn me on, off, on, off, until I am crazy for wanting you." He paced the floor in despair, wringing his hands. "Roberto does have some honor. He does not set out to lure innocent virgins to his apartment."

Beth covered her face and cried.

"Cara Mia, Beth," he pleaded tenderly, "please do not cry. I cannot stand a woman's tears." He was on his knees on the bed, gently stroking her shoulders, then holding her sobbing body against his chest.

"Do you not understand, Bella Rosa Mia, you are a woman with intelligence? With proper upbringing, talent, beauty? You are only woman I could fall in love with, but love ruins everything. I do not wish to fall in love. I wish to be free to live and make love. . . . " He reached for her hand. "Come, get dressed, I will take you home. I am sorry."

"No, please," Beth sobbed. She shook violently while she threw herself together. Completely disheveled, she ran blindly past Roberto, who stood helplessly as she ran out the door, tears streaking her face.

The three French girls were sitting on the steps, laughing as she raced toward them from the direction of Roberto's apartment.

"She didn't like his etchings," one of them sneered.

4

A chill spring rain sent its tears, weeping slender streams down the windowpane. Beth's shroud of misery hovered over her like the morning mists that smothered the Seine. She could not bear the thought of venturing out of the safe cocoon of her apartment, of the bruising cruelty of mocking eyes awaiting her.

The refrain of the love song, "April in Paris," that she and Roberto had once danced to played over and over in her mind. Beth covered her ears and burrowed deep in her quilts, as if to shut out the romantic melody that had gone sour.

"Blithering idiot," she cursed herself. "You played a game without knowing the rules. It's your own fault you got hurt. You'll never be able to look at Roberto again—you've made such a fool of yourself."

A persistent rap at the door demanded an answer. A young French delivery boy grinned, "For you, *Mademoiselle*." He placed a bountiful bouquet of pink roses in her arms. She was too dazed to say anything or think to tip him.

The card read, "Please forgive me, *Bella Rosa Mia*. I am so sorry . . . Roberto."

Beth broke down in tears again. Roberto's dark eyes and handsome face loomed before her. "I can't blame you too much, Roberto," she whispered. Her heart twisted, and her mind churned in confusion. "I thought it was love—we have so much in common, yet we're worlds apart." The momentary ecstasy after she had stopped struggling and surrendered in his arms was overshadowed by a sense of shame and stupidity. The very thing she had determined not to do was done.

The ring of the telephone jarred her. "Beth, are you ill? It's Ruth. I've never known you to miss a class."

Beth choked out the words. "Thanks for calling . . . I'm, I'm all right. Talk to you later. I need to be alone right now."

"Is there bad news? Is it your family?"

Beth didn't want to talk to anyone, not even Ruth. "No . . . they're all right, thanks." She hung up the phone.

Beth mourned the innocence she had wanted to keep for a husband, but also for Roberto's love that could only bring heartache. She had never felt so depressed, nor known that love could be so painful.

The fragrance of the exquisite roses permeated the small apartment. They endured Beth's salty tears upon their velvet petals and caressed her burning cheeks as she buried her face in their cool perfume. Her eyes fell again on the card: "I am so sorry . . . Roberto."

"I'm sorry too," she said aloud. "Come along, girl, get yourself together," she told herself. "Life goes on. Private little tragedies happen every day, and no one else will ever know or care. The French girls with their sneers can just . . . well, I don't care."

Beth splashed cold water on her face and dressed hurriedly. A quick whisk of the hairbrush and a dab of lipstick brightened her spirits. She slipped into her trench coat for a walk in the rain.

She saw herself and Roberto passing the painting stalls of eager artists along the Left Bank, closed now because of the rain. Never again would they stroll together across the Pont Neuf with its golden statues, or wander through the Tuilleries gardens. The Champs Elysees bustled with its usual parade of power and sophistication. Parisians and tourists crowded the avant-garde boutiques and cafes. It looked exactly like a Utrillo painting.

She walked for hours, turning her head aside from every set of oncoming eyes that seemed to question the tears swimming in hers.

At last, she found herself in the Notre Dame cathedral. Here in the parish of the history of France, she gazed in awe of its ancient architecture, the glowing radiance of the thirty-foot expanse of the Rose Window.

A few reverent worshipers were sequestered in the only quiet section of the vast cathedral. Beth slid into a seat. A tour group passed, talking loudly. Slowly, she came to understand. A search for the presence of God had drawn her here. Somewhere among the shadowy mysteries of the ages, hidden among the crowds and the noise, perhaps she could find Him. She had to. The guilt, the turmoil, the explosion inside her soul demanded release.

"I don't know much about You, God," she whispered, "but I do know one of Your commandments says You don't approve of what happened between Roberto and me last night. It's commonplace for others, but You and I know it's not right. Please forgive me. Help me to forget about Roberto. . . . "

A lecturer gathered her tour group a few feet away and began an explanation of the magnificent Gothic architecture and the flying buttresses supporting the walls. Moving on, Beth paused before an awesome golden statue of Christ on the cross. She looked up in silent prayer. "Jesus, I know You died for people like me. You're real to my friend Hope and her family. Would You please, somehow, become real to me? I need You so very much. . . . "

The tense anguish over her lost chastity slowly released its iron knot. With closed eyes she saw the awful mass of confusion, the delusion she'd substituted for the real thing, spiral round and round, like the water in the streets being flushed down a drain. A calm she didn't understand warmed and relaxed her stiffened shoulders as she stepped outside.

Beth often felt refreshed by a walk in the rain. But she didn't know God could wash away the chains of guilt and revive her spirit, just by her asking Him. Healing the heartache would take some time, but at twenty-one she had her whole life before her. She felt calmer, definitely older and hopefully wiser. Whatever had happened in the cathedral was a mystery—a wonderful mystery, for which she would be forever grateful.

One thought about Roberto consoled her. She believed that in his own way, he loved her as much as he could any woman.

She dodged another wave of tourists crossing the bridge to the Left Bank. Through the drizzle the Seine rippled in unperturbed grey-green silence. Beth quickened her step to get back for her last class.

"Beth," Ruth waved from across the hall and came toward her. "You look like a drowned rat. Where have you been? Are you okay?"

"Yes, I'm all right now. A walk in the rain always helps to get my head on straight. Thanks for caring."

"How about going to the ballet tonight? Or are you going out with Roberto?"

"I'd love to go. I'm—I'm not seeing Roberto anymore. That's over."

Ruth's arm slipped around her. "Poor baby, so that's your problem. A lover's quarrel. It hurts, doesn't it?"

"More than you know."

*   *   *

The next few weeks flew by, like the pages of a calendar flipping in the wind. Beth lost herself in her art. Roberto ducked away mercifully whenever they approached each other. It would have been unbearable if he had attempted to woo her into a relationship they both now knew could come to no good end. Once, she dared to look into his eyes long enough to catch a glimpse of pain, or maybe it was desire. She put it quickly out of her mind.

Her only diversion was exercise. The ballet positions and stretching were stimulating. She often studied and painted long into the night, or in the misty early morning light. And then it dawned on her. Her period was two weeks late.

A sickening panic swept over her. She had ignored the tenderness in her slightly more rounded breasts and thought the waves of nausea in the mornings were from not enough sleep.

"You can't get pregnant the first time," she remembered overhearing some of the older girls at the ballet school say.

But they were wrong, because she knew she was.

It was almost midnight. "Ruth, Ruth," Beth called out, knocking frantically on Ruth's apartment door, oblivious to the time.

Still tying her robe, Ruth opened the door. "What is it, Beth? What's wrong?"

"Ruth, I'm pregnant," she blurted out.

"Pregnant? You? You've got to be kidding. No, no, of course you're not. That's not a joking matter. Come in." Beth stood there, clinging to the haven of Ruth's warm embrace, while great sobs wracked her body. "Tell me all about it while I make some tea."

Beth poured out her heart. Between sobs and mopping her tears, she told of her one night with Roberto. "What will I do? Roberto is a lover, not a husband or father. There's no point in even telling him. I do think he loved me, Ruth, but that's little consolation now."

"He still does, Beth. It's written all over him. I see sadness in his eyes when he watches you pass, as though he longs to reach out and touch you, but you're beyond his grasp. But I understand what you're saying. He's not the marrying type. You could go home, couldn't you?"

"You don't understand. Proper young English daughters of prominent families just don't get pregnant."

"Don't kid yourself, of course they do. It's been happening since time began, only it's a well-kept secret."

"I hate secrets, they're dishonest." Beth stepped to the window and gazed absently to the street. "My parents have given me absolutely everything. An idyllic childhood, schooling, theater. Every opportunity to be the best I could be. They just never talked about love or feelings, and certainly not about the facts of life." Beth turned to face her friend. "Ruth, they're very prominent people. Do you know my father's impeccable expertise in antiques and art collections is sought across the continent, around the world? My mother's name is synonymous with the Royal Ballet. Can you imagine how embarrassed they'd be by an illegitimate grandchild? They'd be crushed. It's too unthinkable."

"There's always something else you can consider," Ruth said slowly. "More women than you can imagine have abortions. I'll loan you the money so you won't have to ask for more allowance. Somehow we'll find a decent doctor."

"Oh, Ruth," Beth moaned. "I couldn't do that. It's murder. I could never kill my baby. That's not an option at all."

The words *my baby* sounded so strange. The thought that she could actually be carrying human life was suddenly personal. It involved more than a mere physical condition and emotional experience. Her protective mother instinct had just been born.

The horrible suggestion of aborting her baby suddenly shed a new light on her perspective and determination.

"Ruth," Beth said calmly, "I'm going to have this baby. Just don't ask me where or how."

The silence that followed was a golden gift that required no justification or explanation, only the unspoken assurance of being loved and accepted, whether or not one agreed. Beth treasured that quality in her mentor.

Ruth mutely poured them another cup of tea.

Beth thought of her years of ballet training—and how her body still demanded constant exercise. She knew the intense discipline of mind, the determination to stretch and bend muscle and sinew into unnatural configurations the body was never intended to form. She had endured the bruises on once-tender feet that eventually produced the callouses without which a dancer cannot perform.

Determination. She would have to exercise, stretch and bend her own will beyond all former limits to prepare herself for being a single mother.

Beth came out of her thoughts and looked into Ruth's compassionate face. "You are a love. I appreciate the tea and sympathy, the comfort you always are. Thanks."

Hope, Tillie and now Ruth—she'd been grateful for each of them in her times of need.

"I'll let you go back to sleep now." She stood to leave, giving her friend a hug.

"No, Beth, please. Why don't you just stay here? I'll sleep on the sofa. You need some rest. We'll talk some more later, and maybe you'll change your mind."

"That sounds good. Thanks, Ruth, I'd like that."

Beth drifted off to sleep with a thousand thoughts running through her head. Abortion would certainly be the easier solution. Maybe Ruth was right after all. She would have to consider it tomorrow. She couldn't think right now.

Beth awoke feeling queasy. Ruth gave her an appraising look. "You look a little green. Are you okay?"

"This whole situation makes me want to throw up," Beth attempted humor as she dashed to the bathroom.

"Poor baby, I'll get you some crackers and milk and see if that helps."

Beth felt like a pampered child staying home from school with a tummy ache. "Do you think I should see a doctor? Should I start taking vitamins or something?"

"If you decide to go through with this, you should probably wait until you've missed two periods, or the doctor would tell you it's too soon to confirm pregnancy."

"It seems pretty conclusive to me. Oh, Ruth," the tears came to the surface again, "I've made such a mess of it. I feel like an ordinary tramp. I don't know what to do."

"Only you can decide," Ruth put a comforting hand on Beth's shoulder. "And there's nothing ordinary about you, hon. You're an extraordinary artist and human being. Don't forget, I'm paid by the Metropolitan Museum of Art to recognize genius, so I'm not just being kind. I honestly believe you were too naive to see the handwriting on the wall. Get off the guilt trip. Being in love with the guy doesn't mean you jumped willingly into bed. It was a weak moment. Don't be too hard on yourself."

"It doesn't change the circumstances though, does it?" Beth sighed. "I'm feeling lots better. Thanks for putting up with me. I've got a class in an hour. I'll go home and try to put myself together."

Beth was grateful this was a painting class and not a lecture. A brush in her hand and color on the canvas were always therapeutic. Maybe she'd think of some brilliant way out of her dilemma. She'd have the afternoon free, go for another walk, and perhaps by some magic, she'd see a solution. Maybe something she hadn't thought of yet.

After class Beth couldn't wait to get to the corner coffee house for something to eat, but she dashed first to the post to see if she had any mail. She usually didn't consider mail to be too urgent, but today maybe a sense of security was what she hoped to find.

A letter in Mum's handwriting waited in her box, and Beth knew from the penmanship something was wrong. Mum's ordinarily free and lacy loops were a cramped scrawl. Beth pulled out another letter. Like sunshine, a yellow envelope with a daisy border contrasted the formal gray linen one of Mum's. Hope's letters always arrived when she needed them most, but Beth put this one aside. She'd save it for later, like dessert.

Beth frowned over her sandwich as she read:

My dear Beth,

You should know, love, that the situation here in England is causing us great concern.

That was Mum. Daddy would have begun in poetic verse, avoiding for several lines the awful truth. Mum had a way of jumping right in.

There is worry throughout Britain's business community, anxiety over the direction of our economy with the Labor Party in control. Everyone's uneasy. Coupled with the effects of the war in Korea, I fear the country is headed for rather hard times. You know I have never involved myself in your father's business, you're much more knowledgeable than I. But even the wealthy are cautious. They love to come into Sheridan's for tea and browse just to capture the ambience, but they're not buying.

Jobs are scarce. The Japanese are taking over the auto industry, Germany the textile mills, and England is no longer the queen of the seas and shipbuilding. Britishers are moving to the colonies—New Zealand, Australia, Canada, Rhodesia . . . and San Francisco.

Beth groaned. Never before had Mum talked of commerce. She was a ballerina, without a thought to the outer world beyond the ballet. The tone grew even more grave.

To make matters worse, my dear, our San Francisco store has a catastrophic management problem. Gerald just isn't paying attention to the bottom line.

She didn't know Mum knew what the "bottom line" was.

In short, darling, the cash flow is at a very low ebb, and consequently, your father is dreadfully depressed.

Mum's handwriting became disturbingly shaky here. . . .

Your father's business acumen has never measured up to his marvelous artistic perception. Edward's stability never quite came back after the war here, but of course Sean would never let him go. He just works harder himself. I fear this is too much for your father.

Beth read through the blur of Mum's tears on the page.

Your father's health is failing rapidly. . . .

Poor Mum. Underneath the world-famous ballerina with her strong will for excellence and perfection on stage was a frightened child. Mum's tragedy pitifully overshadowed Beth's. Her letter was a plea. No, maybe it was more. Beth read it again. Between the lines it said, *Come home, we need you desperately.* It also said her schooling in Paris had become unaffordable, and this isn't the time to tell them she's pregnant.

How could her whole wonderful world come crashing down on every side in a matter of twenty-four hours? Yesterday, her life flowed like a melody, rippling merrily toward the promises of bright tomorrows. Today, it loomed in total discord and the incomprehensible clang of painful reality. Beth turned and leaned her head to the wall to hide her tears. Now she was crying in public. "Oh, God," she whispered, "what shall I do?"

Beth peered outside at the morning mists that had become a drenching rain and made a dash for her apartment building. The three French girls gossiped inside the front door but no longer seemed interested in this dull person whose main pursuit was studying.

Chilled to the bone, Beth put a kettle of water on the hot plate for tea. *A cup of tea brightens the gloomiest day and warms the soul,* she told herself. With the lavender afghan Tillie had made tucked around her, Beth gently slipped open the envelope of yellow daisies, anticipating a quiet moment with her dear friend. Subconsciously she wished Hope would offer her the comfort and encouragement she so desperately needed.

Precious Beth,

You are ever in my thoughts and prayers. In your next letter, please paint me a word-picture of the chestnut trees in blossom.

My darling Josh is such a joy and comfort. I praise God for bringing this godly man into my life, especially for what lies ahead. There's no easy way to tell you, so I'll just say it. I had an emergency hysterectomy last week following severe hemorrhaging. The doctors procrastinated as long as they could because I'm so young, and they knew we wanted to have children. But there was no other choice. They feared the tumor causing the bleeding was malignant, and it was confirmed today. But they're sure they got it all.

Beth, please don't worry. I'm feeling amazingly well, but then I shouldn't be too surprised. God will never let me go through pain or suffering alone, and neither will my Josh.

Psalm 139 is a great comfort, more than ever. There's nothing about me He doesn't know or care about. Isn't that neat?

The nurse just came in. I'm sure she's going to tell me the doctor will let me go home today. Write to me soon and tell me what's going on in your life.

God Bless . . . I love you,
Hope

"God isn't fair!" The tea cup flew to the floor. Beth flung the afghan aside, yellow pages fluttering. She stood and pounded the wall, shouts breaking into sobs. "God isn't fair—life isn't fair. Hope, why couldn't we have stayed ten years old forever?" she cried.

"What's going on in there?" Ruth's voice called through the door. "Are you all right, Beth?"

"I'm afraid you pay a high price for being my friend, Ruth," Beth said, as she went to open the door. "How do you always manage to show up when I need you most?"

"Just lucky, I guess," Ruth gave a wry smile as she stepped into the apartment. "Now, make us a cup of tea and tell me what's wrong."

"I'll fall apart all over again if I try to explain," Beth's eyes began to swim. "Here, read Mum's letter first, and then Hope's. I'll make the tea." She watched and waited while Ruth labored through the letters.

"Life isn't fair, is it, Ruth?" Beth asked when Ruth put the letters down. "Hope wants a baby she'll never have, and maybe won't live to spend her life married to a wonderful man. Meanwhile, I'm having an illegitimate baby I can't even tell its grandparents about. And my Mum was never born to cope with adversity. Daddy always does everything for her. She must be frantic. Somehow, my mess doesn't seem as tragic as either of theirs."

"You'll make it, hon."

"I'm going to have to go home, Ruth. They need me. I just hope their crisis improves before I have to tell them I'm pregnant. Even then, they'll be devastated."

Ruth suggested abortion again, but Beth shook her head. "At this point I can't consider abortion. I'm too unstable right now to make such a decision. If I can help Daddy in the store and he doesn't have my costs here to worry about, it may ease his troubles."

"It'll work out. Just take one day at a time. I'm so sorry about your friend Hope. We'll just think positive and maybe the cancer will go away." Ruth looked sadly at her friend. "I'm going to miss you terribly. When are you leaving?"

"I'll call the airlines. As soon as possible," Beth gave Ruth an affectionate hug. "I'll miss you, too."

After Ruth left, her words, "We'll think positive," echoed in Beth's mind. She pondered the older woman's tone of confidence in relying on one's own "good thoughts." Do any of us have the inner ability to be positive in the crisis of an unwanted pregnancy, when a country's economic base crumbles and ruins our lives, or when life itself is threatened by cancer? *That's when I'm least able to help myself,* Beth argued. *I wonder if that works for Ruth when the sky falls in, or if it was the only comforting thing she could think of to say?*

Beth wondered how Hope could be so cheerful with such a peace in her tone, when her illness might be terminal. How could this Psalm, just words on a page, bring that depth of serenity to anyone? She had to find out. . . .

Beth found Psalm 139 in the middle of her Bible.

> O LORD, thou hast searched me, and known me.
>   Thou knowest my downsitting and mine
>   uprising,
> thou understandest my thought afar off.

Beth wasn't too sure how comfortable she was with that.

> Thou compassest my path and my lying down,
>> and art acquainted with all my ways.
> For there is not a word in my tongue,
>> but, lo, O LORD, thou knowest it altogether.
> Thou has beset me behind and before. . . .

Did God know she was going to get pregnant? Why didn't He keep her from ever going out with Roberto? She had said no for such a long time.

> . . . and laid thine hand upon me.

Tears spilled down Beth's cheeks. "Oh, Lord," she whispered with uplifted head. The tears kept coming. "Is Your hand really on my life, and I just don't see it yet?" She read on.

> Such knowledge is too wonderful for me;
>> it is high, I cannot attain unto it.

The knowledge that God cares is *too wonderful*, Beth thought.

> Whither shall I go from thy spirit?
>> or whither shall I flee from thy presence?
> If I ascend up into heaven, thou art there:
>> if I make my bed in hell, behold, thou art there.
> If I take the wings of the morning,
>> and dwell in the uttermost parts of the sea;
> Even there shall thy hand lead me,
>> and thy right hand shall hold me.

Beth now understood the strength Hope drew from these words.

> If I say, Surely the darkness shall cover me;
>> even the night shall be light about me.

Beth thought of her love for light and what a comfort it was for her.

> Yea, the darkness hideth not from thee;
>> but the night shineth as the day:
> the darkness and the light are both alike to thee.

Beth paused and let the truth of the words sink in.

For thou hast possessed my reins:
   thou hast covered me in my mother's womb.
I will praise thee;
   for I am fearfully and wonderfully made:
   marvellous are thy works;
   and that my soul knoweth right well.
Thine eyes did see my substance,
   yet being unperfect;
   and in thy book all my members were written,
   which in continuance were fashioned,
   when as yet there was none of them.

Chill bumps leaped down Beth's whole body. Her eyes were wet, but her vision was never clearer. *I never knew God had such intimate things to say to me in the Bible,* she thought. *It's like a personal letter. If God knows all about my baby, then He knows where it's going to be born, where we'll live and how I'll take care of it. He knows things about me I wouldn't want anyone else to know, but if He's going to plan my days I suppose He has to.*

The verse, "If I take the wings of the morning and dwell in the uttermost parts of the sea; Even there shall thy hand lead me," floated like a melody over the rivers of her mind, swirling into a spectacular drama she longed to put on canvas. *When I can paint the hand of God,* she told herself, *I'll be an artist.*

The phone rang three times before it shook Beth from her thoughts. "Hello."

"Elizabeth? I began to think you weren't there. Did you get my letter?"

"Yes, of course, Mum. I'm sorry things are going so badly. How's Daddy?"

"I've never seen him like this, Beth," she sighed. "You two are so close. It's been hard on him having you away. Of course, it's just what he's wanted you to do, love. His little girl had to grow up sometime.

"It's like he's lost his spirit without his regular customers coming to him. I assure him the wealthy will always be there and this slump will soon pass. Can you imagine your father without his usual bustle of enthusiasm? I don't know what to do."

"Mum, how are you?"

"Other than dreadfully worried about your father, splendid—but rather stressed in an exciting way. Have you heard, the Royal Ballet has been invited to a historic visit to Russia? It's quite incredible, and frightfully demanding. I don't have a minute for anything else."

There's nothing new about that, Beth thought. "How thrilling, Mum, to perform in Moscow. That's the ultimate compliment. I didn't know the Soviets recognized any ballet company but the Bolshoi. That's marvelous!"

The long pause in the conversation meant it was still Beth's move. "I'm coming home, Mum," she said at last. "Would that help? Perhaps I can lend a hand to Daddy in the shop. I thought if he didn't have my school expense that would help, too."

The words stabbed when she heard herself volunteer to come home. It was the last thing she wanted to do. But she knew she must.

"Thank you, Beth," her mother sounded relieved. "I had hoped you would come home without my asking. Frankly, I don't see any other way. When will I see you?"

"I'll check the flight schedule and pack my things as soon as I can and let you know."

"You always have known the proper thing to do, Beth. I'm very proud of you."

How proud will she be when she learns I'm pregnant? Beth wondered as she hung up the phone. Yesterday a doctor had confirmed the obvious, and Beth was mortified at the examination. Now Mum's confidence in her only made her feel worse.

Air France had a daily flight into Gatwick. Even the new airport would be a strange experience. It had been completed after she left London. Beth made reservations, allowing only two full days to pack. She began at once to drag out her footlockers and suitcases.

The phone rang again. "Beth, I know I don't want to hear this," Ruth said, "but did you schedule a flight?"

"Yes. Thursday, leaving Charles de Gaulle at 10:00 A.M. to Gatwick."

"That's so soon—I can't stand it."

"I want you to seriously think about coming to visit us in London when the term is over next month, before you go back to New York. Besides, Ruth, it'll be better this way. I'll be so busy packing I won't have time to think. I only dread the thought of checking out of my classes in the morning."

"I'll come help you pack, and plan on me driving you to the airport."

"Ruth, what would I do without you? Thanks, love."

Side by side, Ruth and Beth crammed things into Beth's suitcases amidst tears and laughter until after midnight. "Don't pack the tissue, I'm not through with it yet," Ruth chuckled. "We'll work some more after my early class and your meetings with your instructors."

Beth reported happily the next day, "Ruth, my instructors all gave me such encouragement. It's not possible to give me a final grade, but they'll send excellent references if I need them."

Late that afternoon, an exquisite single pink rose was delivered by the boy from the florist. The note read, "I wish you to be happy. Maybe it is best this way for us. My life will never be the same. It is painful to be near you without you to be my own *Bella Rosa. Addio.* Roberto."

Grazie, Roberto, Beth said to herself. *You'll never know how much you changed my life. . . .*

Beth handed the note to Ruth. "I wonder if he really knows what pain is all about," she commented.

*   *   *

The sun shone brightly for Beth's dreaded day of departure. Ruth supervised some boys she had enlisted to carry the luggage to her big sedan at the curb.

Beth gasped when she reached the sidewalk. Roberto stood across the street. When she appeared he blew a kiss, then walked away. It seemed she had lived a lifetime since that day two and a half years ago when he and François had carried in her bags.

Roberto had already said it . . . their lives would never be the same. But for totally different reasons. He'd had many women before her, and no doubt many would come after. But she wondered if he would ever again bare his heart, his innermost feelings, his passion for art as he had with her.

If he merely pursued passion and forever denied love, he'd be a lonely man. It gave Beth no comfort to think of Roberto one day reigning proudly over the Villa Cabriollini art empire—alone.

She resisted looking sideways as they passed the suave Italian aristocrat turning the corner.

5

Sean Sheridan made certain he reached the passengers' arrival gate early. In his mind's eye he had seen his daughter running toward him a dozen times, always wearing violet. Through the crowd he spotted her, hurrying through the tunnel toward him in a softly tailored lavender wool suit, silk violets pinned in her black hair.

Beth's legs couldn't carry her fast enough. She'd fought nausea and the fearful anticipation of the toll of her father's exhaustion the whole trip. Daddy's white mustache and his snowy white hair parted in the middle distinguished him in any crowd. He epitomized impeccable English tailoring in his Bond Street suit.

In a moment, they were in each other's arms.

"Let me look at you, love," he held her at arm's length proudly. "That's my pet, willowy, yet more womanly. I'm delighted to see you."

"Oh, Daddy, I'm glad to be home." The reluctance to leave her art studies in Paris melted at the warmth of her father. Tired lines etched his face. She'd never thought of him as fragile before. Yes, she was glad she'd come home.

"It's wonderful about the Ballet's trip to Moscow, isn't it?" Beth asked.

"It's amazing the Russians would invite them. Mum's rehearsing and teaching most of the time, however. We sort of pass in the night. I feel rather bandied about, you know?"

Beth knew very well.

"How's Tillie? I'm so anxious to see her!"

"Tillie's splendid, wonderfully efficient. Edward and Ann come out to see her regularly, but she still won't set foot in the city."

The conversation continued light as they headed toward London. Beth never considered the city's familiar antiquities commonplace, so Sean didn't hurry. She caught a glimpse of the Coldstream Guard and their towering black bearskin hats as they went through the formality of changing the Guards at the palace.

"I see the queen's home—the flag's waving at us! Just like my favorite storybooks, Daddy. And Kensington Gardens—look, the bulbs are in full bloom." She had an impulsive urge to jump out and run up and down those manicured paths.

"Don't mind if I take you to the store first, do you, love? I want to show off my girl. The staff thinks you're tops—that you could take over one day with a bit more experience. That's quite a feather in your cap, I hope you know."

"Since Sheridan's is known all over the continent, probably the world, yes—I'm flattered. When people ask where I'm from and I say London, they instantly connect the name Sheridan with the shop."

"Well then, you're jolly good public relations. Here we are, pet." He jumped out of the Bentley and came around to the left side to open the door and escort his passenger through the massive carved doors.

"Here's my lovely," he announced proudly, and stood back as the staff surrounded her with hugs and greetings.

"The shop is just as I remembered," Beth looked around. "How many rare vases do you have in stock? You'd better hide them all, the little bull's back."

"It'll liven up the place," Edward smiled at her. "It's too bloody quiet in here lately."

Sean's expression fell. He didn't want to be reminded of the lack of customers. "Come here, pet," he said, hoping to change the subject. "Look at this exquisite silver tea set, early 1800, from Belgium. Lovely, what?"

"Fabulous," she said, remembering the fun she used to have with the tea sets on those special Saturdays. "Daddy, where are we going for lunch? I'm famished."

"The Dukes'?"

"The Dukes' it is," she agreed.

George himself came to their table to welcome them. But even the familiarity of people and places couldn't alter the feeling—one cannot go back. She was no longer a little girl. In fact, she almost felt like a parent. A careful eye on her father watched for indications of failing health. Had Mum exaggerated? The trembling hand as he made a toast, the meager appetite, the weary expression behind those watery blue eyes—the evidence was there. It overshadowed their pleasant lunch, but neither acknowledged it.

"Daddy," she said as they drove west, "do first impressions stay with you as they do me? I'll never forget the drive to Hampsted on the Heath when you first brought us out to see our new home."

"Yes, love. Do you remember how gorgeous the spring flowers are around the next bend? And wait until you see Tillie's tulips and daffodils, and oh my, the hyacinths. . . . "

Tillie stood by the gate, watching for them. The frightened young woman who once took so lovingly to a lonely little girl now approached middle-age. Threads of gray peppered her plain brown hair. Beth had never been so aware of change. Could that be a sign of maturity, or an acute sensitivity because of the changes in her own life?

"Miss Beth," Tillie squealed and ran to open the door of the big Bentley. "Welcome home. I baked your favorite scones for tea."

"Oh, Tillie. What a dear. You'll have me roly-poly the first day home if we're not careful." Beth had savored the French cuisine and found English food not too difficult to resist. But now, for the first time in her life, she might have to watch her weight.

"Tillie, show Beth the garden when she gets settled. There'll just be time before tea."

When Tillie and Beth came back in from their garden stroll, they found Sean asleep in his big buttery-soft leather chair in the library.

"He's napping more these days, Miss. It'll do him good."

"He's an old sixty-one, Tillie," Beth said sadly. "He's aged so much since Christmas, I can't believe it. What's happened?"

"My father never has been the same since the war," Tillie said wistfully. "I know he isn't the help Mr. Sheridan needs, Miss. Several of his best people have left London altogether. And your father's been lonely since you went away. You're the light of his life, you know, and the spark just about went out after you went to Paris. Your mum isn't home that much—her life with the Ballet consumes her. Whenever I hear them talking, it's mostly about the trouble the San Francisco store is in. A pity. I'm sorry, Miss Beth, that you had to come home from the art school when you loved the studies so much. But I'm glad you're here. Wish you could be two places at once."

"Thank you, Tillie. I can always count on you for straight talk. I'm glad I'm here too." And she was. Her father had sacrificed greatly to send her to the *Beaux Arts*, and, left to him, he would have absorbed an even greater financial hardship to keep her there.

Sean awoke with a start. "My word, girls, it's 4:30! Why'd you let this old man sleep past tea time?" He stood up and smoothed his hair and vest, once more in command of his immaculate bearing.

Tillie had tea spread out in the parlor on exquisite snow-white Battenburg lace. Beth licked her lips at the fragrant scones, blueberry tarts, Devonshire cream and strawberry preserves.

"May I pour?" Beth asked. She didn't want to invade Tillie's territory the first day home.

"Of course, Miss," Tillie looked pleased.

"Daddy—is this one of the tea services from the San Francisco store I used to play make-believe with on Saturdays?"

"It is, love. Of everything in that shop, you always came back to that tea set to daydream. I saved it for you. Someday when you have a home of your own, you shall have it."

Tears quivered in Beth's eyes. "Oh, Daddy, you are such a softie."

Words and feelings Beth wanted to speak were buried beneath the lump of sentiment in her throat. The heady sweetness of fresh lilac blossoms danced with English chintzes in a misty blur around the cozy parlor. She longed for her father to share his concerns, articulate instead of glossing over problems. It seemed so strange he hadn't questioned her coming home. He'd just accepted the arrangements Mum had made and his delight was more than obvious. She would have to take the initiative. . . .

"Daddy, when can I come and work at the store like I did when I was on school holiday? I think it would be such fun."

"Is tomorrow too soon, love? You have a good eye for floor arrangement, and we need to change the armoires, move some of the larger stuff around and give the old place a fresh appearance. We've a case of the doldrums. I just haven't had the old Sheridan inspiration."

"Everything I learned, I learned from you. I'd love to help. Yes—let's start tomorrow."

Sean looked years younger the next morning. *He's still the most distinguished gentleman on the train,* Beth thought, as their train sped them into the city.

Together they directed the changes in the shop. Creativity sprung back into Sean's decisions. Beth's contributions to the placement of the accessory items, especially major silver pieces, the samovars and paintings, stimulated the whole staff.

"Jolly good, pet," Sean remarked when the project was completed. "We've done it, and in record time. Only took a few days, and I've been procrastinating forever. It looks splendid, like all fresh merchandise. Now, if I only had such a fine solution for the San Francisco operation. What it needs is you, Beth."

"Oh, Daddy, that's a large order," Beth said, taken aback. "Do you really think I have enough smarts to pull it off?"

"It just popped out, love. Never really thought about it until now." His face dropped. "I've just got you back again—I hate to think of losing you so soon. But the San Francisco shop is rather a crisis, my dear. We're in a dreadful dollar loss."

Just enough hesitation crept into his voice to make Beth think he might consider it. Going to San Francisco had popped into her head, too—this might be the way out for all of them. More than anything in the world she dreaded telling her father she was pregnant, and Mum would absolutely die. San Francisco might be the answer. *God*, she thought, *if You're there, show me what to do.*

"Beth, you've always had an amazing head for figures, although don't ask me how a dancer and artist could have business sense too," Sean looked at his daughter. "But if you wanted to, love, I think you could manage it."

"Daddy, that's all I need," Beth hugged her father. "If you think I can—I can. I've got a lot to learn, but I'm willing to give it a shot."

The next few weeks were a crash course on inventory sheets, pricing, markup, customer follow-up and charting the bottom line.

"All this stuff you've been cramming into your head will just help you see the progress," Sean instructed. "The staff can handle all of that. What you need to do is transfer your enthusiasm to them. They just need pepping up a bit. Shake up their complacency. Our buyers in San Francisco and from around the country are a sophisticated lot . . . it's keeping them happy that counts. We've jolly well got the reputation for finest quality.

"I've instructed Gerald to work with you," Sean continued. "He's a good chap, an able assistant who managed very well after Harrison Caldwell passed on. But personal problems have devastated the poor fellow. He needs some heavy assistance these days.

"Aaron is the bookkeeper, so the rest is up to him. And pet, don't forget to serve tea at four o'clock. I'll bet you a chocolate biscuit Gerald let that go by the wayside. Do you suppose that was his downfall? How can the rest of the world carry on without tea?"

Daddy is himself again. His color is back, his spirits are up, Beth thought. *Just when he's up, I can't knock him down with my news. Besides, he'd worry about me being so far away, and whether I should be working when I'm pregnant.*

"We've struck upon a capital idea, love." His tone was pleased, an almost boyish twinkle in his eye.

It's an absolute miracle, an answer to all our problems, Beth told herself. At least for the moment.

"California, here I come, right back where I started from," Beth sang to her father on the trip to Gatwick Airport. Joy and sorrow played a mixed tune in the atmosphere in the Bentley. Daddy had put her favorite pink rose in the crystal bud vase, so typical of Bentley accessories, and so typical of his thoughtfulness. He had a penchant for perfection in luxurious, loving details, especially concerning his only child, and she loved him all the more because of it.

It's only the big things he can't verbalize, she thought. *Like telling me about life in the real world, and how his world had been falling apart.*

When they kissed goodbye at the departure gate, he instructed, "Gerald will be there to meet you. Look for a little man of about fifty with brown hair, spectacles and a white carnation in his lapel. Gerald always wears a white carnation. Part of his Sheridan's image, he'll tell you."

*　　*　　*

The American Airlines Boeing 707 jet, the latest in faster, safer air travel, screamed into the air. Beth held her breath at the deafening thrust to become airborne and her introduction into the "Jet Age." Gatwick, with its longer runways built to accommodate the jets, had felt so sterile and unfamiliar. In her mind, the world and everything in it whirled in the process of change, swifter than she could comprehend.

Beth peered down at the country she came to love during the most impressionable years of her life. *The British are such fascinating people,* she thought, *and my father epitomizes the "islanders," as they call themselves. They appear as though they don't give a fig for others' opinions, while in their own way, they care tremendously.*

She had been amused by the Britishers' consistent preoccupation with weather, their love of pomp and pageantry, their enjoyment of practical jokes and their unshakable self-esteem and vanity. How she would miss all that.

This incredible little island, only three hundred miles at the widest and six hundred miles long, had admirably and honorably defended itself and survived the devastation of a tragic war. Old war movies always made her cry.

She had fallen in love with the whole of it. The White Cliffs of Dover—that protruding wall of chalk that underlies the undulant towns in

Sussex and Kent; Canterbury and its majestic cathedral; the Universities of Oxford and Cambridge, which had shaped the English character of Britain through the ages. Her love of history, assimilated from living in the midst of so much, would forever enrich her life.

Beth loved England's meadows, shimmering in the rain. Swelling cities and spreading industry encroached somewhat on the rural atmosphere, but the countryside could never change. How could she leave all that? Her throat closed at the thought.

The newspapers, which she now read with great interest, had been full of speculations on the economics of the Empire, none of which appeared too bright. The "Age of Affluence," which followed the post-war recovery, had been short-lived. One commentator on changing moral values had been quoted in the morning *Times* she'd brought to read. She picked it up in hopes of fending off the wave of homesickness that threatened to overwhelm her.

> Most people today lack religious conviction; in its place there
> persists a leftover jumble of ethical precepts, now bereft of their
> significance, and the widespread habit of occasional private
> prayer to a god in whom most people only half believe. . . .
> Popular morality is now a wasteland, littered with the debris of
> broken convictions.

She put the paper down, thinking that observation even more depressing than the country's economic outlook.

Beth reminded herself she'd been born in America. She must now shift her mind to life in the United States, from Buckingham Palace to the White House. John F. Kennedy had been inaugurated as the thirty-fifth president just six months ago, in January 1961. "Jackie" brought new style and grace to the executive mansion, and women across the country were wearing slim A-line sheaths and pill-box hats. Beth would now have to adapt to American styles.

Thirteen hours in the air permitted the only time she'd had in weeks for deep introspection into the future and of the life within her.

God, I know You're up there, somewhere, Beth silently prayed. *What shall I do? Whatever the newspaper article says, I do believe You exist, and I know You have the right answers. Show me.*

Is it You, God, or my own inner voice that repeatedly haunts me with "If you love your baby, you'll give it away and give it a chance for a whole life, with two parents"? I've seen too many kids with divorced parents, God. They came from broken homes and have lived shattered lives. Oh, it sounded fashionable to ski in

Switzerland over Christmas vacation, or go to exclusive camps or Grandmother's for the summer. But the truth is, these kids are tragic, displaced persons who long for a family and stability, for two parents who'll be there when they're sick or stub their toes.

That's what I want for my baby, and I know I can't do it alone.

Beth turned her face to the window and the infinity of space. "God, I trust You to find a good home for my child," she whispered with tear-filled eyes.

A little man of about fifty with brown hair, spectacles and a white carnation in his lapel waved anxiously as Beth came through the passengers' tunnel at the San Francisco Airport.

"Welcome home. I understand you're on native soil, Miss Sheridan. I'm Gerald Ormsley. I have a car waiting to take you and your baggage to the apartment."

"I'm pleased to meet you, Gerald, and very grateful. Forgive my rudeness in using your first name," Beth added quickly. "My father always speaks of you as Gerald."

"Then I'd be pleased if you'd call me Gerald, too. However, I feel it is appropriate that I call you Miss Sheridan," he said politely as he guided her toward the baggage claim.

Gerald deftly maneuvered the Mercury station wagon out of the crowded airport toward the city. Whenever Beth spoke, her voice nearly cracked with exhaustion. She felt suddenly limp, as though a plug had been pulled that drained her of every ounce of energy.

"I'm sure you'll be delighted with my mother's apartment, Miss Sheridan," Gerald was rambling. "You'll feel right at home with her art and antiques. She has exquisite taste. And I'm without modesty in admitting that the pieces she didn't inherit from our English ancestors, I procured for her through Sheridan's."

"Am I going to live with your mother?" Beth hoped she'd successfully hidden the shock in her voice. She knew her father and Gerald had arranged a place for her to live. Beyond that she had been too consumed with cramming information on the business into her head to care about further details. But living with an elderly stranger was beyond her comprehension.

"Oh, I thought your father told you," Gerald realized an explanation was in order. "Mother has been in a convalescent home for almost a year since she broke her hip, but she won't hear of giving up her apartment. Thinking about coming back to it gives her something to live for, she loves it so. I'm afraid she never will. Facing reality at the age of eighty-five is often brutal.

She's happier to live in a fantasy land, and she hasn't a practical bone in her body. She owns the building outright, but her own resources have dwindled, so I've been keeping up the maintenance and taxes, which frankly isn't easy. The rent from the other apartment helps though.

"Your father may have mentioned I was having personal problems," Gerald's brow creased in a frown. "I feel I should tell you that my wife left us ten months ago—us being me and the four children. Two boys and two girls, from ten to sixteen. She got tired of me looking after Mother's needs.

"I married late because of providing for Mother. She was a fashion designer—the Coco Chanel of San Francisco for nearly fifty years. But she was a terrible businesswoman and now has little to show for it. My wife, Clara, had always been jealous of the only-child relationship. Called me a mama's boy. She never cared a hoot about her own family and simply cannot understand such devotion to my mother. Maybe I shouldn't have pampered Mama so, but my father died when I was ten, and I owe it to her.

"My, my—I have rattled on, haven't I?" Gerald shifted uncomfortably. "Perhaps that's my way of making excuses for failing your father."

"I think he's as concerned about your personal welfare as he is the gallery, Gerald." Beth appreciated his candor. It would make working together much easier.

"While I'm being so up front with you, Miss Sheridan, let me set the record straight. You have my full cooperation, so don't worry about me resenting a young woman as my superior. I feel like just about everyone is superior to me right now—I've really fouled up," Gerald's tone was low. "Your abilities are quite impressive, and I trust your father's judgment enough to think his summation of them is more than mere parental pride."

"I'm a true neophyte, Gerald," Beth laughed to lighten the mood. "And I understand how you feel about owing your mother your utmost devotion. I feel the same way about my father. If there's any way I can repay him for the sacrifices he's made for me, and if he thinks I can make a turnaround with your help, I'm more than willing to try."

"We'll be a fine team then," Gerald returned her smile. "Right now, I'm financially over my head. Quite frankly, the rent your father is paying for Mother's apartment will relieve me enough to be able to concentrate on business."

"It sounds like the perfect solution for us all." Beth hoped she sounded encouraging. It took a lot of fortitude to be as open as Gerald had just been. *I appreciate that in a person,* she thought, although waves of weariness pulled at her eyelids.

"Where is the apartment?" Beth hoped she wouldn't fall asleep before he answered.

"Do you remember the area not too far from Nob Hill where you lived as a little girl, called Russian Hill?"

"Vaguely."

"It's a stately neighborhood of well-preserved and restored Victorians. Many of the grand old dames have been divided into apartments, and Mother's is on the top floor. It has a splendid view of the Bay and all the lights, especially on clear nights."

"This is definitely not one of those clear nights," Beth commented as they crept along Highway 101 toward the city. "The fog makes me feel right at home, like I'm still in London. But I must confess I'm too tired to care whether it's foggy or not."

"Take a little nap. I'll let you know when we're there." This kind man sounded just like her father.

Gently, so as not to startle her, Gerald jiggled Beth's shoulders and steadied her as she groggily stepped out of the station wagon. Beth looked up at the soft welcoming glow of a Tiffany lamp shining through lace curtains in the turret of the blue and white gingerbread house.

"This is your new home, Miss Sheridan," Gerald beamed under the street lamp. "Your bags are in, and the water's on for tea."

"Gerald, it's adorable. And you're so kind."

"I think you'll be comfortable here."

Gerald paused in the inviting entry to allow her the full effect of the Austrian crystal prisms of the chandelier.

The banisters of the graceful staircase were buffed to such a sheen she could almost see herself.

"It's a doll's house," Beth said in delight at the sight of the parlor. Even in her tired state she noticed the cerise pinks in the wallpaper contrasted by the wide white crown moldings. And the furniture—pure Victorian. "It's wonderful. Gerald, I love it."

With the dignity and decorum befitting the best of English butlers, Gerald bowed from the waist. "And when do you wish your driver to come for you, Madame?"

"How about the crack of two tomorrow afternoon, since it's now midnight? I think I'll be rested by then. I'm so anxious to see the shop and go to work. And Gerald, thank you for everything. You know, I think we can do it."

"I'm going to try, Miss, believe me I am. I've needed some inspiration, and I jolly well think you're it. Sleep well."

Sleep would come easily under the fluffy cream satin-covered down comforter and lace-trimmed sheets. Beth blinked appreciatively at the heavy antique damask canopy of the Queen Anne four-poster bed and said good night to the first day of a new life.

"If the staff is as amiable as Gerald and shares his spirit of friendly cooperation, we'll do well, Daddy," she whispered into the night, and fell instantly asleep.

Much to Beth's frustration, the zipper on the skirt of her lavender wool suit resisted her tugs, then suddenly decided to cooperate. The fashionable jacket camouflaged her slightly rounded tummy nicely. Beth assessed her image—front, back and sideways—in the full-length gold beveled mirror. The final verdict on her appearance: feminine but professional. "No, you don't look pregnant, yet," she told her reflection. "And you no longer look like a carefree art student. Hopefully you look competent to direct San Francisco's most renowned art and antique gallery." She realized that if she dwelt on that last thought for more than a moment, she'd be terrified silly. Besides, there wasn't time to think. Gerald was at the door.

"You look smashing—as fresh as your white lapel carnation, Gerald," Beth greeted him. "You were right, I do love your mother's flat. It's so elegantly homey. Are we ready for my debut?"

"Don't be nervous, Miss Sheridan," Gerald guided her to the car. "Your father's letter of introduction to the staff and explanation of what he expects of all of us have paved the way nicely. For the most part, they've been tolerant but not too innovative with solutions to help the shop as I've gone to pieces over my family problems. Each staff member has unique areas of expertise, but none are capable of the overall management I should have been doing. I feel I've just lost it, along with everything else." Gerald cleared his throat. "That's mighty difficult for a dyed-in-the-wool Britisher to admit, eh? Mr. Sheridan is jolly well loved, and we'll all do our best, with your help, to turn the profits for him."

"Gerald, that's the loveliest bit of confidence-building I've ever heard," Beth smiled. "And I truly appreciate it."

Her mind was temporarily occupied by the remotely familiar streets of San Francisco as they roller-coastered down Powell Street and watching passengers leaping on and off the trolley cars. She strained in an attempt to remember the names of the flower vendors and recapture the delights of those memory-making Saturdays when she and her father made their way down to

Sutter Street. Even at ten, she had known San Francisco was her town. London and Paris claimed her strong affection, but the earliest awakenings of her hopes and dreams were born here. San Francisco was home.

The grand leaded glass and oak double doors of Sheridan's gleamed in well-kept splendor. They issued a dual invitation—to step back into time and to take hold of the present and future which lay before her.

Gerald swung the portals wide. Beth took a deep breath, put on her brightest smile, and took that giant step to meet the staff of Sheridan's, who stood ready to welcome her.

"This is none other than Miss Elizabeth Sheridan," Gerald announced in a stately yet warm tone. "Miss Sheridan, your staff of specialists.

"This is Clarence Tubbs. He's been with us nearly a year and is a veritable encyclopedia on eighteenth-century European antiques. He replaced Mr. Worthington, whom you may remember from your childhood."

Beth concentrated on masking her initial reaction to the jovial-looking Mr. Tubbs. His seedy Harris tweed jacket and dingy white oxford shirt barely covered his ample front. Her peripheral vision told her the shop didn't look any spiffier than Mr. Tubbs himself.

"I'm glad we have your expertise to draw on. I'm sure I can learn much from you, Mr. Tubbs," Beth smiled graciously.

She almost winced at the couple Gerald now turned toward. Both were smartly and immaculately dressed, but exuded the friendliness of Dracula and the dragon lady.

"This is Mrs. Claudette Bouvier, who with her husband, Henri, oversees the art gallery. They were both educated at the *Beaux Arts* in Paris before coming to San Francisco almost ten years ago. You'll have much in common."

Claudette reminds me of an older rendition of the French girls I knew there, Beth thought.

"I'm looking forward to going through the gallery with you," Beth acknowledged, with all the courtesy she could muster.

"You'll find Eileen Adams exceptionally bright and helpful," Gerald motioned toward a pretty blonde woman of about twenty-five. She was slim, with an efficient manner and appearance in a tailored grey wool suit, white silk shirt and pearls. "Eileen is our girl-Friday—a lovely receptionist, and she helps in sales when necessary. She's learning antiques very quickly."

"Eileen, I'll look to you to help me get acquainted with our clientele. Glad you're here."

"Now, last but not least, Aaron Abramson, our bookkeeper, who may not be quite as glum as he looks, now that you're on board, Miss Sheridan. We're all going to try to make Aaron smile and not see red anymore."

"That's right," Aaron extended a warm, manicured hand. "We'll get well acquainted, Miss Sheridan. We have a task ahead of us."

"I'm delighted to be with all of you," Beth assured them, "and I look forward to learning the various facets of how each area and individual functions. I anticipate us working as a team, and I'll appreciate your help."

Claudette, her sleek black coiffure complementing a Dior black wool crepe suit and satin blouse, turned on three-inch heels and clicked away without a word toward the gallery. Henri twirled his slim well-groomed mustache and followed close behind. Gerald shrugged his shoulders in acquiescence to the pair—an unspoken dismissal to the group.

Eileen registered Beth's questioning glance with an amused explanation in confidential tones, "Claudette's on her best behavior today. She didn't say anything. But even so, she always has the last word with Gerald."

"Thanks for the clue," Beth whispered.

Now what I need is a clue as to how and where to start to get this house in order, Beth thought. She surveyed the collection of rare treasures meticulously selected from European markets by her father. The gleaming showroom in her memory as a child now appeared as in a clouded and musty mirror.

And that's why I'm here, Beth reminded herself. *Somehow, we have to wipe away the film of lassitude in this dull and dreary place.*

On her notepad Beth wrote simply, "Bring back the sparkle."

The Westminster chimes of a grandfather clock struck four. Since there were no preparations in sight, on the next line Beth wrote, "And bring back four o'clock tea."

6

August 15, 1961

Dearest Daddy,

Our telephone conversations and various communications seem rather incomplete to relate to you the progress at the shop. I'm excited, and I need your further input.

In the past month, our plans have worked out well. When I arrived, I asked myself, "How do we recapture the sparkle?" First, it was a matter of housekeeping. Gerald's nervousness due to poor sales caused him to let the janitorial help go. Our staff of "professionals" disdain the task of mere housekeeping, so I temporarily reinstated a service to do that. (This staff doesn't know it yet, but they will gradually learn the fine art of housekeeping, just like your people in London have.)

I studied the showroom and we jointly decided which pieces and collections to emphasize, as you and I did in the London shop. The staff became enthusiastic—each got involved with his or her own area. To my surprise, even the Bouviers rose to the occasion. It seems everyone needed a challenge and an upper hand, which I endeavored to exercise gently but firmly. Being the boss's daughter does have some clout!

I hope you don't think I was too aggressive, but instead of a flat salary, I offered them a lower base, which you agreed with, and set up a higher commission—it has worked well. But I cautioned them, if our clients are caught in the middle by a strong sense of competition that disrupts staff harmony, we'll have to change to another plan.

Daddy, I wanted the changes to be considered positive. You liked the idea of an "Open House," and it was indeed a gala event. It previewed the "new look" for the showroom and was a smashing success. I'm glad you were impressed with the sample of the invitation I sent you. Eileen wrote the copy, and Gerald knew a creative printer who designed it. Did you like the new innovations it featured? How did you like the mention of the addition of Miss Elizabeth Sheridan to the staff?

The important thing is, it's working. At the open house we created a delightful rapport and conviviality with our clientele by serving an elaborate tea. They adored it and the special attention we lavished on them. You should have been here—you'd have loved it! Ever since then, we've been presenting tea at four o'clock, prepared by a caterer and served by us. The response has been exceedingly rewarding. We've stimulated an impressive number of clients who had fallen away and attracted new ones.

It's amazing that without adding new merchandise, the showroom looks so transformed. It recaptures my childhood fantasy and enlivens the romanticism of past centuries with elegance and grace. Daily traffic has increased considerably. The staff has a whole new attitude from what I saw the first few days. Even Mr. Tubbs looks as dapper as Gerald, without even having to be asked to sharpen up!

Aaron has already tracked sales on an upward trend in these few weeks. He doesn't think the expenditures are at all out of line with the results. It won't happen overnight, but we're making significant progress. He says, "If it continues, the second half of the year looks promising," but you'll see that in his report.

You asked about Hope and her recovery from cancer. She is as sweet as ever and says she's doing well. I've only spoken to her on the phone, but plan to see her and meet Josh soon, now that the staff is getting organized.

Thank you, Daddy, for this opportunity to spread my wings and test whether the education and benefits you've showered upon me have any practical value. I think they have, and I hope you will think so too. It's hard work, but I love it. . . .

I look forward to hearing from you soon with all your wonderful inspiration that founded Sheridan's. I love you, please take care of yourself. Give Mum and Tillie, Edward, et al., a big cheerio for me.

Your loving Beth

"*Bonjour,* Miss Sheridan. You have already been hard at work today," Claudette paused as Beth stepped out of her office. She actually had a feather duster in her hand. *Amazing,* Beth thought.

"*Bonjour,* Claudette. And you're very productive this morning also. The gallery is looking splendid. Congratulations on the sale of the Helleu paintings yesterday. A nice choice for Mrs. Huntington's bedroom."

"*Merci.* And today, I have another big appointment," Claudette looked smug.

Beth smiled and stepped over to Gerald, who had been adjusting a Louis XV carved walnut mirror. "Claudette appeared to be my toughest challenge, but she and I seem to have established a mutual respect and easy rapport. She's come around nicely, *oui?*"

"Nicely indeed, for you. I'd never have thought any of this was possible. You've done a splendid job and given me fresh inspiration. But, if I may say so, Miss, you look dreadfully tired. Why don't you take the day off?"

"Now that you mention it, Gerald, that's a capital idea. I believe I will."

"Is this Josh?" she inquired of the male voice on the phone. "This is Beth Sheridan. I can't wait to meet the husband of my dearest friend. I finally have a free day and wondered if you and Hope were going to be home. May I come down?"

"Wonderful!" Josh exclaimed. "Yes, we're both here. Let me give you directions."

"Mercy," Beth cried. "I just thought of something. I've never driven in this country before. I only know how to operate our old Bentley. I've never even thought about getting a driver's license."

"Then you'd better take public transportation," Josh laughed, "and we'll meet you at the stop. Here's how you get to San Jose from the city. . . ."

Beth listened carefully.

"That shouldn't be too difficult. Thanks, Josh. May I speak to Hope?"

Beth could hear Josh calling to Hope.

"Beth, is it really you? Here?"

"We always knew we'd see each other again," Beth said, remembering their childhood promise. "Hope, Josh sounds wonderful. He put me at ease already. I'm dying to see you."

"Stay all night with us, Beth," Hope invited. "We'll make believe we're ten again, and Josh is our prince charming. It'll be such fun."

That afternoon, the two women flew into each other's arms in an embrace long and dear. Josh towered over them, his arms like protective wings encircling their reunion.

"All right, you two," he laughed. "It's my turn. I get a hug too, Beth, because I feel I know you almost as well as Hope does. Is there anything you haven't told me about this girl?" He grinned at his wife.

"I'm sure she has lots to tell both of us. Let's go home and get cozy."

Josh drove them to a tract of modest but well-kept homes and parked their '52 Chevy in the driveway of a small yellow house with white trim.

"This is adorable!" Beth gazed at the cheery interior with curtains and tablecloths Hope had made. Its simple Early American furnishings and ruffled lamp shades invited her to relax. Beth noticed a picture of a tiny cottage and verse which read, "As for me and my house, we will serve the Lord . . . Joshua 24:15." *Nice*, she thought.

"Now," Hope insisted as she poured them hot tea, "tell us about your work and how you like being back in San Francisco. Tell us about your family. And we want to hear all the things you couldn't squeeze into your letters from Paris."

"We'll get to that later," Beth said. "I want to know about you, Hope. Did the surgery completely take care of the cancer? What do the doctors say?"

"I'm fine, praise God. I took the radiation, which was horrible, but there's no problem now. I'm healed, or at least in remission, which could last forever."

"Josh," Beth turned, "is that true, or is she just being her usual positive, optimistic self?"

"None of us knows how long we have on this earth, but Hope will be with us a long, long time. The hardest adjustment for us has been to accept that we can never have children."

"I'm so sorry." Beth's eyes stung, and the tears spilled over quietly to run down her cheeks. Josh came immediately to her side. This gentle giant of a man she'd only just met had his comforting arm around her, dabbing at her tears with his handkerchief. "It's all right—we'll be all right. God's in control, Beth."

"If He's a loving God, why did He make this happen?" Beth asked. "If any couple should be parents, it's you two."

"He knows what He's doing, Beth," Josh said firmly. "He doesn't cause such things, but He does allow them, and He wants us to trust Him."

"It's just not fair." Beth wiped at her eyes. "And—and, I have to tell you why. You're the only ones in the world I have to confide in. I'm," she took a deep breath, "I'm pregnant," and bent her head in tears. She turned away. She couldn't face them.

The room became silent for several moments. Beth waited for a reaction. What would these friends think of her? Then she realized they were looking at her with compassion and concern, waiting to hear more. She told them the whole story, of Roberto and her lost innocence, her father's failing health, and how it came about that she was managing Sheridan's. She knew Hope would realize how impossible it would be to tell Mum she was going to be a grandmother of an illegitimate child. And she voiced her concerns about raising the child as a single parent.

Hope came to her side. "Oh, Beth. You've gone through this whole thing alone—keeping your pregnancy to yourself while you've been working so hard to salvage the business. You must be exhausted."

"I am." Beth's eyes fell upon the worn Bible on the coffee table. "Hope, in a letter you told me about a Psalm that had given you encouragement. I found it comforting too. Would you read it to me?"

"Psalm 139, wasn't it?" Josh picked up the Bible. "May I?" They listened to his deep mellow voice. It seemed to Beth that the voice of God Himself had searched her out to remind her in a personal way that He knew intimately the innermost parts of each of them—their hurts, their broken dreams, their need and His love. She heard Josh repeating, "If I take the wings of the morning, and dwell in the uttermost parts of the sea; Even there shall thy hand lead me. . . . " He paused. "You see, Beth, He knows, He's in control, He loves us, even when we doubt Him."

"Thank you, darling," Hope glanced lovingly at her husband. "It's true—'such knowledge' is indeed 'too wonderful for me, it is high—I cannot attain unto it,' as the psalmist says. The more I learn about our God, the more I see how awesome He is."

Beth questioned them with her eyes, and asked, "How does one come to feel like God is as real as He is to both of you? It's like there's something inside of you that no one else has. I don't hear even a hint from you that life isn't fair, or that you're afraid, or angry." She looked straight at Josh. "In Hope's letters, she alluded to the possibility of terminal cancer with a calm that's beyond belief."

Hope touched her hand. "Beth, I think you know I've loved Jesus since I was a little girl. I asked Him into my life when I was eight, and He's been there ever since. Remember I used to sing to you, 'What a Friend We Have in Jesus'? He's always there. My parents and I, and even with Josh in the few years we've been married, have had some hardships besides my cancer. We don't have the answers to these problems, but we know the One who does."

Dusky shadows crept across the small living room, while a peachy glow from the summer sun warmed the plain white walls.

"You look hungry," Josh said kindly to Beth.

"I am—I'm starved," Beth answered, grateful that Josh understood her need for time to take all this in.

"How about the spaghetti we had left over from the youth group, Hope?" Josh called on his way to the kitchen.

"Maybe Beth would rather go out. That's all we have."

"Spaghetti sounds terrific! Can I help? I just taught myself how to make a great salad, and I brought you some San Francisco sourdough."

They lingered long at the table over coffee, then sprawled out with pillows on the floor while Beth pondered aloud—questions she had always had about Jesus, but had no one to ask.

"I always believed there was a God," she began, "but I just never understood that Jesus is the Son of God, and that He and God and the Holy Spirit are one. It makes sense, or how else could God meet all of our needs? I've heard of eternal life, but thought that going to heaven just had to do with being a good person. And I surely didn't know Jesus needed an invitation to be part of my life."

Josh referred to Scriptures all night. He patted the Bible and explained, "You know I fly to Mexico to take doctors, medicine, wheelchairs and life-giving supplies to desperate people. But I couldn't have learned to fly without studying the instruction manual. God's Word is our instruction manual. When we believe that the Author lives and that His teaching works, we can't pretend to understand all the intricacies of God's ways. We only know that desperation gives way to His answers for our lives, and the hope that's in Jesus."

A rosy dawn peeked through the sliding glass doors from the tiny patio. "We've been talking all night, and there's still one other thing I want to know," Beth said as she sat up eagerly.

"What's that?" Hope yawned.

"I want Jesus to live within me, too. I know now that I've been weakly searching for a long time. How do I ask Him to do that?"

All of them became wide awake, and Beth felt a quiver like an electric current pass from one to the other.

"You just talk to Him," Josh smiled at her. "He wants to have you know Him personally. Tell Him you love Him and believe He is Lord and Savior. Ask His forgiveness for sin, which none of us are free from until we come to Him. Open your heart to Him. He never says no. He just waits until you're ready."

"I'm ready," Beth said. "It's what I've wanted in my life since Hope's mother gave me that little white Bible. Even as a child, I knew the love that's in both of them came from some greater source outside of themselves. I just didn't know I could talk to Jesus."

Beth prayed aloud, openly, freely, in a way she had never heard before, with words that overflowed from her heart. "And Jesus," she concluded, "will You love my baby, too, and tell me what to do?"

Her dear friends had taken hold of her hands, and among them a look of joy, peace and release rippled around their tight circle.

"Let's get some sleep, and then we'll talk about the baby," Josh suggested.

"Oh," Beth jumped up, "you two don't have to go to work today, do you? I've kept you up all night!"

"No," Hope yawned again. "I don't know if I told you about my job. Since my graduation from Stanford, I've been working with terminal children at Stanford's Medical Center. I love them so much—it's awful when we lose them. But while they're there, they still want to learn and be read to, just like healthy kids. My job is to help them die with peace and dignity. There are none in crisis right now, so I asked for the day off."

Beth flung her arms around her friend. "Hope, who but you could do such a beautiful thing? I don't think I'd ever have that much strength. But what about Josh's job?"

"I leave in two days to take some medical supplies to Mexico. We're mostly loaded, so the hardest part of the job is done. Don't worry about it. Let's get some sleep."

Hunger brought Beth out of the tiny guest room at about ten o'clock. In the sunny kitchen, Josh flipped pancakes on the griddle, and Hope placed crisp bacon on pretty plates glazed with butterflies.

"It smells delicious, and I'm famished," Beth stretched and yawned.

"It's all ready. Let's thank the Lord and feed the lady." Josh held up the plate of pancakes.

"Beth," Hope began, swallowing the last bite of syrupy pancakes and pouring another cup of coffee, "Josh and I have talked and prayed about this all morning. We didn't sleep a wink. You said you thought we'd be good parents, and if you're sure you shouldn't raise the baby yourself, could we take care of it? Or if you're very sure, maybe adopt the baby?"

Beth's dark hair hung over the breakfast plate. Her shoulders shook with silent sobs, tears splashing into her tea cup. Her lips quivered as she looked up with love in her eyes.

"There are no two people on the face of the earth I'd rather have adopt my baby." She was overcome. "Of course the thought crossed my mind, but because of Hope's illness, I didn't know. . . ." She couldn't finish the sentence.

"Hope really is well enough," Josh said. "But we want you to be sure. Maybe it would be better if we just took care of the baby until you can find a nanny or another solution. You still have almost five months before it comes."

"No." Beth straightened up, her practical nature and the resolve she had from the beginning of her pregnancy surfaced above the sea of emotions she felt. "I vowed my baby would have a whole family, not be torn between the confusion of a single parent, adopted parents and all that. I don't have to think about it. I know what's best. I want a legal and final adoption."

Hope took her hand. "You should take your time, Beth. We don't want you to rush into such an important decision."

Beth had gained complete composure. "What's best for the child is what's important. I'll take care of the attorney's fees and all the arrangements, but I want you to promise me you'll never reveal I'm the birth mother. It wouldn't be fair to anyone. Let me be godmother, friend, Auntie Beth or something. And if I may, I want always to be nearby, to have a small part of his or her growing up. Is that too much to ask? If that would be hard on either of you, it doesn't have to be that way."

Her eyes filled again, but she continued, "I know my baby will have a wonderful life with you. I'll be eternally grateful." She paused and looked upward. "Thank You, Lord."

"Amen," Josh beamed and stood up. "I guess we'd all better put ourselves together."

"Yes, you've got mighty stuff to take care of today, Josh, and I should get back to the city."

"Let me know when you're ready, and I'll drive you. No, we'll both drive you into the city and talk baby some more," Josh called out while he took the breakfast dishes into the kitchen.

*   *   *

"Beth, we thought that, if the baby has our last name, you should choose the first and middle names," Josh said as he drove the three of them to the city.

"Are you sure? I'd love to. Sterling is a beautiful last name. It'll be fun deciding on first and middle ones to go with it. I want to find an attorney as soon as possible, unless you know of someone already, Josh."

"I think I do," Josh said. "Since Sheridan is a well-known San Francisco name, it would probably be better to use someone here in San Jose."

"Yes, you're right." Beth agreed. "Also, I want you two to decorate the nursery the way you want it, but I'll buy the furniture." She held up her hand to stop any argument. "Oh," she suddenly remembered their little house, "which room will be the nursery?"

"Well, since our little one will be the permanent guest of honor, it'll be the guest room. When you come, you'll have to sleep on the sofa," Josh laughed.

"That's fine with me." Beth couldn't remember when she'd felt so truly filled with joy and happiness. The cloud of uncertainty that had hovered over her baby's future was replaced with the sunshine of a perfect solution. And above that, she had Christ in her life.

"The trip into San Francisco never seemed this short, we've had so much to talk about," Hope said as Josh parked in front of Sheridan's.

"And now, I have to go back into the world of business and pretend nothing extraordinary is happening. I detest secrets," Beth managed an almost simultaneous frown and smile. "How does one say thank you to two angels like you?"

"Thank our great God, and take care of our baby until it's fully baked." Josh grinned and waved goodbye.

*   *   *

"You look positively radiant," Eileen observed when Beth came in. "Wow, you should take a day off more often."

"I took more than a day, didn't I?"

"No, you didn't, just parts of two days. Have a good time?"

"Eileen, I can't tell you how wonderful it was to be with those friends. It was very special. Anything exciting going on here?"

"Gerald's mother fell again. He was pretty upset. Claudette only made things worse. She honestly didn't realize what kind of a state he was in, and the fur flew with her for a little while. Gerald always goes off like a whipped puppy. He's with his mother now. She injured the hip that had been broken before. He doesn't know if she needs surgery or not."

"She's been through so much, and so has Gerald—let's hope she doesn't." *Poor Gerald,* Beth thought. He had so much talent, was such a good guy, and it annoyed her that Claudette could be so beastly toward him. "Any messages?"

"Nothing you need to bother with. Why don't you go home? A little more relaxation won't hurt at all."

"Then I'll be in early in the morning. I'll see you."

Beth was more tired than she knew. No one would suspect she was pregnant. Years of dancing and the exercise dancers' bodies demand for the rest of their lives kept her abdominal muscles taut. She'd lost instead of gained weight with the rigorous hours she worked. It would still be some time before she'd really show. But then what would she do?

Happily, everything was different now. Eileen didn't know Beth's radiance came from a new relationship, an inner glow she had never felt before. "I'm learning that with God I only have to handle one day at a time," she whispered and snuggled into the down comforter. Instead of a little nap before dinner, she slept twelve hours, almost without moving.

"You look bright and fresh this morning, Miss Sheridan," Gerald greeted her as she came in the door.

"And you're here awfully early, Gerald. How's your mother?"

"I came in to prepare the paperwork for Eileen on that rare Wooton secretary desk and the leather Victorian swivel chair for the Arringtons. They're still deciding on the rosewood étagère and Italian marble mantle. Their final decisions are usually made over a cup of tea. They'll be in about four."

"How's your mother?" Beth repeated.

"I'm leaving in a few minutes. The doctors are going to decide this morning if she's strong enough for surgery on that hip again."

"Well, I pray she'll be just fine, Gerald. You need to be with her. I'll take care of the Arringtons."

"I appreciate your understanding, and the prayer," Gerald said with relief.

"You came in early and it looks like you're the last to leave again," Eileen chided Beth after a long day.

"I know, but I'm working on some new ideas. Have a good evening."

"Are you still here?" Aaron peeked into Beth's office. "When do you sleep? And how about going to dinner?"

"I'm not quite through yet, Aaron. And thank you, but I've sent out for dinner. Where's your wife tonight?" Beth had no intention of having dinner with a married man, whatever the hour.

"I called and told her I'd be late," he replied with disappointment. "We're climbing out of the red, you'll be happy to hear."

"That's good news. You're doing a great job keeping us on line. I appreciate that."

"That's because you've got us all humming. I've never seen everyone so enthused, except for Claudette, but that's to be expected."

"She's producing, and I don't want to deter that. If only she'd be civil to Gerald."

"It's a matter of respect. She's almost decent to everyone else when she has to be."

"Well, we're not going to solve that tonight. Have a good evening, Aaron."

"Don't work too late. Good night."

What was she going to do with Claudette? Beth sighed and pushed her hair back from her face.

"You need a rest, Miss Sheridan. You were here too late, and now you're in too early," Eileen told her. "But that bright pink is a great color for you. I'm amazed you even took enough time for yourself to shop. The easy style of your new wardrobe is great. It looks so comfortable. But if you don't mind my saying so, you're burning the candle at both ends. How long do you plan to keep this up?"

"Until we get the job done," Beth smiled wryly. "The economy in Britain is so bad, I'm trying to keep our sales up to offset it. Don't worry about me. I love a challenge."

"I hope we don't find you in a little heap some day."

"Eileen, you're a darling. Thanks for being concerned. I want Gerald to be able to do all he needs to do for his mother. She's recovering well, but she needs him by her side. When he's back full time, I'll take it easier."

The days slipped into mid-October. Eileen came smiling into Beth's office with a silver tray of tea and croissants. "You need a morning break with some nourishment. And here's dessert." She waved an envelope bearing Sheridan's London address. "Something from your father."

"Marvelous," Beth's face shone. "Thanks, Eileen—you take good care of me."

"It's not easy . . . " Eileen shook her head and left.

Beth tore open the treasured letter.

My Pet,

You're a wonder! I've studied Aaron's report, and I think you've performed a miracle. Bravo! From Gerald's statement, and as I read between the lines of your letters, I must commend you on a splendid job.

My little girl has turned out to be quite a businesswoman. What good fortune that a daughter who is so talented and lovely can also be so astute.

Now listen carefully, pet. I think you've done a remarkable thing there. But this is an order. I've had Gerald compile information on cabins in Lake Tahoe and cottages in Carmel. Temporarily, at least for a month, you are hereby relieved of your duties for an extended rest.

I'm worried about you. You've endeared yourself to the staff, and every one of them, except Claudette and Henri, has contacted me regarding how haggard you look.

My business is important, but not as important as my daughter. Pack your bags, young lady. Until you put on some weight and look like my girl again—you're fired!

Sincerely,

Sean Sheridan
President, Sheridan & Co., Ltd. London

P.S. I love you. —Daddy

Gerald strode into her office, waving brochures with colored pictures of places in Carmel and Tahoe. "You've got your marching orders, righto? And I have all sorts of good news."

"What?" Beth reserved her enthusiasm.

"For one thing, this fall of Mother's was a blessing. It must have been your prayers, but her recovery from this surgery is nothing other than a miracle. It corrected the complications from the last surgery. She hasn't been this good in years. With a nurse and a walker, she can move back into her apartment. Of course, it'll be a long time before she can go out, but can you believe it?"

Beth sat in stunned silence.

"So you see, you have absolutely no argument," Gerald continued. "You're being evicted, at least for now," he smiled, waving the brochures.

"Look these over and tell me what you think. Or is there somewhere else you want to go?"

"Now just a minute. This is collusion," Beth protested. "I'm in the habit of thinking I'm indispensable, and you're all shoving me out the door!"

"Daddy's orders. We care too much about you, Miss Sheridan, to let you ruin your health. I'd like you to be available for consultation and report to you by phone just to make sure we don't drop the ball now that you've put us in scoring territory. But please trust me. I've got myself together now, even though I've been gone a lot lately. Look these over, and tell me where to make reservations."

Beth sat in disbelief as Gerald strode out of her office. His voice bore a new tone of authority. *If he could speak to her like that, he could probably handle the others,* she thought. Besides, it didn't matter what she thought, the decision had been made.

"God," she whispered, "You've rescued me again, just in time. I must think of the baby, or it'll be a poor, pitiful skinny thing. It only has two more months to get 'fully baked,' in Josh's terminology. Hope was right—You are awesome, Lord. But can I ask one more thing? I'll need two and a half months away from the shop instead of one. Would You do something about that, too?"

7

"*he Cozy Cottages of Carmel*"... *they're delightful, according to the brochure,* Beth mused, *and dialed the number to inquire about cost and availability.*

"Perfect," she told the proprietor, a Mrs. Olson. "Is Bluebird Cottage, the one with a fireplace and little sitting room, available? Wonderful, I'll be there on Saturday."

The tasks of the week were accomplished on a strength Beth knew was not her own. Exhausted, she packed cardboard file boxes with sales reports and comparisons, clients' files, staff production and forms to work on commission schedules—everything she could think of to get the job done while she was somewhere else. Finally, on Friday, she went over last-minute plans with Gerald.

He eyed her with concern. "You need a vacation after all that packing and moving from Mother's apartment. We can keep your paintings and the art supplies you're not taking to Carmel here in the storage area of the shop. Are you sure you want me to put your landscapes and still lifes in the gallery for sale? They're really too magnificent to part with."

"One way to test the quality of one's talent is to see if someone wants to buy it," Beth pointed out.

Gerald nodded. "I can't argue with that. I don't doubt there's a market. They're excellent."

"Our gallery has traditionally carried contemporary painters. I'll talk to Claudette. I think she'll agree they're compatible with the impressionists' groups." Beth stopped looking through the paperwork on her desk. "Gerald, it's a dream of mine. When I was a little girl, coming into this store with my father on Saturdays, I fantasized that one day paintings by E. Sheridan would hang on the wall."

Gerald had no idea that there was more to selling her paintings than the fulfillment of a dream. She had a specific plan for the money. The inspiration had just come to her. It was worth a try.

"One more thing, Gerald," she explained carefully, "I'm putting a sold sticker on the English oak nursery furniture for my friends in San Jose. They're adopting a baby. The invoice will be on my personal check, and it goes to Mr. & Mrs. Josh Sterling for delivery in late December. Here's the address."

Inwardly, Beth bubbled with excitement. She had loved the Victorian crib and wanted it for her baby the moment she saw it. Hand-carved flowers and ribbons festooned the head and footboards, with a canopy of ivory lace. A high chair and attached wooden tray had the identical design carved on the back. She hesitated, with a silent prayer that her paintings would sell quickly, and then added, "and Gerald, please hold the wicker changing table, too."

This is a historic moment, she told herself. *It's the first furniture I've ever bought.* It was an extravagant but irrepressible decision, since, even at whole-sale prices, she had nowhere near that amount of money in her checking account. But giving up her baby was extravagant love. She prayed she'd be able to pay the price of what that involved in the years to come.

She'd have to be frugal these next two months, but she was so thrilled about buying these things for the baby, nothing else mattered.

*   *   *

On Saturday morning Gerald surveyed her considerable baggage in the entry hall. "I'd say you're ready, and what you don't have you probably don't need," he said wryly. "Nice of your friends to drive you to Carmel. When you come back, rested and relaxed, I'll take you out in the station wagon and teach you to drive American style. You really don't need a car in Carmel, though. Everybody rides bicycles."

Even pregnant women? she wondered. "Please thank your mother again for the joy of calling this apartment home for awhile. I'll write her a note when I get settled. I hope she does well, back in her own little dollhouse."

Josh and Hope arrived in the '52 Chevy with its spacious backseat and cavernous trunk space.

"What's this?" Beth looked at a huge book bag bulging with an assortment of reading material.

Hope had that familiar twinkle in her eyes. "They're gems. Great books we've loved through the years. You'll enjoy them in your quiet moments."

"Mmm, thanks. You can't imagine how I look forward to leisurely reading, especially in Carmel. The last time I was there, I was eight years old."

Josh tipped an imaginary chauffeur's cap. "Your chariot awaits, Miss."

"Oh, am I ready!" Beth sighed. As Josh whipped down the steep San Francisco streets to Highway 101, Beth burst into a full description of the nursery furnishings.

Hope giggled. "I think we should put the baby's things in the living room. It'll be the most beautiful furniture in the whole house. What do you say, Beth?"

"She's sound asleep, honey," Josh looked in the rear-view mirror. "She looks worn out. We should let her rest."

Beth stirred sleepily as they came into Monterey, through Pacific Grove and along the spectacular Seventeen Mile Drive.

"Look at that fascinating old mansion planted on the edge of the cliff among the cypresses—like it has always been there," Beth commented.

"Someone told me a filthy rich San Francisco banker owns it," Josh commented. "It looks lonesome." He continued along the magnificent drive of stately homes and awesome views of the rugged California coastline. In Carmel, he crossed Ocean Avenue, in search of Bay View.

"There—there's the sign, 'The Cozy Cottages of Carmel,'" Hope pointed out.

"They're charming, like thatched-roof little provincials, with vines and English gardens. And it's only one block off the main street and two blocks up from the beach. Perfect!" Beth jumped out as soon as the car stopped. "I'll go in and find Mrs. Olson and see where to park."

A small, plain, handsome woman with long, straight blonde hair, probably not yet thirty, approached and spoke to Beth. A small boy, with enormous dark eyes and dusky complexion, clung to the woman, who motioned to them. "She's not at all what I expected," Hope whispered to Josh.

"'The Bluebird Cottage' is there in the middle. And you can park in front of it," the woman instructed. "I'll get Miss Sheridan registered, and you can take her luggage right in."

"Thanks, you two, for unloading my things. Isn't this cozy?" Beth beamed in the doorway. "There's even a desk with good light. I'm going to love it."

"Josh lit the fire for you, and we're going to scoot right back. He has to fly tomorrow and still do some loading tonight. I think I should tuck you right into bed, little mama. You look like you don't have an ounce of energy left."

"I can put myself to bed, love. I'm going to take a long, hot shower first. You're both marvelous. What can I do to say thank you?"

"Oh, nothing much," Josh teased. "Just make us a beautiful baby."

"I'll do my best. I promise."

Sunshine filtered through the blinds. With one half-open eye, Beth looked at the clock on the pine nightstand. Two o'clock! She couldn't remember ever sleeping into the afternoon. It felt wonderful. Excited to explore Carmel, but more interested in food, she quickly dressed in her warmest slacks and sweater.

Mrs. Olson and the child were in the garden. "Hello," Beth called. "Can you tell me of a good little restaurant for mid-afternoon? Something French maybe?"

"Yes, of course. There's a charming place around the corner—Le Petit Fleur."

"Thank you. I'll try it." Beth breathed the fresh ocean air deeply and quickened her step. She felt starved.

Steaming French onion soup bubbling with stringy cheese and croutons, thick buttered hot bread, salad and a chocolate eclair satisfied her completely.

The intriguing shops beckoned to her, but she walked briskly down to the beach. The ocean shimmered like molten, sea-green silver while sandpipers played games with the incoming waves. The curve of the bay invited her in both directions. She decided on the right. Friendly men, women, dogs and children strolled the sands, exchanging cordial smiles or a word of greeting. The beach was almost a community unto itself. Scanning the cliffs above, she stopped to admire the golf course—the famed Pebble Beach. Its treacherous traps held the ever-present possibility of placing an errant ball in the iceplant if one sliced. Beth marveled at the skill of the players in directing that tiny white ball. *I'd rather paint,* she thought, and itched to get out her sketch pad and easel.

Spellbound by the late afternoon's magical rearrangement of hues and patterns, thoughts more pragmatic enticed her back to the gourmet shop before sunset. She envisioned her first homey supper by the fire at Bluebird Cottage. The little life within her was making its presence increasingly known. "I promise to feed you well and take good care of you, whoever you are," she murmured with her arms full of groceries.

Mrs. Olson and her boy were out picking up the evening paper. "How are you this evening?" the blonde woman inquired. "Haven't seen much of you today. You're going to be with us awhile. Is there anything you need to know about our beautiful little community?"

"Lots. I haven't been here since I was a child." Beth hesitated, "You might just be able to tell me of a good doctor, preferably an OB/GYN. I'd like to find a woman doctor if I could."

"I hope you're not having problems," Mrs. Olson scanned her tall, thin frame under the loose bulky sweater. "My doctor is very satisfactory and a woman—Dr. Adele Mason, up on Sixth Street. I went to her when I had Ali and still go to her for annual checkups. Anything else?"

"Not at the moment, thank you. Good evening."

Beth laid a fire, made some tea, unpacked her clothes, arranged her desk, and felt totally content with her solitude and simple supper. On day two she'd get organized: Make a doctor's appointment, check on the location of the hospital, make the necessary preparations for this blessed event.

Each new day brought its own rewards. She never tired of breathing in the sea air in the morning mists on the beach and watching the golden veiled sun slip out of sight at evening tide. Sometimes she'd sit for a few minutes and watch the golfers. About half made the green without putting the ball out of bounds. Mostly she painted, but only after she made her daily call to the shop and talked to Gerald, satisfied all was running well.

In all her precisely structured life, ever since she was a three-year-old budding little ballet student, she'd never luxuriated in such self-indulgence. Even her energetic plans for setting up new systems for the shop seemed less critical.

Mrs. Olson and Ali were pleasant, yet Beth's capacity for becoming totally engrossed in her own activities obscured any need for lengthy conversation. Her exhaustion had at last been overcome by the return of exuberant vitality. At moments she felt like leaping into an impromptu arabesque or leg lift high over her head, but in her present condition, the thought made her laugh. At last she was at peace with herself, her God and the reality of having a baby. She wondered if Mrs. Olson had noticed, or was curious about her.

Beth called Gerald for the Monday report. "How were sales last week? Everything all right? How's your mother?"

"Marvelous. Her recovery is incredible. Aaron reports nearly a 10 percent increase each week. The holidays are bringing in a lot of business. I wish you were here to give us your expertise on decorating the showroom, but Eileen is creative, and she's almost finished. Wreaths and Victorian garlands everywhere. It's smashing."

"How's the rest of the staff?"

"I've never seen them so enthused or productive. They like making money on the new commission setup. Claudette's name is still trouble, but she has an interested client for two of your paintings."

"Oh, that's fabulous. About the paintings, I mean. I hope she sells them. And Gerald, just don't let her get the best of you." With higher sales and her encouragement, Gerald was regaining his competence.

Oh God, please let the paintings sell before the end of December, Beth pleaded after Gerald said goodbye.

And God, I haven't spent the time with You I thought I would, but thanks for keeping Your promise I saw in Psalms, "Day by day I shall refresh you like morning dew"—and for the other good things happening.

One sunny afternoon Beth sat on a beach chair painting two tow-headed tykes building a sand castle. Mrs. Olson and her son paused on their walk to admire her canvas. Beth glanced down at her pregnant form, like a small beach ball concealed under her sweater, then caught the other woman's knowing expression.

"Hi!" Mrs. Olson greeted. "That's a beautiful painting. Carmel is quite an art colony, and I'm impressed."

"Thank you. I love to paint." Beth smiled invitingly.

She'd be happy for Mrs. Olson to stay and visit. She'd been curious about this fair young woman with the beautiful dusky-skinned boy.

"Excuse me, but you've been with us for almost a month, and I'd like you to call me Annie, if you would. You seem pretty happy, but if I can do anything for you, I wouldn't mind, being as you're by yourself." She hesitated, obviously with something else on her mind. Then she plunged in. "When is your baby due?"

Beth put down her brush. "I'll call you Annie if you'll call me Beth. This Mrs. Olson and Miss Sheridan business is a bit silly, isn't it? Dr. Mason said mid-January. She's not quite sure of the date."

Beth suspected they had more in common than living at the cottages, but she never imagined Annie would be so direct. At least any pretense was over. This near-stranger was only the third person, other than Dr. Mason, with whom she shared this phenomenon of having a baby. Annie's blunt question and her openness paved a way to friendship.

"Technically, I'm not a 'Mrs.' either," Annie blushed. "I don't have a husband—it's just easier on Ali and me this way. Fewer raised eyebrows in this rather staid community. Is 'Miss' for professional reasons, or are you unmarried?"

Beth smiled in amusement at this refreshingly frank confrontation, and sank into a more comfortable position on the sand. She gave Annie a quick sketch of her whole life. All except the connection with Sheridan's Antiques of San Francisco and London. Annie didn't press her for those details.

"How long have you lived in Carmel?" Beth asked.

"Almost five years. Ben, Ali's father, came here with me. We were going to get married before the baby came, but he decided he wasn't ready for the responsibility. Men are strange creatures, aren't they? Mama told me, 'It's the woman who pays,' when she learned I was living with Ben, but I found out the hard way. With you, I'll bet it was different."

"I was just too naive to know that when you play with fire, you usually get burned." The very thought of Roberto's passionate kisses still made her limp. "How's it been for you, being a single mother?" *Am I doing the right thing to give up my baby? Am I being a coward, and taking the easy way out?* Beth thought to herself. These questions had burned in her heart.

"My mother tried to convince me to get an abortion, and so did Ben, but I thought that was wrong. I'd die for my little boy, he's so sweet. But let me tell you, it isn't easy. I worry about him, growing up without a male role model, someone to play baseball with, you know?"

"Is Ben totally out of your life? Did you love him?"

"I thought I loved him. He's very handsome, but very selfish. We met at the hospital. I feel so stupid. You'd think I'd know better than to get pregnant, but I won't go into that. I was an obstetrical nurse in emergency, and he was an intern. Then he got a staff position in Oakland, and at the moment I don't know where he is. This is a good job here, great because I don't have to leave Ali with someone else, and a delightful place to live. We manage."

Beth shivered, her silky black hair billowing across her face. "It's getting chilly. Would you and Ali come and have tea and goodies with me?"

Annie's stoic expression of a moment ago brightened. "Shall we go have a tea party with Beth, Ali?" His big eyes widened as he shyly nodded yes.

The tea party was the prelude to a deepening friendship. Beth appreciated Annie's tender compassion, but she was even more thankful that her friend knew all about the mysterious process called birth. "Count on me to take you to the hospital when it's time," she insisted.

The lights intertwined in the barren wisteria vines around the cottages twinkled through the fog as Beth bid her guests goodbye at dusk. The quiet was pierced by the telephone's ring.

"Are you ready for some good news?" Gerald asked.

"Always. Tell me quick."

"We just hit the jackpot. We're out of the red. Aaron finished the balance sheet of the week's report. Bravo, Miss Sheridan, bravo!"

"Oh, Gerald—that's marvelous. Bravo to you. I hope you're going to have a staff celebration. I wish I could be there!"

"You stay right where you are. Oh, by the way, there's something else."

"Yes?"

"Your paintings sold. All of them. Are you doing commissions? Clients will be standing in line. It's the first time we've had a flurry of interest in a contemporary painter. You created quite a stir, young lady. Your check is in the mail."

"Gerald!" she screamed. "Really? Oh, oh my, that's wonderful." Instantly she calculated. It would be more than enough to cover the price of the baby furniture. "Does my father know about the entry into black ink?"

"He knows everything. He'll call you tonight. Says it's a bitter winter in London, and your mother has a dreadful cold."

"I'll be anxious to hear from him. Oh, Gerald, what a wonderful Christmas present this news is. I hope you don't need me in the shop though. I'm almost beginning to feel like the real me again."

"Frankly, I'd like it fine if I could run it on my own a little while longer. My relationship with the staff is improving all the time. They even seem to respect me. Except for Claudette, and Henri's a wimp anyway. Wouldn't you like a relaxed Christmas? We're going to be swamped, but I'm thriving on it."

Oh, God, she thought, *if Gerald only knew the relief I feel, not to have to make up excuses for extending my leave.*

"I'd love it, Gerald. That's marvelous. I'll come back with another painting. Maybe two."

"I'm going to say goodbye now. Your father's probably trying to call."

Within five minutes the phone rang again. "Cheerio, love, have you talked to Gerald?"

"Yes, Daddy, isn't that fabulous news? He's done a smashing job. I'm thrilled!"

"You did it, pet, but they've kept the ball rolling. I'm pleased as punch with all of you. It's a ruddy miracle, that's what it is."

"Daddy, Gerald says it's freezing in London, and Mum has a horrible cold."

"Yes, love—with the shop doing nicely, it might have been nice for you to come home for Christmas. But it's frightfully unpleasant here, and Mum is too sick. You should be painting for a one-woman show, eh? Congratulations—nice bit of change for yourself."

"I'm worried about you and Mum. Are you sure you're all right?"

"Not to fret, dear. Oh, there was a young Italian Count, the heir to the Cabriollini Villa and art fortune, in the shop inquiring about you. He's searching Europe for a certain seventeenth-century Italian marble mantle. Says he met you at the *Beaux Arts*, and to say hello. I gave him the San Francisco store number. Nice chap. Do you remember him?" Beth was silent. "I say, do you hear me, pet?"

"Uh, yes, Daddy—I hear you. I remember Signor Cabriollini, nice chap indeed. . . . "

"Tillie sends her love. Mum too. Cheerio for now."

"I love you, Daddy—love you all. Bye. . . . "

In the soft firelight a tear glistened in Beth's eyes, but Roberto wasn't important right now. The baby's position had shifted to an outrageous one-sided point, followed by several boom-boom kicks into a more normal configuration.

Oh, Daddy, she thought. *You'd be such a precious grandpapa. I'm sorry I'm cheating you of that joy. It can't be any other way. It just can't. Annie's right. A child needs a father too—one like you, like Josh will be to my baby.*

The telephone rang again. "Hello, little mama. How are you and our baby?" Hope's voice cheered her.

"Oh, praise God, it just has to be His doing. You can't believe how beautifully everything is working out." Beth told her about the shop, the timing with Gerald, how secure she felt with Annie nearby, Ali's huge dark eyes, and that the three of them were going to celebrate Christmas together.

"About three more weeks, do you think? Are you gaining weight and feeling good? Everything okay? Have you read all the books yet?"

Beth groaned inwardly. "Oh no—I haven't read the books at all, but I will before the baby comes. I really want to. I've been painting much of the time, and getting my exercise walking several miles every day, but I'm looking a bit top-heavy. I'm eating healthily too, you'll like to know. Has the nursery furniture arrived?"

"We received a delivery notice—next week. Our friends are so excited. They're giving the baby a shower the first week it's home and after we know who's coming—a boy or girl. What are the names?" Hope's voice trilled with elation.

"For a boy, what do you think of Sean? Sean Sterling sounds melodious, doesn't it? And for a girl—I love Kerry. Can we do Kerry Elizabeth? Elizabeth may be the only outward link I'll have with her. Kerry is for Kerry County, my father's birthplace in Ireland, even though he's thoroughly English."

"They're beautiful names. Oh, I'm running late—we have the high school group coming for Bible study tonight, so I'll say goodbye. You take care, hear?"

"I hear . . . you take care too, love."

Beth took out Tillie's lavender afghan, stoked up the fire and rummaged through Hope's books. They'd tucked in a new Bible, with more references and information than she could imagine, and all the books looked interesting. She read long into the night, and the next day, and the day after that, breaking only for simple meals and brief walks on the beach.

I never knew the lessons in life for these very days were to be found in the Bible, Beth pondered. *The answers are in the now—not the ancient pen of an ethereal hand detached from human understanding. This was the Creator, Father God, speaking to His children, the awesome God Hope and Josh loved so dearly.*

New thoughts about God traveled through the corridors of her mind. Beth discovered there was so much more to come after she asked Jesus into her life. She'd heard people say they didn't want to be Christians because you couldn't have fun—it was dull, drab, boring. They were wrong. She agreed with all she read. Zest for life, true quality and not being satisfied with mediocrity were definitions of a life with God.

"Thank You, Lord," she prayed. "I know this will be a wonderful Christmas, because now I know what it's truly about."

"Annie, I'm a long way from being a cook, but would you and Ali have Christmas dinner with me? I have a few little gifts for you under my tiny tree, we'll sing some carols, and have a lovely time."

"Okay, Ali? Would you like that?" His mother asked gently. The big eyes spoke for him. Beth didn't know children could be that shy and quiet at three years old. "Let me bring some ham and sweet potatoes, and you can do the rest," Annie accepted for both of them.

"Silent night, holy night. All is calm, all is bright," they sang in the glimmer of the firelight. Beth would not have imagined such contentment in these circumstances and simple surroundings. *Thank You, Lord, You meet my every need.*

The New Year came in the blink of an eye, with Annie and Beth wondering what it held for all of them.

January's chill wind swept the beach, enveloping it in a shroud of fog until late afternoon. Determined to get her daily exercise, Beth bundled up warmly. She jaunted quickly past the boutiques on the village streets, eager to return to her cozy nest in Bluebird Cottage—to wait.

Beth had carefully selected an exquisite but small layette, which she rearranged daily. Gerald reported a whopping 28 percent increase in sales compared with a year ago December, and she'd completed the commission schedules and spring promotion plans. Claudette remained the only obstacle to Gerald's total satisfaction. The Cozy Cottages of Carmel and their lush gardens were eternally captured on canvas, steeped in sentiment and surprisingly few regrets.

I'm glad, Beth thought, *that I've always been able to accept circumstances as they are, and not as they might have been. Yet only the Lord can give me patience for several more weeks of waiting.*

It was three o'clock in the morning when Beth groped for the phone. "Annie—Annie, I think something's happening."

"What? First babies are usually early, but you don't look ready yet. I've noticed you're carrying this baby low, but you're still so small."

"I've had this lower back pain since early yesterday. I'm sure the water broke, and I started having contractions about midnight. I've heard of false alarms. Do you think this could be the real thing?"

"How far apart are your contractions?"

"Five minutes."

"I'll be right over."

"Annie, I don't know what your spiritual beliefs are," Beth said as her friend entered the cottage. "You're pretty private about that, but I do believe God brought me to the Cottages just because of you." Beth's eyes stung with tears as Annie's deft hands gently evaluated her swollen abdomen. "I'd feel so alone right now without you."

Ignoring the preamble Annie assured her, "I'm glad I'm here for you."

There were those words again—"here for you"—like Tillie and Ruth had been in her most desperate needs. But what need on earth could be more acute, intense, real or demanding than the prolonged stab of the last contraction?

When the labor pains were down to three minutes apart, Annie beamed. "I'm going to call Dr. Mason. Unless I've missed my guess—you're ready!"

Annie had been allowed admittance in the delivery room, although she was no longer on staff. Her friend Alinda was on duty that night. Since work was slow, Alinda held and cuddled Ali while he slept.

After more than eight hours, with perspiration beading on her forehead, Beth panted, "They don't call this labor for nothing, do they?"

"We're almost there," Dr. Mason assured her. A sharp contraction wrenched a cry from her very soul, and then another, and then a surge of joy and relief as new life thrust forth into the world.

Beth, gasping for breath and wet with perspiration, studied Dr. Mason's expression, waiting. It was Annie who beamed, "Welcome to our world, Kerry Elizabeth—and look at those eyelashes! I've never seen a newborn with eyelashes like that!"

"She's beautiful," Beth smiled, exhausted but happy. "All six pounds of her," Annie agreed. "Well done, Mama. She's the most gorgeous little creation I've ever seen."

Alone with her baby, Beth prayed, *God, even though I can't give Kerry the home I want for her, how could any woman have an abortion and snuff out a little miracle such as this? You have given me precious gifts, Lord, the birth of my baby and the birth of my new life through understanding who You are and how much You love me. And, Lord, I need Your strength to part with her.*

B eth sat on the edge of the bed, delicately twirling Kerry's silky black hair into ringlets. "Two days in this world, and you have me willingly wrapped around your baby finger, little one," she whispered.

A nurse rapped softly on Beth's open door and smiled in at the tender scene. "I've heard about this baby's incredible eyelashes—my, my, they look like they're an inch long!" While Beth beamed proudly the nurse went on, "Look at her, done up in pink ribbons and frills, like a tiny porcelain doll, all prettied up for bye-bye day," she cooed. "Except for weighing six pounds, she doesn't look like a newborn. Her complexion's so clear and creamy. The nurse that takes the prints of her hands and feet will be in soon, and the one with the release papers right behind her. Then you can take your dolly home."

Tears filled Beth's eyes as the nurse went out. *Why did she have to say that, just when I thought I was under control? I wish I was taking my baby home,* her heart ached. *If Hope and Josh don't come in right away, there's no way I can let her go.* Tenderly, Beth picked up her baby and held her closer than any other human being had ever been to her heart, walking about the hospital room with Kerry's satiny soft head against her cheek.

Josh's laughter filled the hallway at the same time the records nurse came in. "Thank heaven, they made it before I weakened and changed my mind," Beth sighed under her breath.

Hope took one look at her dear friend. "Before we take another step," she hesitated with sweet understanding in her voice, "are you sure you want to go through with this, Beth?"

Beth bit her lip, gently handed the baby to Hope, then turned to cry in Josh's waiting arms. "I'm—I'm sorry. I didn't want to break down like this," she apologized, dabbing at her eyes. "Whatever I feel, this is best for

Kerry—and I won't change my mind. Please don't worry that I'll put you through this agony after you've come to love her too."

"We love her already," Josh looked adoringly at Kerry.

"The adoption papers are all in order, but you do have a period in which you can legally change your mind."

"I promise, I won't do that to you," Beth couldn't take her eyes off Kerry. "Josh, see what you can do to speed things up—I need to get this over with as soon as possible."

Within another fifteen minutes, Josh and Hope were taking their soon-to-be adopted daughter, Kerry Elizabeth Sterling, to a home filled with love and laughter, with two devoted parents—just the way Beth had planned.

"Annie, bless you—your timing is perfect," Beth said to her friend who had come in after the room had cleared. "Thanks for coming to take me home. I'd like you to meet Josh and Hope someday, but for now, I have to keep the formalities as simple as possible, or I couldn't go through with it."

"I think you're terribly brave, Beth. I really do," Annie gave Beth a little hug. "And I understand."

"I know you do, friend. And I love you for it." Beth picked up the small overnight bag she had taken to the hospital. "Now, I've got to get on with my life . . . and I've got to call Gerald as soon as I get home. He'll wonder what happened to me the last two days."

Once inside the cottage, Beth headed straight for the phone. Annie interceded. "Let me make you some tea first. I'll bring over some hot soup, and Ali picked flowers from the garden for you." Before Beth could protest, Annie continued, "Listen to an old pro—you'll need a few more days to get back on your feet, so don't make any rash promises."

"We'll see. You remind me of Ruth, a wonderful, caring friend I met in Paris. You're two of a kind." She'd have to remember to find one birth announcement and send it and a picture to Ruth in New York. After all her tender kindness, she would appreciate knowing Kerry had arrived.

The phone rang before Beth could sit down. "Hello, Gerald, I was just going to call and ask how the January inventory's going."

"Well, thank you. That's not the problem. I wanted you to know," he stammered nervously, "I let the Bouviers go today."

"What happened?" Already she knew that would leave him short-staffed, and he'd want her back sooner than she'd hoped.

"I can put up with a lot of insults, Miss Sheridan, but Claudette pulled her temperamental prima donna act and got uppity with the Arringtons over the date of a Renoir painting. They were offended, and they know their art.

She was totally out of line and refused to make an apology. I decided she'd gone too far."

"I see," Beth could picture the whole incident in her mind.

"Henri's the one I'll miss. He's a mouse, but he's great at providing the clients with art history and discerning what an unsophisticated client should buy. I've been worried you might think I acted hastily."

Poor Gerald, he would, Beth thought. "You've been remarkably patient, Gerald. When a Sheridan employee insults a client, it's all over. That's policy. You did the right thing. Have you smoothed it over with the Arringtons? They're valuable patrons and really sweet people."

"They felt terrible that Claudette and Henri lost their jobs over the incident, but admitted it was an ugly and regrettable confrontation to endure. In a way, it was fortunate it happened with them instead of less understanding folks."

"It sounds like you've handled the situation well," Beth said. "I'm just sorry you had to do it alone."

"Don't worry about me when you're trying to get some rest. How are you? I hear that tired sound in your voice. I thought you'd be like new by now."

"It's been heavenly, Gerald. I'm glad I chose to come to Carmel. I could stay here forever. Today was an exception, and I am exhausted." *That's a major understatement,* she thought. "But it sounds like you need me. Any ideas on an apartment?"

"As a matter of fact, yes. Mother has a friend who lives alone right around the corner from her. Mrs. Trillingham is in a situation that was similar to Mother's. She had a mild stroke and will have to be in a convalescent home for a while, and she doesn't want to sell her Victorian. It's a little bigger, quite elegant, and she worries about it being unoccupied. Interested?"

"Very. Please get me the details. I'll get my things together and be back in the city in a week. Sorry I can't make it sooner, but I have a commitment until then. I'm anxious for you to see my new paintings." Beth heard her voice quiver with fatigue and realized she was near collapse.

The birth itself hadn't been too difficult, but emotionally she felt as fragile as the early evening moonbeam that had slipped through the winter fog to frost her windowpane.

I have one sure thing to cling to, she thought. *For the rest of my life, I can look to this day and remember, I survived. Nothing on earth could be more heart-wrenching to endure than giving away my baby.* "But God," she whispered, "with You, even the impossible becomes possible."

"The California coast is magnificent," Annie exclaimed as she drove Beth up Highway 1, then over to 101 into San Francisco. "We've never been up here to the Golden Gate, have we, Ali? It'll be fun getting Auntie Beth settled into her house and staying a few days."

"Soon, I'm going to learn to drive a car on the right side of the road," Beth laughed as she directed Annie up Van Ness Avenue to the top of Russian Hill. "Let's turn right on Green Street—it should be just around the corner. Ahh, here's the address. Looks very much like the house I grew up in here in San Francisco." The gingerbread classic had fish-scale shingles and delicate woodwork around the turret, gables and porches. Even an eyelash window.

"I've never been in a house like this. It's out of a storybook," Annie gasped.

"Here's the key, under the mat just like Gerald said it would be." Beth opened the door and led the three of them inside.

"I not only feel like an intruder, but that we've stepped back in time, to a different era," Annie gaped at the ornately curved velvet sofas, beaded lamp shades and hand-painted tea cups. "It's gorgeous, but Ali and I will feel like bulls in a china shop. I don't think we should stay."

Beth feared that her friend, so accustomed to the strictest simplicity and always so direct, meant what she said. She wouldn't try to dissuade Annie if it would make her uncomfortable.

"When you leave for work tomorrow, Ali and I will be on our way," Annie said simply. "I'd like him to see the trolley cars and the aquarium at Golden Gate Park, but let's face it—I'm really not a city girl. And I need to get back to the Cottages."

"You've grown very dear to me," Beth knelt down to give Ali a hug. "And so has your mama. I'll never forget your kindness and friendship as long as I live, Annie. Let's stay in touch. I hope I can come back to Carmel often."

Beth had taken extra special care with her hair and makeup because she had to admit to herself, she was more than a little nervous to walk through Sheridan's heavy oak doors once again. She still felt a little weak, but she supposedly was returning refreshed and rested, so she had to make every attempt to appear so.

Eileen, Mr. Tubbs, Aaron and, of course, Gerald gathered to greet her. They hovered around, waiting to extend their welcomes.

Beth smiled as she searched each of their faces for a reflection of what they saw in hers. Her eyes swept over the shop, and then she saw it. Pink roses! A whole bower! "What a beautiful homecoming! Did you have a special reception or something I don't know about, or are these just for me? Roses always make me feel so special." She walked over to inhale their fragrance, and then she noticed the card: *"Signorina Elizabeth Sheridan. Con Amore, Roberto Cabriollini."*

"You look like you've seen a ghost, Miss Sheridan. Are you all right?" Eileen's eyes registered concern. "I suppose you remember this Italian Count. He said you met in Paris."

"Was—is he here in San Francisco?" Beth asked weakly.

"He was, last week, but had to return to a grandiose-sounding art exhibit at Villa Cabriollini in Lake Como. He regretted he missed you, and asked us to call the florist to deliver the flowers when you returned. Said he'd call you on his next visit to the States," Gerald explained.

"You look pale, Miss Sheridan. Let me get you some tea," Eileen offered. "Just who is this handsome Italian Count that he has such a devastating effect on you?"

Beth felt embarrassed at her transparency. She had written Roberto out of her life, never suspecting that he would follow her. What did he want? She was glad she hadn't told him about Kerry. In spite of all Roberto's charms that made her heart race, he would never get outside himself enough to be a real father.

"Just a handsome Italian Count, that's all. I never expected to see him again. And I surely didn't expect to come back and find a flower shop to greet me." Beth made a concentrated effort to perk up. "Well, how are all of you? Looks like you managed beautifully without me."

Beth observed Gerald's subtle glance at the other three, an obvious dismissal to resume their work. *Good,* she thought, *a healthy sign of leadership.*

"There is one client I especially want you to work with, Miss Sheridan," Gerald turned to business as they sipped tea. "Perhaps you met him at one time in the London shop. He hasn't been in here for over a year, but your father will certainly recognize the name. He's one of San Francisco's leading citizens, and our most impressive client."

"Gerald, I hope you're going to tell me his name soon, or is this a guessing game?"

"Do you recognize the name Charles Townsend?"

"Townsend . . . Tyler Norton Townsend? The multi-billionaire financier of the Townsend Bank Building on Montgomery Street?"

"You're half right. TNT, as he's known on the *Examiner's* financial page, is the explosively ruthless president and CEO of Townsend Bank and holding corporation. His name has been in all the San Francisco papers lately for acquiring majority stocks in several old-line companies and crushing them in hostile takeovers."

Beth shuddered. Not a pleasant-sounding client. Gerald continued, "Townsend Towers, the elegant high-rise of executive suites, also on Montgomery, is owned by Charles Townsend and is totally separate from his father's financial empire. Except for the same name, and the fact that they both have the affinity to turn everything they touch to gold, there's no similarity between the father and son. People in the know say TNT made his billions by running over everyone—Charles by building them up. Charles is a prince of a fellow."

"Is Charles a banker too, then?"

"No, though he's brilliant with money. He's mainly an architect/builder/developer. His buildings around the world, some unique projects from Rio to Rome, have captured architecture's highest awards. And he's also designed prototype affordable housing in St. Louis in hopes of a practical solution for replacing slum areas. An extremely versatile chap—amazing really." Gerald was obviously impressed with Mr. Townsend's accomplishments.

"Sounds fascinating. What can we do for him?"

"He has a passion for seventeenth- and eighteenth-century English and French antiques and fine arts. But I think he's particularly looking for several commodes from the Louis XV and XVI periods. The man's taste is as diversified as the man himself."

"Gerald, what's he going to do with such a collection? Are they for his home? Is he married with a family?"

Gerald shrugged. "He's personally developing and designing the interiors of his private corporate penthouse suites in the Townsend Towers. I suspect by the time he finishes, he'll have another coveted award of some kind."

"It sounds challenging," was Beth's guarded comment. "Townsend Towers isn't a new building, though. I'm not sure I understand."

"When he completed the construction several years ago, he left the entire top floor unfinished. He had a cultural arts building in New York underway and several international commissions on the drawing board. He told me he had shelved this project until he had time to savor it. A client with exquisite taste and a no-holds-barred expense account is everyone's dream, isn't it?" Gerald had a gleam in his eyes.

Beth's trembling hand was a sure giveaway of how weak and shaky she felt, so she put her tea cup down. She had hoped January would not present any spectacular challenges. She had wanted to carry on a convincing facade of physical recovery and merely coast along until she'd recouped the drain on her emotions. *God,* she thought, *I'm not sure I'm ready for this.*

"Miss Sheridan, you don't seem duly impressed," Gerald sounded greatly disappointed. "Just this one account could be a feather in our cap for Sheridan's new image. Mr. Townsend is a prestigious, longstanding client, but this will be our most extensive commission for him. If the photographs of the project wind up in an architectural design magazine, which they surely will, it will put us in an extremely admirable position."

Gerald's tone virtually begged her to compliment him for his knowledge and insight of *the* Mr. Charles Townsend. "It's absolutely splendid, Gerald," Beth praised him. "I'm just trying to digest all you're telling me. How fortunate you're so well-versed on his background and comprehend the potential here. Don't you think both you and I should work together on this project?"

"Well, of course, we'll all be involved, and I'll assist in every way. But I'm already committed to three other clients' projects, and you possess the artistic flair and creativity to satisfy Mr. Townsend. I'd like to see you work directly with him—I'll be in the wings."

"Has he indicated a time schedule?"

"Mr. Townsend's secretary wanted us to be aware of the general scope of the project, but she'll call for an appointment to put together the details. Believe me, Miss Sheridan, if Townsend comes through—and I have no reason to doubt he will—1962 will be a very good year."

"That's wonderful, Gerald. We're ready for it. And ready for Mr. Charles Townsend too." She thought, *What I'm ready for is an escape into my office for a nap before I drop.*

Closing the door to her office, Beth gingerly lowered herself into the soft leather executive chair behind her desk.

For the first time since the moment she realized she was pregnant, there was no more anxiety, no more deception. Her secret was safely entrusted to a precious few, her baby healthy and safe in a loving home.

Beth tilted back in the desk chair with closed eyes, letting the relief penetrate her consciousness. *I'm no longer a student, waiting to become something else,* she thought. *This is Elizabeth Sheridan, businesswoman. Charged with maintaining one of the world's best rare antiques and fine arts galleries, at the age of twenty-two.*

She wouldn't dare delude herself that her position would be possible without Gerald, but he hadn't been able to do it without her either. She no longer wandered through the maze of little-girl fantasies; she was a woman now. Saturday morning daydreams had given wing to a new era of her life—and she liked what she saw through the windows of her mind.

But the cost. The sacrifice she had made for her baby—striving for personal excellence was so deeply ingrained there had seemed no alternative. This offered the only justification for the raw pain in her heart. Next to that, her physical weakness seemed as nothing. She closed her eyes. . . .

"Miss Sheridan, Mr. Charles Townsend is here to see you," Eileen buzzed on the intercom.

Beth gulped. Was she dreaming? "Here, now?"

"Yes, Miss Sheridan. He's here and Gerald is out."

"Please serve him tea, Eileen, and tell him I'll be with him in a few minutes."

Beth slipped out her back door into the ladies' room. As an artist shades colors from a palette, Beth deftly stroked rosiness into her cheeks and blended Pink Lightning into her lips. Under fresh eye shadow her violet-blue eyes sparkled like sapphires. A flick of the hairbrush through her black silky mane brought her final approval. She dabbed Chanel #5 behind her ears and winked at the mirror, "Let's go see what this Charles Townsend is all about, Miss Sheridan."

Eileen's eyes directed Beth to the man browsing through the Impressionist paintings with his back to her. He wore an impeccable European-cut gray flannel suit. The expertly barbered, thick, sandy blonde hair would have caught her attention in any setting. He was well built, possibly a bit heavy in the middle, it was hard to tell, slightly over six feet in height.

"Good afternoon—Mr. Townsend?"

The man turned. Kind eyes, the lightest, clearest crystal blue she had ever seen, met hers. "Good afternoon," he smiled warmly. "You must be Miss Sheridan. I could never forget your face, even though you've changed, wonderfully, since I saw you last." She looked puzzled, and he continued. "Of course you don't remember, you were only a little girl. I saw you in the London shop in 1952. I remember because that's when I bought my first really important painting from your father. It was the beginning of a passionate love affair with collecting fine things."

He's not at all what I expected, Beth thought, assessing his conservative white on white striped shirt, the plain burgundy silk faille tie. He wore no rings on his long, tapered fingers. A slim gold Patek Phillippe watch was his only jewelry. *He's simply elegant,* Beth noticed. *He reminds me of my father, but he can't be more than mid-thirties.* There was not one iota of personal ostentation about Mr. Charles Townsend.

"Mr. Ormsley gave me a brief background of your design objectives for the Towers. How can I help you?" Beth asked politely.

"The wall color of the penthouse is a similar shade of deep crimson to these walls," he gestured. "A French textile mill is weaving it in linen. I see over here an Italian giltwood table with scagliola top, perfect for the foyer. I believe those are nineteenth-century Italian blackamoors? Both of those are exactly what I want." Beth followed alongside, taking notes. "I'm a rare clock fancier—aha, that's the one." He stopped in admiration of an elaborately ornamented Louis XIV ebony-and-Bouelle clock and pedestal. "Bouelle was a genius in perfecting the technique of brass and tortoise-shell marquetry. These are exquisitely exciting pieces."

Beth was amazed by his knowledge of antiques. "Tell me, Mr. Townsend, isn't it rare for a developer, even if he is an architect, to be so well versed in fine art?"

"Perhaps. I grew up wandering through the museums, palaces and galleries of Europe. I acquired a love for beautiful things by osmosis. I studied art and architecture in Florence and Venice—so you see, it isn't so surprising."

Everything about this man is surprising to me, Beth thought. *He's so like my father, except without the eccentricity of his British humor.*

"I had a few spare minutes today, Miss Sheridan, so I walked over unannounced. I hope I didn't disrupt your day," he smiled apologetically. "The Towers is just around the corner of Sutter from here on Montgomery, you know."

"Yes, I know," she said, "and you were no disruption."

"In the future, I'll call for an appointment," he smiled his warm smile again. "I'll get you the blueprints and sketches, along with a furnishings list. I'd like you to keep your eyes open for fine oriental carpets in large-scale sizes, would you?"

"It'll be my pleasure, Mr. Townsend." She looked up into those incredible light blue eyes, at a loss for something more intelligent to say.

In the next few weeks, Beth burned up the phone connection between San Francisco and the London gallery. She conferred with her father as well as Gerald in locating the Louis-period commodes, carpets, antique leather sofas and wing chairs. Tapestries and outrageously unique *objets d'art* presented further challenges.

"I never dreamed working nearly ten hours a day for weeks on end for one client could be so much fun," she sighed to Gerald. "I'm meeting Mr. Townsend at the Towers at five o'clock. It may be the last consultation before the actual deliveries and placement.

"Any client after this project is going to be boring by comparison," she laughed as she prepared to leave. "The man is a walking history of art textbook, and much more fascinating."

"You are positively amazing," Charles Townsend smiled at Beth. The soft clarity of his icy blue eyes always made her stare. "You've done a fabulous job. Everything is going to work out beautifully." Again his blue eyes held Beth in their gaze. "Now I have something else I'd like to discuss with you. Over dinner, if that would be all right." Beth nodded. "How does some good old San Francisco seafood sound? Sam's up on Bush Street has the best food in town."

Charles Townsend's driver opened the huge door of the black Cadillac Fleetwood for Beth. Escorted by Charles Townsend, Beth felt as queenly entering Sam's with the black-and-white linoleum floor and austerely paneled walls as if they were at the Top of the Mark or the grand ballroom of the Fairmont.

Though the atmosphere lacked even the basic rudiments of style, Sam's had the best seafood in all of San Francisco, and that's where Charles Townsend felt like eating. "Would the lady care for something to drink, Mr. Townsend?" the tuxedoed waiter looked slightly overdressed for the surroundings. Charles looked at Beth. "Oh yes, coffee would be nice," she smiled.

"And the regular black coffee for me, please, Max."

Oysters on the half shell, followed by clam chowder, salad, fabulous grilled sea bass and irresistible cheesecake were served promptly. No waiting, no ceremony. Over coffee, Charles brought out several photographs and some sketches.

"I have a dream," he said, spreading before Beth pictures of a serenely beautiful valley. "Other than my education, this land is the only thing of value I've ever accepted from my father." His face clouded at the word *father*.

"It's gorgeous. Where is it?"

"About twenty-five miles south of San Francisco. Not too far from Stanford, my alma mater, in a rather exclusive rural area. There are thirty acres, and I'd like to develop it." Beth raised her eyebrows. "I don't mean subdivide," he continued, "that's not my thing. I mean a private estate. Here are some rough sketches of the main house—Tudoresque architecture as you can see. The drive swings through this existing row of cypress, the house sits here, then there are about sixteen acres of gardens I'd like to develop around it. The rest will be natural terrain."

"This looks like a mansion," Beth observed in amazement. "How big is it?"

Charles Townsend came as near to a blush as a sophisticated gentleman can come. "About 30,000 square feet. I have big plans for it." His blue eyes smiled. "The inside is where you come in. I've seen your paintings. You're truly a magnificent artist. See this area here? It's across from a grand staircase, two stories high. I'd like you to design a rose window to be done in stained glass. The theme of the mansion will be the Tudor Rose—a haven from the outside world. I'm going to call it 'Rosehaven.'"

Beth sat in silence. A whirl of questions flew through her mind. In the course of conversation, she had alluded several times to his father, but Charles refused to discuss him. "Money is all that matters to TNT," Charles had said almost bitterly. Yet she sensed something even deeper than the pain caused by a ruthless man. What was it? Fear? Hatred? It seemed inconceivable that one as kind, gentle and sensitive as Charles could hate his own father.

His elegant slender fingers lay across her hand. "What do you think of it?" he pulled her out of her reverie.

"I think," she said pensively, "that it reminds me of our home in Hampstead on the Heath, only on a ten-times-grander scale. As enormous as it is, you've sketched in a homey feeling."

What she didn't ask, what she was dying to know, was, *Who are you building this for? A client? A wife?* She looked into Charles's ice-blue eyes. *I could fall in love with this man,* Beth told herself. *Maybe I'm already in love with him, and maybe I don't really want to know who he's building it for.*

"Beth, you're so quiet," he said gently. "Would you work with me? If you will, I'd like you to go through every bit of the design phase with me. You can think about it as long as you like. I'm not asking anyone else but you."

Was this the manner in which the renowned Charles Townsend always engaged the most skilled and qualified artisans to work on his projects? By being so charming and sincere no one could resist? How could she refuse? The house was a dream. And so was he.

9

Afrigid March wind blew across San Francisco Bay. It reminded Beth of her parents in London, and how they had suffered through the coldest January since 1740. Beth clutched her coat tighter and continued from Sheridan's up Stockton toward Gumps' store on Post Street.

Perhaps the fascination was a carryover from her childhood, but the variety at Gumps', from well-made toys to outrageously exotic jade, never lost its attraction. Sheridan's and Gumps' both were the ultimate in unique visual experiences. Just browsing with no high purpose felt strangely luxurious. From Gumps' she walked over to I. Magnin's for the sheer delight of buying Kerry something for her two-month birthday.

The inner stirrings that had tugged at her on her morning errands brought her to a standstill across from Union Square. Beth shielded herself from the chill and stood in the protection of I. Magnin's in deep thought.

Her earliest ideals had been gained in this cosmopolitan city. Now she sensed that within its heartbeat seethed a vortex of contradictions. Did the whole country feel this way? Or did it strike her in particular because she had just registered to vote for the first time? Was she super-sensitive because she had a child growing up in a society with frighteningly shifting values? Or were these distressing questions the signatures of her own maturing process? Until a year ago, only fine arts, ballet and a handful of select human beings had a place in her world.

The world of business, responsibility and disturbing social issues now flooded her thoughts daily.

On the one hand, the nation was charmed by Kennedy's "Period of Grace," a "return to Camelot," as it was glamorized by the press. The arts had rarely seemed so fashionable—with master cellist Pablo Casals, ballet performances and Shakespearean actors entertaining at the White House. This she understood.

On the other hand, frightening demonstrations often took place right here in Union Square, protesting the invasion of Cuba or the war in Vietnam. Her mind struggled in confusion, unable to identify with her own generation.

"Are you lost, Miss? A stranger in the city, are you? How about having a drink with me to get out of this cold weather?"

An eager-looking middle-aged man, wearing a Brooks Brothers suit and pink shirt, leered at her.

Beth looked up, startled at this invasion of her private thoughts. "No, no—I'm not lost, uh, thank you."

She hurried away before he could say anything more, then laughed as she braced against the wind going east on Geary Street. *Thank God, I'm not that lost!*

Beth turned left on Market Street and north on Montgomery toward the financial district. She smiled all the way, thinking what fun it would have been to tell that old flirt, "I have an appointment with Mr. Charles Townsend in his penthouse executive suite, where he is eager to consult with me regarding my expert opinions on works of art." And he'd say, "Sure you do, kid!" *It's incredible,* she thought, *I love what I'm doing and being who and what I am. . . . It's only the rest of the world I'm not so sure about.*

*　　*　　*

The express elevator brought Beth to the top of Townsend Towers. To the left was a door marked private. Ahead, a circle of craftsmen hummed with the installation of a parquet floor that would surround sculptured carpets. Paint, fabric, foil and leather wallcoverings lay scattered about for the various suites. Beth stepped out of the way for the copper hood two men were carrying into the fullscale kitchen, while saws buzzed, making precision cuts to fit carved, antique French, walnut panels into the executive dining room. And there in the heart of it all sat Charles at a makeshift drafting table, loving every chaotic bit of it.

"What are you doing down there?" Beth called, stepping around boxes of marble for the bathroom floors.

His gentle ice-blue eyes stunned her every time they met. "Come and see, and tell me how you like it," he beamed, pulling her beside him at the drafting table. "Look at my staircase, across from the rose window, the way its sweeping curve flows into the living room. Are you impressed?"

"I don't read blueprints that well, but of course I'm impressed. Only I thought you were concentrating on Townsend Towers. This blueprint looks like Rosehaven."

"I think more creatively sometimes at the front lines of the battle," Charles smiled. "We have some areas to discuss today, but you've almost completed this," his hands gestured to the chaos around him. "The rest of these people are merely executing it."

Beth wasn't about to argue the point, but Charles was exceedingly generous in giving her the credit for the exquisite interior design and furnishings of the Towers. "I'd like you to notice," he pointed again to the blueprints, "here is the elevation for the entry and courtyard of the main house. But this path leads to a little tea house in Italian Renaissance style for garden parties and receptions." His little-boy excitement drew Beth closer.

Charles Townsend's latest architectural triumph had appeared in this month's leading design trade publication. And here he was, looking at her with those wonderful blue eyes, asking her opinion.

The Townsend Towers' gala opening reception was rivaled only by the opening of the opera season in September. San Francisco's dignitaries and Charles's architectural contemporaries all lauded his achievement, while Beth gazed up at her handsome escort with unabashed admiration. *Don't fall in love with this man,* her heart repeatedly warned, *this is only for a season.*

Through the spring and summer of 1963, Sheridan's Fine Arts continued to flourish, catering to collectors, galleries, the rich and famous. Sean had written, "Smashing, bravo," of Gerald's performance. "The man is in his absolute heyday," he told Beth. "He knows his business, but it took you, with your people skills and artistic and common sense, to lift him and Sheridan's out of the doldrums."

Beth's heart soared. *This is truly my season of gladness,* she told herself. The two men she most admired, Charles and her father, had paid her high compliments. That boosted her confidence for the testing of her talents Rosehaven would be.

Through the months, Beth and Charles's design work for Rosehaven in his Tower office extended to long and then longer lunches, and often dinner. The mansion was already well into construction, yet Charles required her final approval for every fluted column and every type of wood for the graceful arches and windows. His enthusiasm was intense. Beth struggled to keep her sketches ahead of his European artisans who were carving Tudor rose designs throughout the house. And all the time she wondered: *Who is he building Rosehaven for?* But there was never a clue . . . and it seemed totally inappropriate to ask.

Charles and Beth's father shared an impeccably rare artistic sense, an elegant yet conservative manner of dress, and easy good humor. Both were gracious conversationalists. Yet while Sean's business acumen left something to be desired, Charles's surpassed the genius level. She felt Charles's protectiveness in hard-hat areas, and also knew he would be the first to jump overboard if someone were drowning. But the quality Beth came to love most in Charles was his ability to talk about things that mattered most in life—things of the heart. Only two areas seemed to be taboo—his father and the occupants of Rosehaven.

"How did you come to be an architect?" Beth asked over dinner one evening.

"I couldn't be anything else," Charles answered simply, "although it caused an unalterable rift with my father. He thought real men engineered bridges. My love for art and architecture came from my mother."

"I've never heard you speak of your mother before. Is she living?"

"She's still alive, if that's what you'd call it. She was very beautiful once—a stunning woman with brains, sweet and naive, from a family of alcoholics. My father swept her off her feet. He showered her with flowers and the considerable charm he can turn on when he's in the mood. Then diamonds and furs and all that. She really adored the man, and they married. Then she discovered money was the one and only love of his life. Her stunning face and figure were the perfect foil for him to show off his wealth by dressing her in expensive clothes and designer jewelry. But she would have thrown all the diamonds and furs away for even a little bit of love." Charles sipped his coffee, a look of deep sadness on his face.

"Where is she now?"

"In Rome, I think. It's hard to keep track of her. She rambles all over Europe, still running from a broken heart into the arms of a bottle. All the years she waited for him to love her, she courted Mr. Martini—Bombay gin on the rocks, no olives, please."

"Is that why you don't drink?"

"I saw what it did to her. Growing up here in San Francisco, I was her escort—to the museum benefits, opera, ballet and after-theater dinners with her friends. My father liked his wife to be seen in such places. It added to his image, although he never accompanied her. I hated it, though, to see my sweet, sensitive, gorgeous mother dazzle everyone at the beginning of an evening, and then stagger out, slurring her goodbyes."

Beth's sympathy shone in her face. "You have some better memories, too, don't you?"

"My mother loved me dearly, and I'll ever be grateful to her," Charles smiled. "She taught me to appreciate music, the arts, the finer things in life. Since I was small, we'd holiday in Europe the whole summer, unless we went to the house in Carmel. And she bought me the finest books on the art and architecture of the great cathedrals, da Vinci, Michelangelo and paintings by the masters."

"Did you also study in Europe?"

"Mostly in Florence, Venice and Rome, supplemental to getting my degrees from Stanford. I'm an admirer of Sir Christopher Wren, especially the amazing structure of the great dome and nave of St. Paul's Cathedral in London. But I still consider Sheridan's on Bond Street to be one of my great discoveries."

"My father would be delighted to hear that," Beth laughed. "Oh, I should tell you, he's still searching for the rare Wooton desk and the 1800s Belgian silver candlesticks. Are—are they for Rosehaven too?"

"Certainly, as well as an estate collection of English pieces I probably bought right out from under your father," Charles grinned wickedly. "They were offered exclusively to me. The collection includes two fabulous sets of Meissen dinner services."

Beth couldn't bear to think of the time when Rosehaven would be finished. She fought for control to keep from blurting out the anxieties racing through her mind. . . . *You mean too much to me, Charles. You're more than any client should ever be. Surely you know I love you, even though I shouldn't. I'm heading for heartbreak when you go out of my life and on to another project. I can't help myself. You're more of a gentleman than I imagined a man could be. You're a beautiful contrast to Roberto. How can you be so romantic with only a gentle kiss on my cheek? You're driving me out of my mind, Mr. Charles Townsend. . . .*

Instead of all that, she merely asked, "Do I get to see this mystery mansion someday?"

"Is your calendar clear on November first? I'd like you to take the whole day."

"If it isn't, I'll cancel everything."

Once out of San Francisco, the weather turned bright and sunny. "You look very British, right at home in my racing-green Jaguar." He smiled. Beth had no idea where they were going, except Charles had said it was in a quiet valley of country estates. Some of Sheridan's wealthiest clients were in the

Atherton, Menlo Park and Woodside communities. Charles turned off Highway 101 onto 280 and open country. "See that row of cypress? That's the drive," he smiled.

Gardeners swarmed over the grounds, imbedding slate walks, planting hedge borders and flower beds. "All those trees in crates are English yews," Charles explained.

Nestled in the center of the activity, surrounded by gently rolling hills and natural lakes in the distance, the Tudoresque mansion rose up on the crest of a knoll in queenly splendor. Diamond-paned windows caught the tilted rays of the mid-morning sun, blinking a merry greeting.

"Welcome to Rosehaven," Charles beamed with that pleased little-boy look of his, waiting for Beth's response.

"Oh, Charles, it reminds me of Hampstead. I can just imagine the English garden in full bloom, with the clematis draping over the entry in springtime." She took a long look at the mansion. "It's more wonderful than I'd dreamed. It's a castle, but an inviting one. How many rooms did you say there are?"

"Thirty. But it'll take a while to finish them all."

He led her into the entry, a hexagon-shaped room about fifteen feet across and two stories high. A Waterford crystal chandelier hung suspended in the center on a crushed velvet-covered chain from the ceiling. Victorian spindled arches offered an invitation in three directions.

"I've entered into fantasy land," Beth gasped. The lines of poetry carved in the rich walnut arch into the living room read, "Wait not till tomorrow; gather the roses of life today." She glanced at Charles in amusement, "You write poetry, too?"

"No," he laughed, "I stole the lines from an ancient Frenchman, Pierre de Ronsard."

"I can scarcely take it in. I'm speechless, Charles."

"You've been looking at the blueprints and sketches for almost a year—doesn't it look familiar? Come this way. . . . "

He led her through the library, kitchen and enormous dining room, stopping outside two massive walnut doors, deeply carved with roses, ribbons and musical notes, flutes and violins. "Remember sketching that?" he asked.

"Yes, but where do these doors go?"

Charles flung both doors wide open. Beth gasped. "This is the ballroom," he said proudly. "I know you love this pale shade of green. Do you like it?" he asked.

Above the glazed celadon green walls trailed intricate rococo designs in gold leaf. Fluted marble columns flanked gracefully arched windows that caught the reflection of six crystal and gold chandeliers. Deep green Italian marble graced the surround of the fireplace, with pale green and gold urns on the ends of the mantle. At the far end of the room, on the riser for an orchestra, sat a white and gold grand piano.

"On Christmas Eve for the rest of our lives, this room will be filled with music and love and laughter of family and friends," Charles smiled. His ice-blue eyes pierced her heart, as did his words. It was to be his home then. He had never said he didn't have a family. Tears she fought to control filled her eyes, her throat throbbed with pain, she couldn't swallow.

Beth turned away—desperately wanting to run, to be far from this man she'd so foolishly come to love with all her heart. Was she forever destined to fall in love with the wrong man?

Charles took her in his arms, searching the depths of the tears she tried to deny. "Beth," he began tenderly, "I've waited too long for just the right moment to tell you. . . . "

I can't bear it, she thought. *I don't want to hear.*

Charles tipped her chin upward, brushing her forehead with his lips. "What are you doing the rest of your life? I've prayed you'll spend it with me. My love for you inspired Rosehaven . . . You're the only woman I've ever loved."

His lips were upon hers with a deep and tender passion, born of a selfless love. "My proposal lacks the eloquent phrases I've rehearsed a thousand times, my dear Beth. But I'm asking you to be my wife."

With her head nuzzled on his shoulder, Charles deftly removed the pins holding her coil of silky black hair, stroking it softly. Time stood still, nothing else existed. He lifted her face to a gentle kiss. "Aren't you going to say anything?"

"I'm trying to decide if I've died and gone to heaven," she laughed through tears. "Oh, Charles, I love you with my whole heart. I'm going to say yes, before I discover it's only a dream."

"I suppose I went about this backward." He led her to sit beside him on the steps of the orchestra platform. "I fell in love with you the first time we met. No, not the first time when you were only a child of twelve and I was twenty-four. But when I saw you in San Francisco and discovered how much alike we are, I knew I wanted to build a home where we could share a lifetime. I've been terrified of marriage, Beth. Of ruining lives like my father has," Charles's tone had grown solemn. "It seems strange to you, perhaps, but I designed this whole plan so you'd fall in love with Rosehaven and with me. I've not been without success in my other ventures, but if you'd have said no, I'd consider myself a total failure."

"You could never fail at anything, Charles," Beth put her hand on his.

"One of my fears is that you'd think I'm just an egomaniac, building a monument to myself and my own success with a home like this. Beth, I have to make you understand something very basic about me." He looked very seriously into her eyes. "When I turned twenty-one my father deeded this property to me. He had bought it when the Stanfords and other prominent families began to build their country homes in this area, but he had absolutely no use for it. If it had meant something to him, I'd probably never have accepted it. While I'm grateful for the education and lifestyle he afforded my mother and me, I've never wanted anything of his—not even his name.

"I've inherited the Midas touch of making money, but unlike my father, I don't have to ruin someone else to do it. I work hard and use the talent I've been given. The power of wealth has a different meaning for me than it does for my father. Beth," Charles's voice became intense with emotion, "I have more money than I know what to do with. With you by my side, I see Rosehaven as a place to share precious art of past centuries in a setting for us and others to enjoy. I've given away more money than I've kept. Is it wrong for me to want to do this with the rest of it?"

There was a quiet pause as Beth realized she had just been given a peek into the soul of Charles Townsend.

"Before you came into the gallery that first day," she said softly, "Gerald told me you were a prince of a fellow. He was right. You're my prince charming and Rosehaven is our castle where we'll live happily ever after."

Charles smiled in gratitude for Beth's understanding. "Shall we begin with a June wedding?" he asked. "I designed the staircase for a bride, namely you, and the house and gardens are scheduled to be finished by then."

"Now I know why you're such a success."

"I do my homework and set high goals," he stood, pulling her up into his embrace and kisses, "but all else pales compared to winning you. Come along, I have something else to show you."

Their footsteps resounded with happiness and introduced echoes of joy to Rosehaven. Charles led her through the main floor level around various craftsmen to the rear garden side of the house. Sunlight streamed through the French windows of an intimate dining area off the kitchen, overlooking a future garden. Two Victorian white wicker chairs faced a floral-skirted table, set with crystal stemware. The caterer had fresh flowers in silver bowls and a platter of fresh fruit on the table.

"Luncheon is served," Charles announced, pulling out the chair for Beth. On her plate, a small box wrapped in silver foil and pink satin waited. "Open it," Charles nodded.

The card read, "Come live with me and be my love and I will make thee beds of roses and a thousand fragrant posies."

"Oh Charles, you are a romantic! Are you the poet this time?"

"No, Christopher Marlowe is. He's a bit before my time—sixteenth century, to be exact. Open the box."

Nervously, Beth tore the foil off a Cartier box. "Charles, you designed this, didn't you?" He nodded, his pleased-little-boy look spread across his face as he slipped the ring on her finger. "It fits perfectly," Beth sighed, admiring an exquisitely faceted and flawless diamond set on a band of carved platinum roses.

"Do you love me?" Charles asked.

"Oh, I do. I do."

10

The assassination of President John F. Kennedy on November 22, 1963, rocked the world in horror. Within hours, Vice President Lyndon B. Johnson had become the thirty-sixth President of the United States. A nation in shock reeled with the news just forty-eight hours later that Lee Harvey Oswald, Kennedy's murderer, had himself been shot and killed by Jack Ruby while under police guard.

Television sets droned almost around the clock for days, covering the latest developments, the presidential funeral and a nation in mourning.

Only events of such magnitude could blur Beth's joy. She delighted in buying presents for Kerry's first Christmas, scheduling a trip to London with Charles to celebrate Christmas at Hampstead, designing the interior of Rosehaven, and making arrangements for their wedding.

"Charles," Beth suggested, "could we drive down to San Jose early on the Sunday before we go to London to celebrate Christmas with the Sterlings? You've heard me talk so much about Hope and Josh and baby Kerry—I want them to meet you, now that you're a permanent part of my life. They're my dearest friends."

"If they're dear to you, they're dear to me. I'd love to meet them."

Hope bubbled with excitement at their coming. "Beth, Kerry is sooo thrilled about Christmas. It'll be such fun. Come to church with us—you'll love the Christmas cantata, and I'm singing a solo. Why don't you meet us at the church? It will be wonderful to all be there together."

"You have a beautiful voice," Charles complimented Hope after the service. "I enjoyed the informality of the worship. It seemed more meaningful, closer to God than the formal churches I've been to." He led the way to the car. "Everyone must be hungry—where would you like to go for lunch? My treat."

"I've put together something simple at home," Hope said as she loaded Kerry into the car. "Kerry will be ready for her nap soon. I'm not sure she'd make it going out for lunch." She noted Charles's reluctance. "Don't worry—it's no trouble. And we'll probably feel cozier in our living room than at a restaurant."

Beth held or played with Kerry every minute they were there. The cuddly teddy bear, so soft and big it flopped its arms around her, became Kerry's favorite of all the clothes and toys Beth brought.

While Charles, Hope and Josh engaged in adult conversation after lunch, Beth rocked the sleeping baby cradled in her arms. A look of compassion shot between Josh and Hope. Later, in the kitchen, Beth and Hope chattered like schoolgirls about wedding plans. They also overheard Josh and Charles in deep discussion in the small living room, mingled with Kerry's peals of delight when Charles gave her a horsey ride on his foot.

"Beth, do you want to reconsider?" Hope made the offer with misty eyes. "With Charles you could give Kerry a stable home, love, all the things you wanted for her, even more than we have to give."

"Hope, I just couldn't do that. You and Josh were there when I needed you. I can't hold other people's lives like a yo-yo on a string while I get mine in order," she gave her friend a reassuring hug. "I do feel guilty, though, that Charles is on the outside of our secret. But I've made my decision, and I'll live with it."

"You were right about the Sterlings, darling," Charles said on the way back to the city. "I've never been in such a humble home, yet so rich in love and hospitality."

"Isn't Hope adorable?"

Charles nodded. "That gentle little wisp of a woman is full of both wit and wisdom. And I greatly admire Josh. I'd welcome a man with his organizational talents in any one of my businesses. His abilities would command a handsome salary in the corporate world. Yet they're content to live on big faith and a small income."

"You two had quite a chat, didn't you?" Beth's adoration shone in her eyes.

"They're rare, Beth. Most people I come in contact with have a great deal of money and little real happiness. Josh and Hope are wealthy in things that really matter. He and I are going to play golf soon."

"I didn't know you played golf," Beth gave him a playful punch in the arm.

"There's a lot you have to learn about me, my sweet. If you'd open the trunk of either the Cadillac or this Jag, you'd find a set of golf clubs and clothes. One never can tell when the opportunity will present itself." He laughed and they settled into a few moments of silence, enjoying the scenery on a beautiful winter day. "I liked the church's worship service this morning," Charles finally ventured.

"I'm really happy you did." Charles's generosity, his kindness and consideration of everyone were qualities that set Christians apart, but Beth had never heard him mention his beliefs. This was the man she was going to marry. She had to know.

Beth tried to sound casual. "Charles, I think I know what your answer will be, but you've never actually said it. Are you a Christian?"

A cloud came over his face for several seconds before he answered. His expression was troubled. "You may *never* hear me say it. My father, mother and I are members of the largest and wealthiest church in San Francisco, but the walls would probably fall down if any one of us walked in. I'm sure TNT writes it a big check once a year and writes it off on his taxes. He's told people he's a Christian businessman, and then cheated them out of millions. People will know if we are real Christians by our love and how we live, more than by what we say."

Beth took his hand and held it tightly. By his tone, the subject was closed. For now, that was all she needed to know. Not a soul on earth could be of a more loving nature than Charles.

"If Kerry were a few years older, she could be flower girl for our wedding," Charles smiled, ready to change the subject. "She's adorable with her dark curly hair, those huge brown eyes and her knock-out eyelashes. And so sweet. I noticed you couldn't stop kissing her."

Beth blinked back tears he couldn't see. The secret she gladly bore to protect those she loved would forever tear at her heart. It would never be easy. "Charles," she began slowly, "you do want children of our own, don't you?"

She watched the cloud etch his dear face with pain. "As much as you do, but. . . . " His voice broke. He couldn't finish for several awkward seconds, until he found the words. "You did notice the blueprints of Rosehaven included a very large nursery, didn't you?" he brightened.

This happy day must not be marred by make-believe troubles. Beth put Charles's hesitation out of her mind and turned to thoughts of going home to Hampstead for the holidays.

"The weather's quite decent for December twenty-third. You can almost see the sun," Sean chuckled as he embraced Beth and shook Charles's hand at Gatwick Airport. "We're all set for a jolly Christmas. You've never tasted anything like Tillie's roast goose and plum pudding, Charles," he said as they set out for Hampstead.

"Tillie!" Beth squealed with excitement when she opened the front door. "Meet my wonderful Charles. Oh, the fresh green garlands smell heavenly, and I can tell," she sniffed, "you have scones in the oven." Shy Tillie showed obvious approval of Charles. Beth's attention was drawn to the staircase. "Mum! You look fabulous." Margaret Sheridan descended the stairs, elegant as always, wearing deep green velvet, every hair smoothed back off her classic forehead into a French twist.

"And I haven't seen you this radiant since you danced Tatania in *A Midsummer Night's Dream,*" Margaret kissed her daughter's cheek. "Charles, welcome to our home and family."

In a few moments they all gathered for tea. "Charles, I have to tell you about this tea set," Beth began.

"As a little girl," her father interrupted, "our Beth would spend her Saturdays in the shop, serving make-believe tea to the queen!" He laughed. "This set she always had her eye on."

"It's extraordinary," Charles agreed.

"And now it's yours," he said proudly. "The first wedding gift for the future Mr. and Mrs. Charles Townsend. You know, my boy, Margaret and I are delighted. Beth takes her work very seriously," he winked. "But love, did you have to promise to marry our number-one client to get him to place all those orders?"

"Mr. Sheridan, you'd be extremely proud of your daughter if you could see the magnificent work she's done for the Towers and Rosehaven." Charles beamed with a pride of his own.

"We shall jolly well see it all in June when I come to give the bride away," he beamed, "and Margaret and I claim the finest son-in-law we could hope for."

The Christmas holidays seemed wrapped in ribbons of yesterday's memories and tomorrow's dreams. The days sped by all too quickly, but by the time they were on the plane back to the States both Beth and Charles were anxious to get home to Rosehaven.

One week after New Year's they were back in San Jose for Kerry's first birthday party. Charles adored her. Beth felt reassured, knowing he, too, would always want to be there for Kerry's special days.

The months between January and June disappeared like vapor. Rosehaven's future residents fell more in love with each other and their home as time went by. Flowers bloomed in varied masses in the English gardens outside and country English chintzes and plants inside.

Blueprints, sketches, fabric swatches, every kind of building sample and craftsmen, painters, gardeners, and furniture movers at last blended into the glory of the completed Rosehaven. To Beth, it symbolized giving birth again—to the promises of an enchanted life that lay ahead.

The week of the wedding, Sean, Margaret and Tillie arrived from London, Ruth from New York, and Annie and Ali from Carmel. There was ample room for them to stay with Beth at Mrs. Trillingham's comfortable Victorian in the City. The days exploded with the joy of sharing all this with her family and friends.

Of course Sean couldn't wait to explore every detail of Rosehaven. "This is terrifically inviting, you two," he gave his respected opinion, "this drawing room combined with the library—I suppose what you Americans would call the *living room*. Ahh, it's delightful to see the antique Brussels tapestry carpet we ordered in so perfect a setting."

His experienced eyes critiqued the forest green silk velvet walls. And Beth watched her father survey the sofas and chairs covered in a variety of materials: some in rose-splashed chintz, gathering together shades of lavender, raspberry and greens; some in rich cranberry velvet with wool fringe; others in fine tapestries. When Sean smiled, she smiled.

Beth's own paintings graced several walls in gilt Baroque frames, complimenting potted palms and an abundance of fresh flowers everywhere. Sean's admiring gaze traveled up to the deeply carved crown molding against the thirteen-foot ceilings, down again along the architectural woodwork and fluted columns.

"Marvelous," he beamed. "Absolutely marvelous. For all of its massive grandeur, you've pulled off rarified taste, without a breath of stateliness. It's a romantic vision of life in a great house, set in a vast English park. Any less genius for warmth and comfort would have resulted in one feeling like he's in a museum. This place captures the slower pace of the yesterdays none of us ever knew, but only dreamed of. I say," he practically burst a button in pride over his daughter's accomplishment, "it's an inspired background for real living."

At two o'clock in the afternoon on Sunday, June 14, 1964, Beth paused breathlessly at the top of the curving staircase. She felt extraordinarily beautiful, as a bride should.

She was a portrait in white satin, crowned by a frame of silky black hair. It was caught up at the sides into a headband of delicately filigreed pearls and satin rose petals, then cascaded to her shoulders. Gossamer clouds of fine tulle veiled her porcelain skin with the delicacy of a cameo. The rosy glow of happiness, the richness of bridal satin all heightened the sparkle in Beth's deep blue eyes. Under a fringe of dark lashes, her reflection in the gilt-framed mirror on the stair landing returned a smile. She paused to check every detail, while Hope sang "I Love You Truly" in the parlor.

San Francisco's finest couturiers designed her Victorian gown. Its high soft lace band at her throat melted into the bodice with a deep V of Alençon lace on net. A wider Alençon framed a rose design, encrusted with hand-sewn pearls and crystal droplets. Poufy Bishop's sleeves, inset with roses of lace and pearls, fastened at the wrists with tiny buttons. Scattered satin roses and pearls danced down to the deeply scalloped hemline.

Beth turned to the side to enjoy the soft folds of the butterfly bow in the back that made her waist look as small as Scarlett O'Hara's.

Charles had carefully chosen her bridal bouquet, a bountiful nosegay of white and pale pink roses, white orchids, sprays of lily of the valley, forget-me-nots, and the polished petals of stephanotis, graced with trailing satin ribbons.

Beth breathed deeply of the flowers' sweet sentiment and heady fragrance. This cherished moment, the dear, handsome man about to become her husband—all of this—was a precious gift from God. For this fragile moment in time, dearer than her loftiest dreams, she whispered, "Thank You, Lord."

Poised at the foot of the stairs stood Hope as her matron of honor. Ruth and Annie completed the lovely wedding party in shell-pink lace Victorian-style gowns. Ali made a handsome little ring bearer in a white dinner jacket, just like the men.

As strains of the wedding march floated through the rooms below, Beth appeared on the arm of her father in a shimmer of satin and billowing veils. Charles beamed at the vision of his bride he would treasure forever. On her descent, the wedding party proceeded out the French doors to the terrace, followed by their guests. Here Charles and Beth exchanged their vows beneath an arbor thickly entwined with masses of roses.

The woman Charles promised to love and cherish until death came to part them yielded her lips to his, and they were pronounced man and wife.

The garden of many moods, strewn with passionate bursts of color, provided the setting for a Baroque string quartet. Beth's favorite melodies by Bach and Vivaldi wafted over the shifting shadows of the emerald lawn.

A white lattice gazebo, lavished with ferns and flowers, displayed a table draped with volumes of pink netting. It bore an elaborate arrangement of sliced melons, strawberries and other fruits. Servers with silver trays offered paté de fois gras and other delicacies. The bridal couple moved graciously among their guests during the garden reception and after the gourmet sit-down dinner on the terrace.

Dancing in the magnificent ballroom stretched far into the evening. Then the limousine arrived to take Beth's guests back to Mrs. Trillingham's, and the bride and groom were finally alone.

Charles took Beth in his arms. Their eyes spoke the tender words their hearts felt, anticipating the culmination of the deep, abiding love they had for each other. They ascended the stairs as husband and wife to spend the first night of a lifetime together.

Tales of the Townsend wedding, with its guests limited to an intimate few, soon became a legend among San Francisco's social set. Over coffee in the garden-like breakfast room, Charles laughed at the society column's account of their wedding in Tuesday's *Examiner*. "The Townsend/Sheridan wedding at Rosehaven mansion, with a small elite guest list, topped a season of brilliant social events," he read. "Then it describes who wore what, and so on."

"For heaven's sake," Beth sighed, "you'd think we were the king and queen of England."

"Ha!" Charles laughed again. "Must have been a spy reporter. I didn't know anyone from the paper was here, did you?"

"Eileen said a columnist called the gallery wanting information," Beth replied, "so maybe we did have an undercover agent lurking among us."

"Well, hopefully we won't have anyone climbing over the walls to spy on our honeymoon hideaway." Charles pulled Beth into his lap. "I want you all to myself."

"You've got me," Beth giggled.

"Then, if we ever get too tired to make love all day long," Charles began to make plans, "I have business in Rome and I want you to come with me. I'd hoped to locate my mother, but so far I haven't. After that, we'll go to London for the Art of a Decade exhibition at the Tate Gallery, and of course see your parents. Would you like that?"

"Sweetheart, wherever you are is where I want to be." Beth gave him a tender kiss.

Charles tickled her nose with the lace of her negligee. "Beth, I'd begun to think I'd never marry, and I need you to teach me how a real family functions. It's something I've never known, yet long for."

"Charles, God has given me a beautiful husband . . . beginning from the inside out," she smiled. "I think being a real family means having a common sense of values, standing together to face the world, forming a circle of love that gathers everyone in. It's a common search for good. I saw those things in you, right off. It'll take a lifetime for you to know how much I love you."

His ice-blue eyes smiled as he reached for Beth's hand. "Darling, I wouldn't mind if you try . . . like right now," and he led her up the staircase. Charles's caresses aroused a desire only God could have inspired between a man and a woman. A tender, reverent, holy, yet powerful passion—so unlike Roberto's impetuous, lustful lovemaking.

San Francisco's art guilds and the cultural, social and philanthropic membership chairpersons wooed Beth with invitations to their fall luncheons and balls.

"I've never been courted as a VIP before," she chuckled to Charles as they drove into the city one morning in late July. "See what being Mrs. Charles Townsend does for a person? I don't know how much time I'll have to play young society matron. Gerald still needs me until he finds a replacement. Business is booming since you came into the picture."

"I've never been out. Sheridan's has been the only game in town forever, for people who know quality."

"Well, I mean since the Towers and Rosehaven notoriety."

Charles pulled off Highway 101 onto a suburban road.

"What are you doing?" Beth questioned.

"I think it's time you learn how to drive a car in America. Practically all you have to do in the Cadillac is point it in the right direction, and remember to drive on the right side of the road." Charles jumped out and opened the door for her. "All right, Mrs. Townsend, slip behind the wheel and drive me into town."

"This is much simpler than the Bentley," Beth adapted to the American way of driving rather quickly. "But don't expect me to toodle off all over the country now. I love my home too much."

"Can you bear to leave it next week until the end of August? They're ready to talk business in Rome. We'll buy you a ball gown in one of the high fashion salons along the Via Veneto. It'll rival anything you've seen in Paris, and we'll be home for you to wear it for the opening of the opera season."

"I haven't been to Rome since I was a teenager. I'd love it!"

"Buon giorno, Signor Townsend. It is always a pleasure to have you with us," the concierge greeted Charles while Beth stood in awe of the grandeur of the Excelsior Hotel.

"This place is fabulous," she said.

Charles's trained eye scanned its richness. "There is something noble in a classic design," he agreed.

From the window of their luxurious suite, Charles pointed out the Via Veneto below. "This intriguing little avenue is similar to the Champs Elysees in Paris, don't you think? See the small sidewalk cafes? They're my favorite places to people watch. That's the Flora Hotel at the other end, and also the Medici Gardens. The American Embassy and high fashion couturiers are in between. There's a world of fascination right here. Also, the president of the Italian firm I'm working with this week has a driver at our disposal any time we want him. He'll take you sightseeing while I'm working. You can spend an entire day in the galleries and gardens of the Villa Borghese."

"Will we have some time together?" Beth asked, afraid she'd be spending their entire Roman holiday alone.

"Of course, darling, you can't have all the fun. I always have to go and stand in awe of the Pantheon and the Sistine Chapel. And the Vatican will take a whole day."

Beth lifted her lips to his. "Kiss me, so I know I'm not dreaming. Is life with you always going to be an adventure?"

"Why don't you stick around and find out? The real surprise is where we're going between Rome and London."

"You're not going to tell me?"

He shook his head and smiled an impish grin. "You'll just have to wait and see."

On the Eurail going north, Beth laid her head on Charles's shoulder. The majesty of the towering alps framed in the window of the dining car appeared as though the mighty hand of God had frosted their peaks with molten pearls, shimmering in the morning sun.

"Charles, northern Italy is so gorgeous. I have this insatiable desire to paint everything I see."

"Try to refrain from leaping into an arabesque when you get excited, will you, please? We're almost at our destination, darling."

A driver from the hotel met them at the station. Beth's heart froze at the sign, *Lago di Como*. Lake Como. Roberto. The incredibility of it numbed Beth's appreciation of the hilly terrain of emerald carpet below the seven thousand-foot alps. The sapphire blue lake stretched far to the north.

Beth noticed a small sign. "Are we going to Cernobbio?" she asked hopefully.

"That's just a tiny village, within walking distance of our destination on Lake Como, the Villa d'Este," Charles explained. "We can't see the hotel yet."

They drove through a hundred-year-old park past colonnades of trees to an ancient building of pink stone, set near the edge of the lake.

"The villa was built in 1568, but I'm not sure when it became this famous hotel," Charles explained as they entered the opulent lobby of high ceilings and crystal chandeliers. "You're pale, Beth. Are you all right?"

"Yes, darling." She attempted to smile. Beth told herself, *Just put everything but Charles and the beauty of your surroundings out of your mind.* That became easier to do in the warm afternoon sun, lounging on the deck chairs by the floating pool and sparkling lake.

"We'll relax today. Tomorrow will be an unforgettable experience," Charles assured her.

"What—what are we doing tomorrow?" she stammered, afraid to hear the answer.

"Nothing, except seeing the finest private collection of art in the world." The little-boy grin told her he thoroughly enjoyed the elaborate plans he'd made.

I may have a coronary before then, Beth thought. *Oh God, help—You always have. Let Roberto be out of the country, or sick in bed. . . .*

It was a sunny, picture-postcard day. The hotel driver paused at the intricate iron gates of the Villa Cabriollini, and then drove along a sentry of stately cypress on the lake edge surrounding the villa.

At the entrance to the villa, Charles gave his card to a formal-looking gentleman, who promptly disappeared.

"I've made special arrangements for Count Cabriollini to take us on a private tour," Charles said. "At first, his secretary told me that was impossible, but then called me back, saying the Count had high regard for my work and would be pleased to meet me."

Beth smiled weakly, unable to reply.

"Beth, are you sure you're well? You're pale."

At that moment, Roberto swept into the foyer. Debonair, suave, deep brown eyes beaming. *"Ahh, buon giorno, Signor* Townsend," he extended his hand with a broad smile. His face fell instantly at the sight of Beth, yet his recovery was immediate, with barely a flicker of recognition.

"Count Cabriollini, may I present my wife, Elizabeth, who shares my preoccupation with the arts," Charles proudly introduced Beth. "We deeply appreciate your graciousness."

Beth could do nothing less than extend her hand, which Roberto cordially took as he bent to kiss it. "It is my pleasure, *Signora,"* as if he had never set eyes on her before, although his gaze traveled up and down in admiration as on the day they first met. And her face flushed, as it had then.

His guile is probably the better part of valor. He's given me no choice but pretense. I should be grateful, Beth sighed.

"Signor, Signora Townsend, be so kind as to follow me, *per favore."* Their heels clicked on the creamy veined marble floors as they walked toward the gallery of rare seventeenth-century paintings.

The Cabriollini collection surpassed its fame, but to Beth it was merely a blur. After several hours, the subtleties of the game Roberto played for her benefit became an unbearable agony. As Charles's attention was fixed in one direction, Roberto would study her from another, with a hurt in his eyes that clearly asked, *Why did I let you go?*

Beth could stand it no longer and excused herself, claiming a headache, promising to catch up with them in a few minutes. When she did, Charles and Roberto were amicably exchanging cordial handshakes, bidding goodbye like old friends.

Both the beautiful ice-blue and deep brown eyes lit up as she came near. *"Signor, Signora,* you have given me great honor to visit Villa Cabriollini," Roberto bowed deeply. *"Arrivederci."*

"Indeed, I hope we do see you again." Charles took another card from his wallet and handed it to Roberto. "When you're in San Francisco, you must give us an opportunity to repay your hospitality. Come to our home."

"Charles!" Beth gasped.

Startled, he blinked. "What's the matter?"

Flustered and crimson-faced, Beth said, "Oh, nothing—nothing. Please forgive me, darling, I do feel rather strange today."

*　　*　　*

At the hotel, Charles ordered hot tea brought to their room. With a tenderness that touched her heart, he gently unbuttoned the sapphire blue linen suit he'd bought her in Rome, "to match her eyes," he said, and slipped her into bed.

"Sweet dreams, my love. You'll feel better with a little nap. I'll be out on the balcony."

I'd feel better, sweetheart, she thought, *if I weren't beginning our marriage keeping secrets from you. But there's no turning back, nothing to be gained by telling, only hurt.*

Oh God, Beth prayed, *the world is too small to delude ourselves, to think we can escape what we cannot change. As surely as the sun rises with each new day, help me to shield my dear husband from what I've vowed to conceal. You are the God of truth and I am Your child, caught in this chain of secrets I cannot reveal without hurting the ones I love. It's impossible to bear this by myself, Lord. But with You—everything is possible.*

11

Hampstead, so close yet so far removed from the hectic traffic of London, seemed to stretch out its arms in welcome to Beth as never before. Its historical past and present tranquility promised sanctuary. There would be no upsetting surprises here.

The countryside was rich with the romance of its famous, and Beth pointed out where Gainsborough, Reynolds, Keats, Shelley and others had lived. Centuries-old, ivy-covered cottages and grand estates bordered the Heath where she had once played. Inaudibly, the whole of it echoed, *Welcome home,* and Charles felt it too.

The walls of the Sheridans' nineteenth-century stone house rang with her father's jolly laughter. And Mum, with her classical style, flowed in harmony with the symphonic music playing in the background. Hampstead nourished the ingredients memories are made of—the tantalizing aroma of Tillie's scones and marmalade; a lavish garden so ingeniously created it represented an art form in itself; eclectic pieces of exquisite furnishings blended graciously into lived-in comfort. But it was much more. Here Beth had always known a sense of belonging.

In the evenings, Sean relished an hour or so of relaxation at The Spaniards' Inn, a historic pub not far from the North End. He proudly introduced his daughter and son-in-law to the patrons who enjoyed this nightly English ritual of their glasses of ale, although Charles and Beth chose ginger ale. Villagers flocked around Sean wherever he went. Yet, in the middle of one particularly gay evening, Beth suddenly realized she was restless. She discovered Charles was, too. They were homesick for Rosehaven's own warmth and ambience, still so new.

Their last evening in the twilight of the garden, Charles said to Sean and Margaret, "You must promise to come to Rosehaven soon, and Tillie too, of course."

"Tillie, you have me spoiled again with your scones," Beth joked. "I'll just have to put you in my suitcase and take you home with me."

Tillie's usually bland countenance brightened. Everyone in the room looked startled as the shy Tillie spoke out, "I'd love that, Miss Beth."

"We'd like nothing better, Tillie," Beth smiled at her friend. "We really haven't found all the help we need, and certainly no one of your caliber. I can't imagine stealing you from Mum and Daddy, though."

Sean and Margaret exchanged glances. Tillie was part of the family—they had come to love her almost as a daughter. They also cared deeply about her happiness. Margaret sent an affirmative nod to Sean, an unspoken accord that only comes with years of knowing the other's heart. No discussion was necessary.

"Tillie," Sean cleared his throat. "I can see you're serious. Would you really like to live in the States?"

"I've loved living here in the country with you, Mr. Sheridan," Tillie said quietly. "It was as far from London as I could get, and you've been so loving and kind. But all the time we were at Miss Beth's and Mr. Charles's wedding, I kept thinking how much I'd like to stay there."

"Mum, Daddy, what would you do without Tillie?" Beth was amazed that her casual, affectionate comment had escalated into an earnest proposal.

Margaret almost blushed. "Your father and I have been going out for frequent dinner dates in London lately. Then we drive home together instead of living such separate lives. I'm afraid Tillie's been rather lonely."

"I'm sure we can find someone to come in a few days a week," Sean said. "Many of the manors around us are having to cut down on household help. A sign of the times—the economy, 7 percent interest and all that. It's brutal. Gums up everything for the aristocrats with titles and no money. Also, we're losing a portion of our domestic workforce to London shops and offices. So you see, we're all in the same boat. Somehow we'll manage."

Sean regarded Tillie closely, then said, "You've been very loyal. We'd miss you, but if you want to go, you have our blessing."

Tillie's decision was transparent, releasing the mask that usually hid this shy woman's emotions. She smiled joyfully at Beth, who instantly jumped up and hugged her.

Charles beamed. "It looks like it's settled, Tillie. Pack your bags."

When they arrived home in late August, invitations poured in for balls, dinners, luncheons and teas. San Francisco's social set had its usually full calendar ahead. Surprisingly, Tillie seemed to anticipate all this with vicarious pleasure.

"I feel as though we're being rushed for a sorority," Beth sighed. "Charles, is this mad social whirl your normal way of life?" The schedule sounded both exciting and demanding. Would there be any private time with Charles? Or to paint?

"I always receive invitations, especially to the Patron's VIP benefit previews. And the Art Institute's League knows I'm good for several scholarships each year. But it's really you they're romancing, hon," Charles smiled at her. "You're young, beautiful, talented and fresh new material for League."

"I'm not sure if I'm League material," Beth gave a wry smile.

"Do you know Merribelle and Henry Matson?" Charles gave her a reassuring hug. "She's about thirty-five, a cute blonde Southern belle. She pours her soul into being popular and sophisticated, and arranging charity benefits. She's not the oldest in League by far, but sort of the matriarch of the social set. Henry's in the mortgage banking business. We'll go to their usual soirée after the opera."

Beth had been to many an opera, but nothing equaled the extravagant splendor of the opening of the San Francisco season, preceded by a gala dinner party, followed by three balls. It heralded the beginning of the social season.

Charles and Beth were among the few first-nighters who were true opera lovers. Most others seemed more attracted to the glitter and glamour, and were more impressed with the who's who and fashion than with the music.

Beth felt like a queen in her draped royal blue velvet gown with a matching cape trimmed in white mink. It had been Charles's choice at the Roman couturier's on the Via Veneto. On the arm of her handsome blonde husband in white tie and tails, she glowed as only a woman in love can.

The Matsons' extravaganza filled the ballroom of the Fairmont Hotel. Merribelle flew toward them the moment of their arrival. "Ah'm delighted as Ah can be to meet you, Elizabeth," she smiled a charming smile. "You've gone and won the heart of the most eligible bachelor in San Francisco. Come, sweetie, let me introduce you to just the nicest people in the world."

"You're a gracious hostess, Merribelle, and your party is as spectacular as ever, but we'll let you greet your other guests first," Charles interceded. Grinning at Beth, he whispered, "I wasn't about to let Merribelle steal you away from me. May I have this dance, Mrs. Townsend?"

"I feel like Cinderella. I've never been to such a glamorous affair." She beamed as they gracefully glided about the dance floor.

"You are definitely the belle of the ball," Charles kissed her forehead gently. "You're a fantastic dancer. I hate having to share you, and here comes Henry, intent on cutting in!"

When they left the party Beth looked up at Charles with stars in her eyes. "I had a wonderful time this evening. I'm so glad we saw *Lohengrin* instead of a tragic opera. It's one of my favorites, and I loved hearing the Wedding March with you next to me. And wasn't Merribelle's party simply fabulous?"

Beth chattered, exhilarated, as Max drove them down Nob Hill to Sutter Street. "Why are we stopping at the Towers?" she asked? "Do you have to get something from your office?"

"You'll see," Charles teased as Max pulled into the Towers' garage and let them out. Charles pushed the elevator button marked "E" for the executive suites, then unlocked the door marked PRIVATE. Before she knew what had happened, Charles swooped her into his arms and carried her into a dream-like bedroom suite of creamy white silk walls and thick carpet. Beyond the filmy fluttering curtains, San Francisco glittered before them, like a sophisticated lady wearing all her jewels at once against black velvet. The room, all white and baroque gold, was exquisite in every detail—just like Charles.

"This is our hideaway when it's late and we want to stay in town." Charles grinned with his pleased-little-boy look.

"I wondered what was behind this door," Beth said in awe. "I didn't know you were capable of such seductive secrets, Mr. Charles Townsend."

"When we were working on the suites I didn't want to tell you about this for fear you'd think I had secret trysts with a mysterious mistress," Charles looked at her with amusement. "And then I decided it would be a fun surprise. Look here." He opened the closet, and there with their I. Magnin's labels still attached hung a blue satin nightgown and peignoir, a complete business ensemble the color of violets and his own attire for the work day ahead of them. In the warm-white marble bath and dressing room her favorite fragrances and toiletries stood in a careful row.

"You are full of surprises, and each one makes me love you more," Beth melted into his arms.

In the morning Charles served croissants and chilled juice from the provisions in the efficient kitchenette. Over fresh-brewed coffee Beth asked, "Has Merribelle said anything to you about having a Christmas benefit ball for League at Rosehaven?"

"Not a word, but I'm agreeable. We built Rosehaven to be shared. League's events need fresh talent, and you're just the one to inspire them with a touch of class. How do you feel about it?"

"I'd love it, but it makes Christmas seem just around the corner. I volunteered to design the invitations, and Merribelle said, 'Ah'd be delighted if you would. Ah know you're a grand artist.' " Beth laughed at her own imitation of a Southern drawl. "I'm going to be busy," she sighed.

"I hope not too busy," Charles laughed. "Save time for us."

"Well, Gerald and I are looking for my replacement at Sheridan's. Today we're interviewing Kent Bradford, another Englishman with an impressive dossier and an excellent reputation in the trade. Unless something negative comes out of the interview, he's the one."

"And are you sure you're ready to give up Sheridan's?" Charles held her eyes in a steady gaze.

"Yes, darling. I just want to be Mrs. Charles Townsend," Beth admitted. "I'm looking forward to what's ahead of us. I'm excited about League, our first Christmas as husband and wife, having time to paint, making plans for Rosehaven—just everything!"

"Uh-oh," Charles looked at his watch. "It's getting late and I have an appointment. I'll have Max pick you up at six o'clock this evening. Hope the interview goes well."

Behind the dark glass of their luxury sedan, Beth relaxed contentedly against Charles's shoulder while Max drove them home through the evening traffic.

"Kent Bradford is definitely Sheridan material," Beth said. "He's thirty-nine, has impeccable qualifications, dresses well, is good-looking with distinguished streaks of gray through his hair. And he is available for training—now. In two weeks I'll be able to retire. How do you like that?"

"I'm glad I found you first—he sounds too attractive."

"He's married with three children."

"Good."

"Darling," she kissed his cheek and snuggled closer, "you're the most beautiful man in the world, from the inside out. No one else even comes close."

From early October on, Beth and Tillie filled Rosehaven with a flurry of activity in preparation for Christmas and the League's ball. Thanksgiving was tucked in between, though every day found them thankful. Tillie and Cookie concocted a bountiful celebration feast. Hope, Josh and Kerry joined them. With bowed heads before dinner, Charles praised God for a time of thanks-*living*.

In the weeks before Christmas, scents of cedar garlands and sprays of juniper with plump blueberries swagged with gold lamé and burgundy velvet bows filled the rooms, creating vignettes of an old-fashioned Victorian Christmas. San Francisco's elite received and responded to the engraved invitations to the Benefit Ball with great excitement and anticipation.

At seven o'clock on the Saturday evening before Christmas, streams of limousines and elegant automobiles flowed through the gates of Rosehaven, softly aglow with twinkling lights. Merribelle scurried about, prodding the catering staff and musicians into their proper places.

Charles and Beth, he in a burgundy velvet dinner jacket and she in the same color gown frosted with embroidered white lace, her silky black hair piled high upon her head, stood in the flower-filled entry to greet their guests.

Christmas greens, white poinsettias and a huge Victorian tree graced the ballroom. Christmas carols, sounds of the big-band swinging years, the '50s, and finally the latest dance music—the watusi—filled the grand room.

"Ah declare," Merribelle came puffing to Beth in a poufy red taffeta gown, "this is the most dazzlin' pahty League has evah had, darlin'. We're raisin' absolutely tons of money for scholarships."

When the last guests had left and the caterers and musicians had packed up and gone, Charles took Beth in his arms and swirled around the dance floor to make-believe music. "Do you know what I liked best about your party, Mrs. Townsend?"

"What, love?"

"For all of its splendiferous effects, you created a welcoming warmth in our home. People were so open and gracious. I didn't hear the usual stuffy party talk. They felt they could be real. That's an art. They didn't want to leave, you noticed."

"It was a success, wasn't it?" Beth curtsied at the end of their dance. "Now I'm looking forward to our own Christmas."

On Christmas day, Hope, Josh and Kerry came, loaded with hugs and presents. "Bif, Bif," Kerry shouted, running on her chubby little legs into Beth's arms. "Kismus twee," she pointed to the glittering tree with delight.

Amidst packages, paper and ribbon they exchanged their gifts of love. After a festive turkey dinner and Tillie's flaming plum pudding with orange hard sauce, they sat around the crackling fire, sharing their praises to God for the blessings past and their hopes and dreams for the year ahead.

"Thank you all for a beautiful and memorable day." Charles stood to propose a toast, " 'The ornament of a house is the friends that frequent it.' Samuel Clements had those words inscribed on his mantel, and I heartily agree. God bless us, every one." Charles raised his cup of eggnog.

"God bless us, every one," they all repeated.

"Merry Christmas, love of my life." Charles kissed Beth when they were alone. "This is the happiest Christmas—the only real Christmas—I've ever known."

Beth's smile outshone every glowing light. "I've another present for you," she paused and softly added, "Merry Christmas . . . 'Daddy.' I've been holding the doctor's confirmation for several days because I wanted to tell you tonight."

Charles's face went blank as though he were in shock. Beth had hinted at her suspicions, but now she guessed that he hadn't dared to think about it. He must have buried the idea somewhere in his mind, not letting it penetrate his heart that they might be going to have a child.

"Did you hear me, sweetheart? We're having a baby!"

Charles visibly fought the cloud that hung over him. "That's wonderful, darling, wonderful," his enthusiasm was visibly forced. "Please take very good care of yourself. Did the doctor have anything special to say about the baby?"

Beth looked puzzled. "Only that we're going to have one, silly. You're a worrier." She attempted to kiss away the apprehension that appeared any time she'd mentioned having a baby.

It was the first of many restless nights for Charles, of tossing, worrying and praying.

"Are you all right?" he constantly wanted to know.

"Charles, stop it!" Beth had grown frustrated with him. "You're being paranoid. I don't even have morning sickness. How can I enjoy basking in the anticipation of motherhood when you're so glum? This isn't like you at all."

"I'm sorry. Forgive me, sweetheart. I want this baby, I want us to be a family, more than you can know."

She'd comfort him as he laid his head against her chest in their bed. As he tossed in the dark she'd remind him, "Darling, we're merely the means God uses to bear new life. He's the architect, the Creator."

One particularly anxious night she switched on the light, reached over on the nightstand for her Bible and read Psalm 139 to him. "See, Charles," Beth said softly, "God knows all about our baby. He knows its inner parts while it's still being formed. He's in control."

Charles arranged his schedule to walk with her every morning and forbade her to use the ballet barre in their exercise room. He made Tillie see that she rested every afternoon and had Max drive her into the city for luncheons and to meet him at the Tower suite when they attended social events together. They'd stay overnight so she wouldn't be overexerted, and then Max would drive her home the next day.

"This is ridiculous," Beth complained to Tillie. "As long as I've known Charles, he's never fretted over anything beyond his control. He's the one who says worrying saps time, energy and productivity. That's why he's been able to accomplish so much. But look at him now. He's a wreck. I'm a perfectly healthy young woman, and he's making an invalid of me."

Except for Charles's anxiety, those were happy months. Beth painted to her heart's content in their exquisite gardens. Merribelle's string of projects and powers of persuasion resulted in Beth's donating several of her paintings for auction and designing League's invitations and promotional posters for special events. Together they planned a summer garden party to be held at Rosehaven in mid-August. The Christmas Ball had been approved by the Board as an annual event.

Merribelle invented every possible excuse to wangle an invitation to Rosehaven. "It's like being in another world—in a quieter more graceful age," she said.

The Townsends' friendship seemed to be a claim to fame for Merribelle. Although only ten years Beth's senior, she promoted her with the fervor of a stage mother pushing a promising dancer. Not that Beth needed a champion. With or without Merribelle, she became the darling of the social set. But Beth genuinely liked Merribelle. She could see that underneath the endless Southern chatter was a kind and generous heart in search of a friend.

From the time Charles learned Beth was pregnant, he had seemed nervous about the commitment he'd made as the keynote speaker for an architectural design convention in New York on June thirtieth. He'd accepted nearly a year in advance and the reservations sold out in six months, so he had no choice but to go. Besides, she kept reminding him, he'd only be gone five days. She had also convinced him she'd be fine during the several short business trips to Rome in early spring. After all, Tillie was with her.

The week after he returned from New York, Charles followed Beth around like a new puppy, playfully attending to her every whim. She laughed at his disappointment that she didn't want him to get her pickles and ice cream at 2:00 A.M.

However, it was at 2:00 A.M. on July 16, 1965 that Beth began her labor, and by six that morning they were on the way to the hospital.

"You must stop looking so worried, Mr. Townsend," Dr. Harmon told Charles. "Your wife is doing fine. She's already dilated to eight centimeters. It won't be long now."

At seven-thirty Beth was in the delivery room. "All right, this is it," Dr. Harmon said calmly at eight-fifteen. "Ah, the baby's crowning—here it comes." Beth was panting and perspiring with involuntary bearing down. "Just a few more contractions . . . there, it's a boy!"

Dr. Harmon had delivered babies for more than thirty years. Beth watched his trained eye evaluate the new life before him. "Is there anything wrong, Doctor?" she asked, after seeing a clouded look pass his face.

"Oh, probably not. It's too soon to tell," he tried to sound reassuring. "Nurse Roberts, would you call in Dr. Michael, please?"

"Doctor Harmon, what's wrong with my baby?" Beth demanded.

The doctor was measuring the baby's smaller-than-usual head, looking carefully at the slanted eyes, examining the crease across its tiny hands. He scrutinized the unusual spaces between its fingers and toes. He listened to the heart again.

"Doctor, what's the matter?" Beth nearly screamed.

"Maybe nothing, Mrs. Townsend," he said with a weak smile. "Let's attend to you and call in Dr. Michael, a specialist in pediatrics. We'll know more within twenty-four hours."

Meanwhile, she worried about Charles, who sat lonely and frustrated in the expectant fathers' waiting room. *It's terrible,* she thought, *for a husband not to be able to comfort his wife through delivery. I wonder if anyone has told him what's going on?*

*   *   *

"Mr. Townsend, you can see your wife now," the nurse smiled at Charles. "She's back in her room."

"What—what about the baby?" He tried to hide his anxiety.

"It's a boy," she answered with an expression impossible to interpret.

"Oh, God," he whispered, walking down the long hall. "Is this the healthy, normal baby boy I've longed for, or the news I dread? Joy, or sorrow?"

He walked into Beth's room. "Hello, sweetheart. How are you doing?" He bent and kissed Beth tenderly. "I love you. Is everything okay?" he searched her troubled face.

"I'm fine, darling. I love you, too. You must have ordered every rose the florist had. They're gorgeous. You've heard, of course—we have a son."

"Will the nurse bring him in, or is he in the nursery? When do I get to see him?"

"I think the nurse will bring him in soon." Dear Charles, he had been so terribly anxious about her and the baby, she couldn't bear to tell him there might be a problem.

She noticed the familiar cloud come and go across his face, as though he had always known there might be something wrong. What was it?

A nurse came in to take Beth's blood pressure and pulse rate. "You're doing fine," she smiled.

"Are they going to bring the baby in soon?" Charles asked anxiously.

"He's on oxygen, but you can go look at your son through the window, Mr. Townsend."

"Oxygen?" Beth sounded alarmed. "Is that unusual?"

"Not at all," the nurse smiled, "Just a precaution."

"I'm going down to admire our son," Charles jumped up. "I'll tell him hello from his beautiful mama." But all he could see was a tightly wrapped bundle in a tiny plexiglass-covered bassinet with tubes going into it.

"Well?" Beth prodded when Charles returned. He looked so tense she almost cried.

"He was turned the other way. I couldn't even see his little face. There will be plenty of time to see him. You look tired. Why don't you take a little nap? I'll be right here." Charles sat in the bedside chair. He was exhausted too, and they both slept for almost two hours.

In the early evening, Dr. Michael came in and introduced himself. "Is there a problem?" Beth sat up anxiously.

"We're watching him very closely. We suspect a slight heart defect which will usually show up within twenty-four hours, if it's anything significant. Why don't you both get some rest? I'll check the baby again in the morning."

Dr. Michael returned about 11:00 A.M.

"Have you reached any conclusions? How does his heart sound today?" Beth questioned.

"It's still too soon to tell, but we're possibly dealing with autosomal trisomic syndrome," Dr. Michael said.

"What?" Beth demanded.

"I suspect some features which would indicate one of the types of Down's syndrome."

Charles buried his head in his hands as Beth fired more questions. "I've never heard of Down's syndrome. What does this mean? What can be done? I don't understand what you're talking about."

"I'll try to simplify it for you. It's a genetic condition. The most common form of Down's syndrome is the presence of forty-seven chromosomes instead of forty-six, and chromosome pair number twenty-one is not a pair but a triplet or 'trisomy' condition. Other rare chromosomal variants are known as translocation and mosaicism, which result in severe retardation. It sounds terribly technical, but there's no easy explanation. We'll need to do some more testing to be certain, but we suspect translocation."

His attempts at simplification were still over Beth's head. "What causes this, Doctor?" Beth asked with tears in her eyes.

"Several things. Risk increases after a woman is thirty-five, and of course, you're much younger, but there's also the possibility of carrier fathers—they can produce normal and abnormal offspring. Fortunately, these incidents are rare, but in the majority of translocations, approximately half are inherited. My first experience with this rarity occurred quite a number of years ago. The father had a balanced disomy translocation in chromosome nine. The baby lived, but it had to be institutionalized. Reminds me of your baby."

The doctor's explanation left Beth's head swimming in confusion and disbelief. Her face was ashen. "In laymen's terms, what is the outlook for our baby? What can be done?"

"We're still in the dark ages on this. There's no easy way to tell you. If it's what we think it is—probably congenital heart disease, polycystic kidneys. We already see malformations, probable deafness and severe mental retardation."

"How severe?" Charles asked.

"Possibly an IQ of forty or below. I wish I could be more optimistic. Sometimes it takes months to detect these symptoms in less severe cases. I hope to God we're wrong, but your baby's indications are quite pronounced."

Charles leaned forward. "What do you suggest? With love and care, what could we expect?"

"I've made a specialized practice in Down's syndrome babies for over thirty years. With your baby's symptoms, through intervention in special education classes and intimate personal attention, he may eventually talk, become toilet-trained and more socially oriented. I wish I could be more encouraging, but with translocation, my suggestion is institutional care. I'm sorry. . . . " The doctor left the room.

Charles dropped his head in his hands and sobbed. He looked up at Beth, his kind, ice-blue eyes reddened with tears, pleading. . . .

"Forgive me for putting you through this. This is my legacy from my father," he said bitterly. "He's a translocation carrier and obviously so am I. I've read medical texts and talked to doctors. There's no way this can be predetermined. It's haunted and hounded me all my life." Beth cried tears of disbelief, reeling from the shock of Charles's disclosure. "The doctor very possibly described my brother, Tommy," Charles continued. "He lived longer than most in the institution. My father never went to see him. Mother and I did, but Tommy didn't remember us from one day to the next. It broke our hearts."

Beth's pain throbbed too deep for tears—for her baby and her husband. Only now did she understand the extent of Charles's agony, the burden he'd carried. It was clear. He'd taken a gamble—and lost.

"Beth," he sobbed again, "will you forgive me for not telling you? I thought we had a 50-50 chance of having a normal baby, but I've since learned that only applies if you're talking a hundred or more babies. I couldn't bear to have you as worried as I was, and there's really no way to know, believe me."

Beth reached for her husband's hand, unable to speak.

"I wanted a younger brother so much," Charles whispered, "to wrestle around with and keep me from being lonely—to have a real family. But sweetheart, I never wanted a brother nearly as much as I wanted a son."

Beth gently squeezed her husband's hand. "Darling," she said gently, "we'll try again."

"Beth, I don't think I could go through this again," he said. "And I won't allow you to."

Beth remained silent, understanding her husband's need to express the pain he felt. "Maybe I'm out of my mind, irrational right now," Charles's agony appeared in every word he spoke, "but I don't want to go to an institution and agonize over my son's condition. It sounds hard and cruel, and maybe it is. Believe me, the child won't know the difference, but I'd be reminded of my father. Can you understand that, Beth?"

Dr. Michael rushed into the room. "Your baby's having a seizure and is on life-sustaining equipment. We'll need your signature to do emergency surgery." His eyes filled with compassion. "You don't have to sign . . . it poses a terrible question."

Beth swallowed hard, choking back her tears, looking to Charles, then to Dr. Michael.

The nursery supervisor came in with a grave expression. As Dr. Michael turned to her, she shook her head. They all understood.

"I'm truly sorry. . . . "

Too numb with grief, too shocked for tears, Beth and Charles silently clung to each other for comfort. "I trust God knows best," Beth whispered.

"It is for the best, sweetheart, I know it is."

Charles stroked and kissed her hair tenderly. After several minutes he said, "I'd like to name our son. . . . "

"Tommy?" Beth interrupted.

"Yes, Tommy."

12

Peter Rabbit whispered a secret to Jemimah Puddleduck. Other Beatrix Potter storybook characters Beth had painted on the nursery walls—Jeremy Fisher, Tom Kitten, the Tailor of Gloucester—cavorted in amusing antics.

There would be no child for them to delight. Even the golden sunshine that bathed the cheery room failed to brighten Beth's aching heart.

She felt incapable of concentrating on anything, even her painting. The dimensions were flat, the colors without life. The beloved recordings of Chopin that usually rippled throughout the house had lost their melody.

Merribelle handled all the arrangements for the scheduled garden party at Rosehaven for Art League, which Beth and Charles elected not to attend. Merribelle, with all her bustling busyness, said repeatedly they could have another baby, but glossed over the loss of this one. Her own fifteen-year-old daughter and Henry's seventeen-year-old son, both embroiled in stages of rebellion, dressed weirdly and jammed their minds full of eccentricities with the aid of drugs. Perhaps that made her insensitive.

San Francisco's high society sent bushels of flowers and cards, but no one called or came to share their pain. In a real sense, they denied Beth and Charles permission to grieve. They didn't understand. No one seemed to, except Hope and Josh.

These dear friends were consolation with skin on. They hovered over them with sweet notes and the assurance of God's power to heal their broken hearts. They called almost daily with invitations to dinner, church, Bible studies, the movies or picnics.

Beth ached to be with Kerry constantly. When they were together she held and cuddled her, yet the nearness of the child she gave up magnified the pain of the secrets she vowed to honor. God's time will heal this, too, she told herself.

Charles adopted an openness with Josh about spiritual things he held private even from Beth. In that respect he resembled her father and mother. Why was it the dearest ones in all the world who held back what mattered most to her?

Josh read Bible passages to affirm for Charles how unending is the love of the Father, and he tried to help Charles release his anger and resentment toward his earthly father.

TNT couldn't be blamed for chromosomes. But a bitter battle raged within Charles against his father—hostilities he swore to himself he had buried. The tragedy of his own little Tommy revealed they were still very near the surface.

The demands of architectural progress as it related to U.S. and international business provided avenues of escape for Charles. They waited for no one's broken heart to put itself back together again. They required he pick up the pieces and get back in the race.

But he worried about Beth. She needed a quiet, new diversion. She withdrew from the center of the San Francisco social scene as they all scurried about, seemingly oblivious to the depth of her heartache. But an even wider gulf separated them—they had no spiritual resources of their own with which to comfort her.

Years ago, Tillie and Hope were among those that promised, "I'll always be there for you." And bless them, they were. Yet knowing her precious Tommy rested in the arms of Jesus was the only comfort that eased the unspeakable void. *Jesus is the one who is always there for me,* Beth assured herself.

One evening, Charles laid a dozen catalogs on her lap, each cover blooming with roses. Then he handed her a pad of graph paper. "What's all this?" she asked.

"With your love for gardens and roses, I thought you might enjoy planning a rose garden. The lawn area on the master bedroom side of the house is ideal. It's nice and sunny," Charles explained.

"Are there real 'Tudor roses' to conform with our architectural theme?" she laughed. "Where did you acquire your passion for roses?"

"Maybe from Shakespeare—'Of all the flowers, methinks a rose is best,'" he quoted with a grin.

"I could really get into growing roses," Beth mused as she studied the gardens in the catalogs.

"I think I'm about to embark on a new project too."

"What is it, darling?"

"The trustees of First Christian, San Francisco's most prestigious church, met with me today," he replied. "They asked me to draw up the contract to do the architectural work for its complete renovation. They want to update the church while maintaining its original Gothic cathedral design. I'm anxious to do it."

"That's your family's church, isn't it? I think I understand why you want to do it."

"I'm glad you do, sweetheart," Charles's face visibly relaxed at her understanding. "Call it an obsession, but I see it as repaying a debt that isn't mine—in an attempt to even the score. I really want to do this."

"Then it's right to take it on," Beth assured him.

A few weeks later, on a Saturday afternoon while Charles and Beth were plotting the final dimensions of the rose garden, he received a telephone call. It was his father's personal secretary, Mr. Ashcroft.

"Your father has had a stroke—apparently a severe cerebral hemorrhage. I thought you would want to know."

"Thank you, Mr. Ashcroft," Charles was stunned. "Yes, yes, I needed to know."

Beth had followed him into the house. At the sight of his ashen face she asked, "Charles, what is it?"

"My father has had a stroke," he said, somewhat bewildered. "He was a ripe candidate. I'm amazed his driving force hasn't blown him to pieces long ago. They haven't called him TNT for nothing." He sat and silently held his head in his hands for several minutes. "I dread it, but I have to go to him, Beth."

"Yes, you do, darling—for him as well as yourself. You may not get another chance."

Charles met Mr. Ashcroft at the hospital. "What happened?" he asked.

"Your father was conducting a staff meeting at the corporate offices until late last night. He exploded into a fiery tirade at Harrison McClendon, who he said bungled a major takeover, and collapsed."

Charles had witnessed his father's temper on several occasions. The scene Ashcroft had described at the staff meeting was nothing unusual.

"He was brought here immediately by ambulance about midnight," Ashcroft continued. "They've watched him very closely. He's lapsed in and out of consciousness, but I think he's awake now. I checked with the supervisor, and his vital signs are holding. It's all right if you want to go in."

Charles hadn't seen his father for more than ten years. Amidst IV bottles and monitors, the man of dynamic power, loathed by many, loved by few, understood by no one, lay motionless in the bed, except for his eyes.

Under a bushy tangle of white eyebrows the stare of subdued rage melted at the sight of Charles. Unable to speak, his gray eyes communicated the helplessness of a caged animal. TNT searched the depths of his son's sympathetic face, as though trying to reconstruct something he'd smashed long ago.

This was no longer a man to dread. Charles could now pity his father. Many others might classify his condition as a just penalty for a ruthless power-monger. But what power did his money have now?

"Hello, Father," Charles said hesitatingly. What could he say that would make any difference? "Can you hear me? Move your eyes if you understand."

The closest expression to tenderness Charles had ever seen swam in his father's eyes, and his eyes moved up and down in a "yes." Charles felt relieved. His father could comprehend.

Charles held the inert hand that had pounded so many boardroom tables and thought of the irony of it all. *God, what should I say?* he prayed.

"Father, I didn't build bridges or live my life your way, but it's been rewarding for me. You may be interested to know I'm going to do the architectural design for renovating your old church. One of my construction firms will do the work. I wondered if that would please you?" He talked simply, as to a child.

TNT's eyes went up and down again. Charles even imagined he saw something close to love in them, but suddenly the old man grew pale and weak. Charles immediately buzzed for help. He may not have much time, and what he was about to say held the risk of a volatile emotional reaction.

"Father, I need to express this and I don't want to upset you. I'm sure you've thought you've been right all these years, but regardless, I . . . I need to forgive you."

The tears floating in TNT's eyes spilled defenselessly down his cheeks. He blinked to clear them and managed to move them up and down in a "yes" one more time. Charles beheld what he never expected. An expression of peace and reconciliation. Then, the eyes that had threatened, pierced, scorned and brought ruin with only a glance, closed forever. Tyler Norton Townsend was dead at sixty. He had reigned over a self-conceived financial empire and lost his soul.

The look on Charles's face after he left the room told Mr. Ashcroft his employer was gone. "I'm sorry. You have my condolences," Ashcroft said dutifully.

"What's to be done?" Charles asked, dazed and without ceremony. He felt numb, with a growing, almost guilty sense of blessed relief. He'd actually asked God to tell him what to say instead of relying on his own gut feeling. The words "I forgive you" had suddenly, unexpectedly set him free. He felt it, deeply. The bondage of anger and hostility had at last been broken and could be buried alongside his father.

Ashcroft brought him back to the present. "As Mr. Townsend's personal secretary, I had the responsibility of drafting the will for his attorneys. Your father specified cremation in his will. No services of any kind. Your only inheritance is the house in Carmel," he said apologetically. "A sizable amount goes to your mother—if we can locate her. Everything . . . I mean everything else is in trust to be divided between some home for the mentally retarded, I'll have the lawyers tell you the name of it, of course, and a grant for research for genetic birth defects. You should have the details in a few days, and later an opportunity for . . . questions." By his tone, Ashcroft obviously anticipated Charles might contest the will.

Charles had a wild urge to hug Mr. Ashcroft, but he restrained himself with a huge smile. For the first time in his life, he was proud of his father. For once, TNT had done an admirable and honorable thing. He knew his son would reject even a portion of his inheritance from the vast estate, but he also knew Charles loved the house high on the cliff in Carmel and the memories it held of his mother.

Three little words, unsolicited, freely given, gratefully received—"I forgive you"—had blown away the black cloud of bitterness. Charles breathed deeply of his newfound freedom, knowing TNT had finally been released from his own worldly tyranny.

The glories of a brilliant autumn brought a new resolve to get on with the business of living. The designing of the rose garden delighted Beth beyond her imagining. From the catalogs, she had shown the landscapers her choices of hybrid teas and floribundas. They were to surround a cherub fountain and tree roses in the center of the formal garden with a low hedge border.

"I should hire you to design the landscaping for my projects," Charles hugged her and kissed the tip of her nose. "The bloom is back in your cheeks too. We're going to make it, darling."

"Of course we are. The catalogs tell me roses have an indomitable will to survive—and so do we." They both knew they were still dealing with the pain of losing Tommy, but they were gaining strength. "Merribelle will be ecstatic with the rose garden for next summer's charity garden party. She's asked us to host a few more benefit teas, too, and in the blink of an eye it'll be Christmas and time for the ball again."

Tillie saw them sitting on the terrace and brought chilled glasses of minted iced tea. They sipped and talked of many things. . . .

"Let's go to First Christian in the city next Sunday," Charles said. "Reverend Goodwin's invited us several times, and since I'm rebuilding the church, I feel obligated to attend."

Beth winced, then tried to cover her disappointment. "Of course, darling . . . we should go occasionally."

Many of their socialite friends attended First Christian, but Beth felt at home in the small community church the Sterlings attended in San Jose. Since Tommy, her greatest comfort and support came from the women in Hope's Wednesday morning Bible group as they studied the gospel of John, Beth's favorite gospel. It consistently gave her assurance—God had her wrapped in His love.

And going to the San Francisco church would mean Beth would miss helping with the Sunday school class Kerry loved so much. It was such a thrill to hear Kerry say, "Bif, Bif, I wanna sing 'Jesus Lufs Me,' " and then recite simple Bible verses. Beth thought about the children she'd helped to cut snow-white lambs out of construction paper. The pastor and the people of the little church in San Jose brought God closer to His lambs and the flock closer to God.

But of course we have to go to the big church, Beth reminded herself.

Reverend Goodwin stood high in the pulpit above the congregation, impressively holy in his black robe, calling the people to worship in perfectly rounded tones. They joined voices with the huge choir's processional anthem, "Come Thou Almighty King," followed by a recitation of the Lord's prayer in perfect unison and a liturgy.

A shiver went down Beth's spine. In the huge old stone sanctuary, she felt so small before a mighty God, a God so worthy of honor and praise and glory. Standing outside of Europe's cathedrals, before she came to know Him in a personal way, she'd imagined services, formal and awesome as this. She recalled the words of the hymn: "Thy sovereign majesty, may we in glory see, and to eternity, love and adore."

The small community church in San Jose sometimes sang that hymn too. They also sang less formal songs of praise, choruses that flowed out of the Psalms. She concluded worship was a matter of style. God would always welcome a heart that sincerely loved and adored Him.

"I call your attention to the fifth chapter of Deuteronomy," Reverend Goodwin solemnly stated, "and the Ten Commandments God repeated to Moses."

She glanced sideways at Charles as the pastor preached on the first commandment—"Thou shalt have no other gods before Me." She guessed from Charles's clouded expression his thoughts ruminated to the idol TNT had made of money. With eyes full of love Beth looked up at Charles with a silent prayer, *Thank You, God, for the husband You have given to me.*

After the service some of San Francisco's leading citizens flocked to Charles. "Townsend, we were pleased to hear Reverend Goodwin announce you're going to handle the renovation," several of them commented. "It'll be done right—and at a fair price. We're sure of that."

The pleased-little-boy expression broke out on Charles's face. He needed to hear that. Beth felt happy for him.

As weeks grew into months, scaffolding and a maze of high steel braces drove the congregation of First Christian out of the majestic sanctuary into the fellowship hall for services.

"It's not the building," Beth tried to explain to Hope one Wednesday after Bible study. "I've come to realize that most of Reverend Goodwin's sermons sound as though God is supposed to conform to human expectations and relationships, like an order-taker. I'm so frustrated. He's telling these wealthy people what they want to hear, to live on their own determination, put their trust in their own positive thinking. He doesn't teach that Jesus is the way, the truth and the life. His message is shallow, Hope. He gives a Scripture verse, and then spends thirty-five minutes espousing his own intellectual opinions before referring to it again. We need to hear the Word of God, not one man. I wish we could come back to your little church where Jesus is alive."

"What does Charles think?" Hope asked with her usual wise calm.

"That's my problem. He's more concerned with what he's doing for the church than the depth of the message. I feel we're spiritually starved at First Christian after hearing your pastor. Charles has been on the inactive membership list for years. If he hadn't been a Townsend, they'd surely have taken him off a long time ago. But he's certainly active now. He even asked me to fill out a membership application."

"And you will, of course?" Hope asked.

"How can I? I feel disloyal to both my husband and my God, sitting there, taking exception to practically every word of Reverend Goodwin's sermon each Sunday. Often I've asked Charles if he thought the sermon was meaningful, but he maintains that spiritual privacy—except with Josh. Hope, if I don't keep these feelings secret, Charles will be deeply hurt. If I do, I'll be a hypocrite. I don't know what to do."

"Let's pray about it," Hope answered.

During the spring of 1967, Beth added other prayers to her list of concerns. Her refuge became the rose garden where she pondered all these things.

To date, their philanthropies had centered on promoting the multiple cultural arts she and Charles both loved and Stanford's Medical Center charities. Huge sums of money had been raised within the walls of Rosehaven.

But Charles and Beth would return from a day in the city to their quiet refuge, shocked at the growing number of "flower children" on the streets of San Francisco. These lost and confused young people bore testimony to overwhelming social issues that cried for solutions no one had answers for. She desperately longed to make a difference at the street level. But what and how?

Oftentimes, her own heartache seemed quite enough. In her gardens, she could confide in God and the roses, exempt from judgment or hurt.

Charles had a gardener's cottage built and close to it a lattice-covered potting shed canopied with climbing polyantha. Enamored of its quaintness, Beth had painted a picture of it.

"If only we had a qualified resident gardener to live in the cottage and oversee the rest of the crew," Charles sighed one evening.

"That's my job, remember?" she laughed. And when Beth wore her straw hat and delphinium blue-pocketed smock, the gardeners respected her privacy as well as her growing expertise.

To the arbor where she and Charles had taken their wedding vows Beth added sweetbriar climbers of pink and yellow, whose foliage perfumed the air with the fragrance of ripe apples.

The first formal rose garden sparked a passion to fashion a bed of heritage roses. Sentiment reigned over the old favorites of yesteryears—Marie Louise, a damask rose, tea and moss roses, and Lavender Lassie, a hybrid musk.

Around the foundations of the mansion, Beth massed monochromatic pink floribundas and miniatures. They further endeared the structure to the site and created the notion that house and gardens were inseparable, having always been there. In the freshness of the morning or among golden threads of late afternoon shadows, Beth and Charles often strolled hand in hand.

"We've a bit of heaven right here on earth, haven't we, darling?" Beth commented along the slate walks that led out to the tea house.

Charles always grew reflective from their favorite bench on the knoll, gazing down through the English yew trees.

"The world is hellish out there, Beth," he commented. "It's a big game of Monopoly, and everyone's willing to kill for Park Place and the Boardwalk. I often wonder . . . for what?"

"I suppose for what we have right here, Charles. But what I cherish most are these stolen moments of quiet contentment together. You and I never grew up deprived of material things. But among the haves and have nots, most never have enough. You're the exception. You haven't a greedy bone in your body."

Charles looked tired. Beth lightened up by putting on her best British accent, "I say, old chap, you jolly well spend as much time contemplating how to give your money away as you do making it." She feigned removing an English monacle. "Seriously, love, you remember the groanings of Solomon when he wrote Ecclesiastes, that to keep striving after material things is as useless as striving after the wind? He found it doesn't satisfy."

Charles paused a moment. "The satisfaction I want, and know you do, too," he said at last, "is to deposit what God has allowed us to have into His account. I don't want to wait until the end of my life to do something decent, like my father did. I want to see it. I suppose that's why this church project is so important to me. I haven't told you, Beth, but I don't intend to submit a bill for any of the renovation. What would you think about that?"

"I think I keep falling in love with you more every day," she gave him a hug. "You might ask yourself, though, if by giving the whole amount, are you taking too much responsibility off the membership? Don't they need to take ownership in the building too? Why don't you contribute all the architectural design and labor, and give the members the opportunity to pay for the materials?"

"How did you become so wise?" he smiled at her. "By reading old King Solomon?"

"Well, that—and by living with you, darling."

That night in bed after they'd made love, their bodies nestled together as one, Beth treasured her answered prayer. In the past ten months, while she sat next to Charles at First Christian, secretly critical of Reverend Goodwin's worldly views, God Himself had been at work in Charles's heart. And tonight she had seen His evidence—Charles shared a spiritual openness, how the Lord worked in his daily life, that they had never had before. "Thank You, God, for keeping me out of Your way," she whispered. "For keeping my mouth shut and my mind open to trust You more. I know now You won't let him be deceived."

One warm July day Merribelle phoned with her usual persuasiveness. "Darlin', Ah want you to come into town for a luncheon Ah'm havin' for a few dearest friends on July 16. May Ah count on you, honey?"

Did Merribelle remember what day that was? Probably not, but Beth gratefully accepted the invitation. She craved to crowd out the pain of remembering a year ago, when their baby had lived in this world for only twenty-four hours before mercifully going to heaven, into the arms of Jesus.

That morning, Beth and Charles blanketed Tommy's tiny grave with a remembrance of Rosehaven's most beautiful flowers. They knelt and prayed. With tears in her eyes Beth said hopefully, "This year has been filled with suffering, but there have been blessings too."

"There certainly have been for me," Charles put his arm around her in comfort. "The pain of Tommy opened my heart. I realized my father must have suffered with his son in an institution, how that wounded his pride as it would have mine. Mother and I weren't the only ones who grieved." Beth wept silently. "Pain also opened my heart to forgive TNT before he died," Charles reflected, "and saved me from the consuming cancerous growth of bitterness. God gave me the blessing of that opportunity. I asked Him for words when I had none of my own. He said, *Forgive.*"

"He did something else," Beth smiled. "It's precious to me that God opened your heart and enabled you to talk with me about Him, Charles."

"That's a bit of His mercy too." A gentle breeze fluttered the roses on Tommy's grave.

"Now, we have to ask God what He wants us to do next," Charles said quietly.

Under a willow tree on the cemetery's grassy hill, they parted in a comforting embrace, with new resolutions of courage and strength.

"Let's make this a really good day, sweetheart," Charles said, kissing the tip of her nose. Beneath the clarity of his ice-blue eyes, question marks searched her face. "Sure you don't mind driving the Jaguar into the city?"

Beth understood perfectly. She usually drove herself, and Max chauffeured Charles as he used his time to make business calls by car phone. The question was merely a transition from the emotions they'd left behind them up on the knoll of Tommy's grave.

"On a gorgeous day like this? You know I love driving the Jag. Let Max enjoy his day off, and you have a super golf game at Hillsboro with your architects."

Beth looked adoringly into the eyes of her husband. "Painful as this year has been, I wouldn't exchange it for what God has shown us. Our wealth goes far beyond possessions. I've thought of the love we've had from the Sterlings and our unworldly family of friends who have comforted us in our grief." She smiled a sad smile. "But there's a multitude of miserable affluent people out there. I'm having lunch with many of them today. They're impoverished because they don't know the Source of that love. We mustn't give up on them. We need to keep praying that someday they'll understand."

13

On the quiet road that wound through the lush, peaceful valley, through the smaller communities leading north to Highway 101, Beth struggled against depression, determined to win.

A life of faith doesn't always mean mounting up on wings to soar like an eagle, she thought. *Living by faith is mostly a life of walking and not fainting.*

The sun shone brightly, even as she approached San Francisco. With a lighter heart, Beth realized that their grief had been burned away by counting their blessings instead of losses, just as sunshine melted off the fog. She remembered the early mornings when she lived up on Russian Hill. The city's skyscrapers seemed to float above the fog, yet later in the day, the white buildings clustered on the hills glistened in the bright sunlight.

San Francisco—her fabulous town. The flower vendors still thrived on every corner. But on the streets formerly crowded with fashionably dressed sophisticates—where all the women once wore hats and gloves and gentlemen looked like Londoners—there now abounded young people who didn't even wear shoes.

Television and newspapers invested incredible coverage on the thousands who gathered that summer for the "love-in" that had overtaken the Haight-Ashbury district. The whole Bay area had become the epicenter of hippie culture.

"The Establishment," which represented family traditions and conformity to responsible standards, loomed as the target of their outrageous rebellion. They called themselves "The Now Generation," or "The Gentle People," but by any name, they were disillusioned and purposeless dropout renegades from the American middle class. Their alleged quest: a more "meaningful" life.

Beth slowed down, astounded at the young adults in their late teens or early twenties sitting on the streets playing guitars and panhandling with signs that read, "Take a hippie to lunch." Over their flaunted grime, they combined motley denim pants with brilliantly flowered shirts, Mexican serapes, Navajo headbands, luminous body paint.

One young man in the center of Union Square seemed to be the high priest of the love movement. He stomped around in buckskin boots with bells, shoulder-length hair and a flowing red beard. Others wore earrings, hats with bright feathers and no shirts. Many of the girls, with long, straight, sticky hair and no makeup, sat on the streets with small babies tucked under their shawls. They waited for handouts with which to buy marijuana, hash, LSD and, one would hope, a little milk and food.

If this spaced-out "Now Generation" of "Gentle People" demonstrated what they believed to be a new expression of freedom, what could their future hold? What would become of those dirty, helpless, homeless babies, some who would be born already addicted to drugs? Many of these girls would choose not to bring their babies into the world and opt for abortion. Pain stabbed Beth's heart again. She and Charles yearned to love and cherish babies of their own, while countless numbers were being denied the right to live.

Beth felt sick at the sight of wasted lives, blindly conforming to non-conformity. This social "now" revolution was committed only to going nowhere. Everything she held dear—family, stability, the pursuit of excellence—was placed in contempt by these outlandish rebels of her own generation. She shared not one shred of identity, only pity. "God," she whispered, "help them find their way to *real* meaning in life."

"Darlin', you look mahvelous," Merribelle greeted Beth as she entered the elegant dining room of the Fairmont Hotel. "Sit heah by me, sweetie. Ah love the way you wear yore gawgeous black hair so simply elegant, while Ah spend hours 'n hours at the beauty shop. Aren't you all just dyin' to snatch her bald?" Merribelle giggled to the others.

"A bald-headed hostess would seem out of place at Rosehaven's lovely garden party next month," a pleasant friend in League named Catherine Chandler smiled. "It's always the most delightful highlight of the summer, Beth. What did we ever do for grand entertaining, ladies, before Beth and Charles and Rosehaven?"

"I read in the paper the Rose Society is also holding their annual show and a tour of your gardens there this year, Beth. How appropriate," Marjorie Alden commented.

"A member of Stanford Medical Center's Auxiliary invited us to a charity ball at Rosehaven in October," another woman said. "You certainly are generous in opening your home . . . seems like some charity's always holding an event there. My husband wouldn't stand for such an invasion of privacy."

"Charles counts it all joy," Beth smiled. "When Charles designed our home, it was with the intent of making his lifelong love affair with fine art and architecture available for other people to enjoy. He wouldn't think it was any fun if he couldn't share it."

"You two certainly can't have any secrets to hide and be as public as you are," Marjorie said.

Before Beth could answer, Merribelle chimed in again.

"Why Beth's life's so perfect. Ya'll know how beautiful she is, inside an' out. There's simply no flaws she has to hide or anything she can't handle," Merribelle boasted, "even—" She stopped, embarrassed at her own insensitivity.

"Even what?" Catherine's tone sounded curious, as one expecting a skeleton to pop out of the closet.

"Why, Ah've gone and put mah foot in mah mouth. 'Scuse me, Beth honey. Ah was thinkin' how well ya'll got over yore baby dyin'. How did you evah survive, darlin'? Wasn't that 'bout a year ago?"

Once more, a stab of pain pierced Beth's heart. Close as Merribelle thought she'd been to Beth, she'd remained impervious to her grief. Beth swallowed the hurt. "Our baby would have been a year old yesterday, and died a year ago today."

Everyone, even Merribelle, sat in uncomfortable silence. All eyes were either on Beth or the floor. Why Tommy died and why they'd never have another child were secrets no one thought she had.

"One of God's promises is that He never allows us more than we can endure," Beth explained. "He has His special ways of binding up the brokenhearted. Jesus promised, 'I will never leave you or forsake you.' Every July 16 for the rest of my life I'll wish we had our baby, but I know time and God do heal everything."

No one said a word, their eyes still on Beth, waiting expectantly.

"The only way I know to overcome grief is to acknowledge it, take my eyes off my cares and give them to God," she continued. "And then get outside of myself. There's always someone with a sorrow as deep as my own. I can't imagine how sick inside I'd feel if I had a child among those throngs of hippies I just saw all over the streets of San Francisco."

"Well, Ah can tell you how sick it feels—it's disgustin'! Henry told his son if he didn't cut his hair, he'd have to get out of the house, and he did!" Merribelle said bitterly. "That ungrateful boy just took his oldest jeans and a few lil' things an' walked right out the dawh, an' if mah own daughtah didn't follah right after him."

"Oh, Merribelle, I'm so terribly sorry." Beth was horrified that she had intruded on her friend's pain. "Have you tried to talk to them?"

"Tawk to them?" Merribelle's face flushed with anger. "Ah have nothin' more to say! We've sent them to the finest schools, skiin' in Switzerland ovah Christmas vacations, an' to the best camps in summer. Mah daughtah had the nerve to say we nevah really cared, only wrote out a check instead of tawkin' 'bout 'meaningful' things. Ah'm furious with the both of 'em, an' they're slitherin' aroun' picketin' 'The Establishment.' Disgustin' is what it is!"

Catherine nodded, "I had a niece and nephew at Berkeley. They're into this hippie cult all the way, which included dropping out of college. My sister was shocked. The family has always discussed everything from Eastern religions to politics to sex, but the kids just say they're doing 'their own thing.' "

"Well, Ah don't care to pursue this revoltin' conversation one bit furthah. Mah land—look what time it is, Ah've got an appointment in twenty minutes. Have to see a caterer for all these pahties. Thank ya'll fah comin', an 'specially you, Beth."

On the way out Beth quietly attempted to console Merribelle. "I'll be praying for your children."

"Well, it's not that bad, honey. It's not like they're dyin', you know. They'll come home when theyah tired of living in the people's park."

Thank God, Beth thought driving home down 101, *this day is going to end on a predictably happy high.*

Hope and Josh had invited them to dinner. When Beth and Charles needed the comfort only understanding friends could give, those two never let them down. Kerry would lighten their lives with her own lyrics and sweet songs. She perceived the whole world as being joyful and full of sunshine, and herself as the one to distribute it. Beth imagined that even the Jaguar seemed anxious to return to Rosehaven, like a horse racing to get back to its stable. The entire staff had the day off, yet the house never seemed lonely or empty when she returned, only warm and welcoming.

A leisurely shower would feel wonderful, she thought. *There will be ample time before Charles comes home from golf and we have to leave again.*

He'd spent more time on the golf course lately, doctor's orders. Today he insisted three of his top architects join him in recognition of a huge project just completed.

"You've got to slow down, Charles," Dr. Eddington had said. "Play more golf, get more exercise, lose fifteen pounds, take time to smell the roses, or you're at risk of a heart attack before you're forty."

The intensity of emotions that began at Tommy's grave site and ended with the disturbing luncheon conversation melted with the scents of her soaps under the refreshing spray of the shower.

Yet, she had the strange sensation that she saw a figure pass the shower door.

"Charles, is that you?" she called out. No answer.

Realizing it was too early for Charles to be home, she indulged in her pleasure several more minutes.

Beth patted her smooth skin dry and wrapped her wet hair in a towel before stepping out of the shower. As she slipped into a robe, a heavy nauseating odor puzzled her.

The bedroom phone rang. She went to answer it, then froze in utter terror. The filthiest young man she had ever seen sat on her delicate satin comforter at the foot of their canopy bed. Beth's heart leaped, pounding the walls of her chest, her pulse thundered in her ears.

The intruder's hand gripped their brass-handled fireplace poker with white knuckles. His face wore a wry, self-satisfied smile that he had so successfully entered and startled his prey.

Beth's fear and fury welled up together at his arrogance, but he made no motion to come at her with the weapon. Her hands and feet felt clammy, her knees weak. She stood petrified, in horror at what he might do next, then sent up a quick silent prayer, *Dear Jesus, protect me.*

Her wild heartbeats slowed to a calmer rate, enabling her to think.

"Do—do you want money?" she asked. "I don't keep much in the house but I'll give you what I have."

The young man stood up. He was tall, over six feet, thin and lanky, with an acrid body odor that almost made Beth gag.

"I'll take yer fancy diamond rings," he demanded, coming a step closer.

Beth gasped.

"Don't worry, I won't hurt you," he said roughly, but Beth noticed his hand trembled as he held out his palm for the rings. "Yeah, I want yer money too—all of it."

Her own hands shook and perspired as she fumbled to get the precious wedding and engagement rings off her finger. *Dear Jesus, help me,* she silently repeated. Beth backed up to her handbag on the dresser for her wallet. His eyes, steadily fixed upon her as though she were the one with the potentially lethal weapon, began to blink nervously.

It was then she realized that this boy was not an ordinary burglar. *He's as terrified as I am,* she thought. Her heart that only moments ago threatened to pound right through her chest quieted. His restrained smile at the $150 she held out confirmed his lack of professionalism.

"Where's yer other jewels? Ya must have plenty," he demanded with a bravado that sounded like he hadn't yet proven how tough he could be.

His eyes lit up as Beth pointed to a silver box of costume jewelry which he emptied into his pockets as smug as if they had been priceless gems. She breathed a sigh of relief. At least he wasn't a strung out junkie. He apparently meant no physical harm and only wanted things he could sell.

Gradually she experienced a strength and assurance beyond herself, an insight of this wretched intruder. He had obviously savored the wait for her to discover how clever he'd been to get into the house. His eye was untrained as to the value of paintings, sculptures and rare collectibles, treasures he could have turned into a tidy fortune.

Beth watched him shift about the room with increasingly awkward hesitation and uncertainty. Then it struck her: *He doesn't know how to get out of the situation. He's stalling.*

Boldly, with heaven-sent courage, she took charge. A quick glance at the priceless gold Louis XV clock on her writing desk told her Charles could be home at any time. It was a gamble, but she had to take it. If Charles appeared, the young man could be challenged to strike out with the poker and Charles wouldn't hesitate to defend her with his life. Beth also gambled that her intruder's male ego wouldn't misinterpret what she was about to say as a come-on.

"Since you've already robbed me of my money, my wedding rings and valuable possessions, young man," Beth said, "why don't you sit down and talk for a few minutes?"

"Lady, you gotta be loony. That's nutty to ask a guy that just robbed you to sit and talk! Whadaya think, we're gonna discuss the stock market?" he said sarcastically. "Yer outta yer mind."

"Now wait a minute, what's your hurry?" Beth remained calm. "You see, I had a son who died after birth a year ago today. He didn't have a chance at a normal life. If he had lived to be your age, he would have spent his life in diapers, seeing things without knowing what he's looking at, talking in his own language to objects that have no ears. You have a chance to do something better with your life than being a burglar. I care about you."

The sarcasm slipped from his face. His eyes filled with tears, which he wiped away with his stained sleeve and jumped up. "I'm gettin' outta here—you're wacko!"

Beth looked him straight in the eyes. *Jesus, help,* she prayed. He sat down again.

"Do you have friends?" she asked gently.

"No—I don't got friends."

"Then I'll tell you about a very wonderful, special friend of mine. His name is Jesus, and—"

The young man interrupted, "Jesus is a dead man. They nailed Him to a tree. I know that much."

"But there's so much more." She had to make her point quickly. "Would you like to have a friend who would stand by you, even in the worst trouble?"

"Nobody's like that."

"Jesus is. How about someone who'd forgive you—no matter what you have done?"

He shrugged his shoulders, staring at the floor.

"Who do you know who loves you enough to die for you?"

"Even Jesus wouldn't do that. For you maybe, but I'm not worth dyin' for."

"Jesus thinks so. He loves you, just the way you are. The Bible says all who believe Jesus is the Son of God and died for our sins will never perish, but have eternal life." She prayed she could help him understand.

"Well, livin' the way I do, I'm not int'rested in forever. I ain't sure what sin is, but I never stole anything before or murdered nobody. Nobody's ever given me nothin', so why should He? An' how can a dead man be a friend? I got no time for this stuff, lady."

"Would you like to have a better life, and peace in your heart? That's why Jesus came."

He shook his head in disbelief. She glanced at the clock again; time was short. "If I may get up and get it, I have something to give you."

He looked amazed she'd want to give him anything. He said, "Uh, yeah, sure. Go ahead."

Beth went to her purse again and brought him a little booklet. "Here, read this. In a simple way it tells you how Jesus wants to be your friend and Savior too. He *can* give you a new life."

The youth could barely speak. "Nobody ever told me nothin' about Jesus. It don't make sense. Why did you say He died for me?"

"Because He loves you."

"Never heard that before, neither. Here," he surrendered the loot in his pockets on the skirted table and held out the rumpled money. Swallowing the lump in his throat, he said, "Here, I can't take this money or your jewels. I'm not really a burglar. I'm not much of anything."

"You keep the money," Beth said. "Since you're not really a burglar, and I won't tell anyone you were here, what is your name?"

"Jimmy—Jimmy Larson."

"I'll walk downstairs with you, Jimmy. How did you get in?"

"Aw—I didn't pick a lock 'er nothin'. You left the door from the garden unlatched. It was a crazy thing for me to do."

By the French doors to the terrace Beth shook his grimy hand. "God bless you, Jimmy Larson. Remember to read that little booklet, and don't forget—Jesus loves you."

Beth locked the deadbolt and sighed in deep relief with her back pressed against the door. She hadn't gambled at all. God was there the whole time.

"Thank You, Lord," she said aloud, "for Your protection and for giving me the courage to tell Jimmy about You. And, please do bless him."

At that moment the front door clicked open and closed, followed by the sound of Charles's footsteps through the entry hall and gallery.

"Well, look at you roaming around down here in your robe to greet me. Mmm, you smell wonderful." He gathered Beth into his arms, holding her in a long kiss and embrace. *What timing,* she thought, and smiled. "How was the game, darling? Did you walk the course or ride?"

"Magnificent. Uh, not the game, I shot eighty-two, which is shabby for a ten-handicapper, but I walked and got some exercise. That's a gorgeous course. We made a good foursome. I've decided, Beth. I am going to mind the doctor and relax more often. We should go down to the house in Carmel. It's spectacular. I'm sorry I haven't even taken you to see it. We should join Cypress Point Country Club—you'd love it."

"Charles, look what time it is!" Beth grabbed his hand and pulled him up to the bedroom. "Kerry will scold us if we're late. You'll want to shower and I've got to get dressed."

Beth quickly sprayed the room with lilac potpourri and opened the windows to let out the odor. She did not intend to upset Charles. He'd only worry about her, and even with his generous nature, he would probably question her sanity. The incident was over, done with, and only good could come of it. This boy needed a chance and lots of prayer.

On the twenty-five-mile drive to San Jose, Charles observed, "You're so quiet, Beth. Did you have a pleasant lunch with Merribelle in town?"

"I guess I'm just tired, darling. It's been an emotionally draining day. I thought I was on top of it when we left the cemetery this morning. But I got depressed seeing the hippies all over town. Then I learned the Matsons' kids have joined them. Life is too precious to waste."

Jimmy still lingered on Beth's mind as they drove. She closed her eyes, deep in thought. God had been so gracious to her. Thinking of His grace magnified the desperation and hopelessness of others. She glanced at the beautiful man behind the wheel. With him, nothing seemed impossible. Together, they had the power to restore hope to the desperate. Wealth was only part of the power. The Source remained a righteous, understanding, loving and forgiving God.

Charles interrupted her thoughts. "Have a nice nap, sweetheart? We're almost there."

"Bif! Charlie!" Kerry bolted to greet them from the steps of the front porch where she'd been waiting. Charles propelled her through the air with whirring sounds, but suddenly winced as though from strain and put her down.

Beth gathered Kerry into her arms and sat on the steps.

"Bif, wanna hear my ABC song? I know all my numbers too. I'll sing 'Away in a Manger' for you." Charles looked sideways and she giggled, "I know it isn't Christmas, but it's my favorite song."

"It's mine, too, love," Beth smiled. "You know a lot for a four-year-old. Let's hear all this wonderful stuff you've learned."

"Four-and-a-half," Kerry corrected, then began her repertoire.

Hope and Josh stood silently and proudly in the background. "Didn't you come to see us, too?" Hope opened her arms to them.

"Come on in," Josh welcomed them with his big bear hugs.

Kerry kept her audience entertained until bedtime. When she was tucked in, Josh turned to his guests. "How are you doing today? This must have been a tough one. We have two sets of empty shoulders if you need them."

Charles smiled. "We had our little cry out at the cemetery this morning. But through this whole year, God has been more real than I ever thought possible. He's blessed us. And so have you dear people. I've never had friends like you before."

"You're always here for us," Beth agreed. "We surely do love you two."

Several hours slipped away like minutes as the old friends talked about life and God's ways. "It's getting late," Beth stifled a yawn late in the evening. "Take me home, 'Charlie,'" Beth tickled his chin playfully, "our buddies have to go to work tomorrow, and so do you."

The next morning found Beth with the landscapers, directing the planting of the newly designed Shakespearean garden.

Tillie came looking for her, her lips pursed resolutely.

"Miss Beth, there's a strange young man here asking for you. I've never seen him before, but he insists on seeing you."

"Can't imagine who it would be. What's his name?"

"Jimmy—Jimmy Larson, he said."

Beth stared in disbelief. She had prayed about Jimmy all night, but never expected to see him again. "Please tell him to come out to the terrace." Tillie stiffened her back in disapproval.

Beth blinked in surprise. Could this be the same Jimmy? Obviously, he'd taken a shower and wore a fresh shirt and clean blue jeans. He'd washed his hair and looked downright respectable.

Jimmy approached her with a gigantic smile. "Hello, ma'am. Hope I'm not disturbing you. I thought a lot about what you said, especially what Jesus done for me. I read that little booklet too. I like to read."

Beth stared silently for a moment, amazed at what she saw and heard. He continued, "And then I found me a friend who'd loan me clean clothes and let me take a shower so's I'd be fit to come back. Could we talk some more?"

"Of course. Let's sit down. If you know who Jesus is, you've made the most important discovery of your life, Jimmy. What do you want to know?" She wondered if he really understood.

"Nobody told me they cared about me before or that Jesus wanted me for a friend. The only friends I have smoke pot and get in trouble all the time. Nobody but you said I had a chance at nothin' but being a loser. That's why I came back. I wanna hear more like what you said yesterday."

"Tell me something about yourself, Jimmy. Where do you live? Do you have a family?"

He looked down grimly. "I been livin' in an old car my uncle gave me for six months now. Couldn't take it at home no more."

"Why not?" she asked gently.

"It's bad: Filthy. Nobody cares about nothin'."

"What about your family?" she asked again.

"Don't have a father. There's five of us kids, don't none of us know who our old man is. Ma has men comin' in and out all the time. Some stay awhile, some don't. Us kids have had runny noses, dirty faces, and run loose since I can remember. I only went through the eighth grade."

Another story of wasted lives, Beth thought sadly. This young kid never had the choice to be a hippie, even though yesterday he looked like one. He'd never known anything but poverty and neglect.

"Have you ever had a job?"

"Who'd want to hire me? I don't know nothin'."

"What would you like to do?"

"I have to admit I sneaked through your gates 'cause the flowers were so pretty," he smiled a shy smile. "I love beautiful flowers. I'd like to learn how to be a gardener. Bet I could be good at it, too."

Beth admired his spirit. "Will you excuse me a minute, Jimmy? I'll be right back."

Beth needed a quiet moment to think and to ask Cookie to include Jimmy in her lunch preparations. "God, don't let me make the wrong decision," Beth whispered.

Jimmy had walked around the terrace admiring the roses. When Tillie brought sandwiches, salad, iced tea and crisp lemon cookies, Jimmy stared in disbelief.

"Am I having lunch with—with you?" he stammered. "Oh man, I never met anyone like you, ma'am. You're too much, treating a bum like me like—like royalty."

"I thought you might be hungry. And Jimmy, maybe you are royalty. If you understood what you read, who Jesus is and what that means to you personally, anyone who invites Christ into his life becomes a child of the King. Jesus is the King of kings and Lord of lords. Do you believe that?"

"I want to, ma'am. I'm just confused right now. If everyone who has Jesus in them is like you, then I do, 'cause you're neat. But I'm not sure what I believe yet, 'cause I've never heard it before."

"I understand how you feel, Jimmy," Beth reassured him. "But remember, He's the only one who can give you a new life—eternal life. You can't buy it or earn it. It's a precious gift. I'll get you a Bible and you can read some more, and we'll talk about it again."

"Thank you, ma'am. Thank you."

"Do you have a place to live now?"

"Just my car."

"See that little cottage over there?" Beth pointed to the garden. "We built it for a chief gardener to live in, but we haven't found anyone qualified yet. You're not ready to be chief yet, but you may live there and work here if you really want to be a gardener. I think you'll be a good one."

"You gotta be crazy, or an angel, or both!" Jimmy exclaimed, shaking his head in disbelief. "Who ever heard of anyone hiring a burglar? Ain't nobody ever believed in me before. I'll be the best gardener you ever seen!"

"You couldn't be a real burglar if you tried, Jimmy. It's not in you. We'll keep that our secret. Don't live in the past, only the present and the future. No one will ever know about yesterday. That's gone. That's the way it is with God, too. He doesn't just forgive. With Him, it's like it never was. Okay?"

"Okay! I promise, you'll never be sorry you believed in me. Thank you, ma'am. Thank you."

"Let me show you the cottage." Beth went ahead, unlocked the door and ushered him in.

Jimmy's face lit up with delight at the small simple room. "I've never seen nothin' so clean and beautiful. Pure white walls an' real curtains on the windows. You thought of everything, ma'am. Even a TV. This is my first real home. Does it have a bathroom too?"

"Yes, Jimmy. It has a bathroom." Beth smiled. "Behind that door."

"I'll take good care of it, and keep it clean, too, I promise. I won't let you down. With the money you gave me yesterday, I should go buy some decent work clothes, so I'll look like a real good gardener, and I can give my friend back his clothes. Huh?"

"Yes, Jimmy. I think that's exactly what you should do. I'll see you later. Here's your key." She pressed it into his hand, triggering a smile that brightened his whole face.

Beth stood near the rose-covered arbor watching Jimmy as he whistled giddily down the shaded lane. She marveled at the transformation in this young man, his words, "Nobody never believed in me before," and "I won't let you down," kept coming back to her.

"I hope with all my heart you're right, Jimmy Larson," she whispered.

14

Two years later, Beth discussed staging arrangements for the Rose Society's annual show at Rosehaven with Jimmy. They spoke as one accomplished rosarian to another. The 1968 show had been a smashing success to the exhibitors, judges and public. To Jimmy, it had been an event so glorious he could think of little else. This year he planned on personally showing four classifications, hoping for the coveted Queen of the Show trophy.

"That's an ambitious goal, Jimmy," Beth commented, "but you've crammed more about roses in these two years than many rosarians do in ten. You've worked hard at it. I'm really proud of you."

He strode among the beds of more than 400 varieties of roses. Tall, tan, good looking, his conscientiousness and zeal for self-improvement and his keen eye for perfection impressed Beth. "I have you to thank, ma'am. You've done so much for me," he gave her an appreciative look. "You know what? I never thought I could like myself, but I do."

Beth smiled. "People aren't too much different from roses, Jimmy. They both need the sunshine of encouragement, proper feeding, water, tender loving care, skillful pruning and room to grow." She looked at the roses surrounding them. "The pruning is often God's job. He clips away shoots that soar out of control, bringing them back into shape so they'll be all the more beautiful when they leaf out. Meanwhile, the plant gets stronger from the inside out. You were a little different, though. The world did a lot of cutting back before you got a good healthy growth, but look at you now."

"Telling me about Jesus was the most wonderful thing you did for me, ma'am," Jimmy admired the flowers with her. "Since I work with flowers, my favorite part of the Bible is in John 15 when it says Jesus is the vine and

I am the branch, and apart from Him I can do nothing. No one knows that better than I do, ma'am."

"I've tried to share the same things with some of my high society friends, Jimmy, but they don't think it's important at all," she stopped to smell a Fragrant Cloud, reminding her of the task ahead of them. "And now we had better start thinking about the show on June 12. We mostly have to decide about the staging area and how to handle the public. The nine committees will take care of the judges, hospitality, registration and all."

Jimmy nodded. "A rose show is a big production, isn't it? Of course everyone wants to grow the Queen. There's so much to know about how to cut and present her, but the tending before all that is the real pleasure. Roses are so responsive. You talk to them, just like I do, don't you?"

"More than you know," Beth answered thoughtfully. "And they don't tell secrets. It's the English love of gardens in me, but they're a splendid return on one's investment. You've read my favorite childhood book, *The Secret Garden*. Remember when the gnarled old gardener said, 'Where you plant a rose a thistle cannot grow'?"

"I liked that. It's true, too," Jimmy nodded. "Well, I've got my work cut out for me today, better get at it."

*   *   *

On this beautiful June morning Charles was working in his study upstairs. Since Dr. Eddington had warned him to slow down, he'd made significant changes in his schedule and worked at home whenever possible. Beth often marveled at his mastery of time. While Max chauffeured him into the city he'd use the drive to record dictation, track production and make calls on the car phone. He'd arrive at the office or an appointment with an uncluttered mind. She'd often thought he should write a book on effective time management.

Beth buzzed him on the intercom. "How about a break? I have some fresh fruit and spicy herb tea for you."

"Sold!" In anticipation, Charles stood at the open door, ready to welcome her. "You're the cutest lil' waitress in ponytail and blue jeans I've seen all day." He kissed the tip of her nose as she passed him with the tray.

"Are you sure? Considering your day begins at 5:00 A.M., I don't know what all you've seen today."

"I'm excited about this redevelopment project for Chicago. My colleagues scoff at me. They're convinced I'm impairing the Townsend image to do low-income housing. But it's time high-tech professionals try to do a better job in meeting these needs." He pulled her over to the drawing table. "Look at this elevation. It's pretty decent, wouldn't you agree?"

Beth struggled to concentrate on what he was saying. Whenever she looked at Charles she fell in love again. His personal elegance dominated even the study, whose walls of deep Venetian red suggested Old World splendor and were enhanced by rare paintings of Renaissance architecture and leather-bound editions in mahogany bookcases.

"Yoo hoo, are you there?" Charles waved his hand before her. "You're not listening. You're off somewhere in la-la land. What are you thinking about?"

"Sorry, darling," Beth was shaken from her thoughts. "It looks great to me. I see quality even though it is low-cost. If it becomes a prototype, it will certainly improve life in redevelopment neighborhoods. I was just thinking about how I love you for caring about this project as much as the prestigious music centers and billion-dollar hotels."

"My contribution to this troubled generation."

"To be able to do something about it by designing a workable solution and putting it on paper is so rewarding. I just get frustrated! There are millions of people, so eager to discard things that don't come easy, judgments of right and wrong, for ones that drift on shifting sand. Whatever happened to absolute values?"

"Hold it," Charles held his hands up with a laugh. "Those are a whole lot of questions. The ones on the drawing board are all I can handle today." Beth smiled. She really didn't expect Charles to have all the answers. It just felt good to express her feelings. "You get back to work, darling," she said. "Let me worry about solving the world's problems."

"Before you go," Charles motioned her to nestle onto his lap, "I've been thinking about something. For our fifth anniversary next week, let's go down to the house in Carmel."

"That's a wonderful idea. I'd love it! We could see Annie and Ali too."

"Sure," Charles smiled. "Okay, break time's over. I have to get down to business or I won't be able to get away. Kiss me."

"I'll be in the garden, helping Jimmy. He's getting nervous about his exhibition specimens."

Jimmy scrutinized his roses like Sherlock Holmes to detect if aphids, thrips, beetles or any other predators were lurking about his precious blooms. "These are nice, strong stems, aren't they?" Jimmy asked as Beth approached. "And look at their unmarred glossy leaves."

"The blossoms are perfect too. I'll be surprised if you don't have a Queen of the Show. I know Tiffany and Dainty Bess will do well, and I'll bet you have several princesses in the climbers. Only two days to go."

Rose Show day dawned clear and sunny. The judges' luncheon on the terrace had concluded and the pre-show instructions had been given to all the committees. Stuart McFarland, the District Director and Rose Show chairman, approached Beth. Jimmy stood nearby.

"Mrs. Townsend, the setting is exquisite. Every one of your roses could be Queen of the Show. I'd like to know who heads your staff of gardeners. It's splendid work."

"You might say I do, Mr. McFarland. But most of the credit belongs to this young man—James Larson—and our thirteen regular gardeners. James has only been with me two years, and I'm fortunate to have him."

"You are indeed. Congratulations. Everything is splendid, just splendid."

Jimmy beamed. Beth knew that even if Rosehaven didn't place in the show, McFarland's praise would be enough.

Hundreds of rosarians toured the succession of separate areas or garden "rooms" beyond the various beds of roses. They wandered freely about the acres leading to the sunken pool, tea house and walled garden. Beth tried to make her way to Jimmy, to give him her support if the judging went badly, but was detained every few feet by praises for her accomplishments and her generosity in sharing them.

The runners and clerks had already delivered the tallies to the judges, who were punching the awards on the roses when she finally reached Jimmy.

"Well?" she asked, out of breath.

The radiance on his handsome young face said it all. It repaid her every moment spent in the bookstores and libraries, over the manuals on the care of roses, or with pruning clippers in hand.

"We have two Blue Ribbons, one red, and one yellow." He ticked them off on his fingers. "And two princesses in the climbers, like you said."

"Did Tiffany get one of the blues?"

"Yes, and Dainty Bess the other. No Queen of the Show, though. Maybe next year."

"Jimmy," Beth's eyes shone, "when I promised to keep our secret and you promised you'd never let me down, we struck a great bargain, didn't we? No one else will ever fully understand what a victory this is."

"This is the happiest day of my life."

"Mr. Townsend will be ecstatic over your ribbons."

"I'm sorry he couldn't be here today to enjoy this special occasion with us."

"He's finishing an important project so we can get away to Carmel next week. Otherwise he would have been here."

"Mr. Townsend's looking tired again, ma'am." Concern crept into Jimmy's voice. "It'll be good for both of you."

When they were ready to leave for Carmel, Beth asked, "Would you like me to drive, darling? You can just relax."

"You may be my chauffeur anytime. You're prettier than Max," he grinned.

Charles put his head back on the leather seat. "Every time I picture the house in my mind I see my mother's face," he sighed. "Such memories—all jumbled up. Happy and sad. She was beautiful and sweet until my father ruined her life. Without you beside me, Beth, I couldn't possibly set foot in the place again. It's too full of the musty smell of dried up dreams."

"We'll shoo them away and let them float out to sea with the ocean breezes, darling. Close your eyes and rest now, until we get there."

"Let me know when we get to the gate of the Seventeen Mile Drive." He closed his eyes.

In a few hours Beth gently touched his cheek. "Wake up. We're at the gate."

Charles talked to the guard about the resident's pass.

"Okay, sweetheart, just go ahead until I tell you to stop."

The estates on the famed drive were magnificent. Around each curve she anticipated the likeness of that imposing castle, private and aloof, etched in her memory over the six years since she'd driven through here with Hope and Josh.

"Turn into the drive here on the right. I'll open the gate. It may be stuck after all this time."

Beth gasped in disbelief. "Is this your house?" The mansion stood solidly poised on the rocky cliff with massive ivy-covered walls enclosing the grounds, thick with stately oaks and eucalyptus. The castle!

"This is the one!" he beamed.

Charles unlocked the medieval-looking wrought-iron gate and motioned Beth to drive through. He became a child again. He dashed about the grounds and up the stone steps to arched doors that were once hinged to a French monastery. Nervously, Charles worked the key, expecting the lock to be stiff, but it opened with ease. With mild groanings from the thick, deeply carved wood, he pushed the doors open.

As if in a trance, he stepped onto the Persian rugs of the entry into the living room. Beth's imagination gave wing to a vision of a silent screen star, such as Douglas Fairbanks, Jr., suavely leaning against the mantle. The majestic rock fireplace soared up to high, beamed ceilings. Beth watched speechlessly as her husband flung aside the heavy ochre damask draperies on iron rings, revealing French windows and a vast view of the cliff and sea below.

She expected dust to fly. But instead her eye caught the card and note left by the security service on the English oak entry table: "Dear Resident: Your home has been regularly cleaned and inspected for maintenance by our expert staff. Please call the number below if we may be of further service during your stay."

While Charles opened all the draperies and rediscovered the grandeur of the house, Beth studied a tapestry, waiting for him to show her the rooms himself.

"I'm sorry, sweetheart," he said, returning to where he had left her. "I was caught in the mystique of *déjà vu*. I even imagined I heard voices of the past, and my mother laughing."

To date, the attorneys had been unable to locate Ava Townsend. Charles ached to see her, and wondered where and how she fared, if she was even alive.

The week unfolded in a maze of enchanted memories Charles shared with Beth, drawing her back in time with him. He discovered that his father had left him a lifetime membership at the exclusive Cypress Point Country Club in his will. Beth rode with him in the golf cart as he played the famous course, excited as a young boy. He reached the green in three on a long five-par, and sank the putt for a birdie. "That just made my day," Charles beamed.

While they waited for the foursome ahead of them at the turn, Charles's eyes filled with emotion. "Beth, now that I see how the gift of the house, the provision for its care and the club membership were so meticulously arranged in my father's will, it's like he's asking my forgiveness from the grave. He would never have done it face to face."

The foursome offered to let him play through. "I'm in no hurry. We're enjoying the beautiful day," Charles told them. When the tee was clear, he smacked a long straight drive down the fairway that even Arnold Palmer would have been happy to claim.

Other days spun by, with more golf or bicycling along the scenic drive. They frolicked on the beach with Annie and Ali, and Beth painted sunsets until the silent hand of another day pulled the great orange ball below the horizon. Then time ran out. It was time to return to Rosehaven.

"I feel like a new man, Beth," Charles said on the way home. "I didn't realize how much I needed that week. It was good to return to the old house. It's the one truly gracious thing my father did for me. I'll be able to enjoy it now, and I'd like to come down often. Let's bring Kerry next time."

"That would be fun," Beth agreed. "And we'll take her to the Aquarium in Monterey too. I can't wait to stop by on the way home and give her hugs and the shells we collected for her. It seems like more than two weeks since we've seen her."

From the time Beth telephoned ahead, Kerry busily drew pictures to lavish on "Bif and Charlie" when they arrived. Hope had fresh coffee, cake and her ever-ready friendship waiting for them.

"Do I really get to go to Carmel in two weeks, Mama?" Kerry asked excitedly as Beth and Charles hugged her goodbye after their brief visit.

Josh answered, "We're invited too, Kerry. Maybe we'll all be able to go."

"We'll look forward to many happy times there," Charles assured them.

That week had provided a welcome escape from the heightened tension of the news coverage of the war in Vietnam. On the car radio, Charles picked up a Sunday afternoon overview and commentary on the current crises. . . .

"The conflict initiated by the Communist-supported forces of North Vietnam since its attacks against the government of South Vietnam in 1957 has escalated into a savage, full-scale war that threatens world peace."

"That's news?" Charles asked, but continued to listen.

"Though war has never officially been declared, there are now more than 532,000 Americans and over 66,000 other non-communist forces fighting against the Communist guerrillas and regular troops. U.S. participation in the Vietnam war marks the longest involvement in our history. Americans have never been so divided on the issues of foreign policy, both on strategy and objective. Many support the Johnson administration's policies. Some think the U.S. should take an even stronger stand against Communist aggression and take over throughout Southeast Asia. Others think we should not be there at all.

"With President Nixon's call for heavy troop withdrawals this year, we are presented a choice of what has been called an unattainable victory or an unacceptable defeat. Clearly, there is no good news coming from Washington or

Vietnam. Our faith in government has been undermined, our faith in the future shaken."

Charles replaced the grim newscast with soft music. "Discouraging, isn't it? And when I go into San Francisco tomorrow there will be hippies carrying signs protesting an 'immoral' war. The throngs of flower children, who have lost faith in everything but making up their own rules for morality, will have multiplied like flies."

"But it's not only San Francisco, love," Beth reminded him. "Daddy writes that Piccadilly has long-haired weirdos and international dropouts swarming all over the place too." She laughed. "If the Apollo 11 mission is successful next month, and man actually can walk on the moon, should we book passage?"

"I just about go into orbit thinking about the mess the world is in," Charles remained serious, "but there are already enough quitters. Remember in the Bible where it says something like, to whom much is given much is expected? I'm just enough of an optimist to believe there's something else we could be doing to help make the world a better place."

"Where would you start?" Beth asked.

"Good question."

"Charles, it must be my English aversion to sudden change," Beth said. "The outspoken minority are so adamant that the country must throw away tradition and stability for what's right in their own eyes. Sort of an every-man-for-himself mentality. Primitive. Sometimes I feel like I want to drive behind the gates of Rosehaven and sit out the next decade or so."

"It's tempting, isn't it?" he raised his eyebrows at the thought. "We could do that you know, if you're really fed up. My holdings and interest earn enough for us to live the rest of our lives in the style to which we have become accustomed. We could become reclusive, not give a rip about the rest of the world." He glanced at her and smiled. "We could lie around all day and make love and not care about a war or protesters. We could just smell the roses." He was still smiling.

"Be serious."

"I am! Sounds better all the time. You don't think that's meaningful?" He laughed.

Beth ignored the question. "When it comes right down to it—if we're honest—we're all searching for the same things the hippies claim they are. A more meaningful life."

"What's pathetically comic is they're expecting it to fall on them while they're strumming their guitars in the parks," Charles agreed.

"But Merribelle and her crowd don't have it either," Beth sighed. "They're still looking for meaning in materialism. And none of them seems to have found satisfaction."

Thinking of his father, Charles answered, "Mmm—it's a terrible thing to discover that money doesn't buy happiness. I thrive on challenge and love my work, but I don't work this hard just to make money. I think satisfaction is a matter of focus, balance—as basic as the form follows function premise of architecture."

Beth thought for a moment. "Darling, this 'meaningful life' business is different for everyone. It's how we identify success, and whom we aim to please—only ourselves, other people or God."

Charles agreed with a nod.

"Just think of the power God has given us, Charles," Beth went on. "I know we can make an impact on our little part of the world in the decade of the seventies. God only knows what's ahead of us. Look what we've done already, in our own backyard, so to speak."

"I'd like to think His plan goes beyond that," Charles said.

"Me, too."

"I feel so charged right now I'd say, let it happen, as long as we do it together. I'm no good in that department without you."

"Charles, I'd heartily contest that statement," Beth laughed, "but yes, we are a team. And that's just the way I like it."

15

M an's giant step on the moon preambled the decade of the '70s and an unprecedented challenge to survive a head-on collision with the future.

Beth felt invaded by the swiftness of change. Sociologist Alvin Toffler's best-seller, *Future Shock,* explored the hidden impacts of change. He and others predicted that shattering stress and disorientation would result unless people quickly learned to control this overwhelming influence on family life and the breakup of society. Some termed the phenomenon as a dislocation of human identity.

Every trip into San Francisco brought Beth the shock of strange new subcultures. They seemed to develop weekly as things familiar were exchanged for new and bewildering standards.

Over breakfasts and the daily newspaper, she and Charles read the world scene. Where would it all end? Peace in Vietnam was still elusive. Armed conflict in the Middle East never ceased. The Strategic Arms Limitations Talks with Russia droned on as a world in the throes of an anxiety attack dangled precariously on the brink of disaster.

They watched on television as President Nixon described the '70s as an era of negotiation, and it became the beginning of the end of an America-dominated Free World.

One note of encouragement in the United States: Militant organizations on campuses and in cities were becoming noticeably less violent. However, inflation bred earlier by the escalation of the Vietnam War brought a soar of unemployment. The jobless rate rose, corporate profits fell, business failures jumped, the stock market dipped, interest rates skyrocketed to the highest levels in a century.

Tillie loved to watch *I Love Lucy* reruns on television, but in June of 1972, the Watergate scandal flooded the news media, morning, noon and night. The Democratic Party headquarters were burglarized under the direction of government officials, searching for evidence of one candidate's purported psychological aberration and treatment. They were charged with violating public trust and other abuses of power in order to maintain positions of authority. In November Richard Nixon was reelected president while members of his staff were being tried for second degree burglary. Meanwhile, the rest of the world judged the break-in as necessary, the "crime" inconsequential, and laughed at politics in America.

In spite of it all, January 1973 marked one very important decade for Beth. Kerry's tenth birthday.

"May I plan Kerry's party?" Beth had asked Hope at Christmastime. "Wouldn't it be fun to carry on tradition and have a surprise for her on Saturday at the Palace Hotel like Daddy did for me? Remember? We'll invite several of her best friends. Then on Sunday, we'll have a party at Rosehaven with all of us. Tillie and Jimmy would be thrilled to be included."

Hope gave her a squeeze. "Beth, plan anything you like. When we were ten, how could we have known we'd have this lifelong friendship?"

"I hope Kerry will have a friend as dear to her as you have been to me," Beth smiled at Hope.

"I think she considers you one of her closest friends," Hope confided. "She adores you. She wants to dance and paint and look just like her 'godmother.' The other day as she brushed her gorgeous dark hair, she said, 'Don't you think I look a little like Bif—except Bif's skin is lighter and creamier, and her eyes are real blue and mine are real brown? Do I look like my real mother, now that I'm growing up?'"

"How did you answer her?" Beth wondered, pleased with the child's openness about being adopted.

"I simply agreed with her on all counts. Then I assured her that a real mother, willing to sacrifice her own feelings to give a baby up for adoption and a better life, did it out of love."

"What did she say?" Beth asked eagerly, although she knew Kerry and Hope had had such conversations before.

"Just what she always does. She thanked Jesus that we were her 'real parents.' She said the dearest thing, 'Real is being there.' Kerry is a precious gift from you and God, Beth, and we thank both of you every day for her."

"I thank God, too, that you and Josh have been such beautiful examples of love to my baby." Tears came to Beth's eyes. "Hope, my heart grieves for the countless thousands of women and the babies they abort. Can you imagine life without Kerry, or Kerry being denied life?"

Before Charles left for the city the Friday before Kerry's party, he opened a froth of tissue from an I. Magnin's box. "I ask you, is this Kerry?" he beamed, holding up a beribboned fluff of a pink party dress with ruffles and lace. "You should have seen me in the girl's department." He grinned, then he produced a petticoat, anklets and hairbows.

"You love pampering her, don't you?" Beth blinked back her tears, touched by the value he placed on a child in comparison to the value of his time at hundreds of dollars an hour.

"We're lucky to have a borrowed little girl to love, aren't we?"

More than you know, Beth thought sadly.

"Oh," Charles went on, "I have a late meeting tonight. I don't know how long this one will go, but if you don't mind I think I'll stay at the Tower and then play catch-up for a while on Saturday while you do girl things."

"You're working too hard again," she warned. "And the paunch is back."

"Hush up and kiss me—I'm fine. Bye, sweetheart."

Beth brought a large but delicate bouquet of pink flowers for the table by the palms at the Palace. Pink pleated nutcups and small gifts for the little guests sat at each place setting. Presents for the birthday girl formed a towering pyramid. When Kerry arrived with Hope, she squealed with delight at seeing her friends at the frilly, feminine table and ran to Beth with open arms.

"It's beautiful, just like you, Bif!" she cried with glee. But in a moment, her dark thick lashes fluttered downward, hiding disappointment. "Does this mean we're not having a party at your house tomorrow?"

"Not at all," Beth laughed. "Today is just for females, something special because ten-year-olds are special."

Kerry's face lit up again as the table of girls chattered and giggled over lunch, ice cream, cake and punch until the party was over.

Sunday afternoon, Rosehaven's rooms had cheery fires that chased away the gray chill, inviting cozy conviviality. Streamers and balloons tied with swirls of ribbon floated from the crystal chandelier in the dining room. The savory aroma of Cookie's baked chicken, mashed potatoes, gravy, mile-high biscuits, and shimmering red Jell-O, all Kerry's favorite foods, wafted from the kitchen.

Hope, Josh, Jimmy, Tillie, Annie and Ali hovered around as Kerry opened her gifts.

At the sound of the doorbell, the adults exchanged smiles and knowing glances. That would be Bobo the clown who had come to surprise Kerry and entertain them with balloon tricks. Beth nodded to Tillie to answer it.

She returned in a fluster, "There's a gentleman here to see you, Mr. Townsend."

Charles wore his perennial pleased-little-boy expression, even though he was now quite gray at the temples. "Please show him in, Tillie."

"I think you'd do well to come yourself, sir."

Tillie's pursed lips affirmed her curt tone.

She's acting a bit melodramatic, Beth thought. Charles chuckled as he went to the entry.

Upon seeing the distinguished gentleman admiring the paintings in the entry gallery, Charles was momentarily stunned. Tillie stood firm, showing her protective agitation at the visitor's intrusion of the party.

The phone call of Friday afternoon, in the midst of back-to-back appointments and heavy meetings with international corporate heads, had been crowded out of his memory. Only now did Charles remember insisting that Count Cabriollini honor him with a visit to Rosehaven during his short stay in San Francisco. He'd even temporarily forgotten Kerry's party that day, but now he rationalized that the Count's presence would only add elegance to the occasion. He knew he could bank on Beth's graciousness to put their guest at ease.

"Count Cabriollini, welcome to Rosehaven. Forgive the briefness of my conversation with you Friday, but I'm so pleased you could get out of the city today."

"Ah, Signor Townsend, it is good to see you again," Roberto extended his hand. "*Grazie,* you are most gracious to have me to your exquisite home. I hear, as you say, festivities. Am I imposing?"

"Not at all. Please, come and join in an American-style birthday party for my wife's godchild."

Beth looked expectantly toward the doorway, bracing herself in anticipation of Kerry's shrill shrieks when Bobo appeared. Instead, she felt faint. Suddenly she saw the room and everyone in it turn nauseous green at the sight of Charles ushering Roberto into their living room. Hope, Josh and Annie shot questioning glances at one another. It took only one glance at the likeness to Kerry to guess who the handsome Italian nobleman was. The timing of his arrival was uncanny.

"Ladies and gentlemen, we have the pleasure of a most illustrious guest joining us this afternoon—Count Cabriollini," Charles announced. "When Beth and I were in Lake Como several years ago, he graciously gave us a private tour of his renowned villa and art collection. I requested the honor of reciprocating with an open invitation to Rosehaven when he came to the United States. Count Cabriollini called my office on Friday, Beth. We've both been so preoccupied I forgot to mention it, but I knew you'd be delighted."

Beth heard herself respond with some rote courtesy, but she didn't know what she said. Numbness engulfed her as she tried desperately not to be rude or embarrass her innocent husband while he introduced their friends.

"This beautiful little lady, Kerry, is our birthday girl. She's ten years old today," Charles said proudly.

"*Si*, she is bee-u-tiful indeed, *cara mia* . . . those eyelashes! *Felice compleanno* . . . happy birthday."

"Thank you, sir." Kerry smiled politely.

The doorbell rang again. This time, Beth sighed in relief. It really was Bobo. While he entertained the partiers with his bulbous nose that lit up when he blew into the balloons and twisted them into animal shapes, Beth struggled to regain her composure.

All the while, she felt Roberto's disarming dark eyes traveling between her and Kerry. Had he guessed? Did he know at the sight of her whose eyes were so like his? Had he ever wondered about the consequences of their one night of passion more than ten years ago, and her departure from Paris before the end of the school term?

She felt clammy, weak, with a degree of outrage at his audacity in accepting Charles's invitation to her home. But his beautiful eyes, as in days past, drew her into their magical spell. Beneath his aristocratic bearing, enormous wealth, elegance and arrogance, lay a deep and pleading look of sadness that engendered her compassion.

Roberto wore diamonds, but no wedding ring. Had the villa, with its prestige and priceless art, filled his nights with the equalled ecstasy of a lifetime love with one woman, or the joy of a child?

Charles took advantage of a break in Bobo's act. "Beth, would you excuse the Count and me for a few moments? I'd like to quickly show him through the gallery and a bit of the house."

"Of course, darling," she smiled. It would be relief from Roberto's scrutiny.

When they returned, Tillie informed them that Cookie's dinner was almost ready, and Kerry excitedly drew Charles away to admire her new Barbie doll.

"*Scusi, Signora* Townsend, I will take my leave." Roberto bowed ceremoniously. "My visit today is inopportune."

"My husband will be disappointed if you do not stay for dinner," Beth replied courteously.

"Another time, perhaps. Would you kindly see me to the door, *Signora?*"

Beth trembled. Again, he left her no choice. In the privacy of the entry, he took her hand and pressed it to his lips. "You are a happy woman, I can tell. It is what you deserve, *Bella Rosa.* The child, she is beautiful too. May she have a happy birthday."

He removed the smaller of his brilliantly cut rings. "Here, I did not know I was coming to a birthday party. Have this diamond set in something suitable for her, *per favore,* and. . . . "

"No, Roberto," she interrupted, "it isn't necessary."

He placed a finger over her lips. "Shhh—do it not for her, but me. I do not have anyone ten years old to give a present to."

They stood as in a hypnotic trance searching each other's eyes. Beth broke it with a gesture toward the door.

"*Adio,* Roberto. . . . "

"*Arrivederci, Bella Rosa.* We will meet again."

She watched him stride toward the waiting limousine he'd hired to bring him from the city, in the same manner he'd walked away when she'd declined his advances the first day they met. Yet the world—their lives—were so different now. Would Roberto continue to pop into her life with such unpredictability? The world was too small, and he was too presumptuous for Beth to think otherwise.

A few weeks later, the cease-fire agreement in Vietnam and the withdrawal of U.S. troops helped ease world tensions. The release of prisoners by the North Vietnamese would follow. But it was only half a victory. Anti-war demonstrations as well as congressional opposition still raged over the continued bombing of Cambodia. Public confidence in government remained on shaky ground.

Everything felt shaky—except her God, her home, her husband.

Over coffee in their garden room on a drizzly February morning, Beth slapped the newspaper and cried out in anguish, "My God, look what they've done!"

"Who? What?" Charles blinked over his bifocals and the financial page at his wife's unusual outburst.

"The Supreme Court legalized abortion."

"That is a tragedy," Charles shook his head sadly. "So many times when I've thought of Kerry and whoever her mother was, I've been grateful she found a loving home for her instead of destroying that precious life. Or think of Jimmy. You said he never knew a father and grew up in a terrible environment, yet he still had a chance to live and succeed."

"I know, darling." Little did Charles realize he was talking so close to home . . . about his own wife. Yet even in her own period of desperation, abortion had never been considered a viable option.

Beth raged on as she read more of the article. "Abortion for reasons of inconvenience? That spells legalized murder! Charles, how could the Supreme Court of a civilized nation adopt such a barbaric practice, let alone thumb their noses at God?"

"I know," he shook his head. "You'd really get upset if you overheard what I hear almost every day in the business community. Sleeping around is quite the norm."

"Yes, I know. Even the supposedly intelligent ones give only slight consideration to the consequences. I've thought about this a lot, Charles. There ought to be a place, maybe like the coffeehouse concept that's catching on now, where women, especially the real young ones in the heart of the inner cities, could go and talk to caring people. When they're pregnant and confused, they need to get help, to know someone's willing to listen. Maybe even have a connection with adoption centers. There should be pastors, psychologists and trained lay people who are willing to reach out to them."

"You just outlined a plan," Charles looked at his wife in admiration. "There's certainly a need. Why don't you do it?"

"Charles, you're serious, aren't you?"

"Are you?"

"Well—yes. Yes, I am." Suddenly she broke out in laughter.

"What's so funny?" he quizzed with a puzzled look.

"I'm thinking about Merribelle. She loves me, I know, but she'd be aghast that her 'queen,' as she calls me, would get involved with 'ordinary people.' Her cavalier innuendoes lack subtlety as usual, but it's obvious I'm to be the recipient of League's 'Woman of the Year' award. The annual luncheon is at the Mark Hopkins next week. I know I should go, but I really don't relish the thought. I don't do what I do for awards."

"You're always my Woman of the Year," Charles smiled his most charming smile, "in or out of League. You've done a fantastic job in supporting and generating new talent in the arts, Beth. I'm really proud of you. But I'm almost more excited about your newest idea."

"Me too. I'll go to work on it right away."

Within the year Beth had the support of several churches, pastors, psychologists and volunteers willing to be trained as lay counselors—herself included. They agreed on the name "House of New Hope," a nonprofit, non-denominational center in mid-city. Women, primarily twenty to thirty-five years old and teenagers already disillusioned with life, came first. Their need to talk with caring listeners in a nonthreatening atmosphere was desperate. They needed listeners who would help them turn their lives around. The immediate response was more than anyone imagined they could accommodate, and then the men began to come.

Each day bore witness to the need. Beth more often than not came home exhausted, burdened by other people's troubles. Yet her heart remained strong because she knew it was worth the effort.

In the course of a lifetime, some years slip away from memory, others are marked deeply with indelible ink. The nation would never forget the disgrace of Watergate or the grueling Vietnam conflict. But regardless, Presidents Ford and Carter played out their roles in history and time marched on.

Beth marched too, almost militantly, against the "do your own thing" movement that was tearing youth, families, the whole society apart. The intensity of meeting the needs sometimes became too much. Charles was the first to see it. During the spring of 1981, he sought more frequent refuge in Carmel. He insisted they take time to absorb the calm, powerful beauty of the sea where he felt such peace while Beth captured its changing mood on canvas.

"One of the wisest things we've done is to schedule these retreats for ourselves," Charles stretched back in his chair. "The most productive time of our lives has grown out of calling a moratorium on routine to get in touch with ourselves—and God."

"I agree," Beth said, contentedly painting the sun's coral glow on the shimmering silver sea. "It's like we come here with our minds as stuffed as bulging suitcases. You're consumed with what you're going to write for *Architectural Digest* or say at your next convention. I have my plans for the center and charity balls, tapes and notes from sermons and books that we haven't yet sorted out."

"That's true. I'm working on a speech right now," Charles set his notes aside.

"But then, don't we begin to shake off the busyness, like a dog shaking off sand, and settle down?"

Beth smiled at the analogy. "I've seen dogs do that. But I see it like emptying out the contents of our baggage, and then asking God how to fit it all back into our daily lives." She added another delicate stroke of the brush. "Have you noticed how often God says, 'Leave it behind'? "

"Mmm," Charles murmured, looking at the stillness of the ocean. "How time does fly. I can't get it through my head Kerry's graduating from high school. It seems like only yesterday she was ten."

"Incredible, isn't it?" Beth brushed the finishing strokes on her painting. "I was thinking we should take a trip to London for Daddy's eightieth birthday, and invite Kerry to join us as a graduation present."

"That would be a present for everyone," Charles agreed. "It's been over a year since you've seen your parents. They'd love it."

"Hope needs some quiet time," Beth added thoughtfully. "She's pale and less vivacious lately. She said something about having tests, but quickly shrugged it off. I'm worried about her. Maybe if Kerry's not there they won't have so many young people around, and she'll take more time to rest."

But there was little time for anyone to rest in the following weeks. They were all excited over Kerry's first trip to London, and there were graduation parties, planning and packing to be done.

Kerry's excitement lifted her through the grueling finals at Valley Christian High where she graduated as valedictorian. The theme of her message to her class, titled "Reaching Out to a Hurting World," brought tears to Beth's eyes and gratefulness in her heart for the sensitive, godly woman her secret daughter was becoming. Beth looked forward to watching Kerry continue to mature through her college years.

On their flight to London, Charles asked, "Is Stanford your final decision on a college, Kerry?"

"Yes, Charlie, I thought you'd heard. I have a full scholarship. Isn't that wonderful?"

"It is, and we're so proud of you."

Kerry looked out the plane's window. "Is it much longer, Charlie?"

"Not too much," he smiled. "I hope you enjoy this trip. You'll love Beth's parents."

Sean Sheridan faithfully met them at Gatwick Airport. Beth spotted him instantly among the slipshod travelers. Kerry immediately identified him with the last of a breed of impeccably mannered jolly Englishmen. Bowler hat, black umbrella, dignity and aplomb, all intact.

"By jove, so this is Kerry, all grown up," Sean gave her a hug. "Splendid, simply splendid. Haven't seen you since you were a little tyke, but I know you intimately. Beth's letters and her annual visits to Hampstead are filled with 'Kerry this' and 'Kerry that.' Now I see why."

He turned to give his daughter a peck on the cheek. "Beth, my stunning girl, you're lovelier with each year, and Charles, old fellow, you're well, I presume?"

With a wink at Beth, Charles escorted Kerry into the front seat. Her eyes widened as Sean sparkled with his typical eloquence in pointing out the sights of London. He chattered all the way as London opened out to the countryside and the heath.

When they entered the house, Beth noticed Kerry warmed instantly to Mum's ageless elegance, which blended so perfectly with the charm and traditions of Hampstead. She also saw the tingle of excitement over the evidence of the lavish preparations for Sean's party, just two days off.

The list of amiable guests at Sean's eightieth birthday party was dominated by longtime friends, titled Londoners and English gentry from Hampstead and Bath. Beth always found them delightful and outrageously amusing. When the British economy became brutal, they would merely sell another painting off their manor walls to Sheridan's gallery. Their consuming interest centered on whom they last saw at Ascot and whether their roses had black spot.

Beth keenly observed Kerry's fascination—the preoccupation with frivolity and impeccable manners.

"I say, I adore the pure 'Englishness' of it all," Kerry confided to Beth, putting on her best British accent. But no one took more delight in the celebration than the guest of honor. At midnight, Sean's eyes still danced as he bid his formally clad guests goodbye.

"A bully party, what? Come have a cognac with me by the fire, love," he invited Beth after the others had retired. She declined the brandy but welcomed the chat.

"Life is good." His watery blue eyes softened. "Yes indeed, God has been superbly good to me." Within moments his head drooped. He was asleep. Beth took the Waterford snifter from his hand and set it on the table, covered him with an afghan and quietly stoked up the fire, letting him dream in the afterglow.

Beth's only regrets on her visits home were that her mother perennially avoided opportunities to talk woman to woman, one on one with her. But then, they rarely ever had. Now that there were a few silver threads in her own hair, she wondered how her mother had felt when she hung up her toe shoes to teach. And about aging . . . and about life itself. What wisdom did she have to pass on?

In the fall, Kerry was off to college with a huge expense check deposited into the bank account Charles had set up for her. Beth had attended Stanford's football games with Charles as an alumnus, but suddenly they became more exciting for Beth with Kerry there. And more spirited, Charles admitted, than his own college days. He'd been too tense during that time, trying to prove himself to his father. Beth and Josh became equally avid fans, but Hope made excuses not to go. She claimed she needed time to prepare her Bible study lectures, or to conserve her energy for the terminal children at the Medical Center. But she didn't look well.

In Kerry's junior year, Beth spotted a new light in her eyes when they all met for the Berkeley game. "Bif, Charlie—this is Bob Daniels," Kerry said with a big smile.

Josh put a huge arm around Bob. "This young man spends a lot of time in our home these days. He's a Stanford grad and now a seminary student." Bob enthusiastically shook Beth's and Charles's hands.

At halftime, Beth had a chance to talk to Josh. "Kerry seems pretty interested in this young man," she said. "Tell me about him."

"Hope and I think he's something special," Josh replied. "He really has his head on straight. After his parents were killed in a car accident a few years ago, he worked himself through college and is now making excellent grades in seminary. He's bright, sincere, just a really nice guy." Josh smiled. "And he treats Kerry with respect and tenderness. We couldn't be happier for her."

"Bif," Kerry confided in Beth after six months of dating, "Bob's the one. He's everything I've ever dreamed of in the man I want to spend my life with."

"Has he popped the question?" Beth's face lit up in anticipation. "He's perfect for you."

"No, but no one else even comes close. First of all, he loves God with all his heart, so I know he'd be a wonderful husband. We'd have a marriage like Mom and Dad's, and that's what I want. He's fun and witty, but he's deep and tender too. There isn't anything we can't talk about. I always dreamed that when I fell in love I'd hear bells ringing, but that after the lovemaking, there'd be a best friend beside me. You and Charlie have that, don't you?"

"Yes," Beth's affection for her husband shone in her eyes. "Charles entered my life like a white knight, and his shield has never tarnished. Marriages like ours and your parents' are rare in these times."

Beth blinked back tears. Her exquisitely beautiful daughter glowed before her, a woman in love, sharing the depths of her heart, pouring out her dreams.

Beth enveloped Kerry in a hug. "I must scoot now. I'm working at the center today. You keep me up to date on your love life. Okay?"

"Count on it," Kerry beamed.

Throughout Kerry's senior year, Beth waited for an engagement announcement, but heard nothing more. Sometimes she worried that something might have gone wrong. Had Kerry spoken too soon?

On commencement day, Kerry and Bob ran toward them after the ceremony. Laughing gaily arm-in-arm, Kerry's black hair flowing and graduation gown flapping about her legs, Kerry flashed a small diamond before Beth's eyes.

"What's this?" Charles feigned surprise, looking at Josh.

His whole gigantic frame seemed to be one enormous smile. "This young man came to us, very proper, and asked for our daughter's hand in marriage. We think it's a fine match." Josh crushed them to his sides with one of his famous bear hugs.

"Congratulations, both of you!" All six of them joined in the embrace.

"When's the wedding?" Beth asked, straightening her hair after the crunch.

Bob answered. "You'll think we're crazy, but—we want to get married in September." Everyone blinked. "I know weddings usually take longer than that to plan, but we don't want to wait. I've been working some extra jobs to save the money I know we're going to need while I finish my degree at the seminary. . . . " His questioning glance around the circle invited comment.

"That kind of responsibility tells me you're going to be a good husband, son," Charles said with encouragement. "I admire that."

"Bif, we'd like to be married at Rosehaven," Kerry said excitedly. "Mother has described your wedding in living color. I'd like ours to be just like it. Could we do that?"

Charles answered. "You've got it. Send me the bill." Later Charles confided in Beth, "The wedding I want for Kerry would be beyond Josh and

Hope's financial ability. I promise, I'll be ever so careful not to overshadow Josh, but I could at least *pretend* I'm the father of the bride." He wrapped Beth in a hug. "For a few weeks we can be the parents of the daughter we never had, or the son that never grew up to cherish a wife."

The following weeks were jammed with a flurry of activities once the announcements were sent. After the wedding rehearsal dinner at Rosehaven, stacks of gifts waited to be opened. Beth, who had been checking the florist's arrangements, came into the room as Kerry lifted a dazzling cobalt blue and gold antique Venetian vase from volumes of packing.

Beth stopped cold. "Who's that from?"

"Count Cabriollini," Kerry answered. "He gave me that beautiful diamond when I was ten, didn't he? How did he know I was getting married?"

"He wrote and invited us to join him for dinner while he's in San Francisco. I declined, of course, but invited him to the wedding," Charles answered innocently.

Exasperated, Beth thought, *Dear, hospitable Charles.* Now she almost wished he knew of their past relationship. But there was too much to do to worry about Roberto now. She just prayed he would have the good manners not to come.

Beth's pearl and crystal encrusted satin gown had been carefully packed in tissue and sealed. She brought it out and it fit Kerry perfectly.

The bride waited in a billow of tulle veils at the top of the stairs on Josh's arm, poised as Beth and Sean had twenty-one years ago, breathlessly waiting for the first note of "The Wedding March," all eyes upon them.

Beth longed to cry out, "That's my daughter," as she watched her float light as a dream descending the stairs. *Now she's fixing her eyes on the rose design of the stained-glass window, just as I did to calm my nervousness,* Beth thought to herself. *See the love in her eyes for the man about to become her husband. . . .*

Charles watched Bob step forward to receive his bride. With a thankful heart, Charles relived the wonder that a God he scarcely knew at the time of his own wedding had given him the perfect mate to share his life.

Hope breathed a prayer of thanksgiving that she had lived to know the joy of this day. At that moment a handsome young usher offered his arm. He united her with the wedding party in a unique procession beyond the terrace to the guests' seats in a crescent around the rose arbor where Kerry and Bob would take their vows.

When the ceremony was over, Beth overheard one of Kerry's college friends sniffle to her boyfriend, "This was the sweetest wedding I've ever seen. I knew they were Christians, but I've never heard a couple ask Christ to be the center of their lives in a wedding ceremony."

Beth smiled, pleased, and paused, intending to talk with them. But Charles came along and took Beth's hand, leading her under the rose arbor before the wedding party gathered for pictures.

His wonderful, clear blue eyes looked into hers. "I, Charles, take thee, Beth, to be my wedded wife, to love and to cherish from this day forward, till death do us part."

"And I, Beth, take thee, Charles . . . oh darling, I'm even more in love with you than on our wedding day."

At the moment they kissed, someone's camera flashed.

Josh grinned. "You're still a beautiful bride, Beth. And Charles is okay too." He circled them in one big hug.

The elegant stranger in the creamy silk suit that had turned the heads of so many guests stepped forward. "*Signor, Signora* Townsend, it is difficult to know who is the bride and groom, you are so bee-u-tiful," Roberto bowed to Beth. "But of course, the bride is a beauty also. So bee-u-tiful she could be your daughter, *Signora,* except for those dark eyes."

Beth's inner rage blotted out whatever else Roberto said. Had he suspected he was actually at his own daughter's wedding? How dare he persist in these uncannily timed appearances from out of the past to haunt her!

"*Blast you!*" she silently screamed. She searched those ravishing dark eyes that had been able to snare her into a swirling whirlpool of passion since the day they met. She searched for a clue to his motives, while her loving husband stood by in innocence and adoration.

But Roberto gave no clues; he revealed no malice or guile. Perhaps he, too, stood innocent, drawn into a circle of warmth and love his world could not offer.

And how could she curse him? He had procreated the everlasting joy of her daughter. She had denied him even the knowledge of Kerry's existence.

Oh, Roberto, have I misjudged you? Forgive me! her heart cried out. *I hate living a life of secrets, but once begun, there is no end.*

16

Bob and Kerry leaped into the back of Charles's Cadillac, ducking rice and waving to their well-wishers. Max grinned, ready to drive them to San Francisco airport for their honeymoon flight to Hawaii.

The guests crowded around the big black sedan. "God bless! Have a wonderful trip!" they shouted. Hope and Josh cheered and threw kisses until the couple were out of sight.

"Maybe we can afford to go to Hawaii someday, honey," Josh beamed at his frail wife. "I wish I could whisk you away right now, to rest and lie in the sun."

"But I'm so glad we could send them," Hope smiled.

Tears of joy slid down Beth's cheeks as the car sped away. But she felt Charles's arm around her stiffen. "Why are you frowning?" she asked, puzzled.

"Josh and Hope can't afford to do that," Charles complained in a whisper to Beth. "It's way beyond their means—such a sacrifice. We should be paying for the honeymoon trip."

"They'll manage, darling. I'm continually amazed at how they make such a modest income do so much." She looked into his concerned eyes. "We mustn't deprive them of this pleasure. You can't imagine what it meant to them to be able to give the kids a honeymoon trip."

A handful of guests lingered in the fading summer twilight, spellbound by the perfume of roses floating on the soft breeze.

Charles scanned the stragglers for Hope. "You look exhausted, little one," he said as he put his arm around her shoulders. "Let's all go in, find a cup of coffee, kick off our shoes and do an instant replay of the video. What an age we live in. We can do something memorable and immediately push a button and watch ourselves do it again."

"That's wonderful," Hope sighed. "Charles, how can we say thank you? I never dreamed our daughter could ever have such a heavenly wedding. But it's like a blur. I'd love to see it again and again and again. Then I'll know it was real and not a dream."

Just when the video Kerry said, "I do," Tillie whispered to Beth. "You have a phone call, Miss Beth." Beth caught her breath at Tillie's grim expression. "It's your mother."

Mum's voice quivered. "Sorry to ring you up on Kerry's wedding day, love, but you must come home. Your father's in the hospital. He developed a severe case of pneumonia after that minor surgery he had a few days ago." Her voice broke its usual calm. "I'm—I'm frightfully concerned, Beth," she sounded near hysteria. "Try to get here as soon as possible."

Beth returned ashen. "It's Daddy. He has pneumonia, and Mum is frightened to death. Charles, we need to leave immediately." Tears slid from her eyes. Josh came to comfort her, pressing her head into his massive chest while Charles phoned British Airways.

The few remaining guests quickly offered condolences and left.

"There's a midnight flight into Heathrow—we can just make it, sweetheart," Charles said when he returned.

"I'll drive you to the airport," Josh volunteered.

"Nonsense," Charles put his hand up. "Max will be here by the time we're ready to leave. Take our little mother-of-the-bride to your room, Josh. She needs to go to bed."

Hope suddenly looked even more fragile, as though she might break. Her thick, brown, curly hair had become sparse from the chemotherapy she refused to talk about, yet she faced every situation beaming her cheerful, ready smile.

The news of her father's critical condition drained Beth's last reserve of energy, yet she could only doze on the huge plane while Charles slept. She studied her husband adoringly. "You are the most adaptable, capable, kindest man in the whole world. Thank God for you and all you do for everyone. And please, Lord, heal Daddy," she whispered.

Once again, Edward met them at the airport and drove them on the motorway directly to the small community hospital where Mum sat beside Sean's bed, dozing in a chair.

Sean breathed irregular rasping sounds under an oxygen tent and connections of tubes. His skin appeared paper thin, his color white as the sheets, glistening with clammy perspiration.

Mum, half-asleep, jumped when she heard Beth and Charles enter the dimly lit room. Wearily, she rose and fell like a frightened, bewildered child into the comfort of her daughter's outstretched arms. They stood, clinging to each other for long, silent minutes.

"What time is it?" Mum asked, befuddled. "Oh, never mind. You're not on our time yet." How long had Mum kept her silent vigil? Her usually sleek silver hair had broken loose from its chignon, spilling about her shoulders, framing her gaunt face and hollow eyes.

Beth held her close for several more silent moments. "How is Daddy?" she asked gently.

"Hanging on by a mere snippet, love," Mum replied wearily. "The doctor thinks if he can make it through the next few hours, he will have passed the crisis. He's sleeping well right now. Let's go downstairs and get some tea."

Twenty minutes later when they returned to Sean's room, a kindly nurse hovered over him, taking his pulse and temperature.

"What's his condition?" Charles whispered.

"He opens his eyes now and then, but he's having a rough time of it, sir."

Sean's eyes fluttered. He recognized Beth and Charles. A sweet smile of contentment spread over his lips. His lids closed again, but the smile lingered. *What pleasant visions were going through his mind?* Beth wondered. Possibly he imagined a carousel, with his beautiful wife dancing on a white horse, his precious daughter rising up and down on a pink pony, and then as a beautiful bride in a gold chariot and Charles, her shining knight, on a bold prancer. His life had been wonderful. He had caught the golden ring and shared it with the ones he loved. A tear escaped and rolled down his illumined face as he whispered, "I'm coming, Jesus," and closed his weary eyes for the last time.

Beth and Charles exchanged startled glances, squeezing each other's hands in grateful acknowledgment at his words. Sean had never been an openly religious man, and Beth had long yearned for the assurance that he was a believer.

Mum's composure shattered. She turned to Beth, who enveloped her shaken mother in her arms, while her own heart felt ready to burst with grief. Then Mum pulled away and turned for the last time to her husband.

"You were always so good." She touched his cheek, then the nurse pulled a sheet over the white face. Mum sat down. "Let me sit beside him for just a few more minutes."

Beth and Charles left silently. Margaret Sheridan, such a private person, needed to say goodbye to her beloved alone.

Beth had tried valiantly to be strong for her mother. But in the corridor, she could weep deeply in her husband's arms for the father who had taught her to pass lightly over the ugly and mundane and cherish life's best and most beautiful.

"What will she do now?" Charles asked with concern while Beth's grief subsided.

"I don't know," Beth pulled a tissue from her purse and dabbed her eyes. "Mum never carried one iota of household responsibility. Daddy's purpose in life was to pamper her. He did everything, adoring her on a pedestal he fashioned of pure devotion for his beloved ballerina. I'm not even sure she knows how to write a check. He made every decision for her except in things having to do with ballet. There, she reigned as undisputed queen." Beth choked on the words as the tears began again.

"And you were the princess, equally adored," Charles added, tenderly stroking her hair.

"He spoiled Mum and me both. But I'm so grateful he taught me how to think. And yes, he always made me feel so special."

"Your father and mine didn't even live in the same universe," Charles sighed. "I loved Sean not only for who and what he was, but also for giving me the most wonderful wife in the world."

Beth smiled. "I loved the way he managed to leave the mundane to someone else while he went for the extraordinary. He'll be greatly missed, Charles. Especially by me and Mum."

In her heart she cried out, *Oh, Daddy, I wish you could have known Kerry was your granddaughter, but I know you loved her.*

Margaret Sheridan rejoined her family. She had wound her shimmering silver hair neatly into its classic chignon, powdered her nose, and appeared every ounce the stunning performer she had always been. "It's not necessary to stay here any longer," she stated matter-of-factly. "I've signed and done what is required. A stiff upper lip, and all that." But hers quivered.

"This great lady even cries with dignity," Charles whispered to Beth as he drove them the short distance to the coziness of her Hampstead home. Inside, the chimes on the entry clock struck four.

"Time for tea." Margaret began to busy herself with the teakettle.

"Here, let me do that," Beth insisted.

"Believe it or not, love, I can actually set a tea table these days. You two must be done in. How long have you been up?"

"Forever, it seems," Charles stepped in. "Almost thirty hours, I think."

Over the Wedgewood tea cups and biscuits, Mum's composure amazed them. Swallowing the lump in her throat, she blinked misty eyes and said, "There's something I know is on your minds. The English are not generally very religious. We're a private people about things like that. Different certainly than your Christian friends we've met who so openly talk about Jesus. Our churches aren't at all like yours, and often have little real meaning."

Beth nodded in agreement.

"What we've never told you is that years ago, at your wedding, Sean and I talked at some length with Josh and Hope," Mum continued, "and saw for ourselves what your Christian life is all about. When we came home, we didn't find a church like yours, but we did ask Christ into our lives."

A smile from deep within lit Beth's face.

"We've come to know a Reverend Wilton, a dedicated Christian, and his wife, Emily, who are changing lives here in our little Hampstead on the Heath. He will officiate at your father's service. You may not believe it, but with God's help, I can and will survive without Sean."

Tears of joy spilled down Beth's face. Charles's eyes were also full. "Oh, Mum," Beth cried, kneeling at her mother's chair, "we're so happy to hear that. Praise God!" She laid her head on her mother's knee like a small child, feeling a greater comfort from her than she had ever known before.

"Now," Mum said with newfound authority, "you both look dreadful. Mattie's like another Tillie. She's popping in to prepare supper. In the meantime, you take yourselves upstairs for a nap. If you don't wake up for supper, not to worry. You need your sleep."

St. John-at-Hampstead on Church Row overflowed with people who came from around the Heath and around the world to pay homage to their friend Sean Sheridan. Writers, artists, composers mingled with lords, ladies, earls, London shopkeepers, and the whole of the Royal Ballet school staff. News of Sean's passing traveled quickly among art circles, with telegrams of condolence pouring in from throughout Europe and the United States.

The altar at the west end of St. John's appeared to be solid flowers. After the service the family found comfort in their beauty and the names of the loving senders. Mum studied the card on a huge easel massed with roses, the largest arrangement of all. "Who is Count Cabriollini?" she asked. "I don't believe I know him, but he surely must be an admirer of Sean's."

While Charles explained Sean's and his own relationship with the Count, Beth wondered if Roberto would permit any major happening in her life to pass unnoticed. Would she forever be jolted with his turning up unexpectedly? Maybe by now she should learn to expect that he would somehow always find his way into her private life. His lavish remembrances, though bordering on the ostentatious, seemed devoid of guile. They appeared to be an expression of a need to have a part in the one thing wealth couldn't buy—a loving family.

"How does she do it?" Charles often asked during the month they stayed with Mum to make sure her affairs were in order. "I hear her crying in her room at night, but I'm totally amazed at how well she's adjusting. I think we can—and should—go home soon. Let her get on with her life."

"I think you're right," Beth quietly agreed. "The life of a ballerina and one who's taught the disciplines of ballet all her life is at least 60 percent determination—the old 'show must go on' doggedness. What's beautiful is that now she says God gives her the strength to carry on."

"I never would have believed any of this."

"Neither would I," Beth smiled. "She's still grieving, but I think she's pretty pleased at finding a competence she didn't know she had. I can see now that it wasn't that she couldn't take care of herself, but that it gave Daddy pleasure to do everything for her. Since you're satisfied she's financially cared for, I thoroughly trust the staff to run the business and the bookkeepers to pay the bills as usual. Mattie runs the house, and Mum can teach ballet until the day she dies. I agree, I think she's ready for us to go home. I'll talk to her tomorrow. Then you can make plane reservations."

*   *   *

Kerry and Bob waited for them at the arrival gate at San Francisco airport while the whole Bay area sweltered in a heat wave, rare even for August. They held up a banner, "Welcome Home."

"We missed you!" Kerry flung out her arms.

"Hi, honeymooners, how was Hawaii?" Charles laughed. "We loved your postcards, and thanks for the encouraging letters," Beth added.

"Hawaii was wonderful. That week in tropical paradise seems like a long time ago though, what with all . . . " Bob stopped abruptly.

"All what?" Beth asked with apprehension.

"Mom went into the hospital the day after we came home from Hawaii," Kerry said. "She couldn't take any more chemo. She couldn't eat and had lost more weight. Surgery's out of the question. The cancer's too widespread, so they gave her blood transfusions and intravenous feeding. She's a little stronger now, but. . . . " Kerry's voice broke and her thick lashes hung heavy with tears.

"What's the prognosis, Bob?" Charles asked, afraid to hear the answer. "And where is she?"

"It's a matter of time, a few months. Maybe longer. She wanted to come home. She insisted on no more treatments or life support, just wants to prepare for her 'graduation day,' as she calls it, with those she loves. 'Home' right now is at Rosehaven. Tillie insisted you'd want her there. She needs air conditioning, which they don't have in San Jose. It's been so hot, you wouldn't believe it. When it cools off she'll go home."

Charles swallowed hard and turned to Beth. "The luggage should be off by now. Let's head down there and they can bring up the car."

* * *

Tillie, Jimmy, Cookie and the rest of the staff who had heard the Cadillac come through the gates lined the driveway to greet them.

Charles broke the tension by saying, "This reminds me of a TV commercial, where the lord of the manor returns with great ceremony. But I don't recall the product."

"In this scene we'll caption it 'loyalty.' They've been wonderful," Bob praised.

Beth saw welcoming enthusiasm intermingled with anguish on their faces, as though apologizing for a sad homecoming and one sorrow heaped upon another. They paused to receive a greeting from each one, especially Tillie, and then went upstairs to Hope's room.

The fragrance of roses, which Jimmy brought fresh every day, filled the light, airy room. Beth had furnished it in peach and yellow prints, especially as a guest room for Hope and Josh.

Josh sat by the side of her bed, reading the Psalms as Hope absorbed the beautiful words with closed eyes.

"Hey, look who's here!" Josh stood to throw his arms around them.

Hope tried to sit up and failed, but her smile lit up their hearts with her inner joy and courage. "Oh, I'm so happy to see you, precious friends!"

Beth held back the shock and pain that threatened to overcome her at the sight of her dearest friend. Only dull wisps of the brown hair that had once been luxuriously thick and wavy remained. She forced a smile almost as bright as Hope's and went to the bed to hold her pitifully thin body. Hope welcomed those comforting arms as Mum had in her hour of need.

"Why didn't you call and tell us Hope was in the hospital, Josh?" Charles asked.

"Because I wouldn't let him," Hope smiled. "You had enough on your minds, and do I look neglected? I'm living the life of luxury here." Hope's voice lowered to above a whisper. "It's been so hot out there—and so cool and comfortable in here. Tillie and everyone has been so kind." She took a deep breath. "Jimmy's sweet. He comes up and shares his favorite verses in the Bible with me every day. I'm spoiled. When it cools down, we'll go home where we belong."

"Hope, you belong right here where we can keep an eye on you. Don't talk about going anywhere," Charles was firm.

Suddenly, Hope's brief brilliance died, like a Fourth of July sparkler at the end of its blaze. Josh sprang to her side. "Say good night, folks. Our little lady had better get some sleep."

"May Bob and I tuck her in, Dad?" Kerry asked. "I know you all want to talk."

Tillie had iced tea and lemon cookies for them in the garden room, so fresh with palms and flowering plants that it belied the heat outside.

The three friends searched for words, but there were none to express the heartache they shared. Josh opened his mouth, but Charles said, "Before you say anything, Josh, we want you and Hope to stay until . . . until . . . well, I mean indefinitely, so we can be near, with plenty of people to help. Hope seems happy here, and . . . " his voice broke.

"Thanks, Charles," Josh said softly. "Rosehaven is truly a refuge for us now. Hope does have some good days, and we'll have a sweet time, I know we will. I may put the house up for sale. I'll need to pay the hospital and doctor bills. Our health insurance won't cover all this, and I couldn't live there alone."

"Give the bills to me, would you please, Josh? And don't list the house just yet. Let's pray for a miracle."

Tillie interrupted before Josh could answer.

"Telephone, Miss Beth. It's Miss Merribelle. Shall I tell her you just got home and you'll call her later?"

"No thank you, Tillie, I'll take it." The last fifteen hours of traveling and Hope's heartbreaking condition had left her exhausted and shaky. *But I'll have to talk to Merribelle sooner or later,* she thought.

"Welcome home, sugar. We missed ya'll. Was your Daddy's funeral nice?" Merribelle didn't wait for an answer. "He had a good long life, and you just can't ask for more than that—isn't that right, honey? How's your mama? She'll be fine. Ah'll wager she's strong, just like you. What Ah'm wondering about is League's annual garden party at Rosehaven—ordinarily, it would be in a few weeks, but ya'll left us in the lurch, leavin' so quick-like, an' of course we wouldn't put out any publicity without checkin' with you first. But it's all ready to go but the date, an' Ah'm sure, sugar, your flowers will still be magnificent no matter when we have it. That's all right to go ahead, isn't it? If not, we'll be in a pickle, sweetie."

Beth stammered, grasping for tact. "It's—it's good to hear from you, Merribelle, but we just came home. I'll need a little time to think about it. My dear friend Hope is terminally ill. They're staying with us, and—"

Merribelle interrupted, "There really isn't time to think long, honey. Ah was just positive you and Charles wouldn't let us down. You know the committee does most of the work."

Beth stiffened, thinking of Hope upstairs. Her very life depended on every moment of peace and quiet. Merribelle's affair would involve the bustle of caterers, musicians and the crowds of people the garden party always attracted. "My first obligation is to my friend who's here with us, Merribelle. We probably won't have her with us next year, and—"

Merribelle interrupted again, "Ah want you to know, Ah'm terribly disappointed, darlin'. It's only one little old day—plus the set-up the day before and dismantling after."

"Every day is crucial when they're numbered," Beth felt impatience creeping into her tone. "I feel it's the right thing to say no this time."

"Well, Ah think you just don't consider League too important right now."

"Not as important as my dearest friend."

"Well, excuse me, honey. Ah thought Ah was your dearest friend. Goodbye."

"You're certainly one of them, Merribelle. I'm sorry you don't understand my priorities . . . Merribelle?" No use continuing, she was talking to the dial tone.

By late September, Hope's strength and blood count had improved remarkably. On her better days she rested on a lounge on the terrace overlooking the vast gardens. She even acquired a little suntan, and occasionally walked about the grounds with Beth.

"We've been in paradise, but now I think it's time to go home," she announced one day.

"It's been perfect for Kerry and Bob to live in our little house, to care for the yard and houseplants, and it's saved them rent," Josh said. "But as long as they're there to help, I think Hope's right—we should go home."

"I'm not sure we can bear to let go of you. We're going to miss you. Especially Josh's jokes," Charles said.

But what they would all miss most were the evening talks. Usually in the peacefulness of dusk they dipped into delicious imaginings of what eternity would be like within heaven's gates. They shared what they'd read of people's out-of-body experiences: of a peach and golden glow, rare and extraordinary as on an autumn afternoon that bathed streets and walls of pearl and jasper; bodies transformed from the deterioration of this world, made new and perfect and without pain. And most wonderful of all—to be forever in the presence of the Master and believers they'd loved so dearly on earth. Sometimes they listed those who had gone before that they most looked forward to seeing: St. Paul, C. S. Lewis, Sean. . . .

Thanksgiving day that year seemed more blessed and bountiful than ever before. The very walls of Rosehaven rang with praise that the ravages of Hope's cancer were miraculously in remission. Ruth came from New York, Annie and Ali from Carmel, and Mum all the way from London to stay through Christmas.

After dinner, Bob ceremoniously tapped a crystal goblet requesting their attention, and raised up Kerry to stand beside him. "We give special thanksgiving," he said, "to announce that—we're going to have a baby!"

Under the applause and joyful congratulations Hope whispered, "God, may I live to see this grandchild."

17

Early one drizzly January morning, over coffee and the newspaper, Beth studied her husband's weary face. During the past seven months they'd experienced the emotions of Kerry's wedding, Sean's death, Hope's remission from cancer, and Kerry's joyful news. Then came League's annual Christmas Charity Ball at Rosehaven, Mum's wonderful visit through the holidays, the Townsends' elaborate corporate Christmas banquet, and countless festivities with family and friends.

Thoughts of what the coming year held in store were on hold. Charles's responsibilities as CEO and president of the Townsend corporations were enough in themselves. The deep lines of fatigue on his face had escaped Beth's notice until now. His hand trembled as he held his coffee cup.

"Charles," she interrupted his scrutiny of the financial page, "I've never seen you look so utterly exhausted. We should take a month off and get away somewhere. Where would you like to go?"

"Nowhere, right now. I'm up to my eyeballs trying to wind up that inner-city project in Chicago. Most of my architectural staff aren't as thrilled about this as I am. There's still only a handful of us in the whole industry who care. Designing low-cost housing that won't fall down in a couple of years isn't high priority." He paused, "I really look that bad for a fifty-five-year-old, huh?"

"I'm afraid I've become accustomed to your tired face," she playfully jabbed. "But yes, I'm concerned. You've been pushing yourself too hard. How do you feel? How's your blood pressure?"

"I don't know how my blood pressure is, but you know me better than I know myself. I think more about what I'm doing than how my body feels. Truthfully, my body feels worn out. Maybe in the next couple of weeks I can turn Chicago over to Richard and Tim. They've really soared in these ten years with me. They're both brilliant. I can't be too far away, but I'd love to go to Carmel. Wouldn't it be nice to just sleep, walk on the beach and golf?"

"Well, let's do it, darling."

A wet winter rain drenched the whole Monterey peninsula their first two days in Carmel. Charles slept through most of it. Secure and warm in their hideaway high on the cliffs, Beth contentedly painted a moody gray-green sea. She captured the spray of the surf dashing and crashing the rocky coastline with such realism, Charles told her he could feel the salty sting.

The evening fire spit and blazed, oblivious to the pelting rain that splashed the window panes. "This is the most relaxed I've felt in months," Charles stretched, "sitting here in my pajamas with you waiting on me. Did you make this fabulous beef stew?"

"Me?" Beth laughed. "I wish. Cookie and Tillie packed up tons of yummy dinners, just for the two of us. We don't ever have to go out unless we find some quiet, romantic restaurant we can't resist."

"It can't get much more quiet and romantic than this, can it? If I died right now, I'd die a happy man. What did I ever do to deserve you?"

"You lavish me with affection. You appreciate me. There are millions of women out there who would give anything to be cherished that way."

The telephone had an especially unwelcome ring, but Beth answered it.

"It's for you. It's Richard," Beth groaned, then carried the dishes off to the kitchen.

When she returned with the coffee, Charles said, "Richard and Tim are hung up on a structural technicality in the design. They're coming down in the morning. We'll do a little work and then I invited them to stay over and play a round of golf the next day. The weather should clear up by then."

Beth looked skeptical. "What's a *little* work?"

Charles ignored her question. "I'll call Rob Hall and see if he can play with us to make a foursome. Do you remember meeting him at the Cypress Point Club members' party?"

"He's a cardiologist, isn't he?"

"The best. Is that plan all right with you?"

"All but the work part. You're really pressing it. But what can I say?"

"Say, 'I love you, Charles,' before I fall asleep again."

"I love you, I love you, I love you," she whispered into his ear. "Good night, my darling."

Charles greeted Richard and Tim exuberantly. "Isn't this a gorgeous morning? Who ever thought the sky would be so clear and blue after last night?" Charles marveled. "I'll bring coffee into the study. Let's go to work, men."

It never seemed to matter to Charles when he was bone-tired. If anyone needed him, if there was a problem, a design to be perfected, it became an open invitation to move in and solve it with his whole heart. Beth thought his capacity to give had a selfless quality she had never seen in another human being, not even her father.

"How's the work coming? It's lunchtime." Beth interrupted the three men laboring over plans in Charles's study. "I'm going to insist you take a break. Here are some turkey sandwiches with the trimmings for you."

"Thanks, sweetheart. We've come up with a revolutionary elevation. Look at this preliminary rendering. Functional without being ugly. What do you think?"

"I like it." Beth turned to leave, then hesitated. "But don't work too long today. . . . "

"We won't," Charles quickly said.

Richard caught the doubt in Beth's raised eyebrows and attempted to reassure her. "You wouldn't believe how the obstacles come down at the stroke of the genius's hand, Mrs. Townsend."

"He's the master, all right," Tim patted Charles's back. "It's a privilege to work with your husband."

Beth went back to her canvas in total agreement. She wondered how much longer Charles would drive himself. At seven that evening she announced dinner, insisting they quit, finished or not.

Charles flashed her a victorious smile. "It's basically done. I predict this concept in large-scale project housing will be the prototype for years to come."

"Right," Tim added. "Its purity of design flows from the first basic law of architecture—form follows function."

Charles spoke to Richard and Tim in a fatherly fashion around the dinner table. "As a boy, I spent summers in Europe. In those impressionable years I ground out thousands of drawings of classical buildings. But it was in Rome, where so many architectural intentions live together, that my understanding of design really developed."

Beth enjoyed the pleasure her husband so obviously derived from his work.

"Throughout my career, I've 'had more than my share of triumphs.' Recognize the quote from the latest article in the trade magazine?" he said with a sly smile. "Beth, I want you especially to know, I've gained more personal satisfaction from this achievement than any other single design. To my colleagues," he beamed, raising a toast with his water glass.

"Wrong, Charles. Tim and I agree with everything you've said, but we can't be called your colleagues. You deserve the credit. You brought out the best in each of us. We were underinspired and over our heads. The inspiration came from you."

"May God forgive me if I'm merely an idealist who only lectures about building for those who have no hope of owning a decent place to raise families," Charles's tone became quite serious. "If this project eliminates even one dreadful slum area in the deteriorating inner cities in this country, our work will not have been in vain."

Charles stood, shook their hands and hugged Beth for her patience with his dissertation over coffee. "Tomorrow we conquer the golf course."

Exhaustion was written all over his face, but even in bed Charles couldn't stop talking.

"You look so tired. We should go to sleep now, darling," Beth cuddled in his arms.

"I'm okay, just wound up." He squeezed her tighter, kissing her cheek. "I was just thinking how amazing God is. He keeps pouring out His blessings to us so we can be really creative with what He's given us. This housing project has been proof of that. All my money couldn't buy me the satisfaction that doing this project has given me." He laughed. "And now, darling, you're right. I've got to get some sleep, or I won't be able to hit the ball tomorrow."

Over breakfast in the exclusive clubhouse, Charles explained not quite apologetically to his associates, "Cypress Point might be a little stuffy, but the course is absolutely magnificent. You'll enjoy Ron Hall. He's about a nine handicap, and a super guy. He'll meet us on the first tee."

He turned to Beth, "Sweetheart, enjoy your bike ride. Say hello to Annie for me. We'll see you at home this afternoon. Thanks for having breakfast with us guys."

Beth turned to Richard and Tim. "Have a great game. And take it easy on him."

"Are you kidding? He's the low handicapper. He'll kill us on this course," Tim winced.

Pedaling along the Seventeen Mile Drive always gave Beth a sense of awesome wonder at the beauty of God's creation. She was thankful that man had set apart this area to preserve rather than plunder.

She hadn't seen Annie since Thanksgiving, yet their friendship had the resilience of resuming the warmth of only yesterday. At the little French cafe, Annie shared how proud she was of Ali's career and his self-confidence even without the example of a father figure. They talked about almost everything under the sun until it was once again time for their lives to take separate paths.

The sea air and pungent blend of pine and cypress expanded Beth's lungs. She lowered the bike's gears for the uphill grade and pedaled toward their castle on the cliffs. Around the bend she saw three figures, Ron Hall, Richard and Tim, waiting at the shaded entrance. As their pained grave faces came into view, her heart lurched in panic. Where was Charles? What had happened? Her mind raced faster than she could pedal. Breathlessly she spun toward the gates at the edge of the narrow road.

Their eyes met. Instantly Beth knew her loss. Charles would not be there to meet her—ever.

"He had a massive coronary, Beth. I'm so sorry," Dr. Hall said. "I used every emergency skill I had. The paramedics responded with heroic efforts. We did everything we could. We couldn't save him."

Dr. Hall swallowed his sorrow with an urgency to tell Beth the rest. "Beth, in his last flickering moments of life, I wish you could have seen the expression on Charles's face. We saw a man totally at peace. He even smiled at us. No fear, no fright in the face of death."

It was merciful Beth had not seen the moment of cardiac arrest and the incredible pain as the heart literally exploded within the body.

Richard and Tim, stunned by grief and shock, stared compassionately at Beth.

"Mrs. Townsend—Beth—your husband had a quality I've long admired," Richard choked out the words. "He was a man's man, with the strength of steel in his convictions, yet so kind. I've never met anyone like him."

"Thank you, Richard," Beth whispered.

"I'll never forget how he faced death so peaceably," he added. "Surely you must know why. Someday, I'd appreciate if you'd tell me. That's what I want in my life."

"Not now," Tim added reverently, "but I'd also like you to tell me the secret of Charles's life."

"There isn't any secret," Beth replied calmly. "Charles loved Jesus with his whole heart, and that makes a person different from the inside out. It would please him very much for me to share that with both of you."

Her mind stumbled. Under other circumstances she would have freely illustrated why Charles's relationship with Christ made him different from other men. Now she must abruptly use the past tense, and she couldn't assimilate the shock. *This isn't real,* she kept telling herself.

All was a bewildered blur as Beth made the sad calls to Annie, to Tillie and their household, and to Josh, Hope, Kerry, Bob, Merribelle and especially Mum. She had dreaded to call Mum, and encouraged her not to come. It was too soon, her own grief still too raw. She quickly threw a few things together and prepared for what she dreaded as the longest, loneliest drive home she'd ever known.

Even back within the refuge of Rosehaven Beth kept thinking, *This can't be real. It didn't happen.* But alone in bed at night, engulfed in the exquisite beauty of the mansion where Charles's design genius lived in every detail, her heart broke. She ached to be able to reach out and touch him, to be held in his arms.

The huge sanctuary and halls of First Church of San Francisco, where Charles had invested so much of himself, thronged with those who mourned the death of this good man. He had deeply touched many of their lives, and they celebrated his memory.

A massive arrangement of roses, gardenias and orchids dominated all others in the immense bower of flowers surrounding the altar. After the service Beth was astonished as she read the card: "My deepest sympathy, *Bella Rosa* . . . Roberto."

She knew the news of Charles's death had quickly reached around the world. Even so, it was as though Roberto again had a hotline on her life. No major event went unnoticed. Flowers had become a pattern, marking his awareness. He did not intend to be forgotten. What part of her life would he seek now with Charles gone? Beth shook the thought away.

Later, at the cemetery in the valley Charles so loved near Rosehaven, up on the knoll next to the tiny unnoticed grave of his infant son, private services were held for only the closest personal friends and business associates. After the brief graveside ceremony, on Beth's behalf, Josh invited whoever wished to come to Rosehaven.

As people walked down the knoll to their cars, Beth paused for a few moments alone. "I'm going to miss you," she whispered. She picked a rose from one of the floral arrangements to put in the memory box Charles had given her. "A rose to remember, my darling." The tears flowed freely. She didn't want to leave his side. She wasn't sure she was ready for life without him.

Beth looked to the clouds and prayed a simple prayer, "Lord, You've worked miracles before. Work one now in my broken heart." A warm peace flooded through her body, consoling her deepest grief. She tenderly blew a kiss to her beloved and walked down the knoll.

A trail of cars wound through the gates of Rosehaven, as they had countless other times on happy occasions. Once inside, Beth became the consoler, the encourager of her faith to the mourners, to the wonder of even Hope and Josh. Her tears flowed along with theirs, yet she had a story of remembrance of Charles's special friendship with each person. She realized her strength was an answer to her graveside prayer.

Merribelle came rushing to Beth with Henry trying to keep up. She flung her arms around her and wailed with red swollen eyes, "Mah poor darlin'. Mah heart bleeds for you, deah. Ah don't know how you will ever get through this. It's a tragedy. Ah can't believe it. Whatevah are you goin' to do without him, sweetie?" Merribelle blotted her eyes frantically, but couldn't hold back the tears. "Ah know Ah should have some words of comfawt fah you, honey, but Ah'm devastated. Simply devastated."

Beth took her friend in her arms, hugging her close. But what comfort could she give to one who couldn't grasp the concept of eternal life and Jesus Christ, who made it possible? When death is all there is, when there is nothing beyond the grave, when heaven is only a figure of speech, there is no comfort.

Richard and Tim had Josh cornered by the fireplace, shooting questions. They sought to understand how Charles had only slipped out of his body into another life and continued to exist in a place for believers called heaven. Richard asked, "Did I correctly understand what you said at the graveside service? Will Christ really come into a person's life and change his old ways?"

Tim didn't wait for Josh to answer. "And was this belief of Charles's the core of his gentle, caring way of life? It was so incredible for a man of such wealth and power." Beth overheard the barrage of questions as she came to join them.

"May I answer?" she asked. "Yes, to all of the above. And you've come to the right man with your questions. Josh knows the answers." She left to talk with others, knowing Richard and Tim were in good hands.

Josh found Beth a little later. "Charles would be thrilled," he said. "Richard, Tim and I went into the privacy of the library. Because of their admiration for Charles's life, they both made a personal commitment to Jesus Christ."

"Oh, I can just see Charles's face. He probably knows and is so glad for them." Beth squeezed Josh's hand, her eyes filled with joyful tears.

While Josh talked with departing guests, Hope brought Beth a cup of tea. "You must be drained, physically and emotionally," she said quietly, joining Beth on the sofa in front of the fire. "Charles would have loved this gathering today."

A moment of silence fell between them as they listened to the soft popping of the fire.

"Beth," Hope ventured at last, "those months when we were preparing for my own 'graduation day' were a time I'll always cherish. I'm grateful we said our goodbyes on this earth and everything we wanted to share with one another. Charles died so unexpectedly," Hope paused, her eyes brimming with tears, "I hope there was nothing between you left unsaid."

"There wasn't," Beth smiled, then added thoughtfully, "He'd become so wonderfully open through the years. Charles didn't know how to hold any of himself back. He gave everything there was to give . . . and we said it all, every day of our lives."

A log slipping in the fireplace sent a spray of sparks upward, breaking Beth out of her reverie. She turned and looked more closely at her friend. "Hope, are you back on chemo? You look—different."

"The doctors want to try it again," she sighed. "God will let me meet our grandchild. That's all I asked, remember?"

Beth put her hand on top of Hope's as the two women whose lives had been so tightly interwoven for more than thirty years sat together in silence before the glowing embers of a dying fire. *The sweet sorrow of another parting may come again sooner than I can bear,* Beth thought. *God, help me, please.*

What does one do after the people leave and everyone else's days return to normal? Beth wondered. Their bedroom felt so lonely, the four-poster so huge and empty.

Charles had always insisted on a purpose for Rosehaven beyond their own pleasure. Yet to hold the charity balls and parties without the congenial host would be utterly unendurable. However, she would hate to deprive the League and the other charities of the hundreds of thousands of dollars from these established annual events. Charles would never abandon support for scholarships for promising students of all the arts. The Rose Show wasn't as difficult, and she would be loathe to deprive Jimmy of his earned glory.

Only God knew the purposes He had for her and Rosehaven, she decided. It was too soon to think about it.

In the meantime, the workload at the House of New Hope could consume every day for the rest of her life. She and the other lay counselors who worked with pastors and psychologists felt great encouragement in helping the increasing numbers who came. Daily they had opportunities to counsel women with the alternatives to abortion.

Everywhere Beth looked she saw needs. The street people were like masses of displaced persons who ran amok in a confused society. Most of her contemporaries had turned their backs on the system of values that molded her life.

Rich, poor, or somewhere in that great in-between, there seemed no regard for absolutes. No time-proven, clear-cut rights and wrongs to trust, to guide and protect them. Instead, society largely chose the horrendous uncertainty of doing that which feels good at the moment. People were like Pinocchio and the children ensnared in the misrepresentation of "Pleasure Island," with similar results.

In relatively few years, Beth had sadly observed the rapid increase of wrecked lives. They gathered in the heart of the cities around the world. In San Francisco, they littered the streets like the flotsam and jetsam along the beaches of the Bay. But when a massive cleanup is in order, the problem is always, where to begin? *Yes, there are more than enough places to direct my energies,* Beth thought.

For the next few months the greatest joy of Beth's life came with thinking about Kerry's baby and buying the layette of tiny cuddly things. She yearned to tell her friends she'd be a grandmother soon. She wanted to have a "brag book" like theirs. But the secret of long ago could never be broken. It must go on forever. So be it. She would be content to brag about her grand-godchild.

Charles's sudden death left Kerry burdened with a terrible sadness and times of depression. Beth certainly knew "Charlie" was one of Kerry's favorite people on earth. Seeing Beth without him must be unbearable. Kerry had never lost anyone close, not even a pet. A few months ago, Beth thought her daughter was somewhat prepared for Hope's inevitable death, but now she seemed far from it.

"It's strange, Bif," Kerry had said to Beth on one of their baby-shopping excursions into the city, "life has to teach its own lessons. There are several widows I've tried to comfort in the Bible study I took over for Mom. I know God's words and promises are real, but it still hurts so very much, doesn't it?"

"I don't think we should try to deny grief, Kerry," Beth explained. "I miss Charles, and sometimes I cry. But at the same time I cherish memories of him—things so sweet they bring pain. It's helping to heal me. It's a process. The trick of it is to trust God to get you through each day. It's learning not to stay too long in one phase. To know that tomorrow will be one day easier—to cherish the richness of the past while getting on with the future, looking forward to new things. It helps to know Charles is alive, already in the future, probably aware of what we're doing, and one day we'll see him again."

Kerry nodded in silent understanding.

"That brings us to happy thoughts," Beth lightened the mood. "It's only four more weeks, isn't it? You still look awfully small."

"Five," Kerry grinned, patting her tummy. "I love to feel his or her little kick, and pat him and tell him I love him. Sometimes I even sing to him," she confided.

Springtime at Rosehaven had never been so beautiful. The mature yew trees and everything that blossomed and bloomed over the lush acres of Rosehaven flourished. The investment of more than two decades of nurturing yielded an abundant return. Gorgeous lavender blossoms and the heady fragrance of lilacs followed hundreds of hyacinths, daffodils and tulips in a profusion of color.

"This is the most beautiful spring ever," Beth said to Jimmy. "I wish Charles could see it." *Perhaps he can,* she smiled to herself. *And maybe in heaven there are flowers so beautiful we can't even imagine.*

"The roses look like they could all be winners this year, Miss Beth. And . . . I miss him too," Jimmy comforted.

In loving admiration he had observed this great lady and understood her need to be out among the roses in solitude. He had watched her pinching back buds before the first blooms, talking and listening to God.

She paused along the garden path, looking squarely into his now mature face, so confident, worlds apart from the tragic boy who broke into her life so many years before.

"Can you possibly know how proud I am of you, Jimmy? You've become a precious part of my life."

"It's all because of you . . . and God, of course. Heaven knows where I'd be, in jail somewhere, maybe, if you hadn't had the courage to tell me about Jesus."

"God and I would be happy to take all the credit," she smiled, "but Jimmy, the decision to become what you are was yours. You've worked hard, and you're no longer a scared boy, but a fine man. Don't you need more of a life of your own now? A wife, or a family? We could add on to the cottage."

Jimmy dug his toe into the ground and blushed like a boy again. "I have taken this young woman out for Cokes after Wednesday night church a few times. Shelly's a single mom with a little boy and works a lot, so she's pretty busy. We'll see. But as always, thanks for caring."

Beth's thoughts turned back to Hope and wondered about her reaction to yesterday's chemo. It was difficult even to pick up the phone—but she had to know. She thought of Job and his series of troubles. She knew her own season of sorrow had not yet ended.

18

With clammy hands, Beth clutched the phone, waiting for Josh to answer. "How's our girl?" She struggled to mask her fear. "How did she do with the chemo yesterday?"

"She's feeling rotten right now, awfully nauseated. She's scheduled to have a few more if she can take it, but she's still smiling. I'm really worried about Kerry. I'm afraid she's more upset than what she's showing."

"How can I help? What do you need?"

"Your prayers. Pray that Hope will live to see the baby. That's what keeps her going. . . . " His voice broke. "I'll talk to you later, Beth. She's calling me."

"Josh, may I come down? I could take a motel room nearby." Their tiny home was already overcrowded with Kerry and Bob there in Kerry's little room. Beth wanted desperately to be available, to do something to alleviate the hardships of this critical time for her dearest friends.

"Thanks, no. Kerry's especially possessive with Hope right now, insists on doing everything. Bible study is over for the summer, so she has the time, but I'm not convinced she has the energy. I certainly will call you, though. Beth, I have to go."

"God," Beth whispered, "please let our dear Hope live to see the baby. Better yet, I still believe in the miracle of healing."

*   *   *

Beth crammed the next week with longer hours at the center. She pored over the details for the Rose Show and annual League benefit garden party at Rosehaven to keep her mind occupied. The void of Charles's support left an ache that could be filled only by the comfort of her Bible and frequent phone calls to Hope.

On a warm Friday afternoon, Kerry answered, and Beth immediately caught the weariness in her voice. She felt so separated from her daughter. Beth suffered the same deep pain Kerry suffered over Hope's illness. Kerry's devotion to her adopted mother was never more evident than now.

"You sound exhausted, love," Beth told her daughter. "I'm frustrated with wanting to help. What can I do?"

"Bif, I do need help. Dad has had to spend more time at the airfield because they're getting ready to fly a medical team to Mexico. Bob is frantically trying to keep up and study for finals. Mom is weaker by the day." She began to cry.

"Kerry, listen to me. I'd like all of you to pack up your necessities. I'll send Max down in the big car for Hope, or even an ambulance if she'd be more comfortable. I'd feel so much better if we were all here together, so we could support one another. I'm totally out of it, while you're all struggling. I can't stand it."

"I love you, Bif. You've always been there when I needed you, and we all need you now. I'll talk to Dad and Bob."

The following afternoon, an entourage arrived at Rosehaven. An ambulance bringing Hope with Josh beside her, Max chauffeuring everyone's luggage while Kerry napped in the spacious backseat, and Bob driving his Volkswagen. That night, Kerry alarmed everyone at dinner with signs of early labor, more than three weeks ahead of her due date. She still looked much too small to deliver a full-term baby. Beth phoned Annie with descriptive accounts of the symptoms. "Call her doctor, and expect a premature delivery," she said. "Better to be prepared than worry about a false alarm."

Bob asked Beth to go with them as he drove Kerry to the hospital in nearby Atherton. Kerry was examined and admitted. "We're going to try to hold this baby off for a few more weeks. Let's get her into a room, at least for a day or so, and see what we can do," Dr. Aldridge advised. "I'll be nearby if you need me," he assured them.

More intense contractions began about 10:00, coming at three-minute intervals by 4:00 A.M. The nurse said, "It looks like the baby's coming, ready or not."

The contractions were even closer and more difficult when Dr. Aldridge returned at 8:00 A.M. to check on Kerry and his other new mothers. Kerry was pale, weakened by the long hours of labor. Dr. Aldridge wore a look of concern. "This little one seems to be in a posterior position. We'll have to turn it around. Kerry, get on your knees and rock back and forth. I know you're tired, but that usually does it."

Bob never left her side. The weeks of Lamaze training for natural childbirth hadn't prepared them for this sort of situation. For the first time, the young couple realized the reality of the term "labor."

Dr. Aldridge continually monitored the baby's heartbeat, concerned that it might not be strong enough to endure the difficulties of being born. At last it reached the proper position, and at 10:22 A.M. a four-pound, six-ounce baby boy, whom they named Theodore Joshua Charles Daniels, came into the world.

No bigger than a baby doll, deep purplish pink, a frown creasing his tiny brow, with barely the energy to cry, he was placed immediately in an incubator. He looked beautiful to Kerry, Bob and Beth, who all breathed a prayer of relief. Kerry's forehead glistened with beads of perspiration, but at last she could rest.

The relieved father and grand-godmother waited until the 2 o'clock visiting hours to come back to see baby "Teddy" and his mama. Kerry had talked several times to Josh and Hope on the phone, describing their newborn grandson, assuring them he was out of danger.

"Dr. Aldridge says he'll have to stay here in the incubator until he reaches five pounds, but we both survived the ordeal," Kerry told her parents. "They do wonders with preemies these days, and he has all his parts in the right places so don't you worry. I love you, Mom and Dad."

Hope's lip quivered with emotion the day Kerry came home from the hospital without the baby. Her disappointment in not being able to hold him now nearly overwhelmed her as her strength faded with each day. Yet she hadn't lost her sweet, patient smile and she didn't complain.

Another two weeks went by. Hope still clung to life, determined to see her grandson. Although Teddy hadn't quite reached five pounds, he was gaining steadily. Dr. Aldridge decided he was progressing nicely and, under the circumstances, could quite safely be released from hospital care.

Kerry and Bob especially were exhausted going back and forth to the hospital, and kept worrying about the formidable mountain of bills.

Beth repeatedly assured them, "The last thing I want you to think about is the hospital bill. I'll take care of it. I have a stake in Teddy's life too, you know," although they didn't fully understand her meaning. "You know it's what Charlie would do, Kerry," Beth mustered a smile and a wink.

"You two have been like second parents, always there, always loving me," Kerry gave Beth a hug. "How can we ever repay you?"

Max drove the new little family home from the hospital, smiling all the way and beaming as if he were a proud uncle. Bob nestled his tiny son in his arms as though he were made of delicate crystal, not too sure he wouldn't break. Kerry glowed with a joy she'd never known. She was going to love being a mother.

Meanwhile, at Hope's insistence, Beth swirled the sparse wisps of hair as becomingly as possible around her friend's thin face. She smoothed color onto pale cheeks, adding a soft peach shade of lipstick.

"I need to look good when I meet our grandson, or I might frighten the lil' fella," she laughed. "Help me sit up a little more, will you please? And get the camera. I want a picture of him. Try and make me look as beautiful as possible, so someday you can show him his Granny Sterling and he won't go 'ughhh.'"

"I'll cuddle and coddle him for the both of us," Beth promised tenderly. Remembering how radiantly lovely Hope had been, she turned the other way to hide the tears. "Josh is coming up with the video camera too."

A few minutes later, Bob bustled excitedly into Hope's sunny room, ushering in Kerry with their little bundle asleep in her arms.

"Teddy, you've met everyone in your family except your grandmother," she cooed to her baby, "and here she is." Kerry kissed Hope's forehead, carefully placing Teddy into the waiting arms.

"Oh, you're sweet, so adorable, little one," Hope couldn't hold back the tears. "You don't know how happy I am to meet you. Did you get his face, Josh?"

Josh focused on Hope and Teddy, catching their expressions for several minutes, then panned the room with Beth, Tillie, Bob and Kerry clustered around Hope, gently rocking her tiny treasure in her arms.

Suddenly Hope felt weak from a combination of nervous anticipation and the delicious excitement of the moment. "Okay, baby, go to Grammy Beth," Hope said, a new tiredness in her voice. "She'll help Mommy and Daddy take good care of you."

Gently lifting the baby, Beth crooned, "Come on, love," while Kerry and Josh eased Hope into a resting position.

"You come back and see me a little later, Teddy, after my nap, all right?" Hope smiled. She had already closed her heavy eyes.

Josh tiptoed out of the cheery yellow room, softly closing the door. His usually smiling lips pursed in concern, and he sadly shook his head and came to Beth with outstretched arms. "May I hold him a minute? I've got to get to a meeting, but I should be back by the time Hope's ready to see him again." With pride he took his grandson. "This is what's she's been living for. It's been a matter of sheer determination, and I just wonder how much longer she can hold on. . . . "

His hands became a gigantic cradle for Teddy's tiny form and he smiled, gurgled and made funny faces, as grandfathers are prone to do. "You're going to have a very special place in our lives, lil' guy," he said, kissing the velvety baby cheeks.

For the next week, in her every waking moment, Hope coveted Teddy by her side. She nuzzled the downy chestnut brown fuzz of his head, as a mare with a newborn colt. She softly prayed over him, covering every phase and direction of his life, even who he would someday marry. She crooned gentle lullabies and tickled his cheeks to provoke a smile, and gazed deeply into his dark blue eyes, certain they'd turn brown like his mother's. She studied his features, forming a mental picture of what he'd look like in a few more months and years.

Often Kerry or Beth would sit by her bed and discuss visions of his future, or memories of their own childhoods. But best of all were the quiet times that took no energy as Hope watched over the sleeping baby beside her.

Early on a warm morning in mid-July, Josh sought Beth in the garden during her quiet time talking to God among the roses. It was part of her morning ritual after aerobics and ballet exercises in the workout room. Her disciplined body retained the slim, youthful litheness of a dancer, yet she felt old as her thoughts drifted back to the vivid memories of being ten years old with Hope.

At the sound of Josh's footsteps on the slate path, she squinted into the bright sun, and knew at a glance by his purposeful stride that this wasn't a casual morning walk. He was coming to tell her something, something they both foreknew and dreaded.

Josh's face was solemn. "This is the day." He swallowed hard. "She woke up, smiling at me as sweetly as ever when I came into her room. She asked me to lift her to the chair by the window for a few minutes so she could enjoy the garden one more time, and said, 'God is so good. He gave me a whole precious week with our Teddy. But my body's worn out, Josh. I'm going home today. Can you stay here with me?'" His voice quivered, "I believe her, Beth."

They fell into each other's arms, knocking Beth's panama sun hat to the ground. After long moments, Beth wiped her eyes with the sleeve of her faded blue garden smock.

"I believe her too, Josh. It's by sheer will and God's grace she's lived this long. The moment she gives up, He'll mercifully let her go home." Beth's eyes shone with the tears. "Let's pull ourselves together and give her our best."

In the sunny room with yellow roses strewn in the English wallpaper, Hope lay contentedly among the pillows while the filmy peach organdy curtains she loved fluttered in the morning breeze. Repeatedly she would smile at them and doze, then awake and smile again, waiting. Then she awoke with a start, as though remembering something of great importance she'd forgotten.

"If Kerry's through feeding the baby," Hope whispered, "have her come in." Kerry came at once, struggling for control. She held Teddy so her mother could see his little face, then handed him to Beth who slipped out of the room with Josh to give them time alone.

For the next anxious hour Beth rocked the baby while she and Josh prayed together in the adjacent sitting room. When Kerry appeared, her face drained of color and contorted with bittersweet tears, she whispered, "She's home now."

Beth put the baby down, and Kerry was instantly in her arms, sobbing, trying so hard to say something, while Josh circled his great arms around them.

"Shh, just let the tears come," Beth stroked her thick dark wavy hair as she had so many times when Kerry had come to her with a scraped knee. "We all share a great loss."

"I know—I know the secret . . . 'Mother.' "

Beth pulled back in shock.

"She told me how she and Dad wanted to but could never have a baby," Kerry went on, "and that you came to them, desperately wanting me to have a whole life with a loving mother and a father. And how you loved me enough to give me away in adoption. Now that I'm a mother, I—I don't think I could ever be unselfish enough to give up my baby. And yet even when you had Charlie and a beautiful home and everything, you kept your agreement and the secret. You've always been there for me, Bif," she choked. "I've had the love of two mothers all my life. Oh, Bif—Mother—I love you so much. . . . "

Josh drew them both closer, his tears of loss mingled with tears of joy for the gift that only Hope could have unwrapped and given to them before she left this life.

"All of your life," Beth squeezed Kerry, "I've longed to hear the word 'Mother' from your lips. Hope released the secret I would have guarded forever. It eases the empty space we have without her." The tears fell afresh.

"You and Hope had such a deep, sweet bond, Kerry," Beth said with tenderness. "And I'll always love her for making a special place for me in your life."

Kerry's thick dark lashes massed together with tears. "Dad, you and Mom have given me such love, I hope we will give that kind of home to Teddy." She paused, "I think I hear him now. He should be ready to wake up."

Josh peered at the baby, then picked him up, praying the grief of letting go of one life would be lessened by this new one.

"Let me take the little guy for a few minutes," he said. "I suspect you two haven't finished your talk." They smiled after him, appreciative of his intuitive understanding when his own heart wrenched with the inseparable twins of relief and sorrow.

Beth embraced her daughter again. "We're still the only ones who know. It's too complicated now. We can't go back. Bob should be told, and maybe someday, Mum. It would be wonderful for her to know she has a granddaughter, especially you, and a great-grandson." Kerry nodded in understanding. "Maybe we've said it all for now, love." Beth hesitated. "Except that someday you may want to know who your father is. Have you ever been curious about who your parents were?"

"No, not really," Kerry replied. "Mom and Dad always told me my birth mother gave me up with a sacrificial love, only because she couldn't give me the kind of home she wanted me to have. That was enough for me. Mom explained that my biological father was an extremely talented artist and a good person, but he had made it clear he could never handle being a loyal husband and father. Is that the way it was?"

"Yes, pretty much," Beth was thankful for the Sterlings' candor as they raised Kerry. "But you do have a right to know who your father is, if you want to."

In her heart Beth dreaded even the thought of divulging that it was the intriguing, sophisticated, self-centered Italian Count who had captured her heart. Their lives were worlds apart. Roberto may have suspected and put the pieces together that Kerry could possibly be his daughter, but Kerry would be shocked beyond all comprehension. How would she accept it?

In the face of all that had happened since just a year ago, the loss of her beloved father, the terrible ache in her heart for Charles, the pain of letting go of her dearest friend, Beth wondered if she could even bear it if Kerry wanted to know. Yet her daughter, if she wished, now had that right. Beth almost held her breath, waiting.

Kerry, still struggling to grasp the realities of the last hour, hesitated, weighing carefully if she could possibly assimilate even a speck more trauma at this point in time. "I—I don't think so, Bif," she said at last. "Not now and maybe never. If he didn't care about us then, he probably doesn't now. So what would come of it but more confusion?"

Beth felt a wave of relief wash over her.

"Some kids I grew up with became angry when they learned they were adopted," Kerry looked directly into Beth's eyes, "forgetting they were specially chosen because they were really wanted. They chose only to remember that their birth parents rejected them, not even taking into account that most of the time they were given up for their own good. I never felt anything but loved. I'd like to keep it that way. And I thank God that you're my birth mother. A real mother is the one who's always there, and I had two real mothers. That is wonderful enough for me."

Kerry reached out to Beth again, to be held in her arms. "I've always loved you and wanted to be like you my whole life. I've felt your love for me ever since I can remember, but you've never been dearer to me than at this moment. Did Mom tell you she was going to share your secret with me?"

"No," Beth said softly. "The three of us made an agreement before you were born so there would never be that confusion and conflict in your life. She asked if I wanted to reconsider when I married Charles, but that would have been so unfair. I couldn't. Annie and Ruth are the only other souls who know you're my daughter."

Kerry's beautiful dark eyes looked at her incredulously, "Didn't even Charlie know? He loved me like he did. . . . "

"Charles knew only that you were adopted by Hope and Josh, my dearest friends, because she could never have children," Beth spoke lovingly of her husband. "He adored all of you, and the desire of his heart was that we'd have a child as sweet as you. When we knew that was not to be, you filled a throbbing void and lent a father role to his life."

"I miss Charlie so much, Bif, but now he and Mom are together." A new wave of tears spilled down her cheeks. "He's probably graciously escorting her all over heaven and lavishing her with her favorite chocolate double-dip ice-cream cones. Mom would want us to be happy for them in that beautiful place where there's no more deterioration, no more death, wouldn't she? So I'm surely going to try." She brushed the tears from her face and gave Beth a brave smile. "We'd better relieve Dad of Teddy. He'll have phone calls to make."

The sun shone brightly on the day of Hope's memorial service. It spotlighted the masses of her favorite yellow roses from the gardens of Rosehaven amidst a variety of other light and summery arrangements Hope would have loved. Every seat in the rural community church in San Jose was filled. Hope had planned the service herself last fall, before she miraculously went into remission.

Pastor Dave welcomed the people, and so did her own voice on a tape recorder, inviting her friends to celebrate with her on her Graduation Day into eternal life.

Josh took note of the startled expressions on the people's faces when they first heard her voice. She sang, "How Great Thou Art," even though it wasn't the rich full soprano it had once been, then asked them to join her in singing, "Great Is Thy Faithfulness." The entire congregation entered into a praise and worship time with a volume that nearly made the walls vibrate.

Pastor Dave, at Beth's request, read from 1 Corinthians 15, beginning with verse 53 (NASB): "For this perishable must put on the imperishable, and this mortal must put on immortality. But when this perishable will have put on the imperishable, and this mortal will have put on immortality, then will come about the saying that is written, 'Death is swallowed up in victory. O death, where is your victory? Oh death, where is your sting?' . . . but thanks be to God, who gives us the victory through our Lord Jesus Christ. Therefore, my beloved brethren, be steadfast, immovable, always abounding in the work of the Lord, knowing that your toil is not in vain in the Lord."

Josh, with misty eyes yet amazing composure, invited people to share the things Christ had done in their lives through Hope. Women from over the years in her Bible study, children who had grown up in the Sunday school classes she taught, and couples she and Josh had helped through the rough spots as well as the good times shared. Many testified that her steadfast abounding in the Lord, her sweetness, patience and courage, her assurance that none of it was in vain, inspired many to the greatest faith they'd ever known.

And when the people left they hugged one another, comforted and giving comfort. Neighbors who had never been to church before asked Josh how to become a Christian. That had been the purpose of her life—steadfast, immovable, always abounding in the work of the Lord, to the very end.

After the service Josh sat alone for a few moments in the empty church. Beth knew only too well how he needed these private moments. Did he envision Hope's sweet smile in the faces of the exquisite flowers, as she did? Did he see her lips form a silent "thank you" that he could almost hear? Or her bubbling with pleasure, saying, "This day was everything I prayed it would be"?

Kerry quietly slipped into the pew beside him. "It was beautiful, Dad. How do people who don't know Jesus ever get through the loss of someone they love, with no hope of seeing them in eternity?"

"Not very well, honey. For them, dead is dead. There isn't anything else. No hope, no comfort." He paused, putting his arm around her. "And that's why I'm ready to get on with the next phase of my own life."

Kerry hadn't given a thought about what he would do next, just supposed he'd continue his missionary work and fly his airplane for the medical teams. Wasn't that enough? There had already been too much change. In these long months she'd ached to settle into a quiet, stable, peaceful life. She asked for nothing more than to enjoy her husband, her baby, and have her father released from the terrible stress of watching his precious wife slip away day by day. To take it easy for once.

"Next phase?" she held her breath.

"Thailand." His voice held a sparkle that had been absent for a long time. "They need me over there right now."

"Thailand!" Resentment, so foreign to her nature, welled up inside. "I need you right *here*. I've just lost a mother. Do I have to lose my father too, to some far-off country?"

Josh dropped his head in distress. More than anything, he wanted to smooth the sharp edge of Kerry's shock and loss. But for months he'd felt stirrings in his own soul, knowing that once the inevitable happened, the Lord would open a door for a complete change—one he prayed would erase the etchings in his memory of Hope physically waning away to nothingness. And now that she had been liberated from the limitations of the body, he ached for those painful images to be dissolved and replaced by healthy productive ones, by getting totally outside of his own pain and loss.

Of all the appropriate settings he'd thought of to talk to Kerry about going overseas, this wasn't it. It just slipped out. But the damage was done. Kerry was devastated. He tried to explain his deep need and the circumstances that would merit his leaving her at a time such as this. . . .

"Kerry, as I've flown to other countries and seen the needs on the mission field, my heart has ached. I've wanted to do training overseas for years, but of course under the circumstances, that was impossible."

Kerry didn't say a word.

Josh continued, "News came through the office that one of the missions couples we know needed help. Tom Regen and his wife, Thelma, have been working in Bangkok with Thai students, leading a special movement on campus at Ramm University on evangelism. They have a dynamic momentum in process, only Thelma has to have open-heart surgery immediately, and they must return to the States. It's imperative to keep that training going. I feel called to do that."

Kerry was numb with anguish.

"Honey, don't look so sad," Josh drew her close. "I'm sorry, this isn't the time to talk about it." He gave her a kiss on the forehead. "I won't be there forever. A few months, maybe. After that I'm not sure. We'll talk more later. The others are waiting. . . . "

19

Beth paced the vestibule with Teddy, jiggling and patting in a desperate effort to pacify the squirming, hot, fussy baby. Each time she passed the open door into the sanctuary, she mutely nodded approval at the heartwarming scene of father and daughter comforting each other side-by-side. It was for such a quality relationship that she had given Kerry up for adoption. Now, more than ever, they would cling to that closeness.

How much longer, she wondered, could she keep Teddy from wailing before she absolutely had to disturb Kerry for his diaper bag and bottle? Suddenly, Kerry burst blindly up the aisle. She almost collided with Beth, seemingly mindless of her cranky baby.

This rare emotional outburst, even in the face of profound sorrow, was so unlike Kerry's gentle nature. Beth gasped at the anger and hurt flashing from her beautiful dark eyes. "Kerry, what's the matter?"

"Dad's the matter," Kerry fumed. "I can't believe he'd leave me. Talk some sense into him, Bif! He can't go. Not now."

Her face crumbled and tears spilled down her cheeks. She dashed out the door, past Bob who stood in the scorching sun thanking parting friends for their support.

Teddy howled, not to be assuaged by mere back-patting while his little tummy twisted with hunger pangs. Beth bounced him frantically to no avail, wondering where his bag and bottle might be, and even more astounded by Kerry's pleading, *"Talk some sense into him."* Where could Josh be going? What could he do or say to cause her such upset?

Josh walked slowly up the aisle. A few minutes ago he'd been so inspired, uplifted by the service. Beth thought the most difficult part of the day was over for him. Now he winced as if in pain. His head wagged slowly from side to side. He seemed bewildered.

Bouncing the baby, Beth said, "Josh, can I help? I've never seen Kerry in such a state."

"My timing's rotten," he berated himself. "I've chosen the worst possible moment to mention the need to go to Thailand."

Beth's mind reeled. Thailand? That was a shock! Her mouth must have dropped in unabashed astonishment and Josh shrunk back in apology again. "I'm sorry, Beth. I haven't had a chance to prepare you either. I had hoped to properly let you and Kerry know what's on my mind."

"I think you'd better try—she's crushed."

"You've always been sensitive to my needs. Beth, your understanding of what I'm feeling now is crucial." He painstakingly repeated what he'd told Kerry—about the training mission in Thailand and why he needed to go there. Their conversation, although important, couldn't compete with Teddy's cries. "We'll have to talk later." Beth knew Teddy's needs demanded attention.

While Beth paced with the miserable infant, Josh continued to wrestle with his thoughts. . . .

When he had heard about the Regens' emergency departure a few days ago, it seemed that God's timing was perfect. They needed someone to replace them almost immediately. Dimly, in dreams of long ago, this was what he wanted to do for God with his life. Through his work of flying for the mission organization, he had the training, the ability and certainly the desire. Hope's illness had made it impossible for years. From her, he'd learned volumes about acceptance and patience and dreams that never come true.

Two days ago, the idea of picking up the pieces of his life and fitting them in to fill this urgency in Thailand made sense—until he tried to explain it.

The crescendo of Teddy's cries caught Bob's attention. He rushed to the rescue, recognizing hunger in his son's wails, with bottle in hand.

"Whoa, there, little fella, Daddy's got your dinner," Bob soothed. "Sorry, Beth, he's been a real handful. I can take him now, thanks." He poked the bottle into the tiny mouth and Teddy at once began sucking and slurping noisily. "As soon as he's devoured his bottle, I'll take Kerry home," Bob said. "She's handled all this beautifully, up until now. I don't understand, and she won't talk to me. It's almost as though she's angry. Even in the darkest hours of Hope's illness, I've never seen her like this."

Josh, standing in the vestibule, confessed. "I'm the one responsible for Kerry's anger, Bob. But I think it's more hurt than anything." He took a few minutes to fill Bob in on the situation. Bob nodded his head. "I'd heard about the Regens' medical emergency at the seminary. Actually, I think you'd be the ideal one to go into the field right now, if only . . . " his voice trailed off. "If only Kerry hadn't always looked to you for strength, and it wasn't so soon after the funeral."

"There just won't be anyone else available for months," Josh tried to explain, but Beth was lost in her own thoughts. *Small wonder Kerry bolted. I'm not too sure I don't feel forsaken, too.* Yet, deep down, even without his explanation, Beth's heart reached out in compassion. He had lived in the shadow of Hope's illness since they were first married. No one knew that better than she. He'd been steadfast, loyal, lovingly supportive, always the encourager, setting aside his objectives for what was best for Hope. Who could expect more of any one human being? And yet, Kerry had never needed him more than she would in the days and months ahead.

Bob glanced out the front doors and, seeing Kerry, quickly excused himself.

Josh and Beth stood face to face in the empty church. As she looked up into his somber eyes, it grieved her to see her dear friend, this man of great faith and courage, drained of vitality on this saddest of days.

The reality of loss struck both of them. Beth longed to reach out and gather him into her arms, to comfort him as he had comforted her countless times through the years. Impulsively, she wrapped her arms around Josh and held him close.

Tears stung and swam in her violet-blue eyes. "Josh," Beth attempted to console him, "I know you wouldn't hurt Kerry or any of us for the world. I'm sure in her heart she knows that too. We've got to go talk this over with her right now, so it won't be a double burden on both of you."

Josh drove Beth to the little yellow and white house where Kerry and Bob and Teddy planned to remain with him, at least until Bob graduated from seminary.

"Am I doing such a terrible thing?" he asked. "Kerry has Bob's love and baby Teddy to pour her life into. She has you to console and mother her. There are supportive, caring friends—all of whom will give her a sense of security in my absence."

"I can't argue with that, Josh." Beth's heart went out to him. Within the last hour, he looked years older.

"She's competent," Josh continued. "I've been so pleased and proud of her. Even though Kerry's young, she's taken over the leadership of the twenty or so women in their Bible study." He paused. "Of this I'm confident—God's Word and His presence *are* sufficient to get her through her season of grieving for Hope."

"And I'm confident she'll come to realize that, Josh," Beth said gently. "Give her a little time."

"I'm concerned for you as well, Beth. In less than a year, three of the dearest ones in your life have been snatched from you. Only God and time and loving support can fill such an abyss. I hope you realize, it's not going to happen overnight."

"I'm discovering that, daily." Her voice was barely above a whisper. *Lord, help me be strong for him right now,* she prayed.

"Beth, I remember the desperate and searching young woman who came to us, so many years ago, pregnant and afraid," Josh reflected. "I'm sure you remember too, the dawn, in our living room, when you invited Christ into your life. How grateful I am now that we have the comfort of knowing only the bodies of our loved ones are dead. Their real selves are alive, and we'll all be together in eternity."

"Eternity's the big picture," Beth agreed, "that takes away the sting of death. I'm having trouble with the hurts of the here and now. . . . "

"I think you're referring to Merribelle. At least in part?"

"We've everything, and nothing, in common that matters. But she's certainly not the only one."

Beth had already been hurt by her society friends. They minimized her losses, expecting her multi-millions, the magnificence of Rosehaven and her prominence among San Francisco's cultural leaders to fill the voids.

"Do you . . . " he paused cautiously, "do you ever feel used by the multiple charities that prevail upon your generosity? What would happen if you ever declined? Would they still idolize, or criticize?"

"Yes."

"Yes, what?"

"To both of the above." Merribelle's caustic comments after Beth's one-and-only refusal to hold the garden party at Rosehaven, with never an apology, was one of those still-raw hurts.

Josh pressed further. "And do you ever grow weary of listening to those who come into the House of New Hope? In numerous ways, Beth, you've created your own mission field. You're as much or more of a missionary acting out God's love as anyone I know."

Beth closed her eyes for a few minutes, digesting what he'd said. "What's on your mind, Josh?"

"So much. You. I've been so uptight and held everything in. I'm just trying to sort it all out. I'm thinking how the course of your life has changed since I first met you. I saw an intensely disciplined ballerina/painter—of necessity turned ambitious businesswoman. Those qualities transformed into motherhood, being a wife, friend, socialite, philanthropist, everything you do. Out of this has emerged a woman determined to allow God to direct her life for eternal purposes. You've had far-reaching effects on many lives, Beth."

With eyes on the road, Josh continued soberly, "You've already been through this. Is there ever any escape? When does it begin to get easier? Hope was ill so much, I've already known what it's like not to have her with me. I've already known grieving, but it still hurts. The shock you suffered with Charles's sudden death is beyond my comprehension."

"I can't fully answer those questions, Josh," Beth's voice was full of emotion. "I'm still not there yet. I suppose it's probably different for everyone. Kerry asked me that too. I think grief has its stages and it is necessary to pass patiently through each one of them and be kind to ourselves as we do.

"Losing a mate is a little like suffering an amputation," she added thoughtfully. "You feel like you'll never be whole again. You'll find others will try to speed things along because your loss makes them feel uncomfortable. But they, like my friend Merribelle, only do that because they don't know what you're going through or how to comfort. Yet you will heal just as I will heal. God will help us."

Beth shifted in her seat, ready to change the subject. "Now, what's this about Thailand? I've been exceedingly patient, don't you think? And I'm burning to know. What did you say to Kerry?"

"Very little. It just spilled out, without setting the proper scene, I'm afraid. Until now, I've never told anyone but I've always wanted to work in an overseas mission assignment. I've felt a special concern for Asia. With Hope's illness, that was out of the question. But now I can go, and I think she'd want me to. Thailand is ripe for evangelism. Every time I've heard about it, I've wished I could be part of it."

"What will you be doing?"

"Working with Tom and Thelma's team of trainers and a group of nationals, about twenty in all. Each trainer has assigned students whom he or she works closely with for a nine-month period. Using a translator, I'd also be teaching classes, basically training them how to train others and tell them about Christ and spiritual life concepts. The Regens' students are really turned on." His face shone with enthusiasm.

"How long do you think you'll be gone?"

"I'll be finishing the Regens' term of about another five months. Possibly I'd stay longer. But right now, I feel I really have to have a change of scenery. Beth," he looked at her with pleading eyes, "am I thinking too much about myself? Are you angry with me too?"

Beth was silent. The lump in her throat made it difficult to talk. *You dear, dear man,* she thought. Kerry had often called Josh their solid gold rock, their foundation. But even to one like him, the future could sometimes feel like shifting sand. *Truly, only God is our rock, our foundation,* she reminded herself. *I can't lean on Josh forever either.*

"I'll miss you, but I could never really be angry with you, Josh." She sighed. "I can't find the words. I think I'd like to be angry. There are even times when I'd like to lash out, kick, scream, holler, have a good ol' tantrum. But who would I lash out to? Certainly not you. Just life, maybe. It's just too tough, sometimes."

Crystal tears shimmered in her eyes. "The worst times are at night, I think. Sometimes even when there's a crowd of people, loneliness comes on me like the darkness. But when the sun comes up it's a new day again. When I count my blessings, I can only say, 'Thank You, Father.' "

She turned to Josh. "And I owe you a debt I can never repay. I saw a stitchery once that said, 'Any man can be a father, but it takes someone special to be a daddy.' You've been a wonderful daddy to Kerry, and a wonderful husband to Hope. Now you need to be free to go and be a wonderful missionary."

He sighed, "Thanks."

"We'll be fine," she reassured him. "I'll mother my Kerry. We'll go through our sorrow together. Something beautiful will come of it. I've learned sunshine always follows showers. It takes them both to make the roses grow." She patted his arm affectionately. "You have my blessing, Josh. When will you leave?"

"I truly thank you. You're so gracious, Beth. I'd hoped you of all people would understand." He smiled, his eyes glistening.

As he drove, his whole being came alive again, like a plant whose drooping leaves had been revived and refreshed by a cup of cool clear water.

Shoulders erect now, he answered her question with that familiar twinkle in his eyes. "I should be in Bangkok by the end of next week."

"Bangkok! So soon? I know very little about Thailand. Where will you live? I mean, under a thatched roof, or what?" She hesitated, "Josh, couldn't you wait just another week—give Kerry a little more time?"

"I'd like to. I don't know. I'll have to see what I can work out." He spoke animatedly now, for at last he could share about his opportunity. Tom had described the city to him as being on a broad plain at about sea-level, straddling the Bangkok river. Canals run through it, which serve as streets, with water taxis and canoes, and jammed with floating markets for the produce that comes from upriver. It sounded colorful, but hot, humid and steamy, surrounded by thousands of acres of rice paddies.

The picture Beth saw in her mind almost made her perspire. She smiled and tried to look fascinated as he glanced at her. She suddenly empathized with how much this gigantic, masculine man needed this adventure. His life had been restrained for so long.

He continued, "Tom said I'd be living at the Alliance Guest House. It's about twenty-five years old, run by Christians, with something like twenty-five rooms. People from all over the world come to stay there. Oh yes, I'll be teaching on the Ramm University Campus, which is about five miles away. You'll get a charge out of this—Tom was given a two-passenger rickshaw motorcycle which he's passing on to me. He says they're only slightly hazardous, if one can avoid a head-on collision."

"Sounds pretty precarious to me. Please promise me you'll take good care of yourself, Josh. I can't handle another catastrophe any time soon."

At that moment, Josh pulled into the driveway.

They walked into his flower-filled living room, fragrant with Rose-haven's golden roses and other bouquets from the memorial service. A Vivaldi tape welcomed them. Bob found it a soothing background for studying while Kerry and Teddy napped. He stood to embrace them, stepping over books and papers sprawled all over the floor. The portable typewriter nearly consumed the coffee table where he had begun to study.

At once Bob volunteered in hushed confidential tones, "Josh, before Kerry gets up, I just have to tell you. She's really upset. I don't know too much more about Thailand than what you told her. Time just hasn't permitted us much conversation on the subject. But Kerry's gone into a shell." Josh shook his head sadly, but he had more confidence now and was better able to think rather than reacting on initial emotions.

"Bob, I know it must seem unreasonable to her, but I have to do this. I also know she'll be fine. The best antidote right now is a huge dose of TLC from you. Encourage her to express all her feelings. Let's pray that God Himself will remind her that her heavenly Father, her truest Father, is able to supply all her needs. . . . "

A faint sniffle from the hall doorway startled them. They caught a glimpse of Kerry, pallid of face, her hair tangled, who had surely overheard. She darted back into her bedroom. A questioning glance shot between them.

Tenderly, Beth suggested, "Go to her, Josh. Just hold her tight. She's running the gamut of emotions right now. Tell her your love is with her no matter where you are in the world. Pray with her."

"Josh, Beth is right," Bob said. "But I think I should go in first and sit with her awhile."

"She needs that from you, too, Bob," Beth agreed.

*   *   *

Cries came from Teddy's crib, and Beth jumped immediately to pick him up. The antique crib and rocker she'd bought for Kerry seemed an even greater treasure now.

"Hi, lil' sweetheart. Ooo, how's my boy? Come on darlin', Gammy Beth will feed you." She kissed, cooed, cuddled and changed the ravenous baby, then settled into the rocker.

Josh observed Beth with admiring eyes as she held her grandson. "Do you know you're a special lady? I'm going to miss you."

"I'll miss you too," is all she could manage to put into words. *That's the understatement of a lifetime,* she thought.

"I'm going home when Teddy goes down for a nap again. I'll see you before you leave, I trust?"

"Of course."

Josh's schedule was horrendously jammed. He had meetings with his replacement here in the Bay area, there were books, papers, clothes and supplies to be packed and shipped to Bangkok, and he needed to spend all the time he could with Kerry. He hoped it would be possible to take Beth's advice and leave the week after next.

Kerry's favorite picture as a child, that of Jesus, the Good Shepherd, with His flock of fleecy white sheep, hung over Teddy's crib. She'd memorized the passage in the gospel of John and taught it in Bible study. Jesus asked Peter, "Do you love Me?" and Peter answered "Yes, Lord, You know I love You." "Then feed My sheep," Jesus said.

Her head told her this was what Josh Sterling had done all his Christian life—loved and obeyed Jesus. But now it was too much for her. Let someone else do it. She was the bleating, bleeding lamb, stuck deep in a rocky crevice.

Don't leave me, Dad. Pull me out, her heart cried. *Let someone else go to the people in Asia. Feed me. Stay with me. I need help, too.*

These were words she felt reluctant to say aloud. During that week, as Josh squeezed in sincere and fervid "I love you" assurances, he also shared how strongly he felt the need to go to Thailand. Yet all she heard was her own anguished silent plea, *Dad, please don't leave.*

He delayed his departure another four days, with every possible moment lavished on Kerry. The only time left for Beth was a phone call.

"I'll write," Josh promised.

Several year-long days passed. Rosehaven, although infinitely more splendid than when it was first built, resounded with vacant strangeness. The years had enriched the patina of its hand-carved woods, mellowed the deep green silks and shades of rose coloured glazes of its walls. Time added reverence to its priceless collection of art and furnishings. Yet it seemed silent. Beth could no longer hear its heartbeat.

For all who entered within its gracious garden walls, verdant with English ivy and mosses, came the enticement to wander forever among the varied moods and fragrances. The romance of the mansion itself whispered, "Linger awhile."

But Beth didn't feel like lingering. She couldn't settle.

She and Charles, the place, and all the joy that occurred there were bound together, as by a three-strand braid of silken cord. Without Charles, it was loosed forever. The years at Rosehaven had woven a rich tapestry with golden threads of love, purpose, fulfillment. Yet now she envisioned the cord sprawled across it, randomly coiled in lifeless circles. As in a mist, the image faded. *I'm just getting old and nostalgic,* she thought.

Another evening, Beth sipped tea alone in the peaceful twilight on the terrace after an intense day at the center. She marveled at God's finger painting in the heavens. Swirls of plum-colored clouds blended into lavender, deepening into pearlish grey-blues etched with silver edges. A blend of vibrant pinks washed over the whole of it. And in a wink, the color vanished, leaving only silhouettes of neutral hues.

In that moment, Beth saw what these melancholy moods had been revealing to her. "My seasons at Rosehaven are over," she whispered.

The sun had gone down on an era. Other days will dawn, she told herself, but for other eyes, for purposes beyond her present imagining.

Charles had discerned it. He had spelled it out in his will, but she didn't comprehend, until now. He had known Rosehaven would one day attain a reason for existing beyond themselves. That's what the clause meant that said at such time when she no longer found it feasible to reside here, the property must not be sold as real estate. It should be held and maintained in a trust, for whatever philanthropy she should choose. *What an overwhelming responsibility,* she thought, but felt no anxiety.

Beth lifted her face upward at the first star, flung like a diamond in the sky, and smiled. With a wavery chuckle she whispered, "You are an awesome God. You've known the plan all along. Just show me what's next."

Sleep came easily that night. As always, the first and last prayers were for Kerry, "God, help me fill the void in her life and heal her hurt."

A sudden September coolness drifted with the morning breeze across the rose garden. Its freshness smacked of the briskness of Carmel, and Beth longed for its saltiness. Inspired, she hurried to the phone in the breakfast room. Through the years, whatever the circumstances, this cheerful room like an indoor garden, where Charles asked her to become his wife, had given her joy.

"Kerry?" Beth was glad to find her home. "I've a splendid notion. Let me cart you and Teddy to Carmel with me for about a week. Bob surely must be buried with all he has to do. It'll be good for us to get away."

Kerry, the formerly ebullient, sunny child-into-woman, had only slightly emerged from the cocoon she entered at the first mention of Thailand. Neither Josh, Bob nor Beth had been able to reach her.

Beth waited. A pregnant pause, and then, still with hesitation, Kerry responded. "I don't know . . . well, maybe. I've almost got Mom's things stored or given away. It's been . . . so difficult to let go." Another pause. Finally "Yes, Bif. I'd like that. When do you want to go?"

"How's tomorrow, early afternoon?"

"Okay. I'll see you then."

Wonderful, Beth thought, catching a hint of a lilt in her voice. She savored expectations of giving and receiving hugs that would heal. Hugs like those that provided the therapy of a mother enfolding her sick child in a cozy rocker, or a toddler gleaning security from snuggling its teddy bear—that's what Kerry needed.

She and Kerry needed to recapture the secrets of the heart between trusted woman-to-woman relationships. Those moments flowed most freely while walking on the beach or curled up in their nighties in the wee hours of the dawn. These were the stolen moments she'd craved with her Mum, that never were.

"Kerry," Beth looked around at Carmel. "I'm so grateful we have this time together. I haven't been here since—since Charles—died. Too many circumstances have prevented it. I've longed to come back, but not alone." Kerry smiled in understanding. "I treasure your being both my daughter and my friend," Beth took Kerry's hands in hers. "Charles and I, Hope and Josh were all more than friends. We've been like family. Honey, I pray you and

Bob will have friends along the way to share a lifetime of joys, and to share the sorrows because we're going to have sorrows. I love the old Swedish proverb that says, 'Shared joy is double joy, but a shared sorrow is half a sorrow.' I know that to be true."

Kerry nodded, but Beth knew her tender phrases slid numbly off the invisible, impenetrable compartment in which Kerry had encased herself, like rain slipping silently down a pane of glass.

Unhurried days followed. With Teddy snug and secure in a pack on Kerry's back, the three of them ambled aimlessly, with no sense of time, along the water's edge. In the afternoons, the sea air lulled the infant to sleep contentedly on his blanket, shielded from the late September sun. Gentle breezes caressed them, while they each read or gazed at clouds.

On their walks, Beth began to paint memory pictures of herself for her daughter. The afternoons she sauntered this beach alone. And how like now she'd thrown sticks for friendly dogs, and dodged children's sand castles. While carrying her unborn child, she'd wondered what the future held for her and her baby.

Beth put her arm around Kerry's shoulders and paused as the water swirled around their ankles. "It seems like the impossible dream to have you here beside me now. I believe the God I hadn't fully met then made this appointment for us long ago."

"I'm learning, Bif, to apply more of the words I've taught," Kerry said slowly. "We truly do have a God of the impossible. And the tensions, hurts and grief I brought here with me are gradually floating away. You've been very patient with me. Never forcing, but creating a refuge for me to release my resentment. I can see that Dad is serving where he needs to be right now. And as much as I hated to let him go, I'm glad he did. He has enough love in his heart to stretch clear around the world. Mom must be glad too."

"I'm sure she is," Beth smiled.

"I've noticed at sunset, the beach is strewn with debris washed up on the shore. The next morning, it's clean and uncluttered again," Kerry observed. "It's like my innermost pain has been washed away with the outgoing tide into the vastness of the sea."

"Who else could do that but God, who understands us better than we could ever know ourselves?" Beth said.

"Only a wise, loving and understanding mother," Kerry beamed.

Smiling and lightened of heart, they walked toward the uphill slope of Carmel's bay. People were beginning to gather to applaud the evening performance of the setting sun.

U pon Beth's return to Rosehaven, a mountain of mail waited on her study desk. Tillie had singled out a letter which she'd propped on the French writing desk in her bedroom, postmarked Bangkok with Thai stamps. Beth savored it, leaving the best until last, like dessert.

Rifling first through the mundane, she came to the League's minutes of their meeting for fall luncheons and the Christmas Ball. Two more response letters came from churches giving encouragement in the form of financial support and pastoral counseling at the center. *Praise God,* she thought.

She opened five invitations to dinner parties. The one to the gala soirée of Merribelle's for the opening night of the opera season must have been lost in the mail or sent out late. It was already past. Just as well. Without Charles, she preferred going to the opera for the love of opera, not the glitzy parties for first-nighters.

Tillie, Jimmy and Cookie hovered nearby, delighted to have the mistress of the mansion home again. The tantalizing scent of Cookie's lemon wafers wafted from the kitchen. Max had shuffled around with nothing to do but get in Tillie's way, so she said. The glint in her eye told Beth she didn't mind as much as she put on. Several phone messages demanded immediate attention.

Finally, Beth retreated to her bedroom with Josh's letter and nestled comfortably in the window seat overlooking the gardens. Then came Tillie's rap at the door.

"It's four o'clock tea, Miss Beth." She put the tray down. "I've made scones and marmalade for you. Jimmy added the rose. Welcome home."

"You all do spoil me. Mmm, smells marvelous. Thank you, and Jimmy, too."

Beth leisurely began to read the letter, amazed at the unexpected speed of the mail service.

September 18, 1986

Dear Beth,

Wanted you to know I arrived safely three days ago. Each day seems to have a week's worth of catching up to do. I've had little sleep but am excited to be here. The humidity is a world apart from the Bay area, but I'm adjusting.

The Alliance House, where I live, is just as Tom described it. Picture a two-story horseshoe-shaped frame structure (no, it doesn't have a thatched roof!) built in the 1960s at the end of a one-lane street. Love the street names—it's on Pracha Utit Lane, which is only a block long, off Praditat Road. It's bustling and congested, across from another hotel. There are houses very close on either side where Thais live and have their little shops. I'm an adventure-lover at heart, but not about food. I'm a meat and potatoes man. Thai food is spicy, but I'll get along fine on rice, rice, and more rice. More trivia later.

I'm anxious to get out and meet more of the people. The Thais as a whole appear to be gentle, patient, lighthearted, independent. I say appear to be because they smile readily. It's part of their culture to wear a smile, hide pain, and not trouble others or have anyone think they are suffering effects of deeds in a previous life. They are reserved, especially toward foreigners. It will require time to build trust. One must understand they are steeped in age-old Buddhist traditions and ancestral spirit worship, which ties them tightly to their own culture. It's a whole new experience for me, and I'm beginning to feel like a real missionary at last.

The team made me feel right at home. Received a phone call last night that Thelma's heart bypass went extremely well, and just in time as she was a candidate for a major heart attack.

I pray for you and my family, and that Kerry will soon forgive me. I'm so happy that you're there for her, as always. Please pray for me, and God bless. Must run—

Fondly,
Josh

She read the short letter slowly several times and searched the lines for what it really said. He was as positive as ever, but probably exhausted, and so busy thinking about everyone else that he hadn't realized it yet. She wished he could instantly know of Kerry's change of heart.

Beth clutched the thin sheets of paper, her only tangible link with the one person who understood her better than anyone else in the world. She thought, *It doesn't matter where he is—in a steamy jungle land, talking to an auditorium of hundreds, or one-on-one. His easy jovial nature and genuine love for all people draw them to him like a magnet. I'm happy for him.*

She laid the letter down and stared out the window, *As for me, it's been twenty-five years since I've felt so uncertain about the future only God knows.* Contemplating that sober thought, she resumed her desk work.

One of the phone messages, marked urgent, was from Merribelle. *Better ring her up right away, or she'll be calling in a tizzy,* Beth decided and smiled.

Merribelle was one of those irrepressible, irresistible characters with a hundred little irritating mannerisms. After all these years in League, some members adored her, some avoided her, others merely tolerated her. None seemed really close. Except Beth, who knew she simply needed a friend. She dialed the phone.

"Ah'm so dee-lighted to hear from you all, honey," Merribelle's syrupy voice cooed. "Ah trust Carmel was wonderful. Ah didn't reckon you to be off somewhere for a whole week. Ah desperately need to talk over League's upcoming events. May Ah come down to Rosehaven, save you a trip to the city, hon?"

How unusual, Beth thought. Merribelle historically expected everyone to jump and run to her. This was a switch, for her to offer to drive down the twenty-five miles and back again. Actually, one day soon she needed to go into San Francisco and sign some papers at the corporate office in Townsend Towers, but better let Merribelle come out. She must have her reasons.

"I'd love to have you come down. When would it be convenient?"

"Ah'd like to see you tomorrow, if it's all the same to you, deah."

Beth smiled. The immediacy came as no shock. She wouldn't have been surprised if Merribelle had said yesterday. "Tomorrow will be fine. Cookie will be delighted to have a guest coming for lunch. My wonderful household help are always frustrated with an empty house."

Merribelle tottered in on three-inch heels at 10:00 A.M., after a perfunctory greeting to Tillie. Her face was as pretty as ever, and like her own, Beth observed, showed a few more lines. Curly platinum-blonde hair, freshly coiffed, brilliantly contrasted the scarlet silk designer blouse and coordinating pants, too snug over her now ample bottom.

Beth looked enviously slim and trim in jeans. Her black hair had traces of occasional silver streaks, and was now classically tied back with a violet ribbon. She greeted Merribelle with a warm embrace.

"Shall we enjoy this lovely warm October morning on the terrace? Tillie will bring us fresh coffee."

"Ah feel like Ah'm still having hot flashes, sweetie," she fanned her flushed face. "May Ah have something cold, in here?" she gestured to the exquisitely inviting library off the entry.

Beth nodded in agreement and followed Merribelle, who headed for the richly carved library table flanked by Regence armchairs. She paused, tracing appreciative fingers over the intricate design in the forest green needlepoint coverings. Settling down to business instantly, she fanned out pages upon pages of notes.

At noon, Tillie appeared, inquiring as to where and when she should set lunch. Merribelle, never at a loss for giving directions, responded with, "How 'bout that lovely spot over there by the French doors?" She pointed to an exquisite lemonwood and ebony inlaid table. "Ah love this room. It's so cool and confidential. Is that all right, hon?" she glanced at Beth who nodded. "In about fifteen minutes? Ah'm famished!"

"That'll be just fine. Thank you, Tillie."

Tillie obediently disappeared, but Beth caught the belligerent set of her jaw. Merribelle's reference to "confidential" implied she suspected Tillie of eavesdropping. She would be fuming, and later Beth would surely have to calm her down after the unjustified accusation.

The theme for the League's Annual Christmas Ball, as well as the florist, caterer, ice carver, musicians and other details, had already passed through committee. The planning had become fairly routine. Beth considered it merely a courtesy that Merribelle ran it by her—an acknowledgment of the fact that this was her home.

The ball remained the single most glamorous social event of the holiday season. Merribelle insisted each year be infinitely more spectacular than the previous one. Wealthy San Franciscans adored the junket out of the city. They arrived in lavishly decorated charter coaches that carried them to experience the wonders of Rosehaven at Christmas.

It appeared that a staggering sum of money was always generated for scholarships and benefits in support of those of artistic promise. However, the actual cost to do so kept gnawing at Beth.

Over the past decade especially, she questioned her part in promoting the indulgence of such ultra-extravagance. She calculated the horrendous expenditures required to raise these funds in the name of charity. And simultaneously, she cringed.

While thousands of dollars went just to the haute couture finery for each gown and tuxedo, Merribelle and the others felt they could not support the work of the center "at this time." The desperately hurting people in the heart of the city who needed help weren't their problem. . . .

Her mind had drifted far from Merribelle's insistent voice.

"Ah do believe you didn't hear a word Ah said, Beth, honey," Merribelle's voice had grown a little sharp. "Don't you think that menu sounds divine?"

"Yes, it sounds lovely, Merribelle. Everything does. It will be another dazzling ball, as usual."

"Well, honey, then that does it. Ah do believe that's all the 'business' we have to do today."

Promptly fifteen minutes later, Tillie wheeled in an elaborate serving table, draped with a crisp white Battenberg lace cloth.

"You've chosen my favorite luncheon settings. It's lovely, Tillie, thank you." Beth smiled.

Merribelle fairly salivated at the delectable menu Cookie had prepared: an apricot aspic on delicately dressed crisp greens, poached salmon with a dill Hollandaise sauce accompanied by a light pasta and puffy croissants. Strawberry mousse tarts waited on the serving table for dessert.

"Mah, mah, isn't this lovely?" Merribelle cooed with delight. "This is so gawgeous. Why, it looks like a special occasion!"

Beth smiled and gestured for her to be seated. "Well, it is. You're a special friend, Merribelle."

But Tillie's glance at Beth asked, *Why?*

Merribelle gushed, "Oh Beth, darlin', you are mah very dearest friend in all the world. This is delightful," Merribelle repeated, savoring every delicious bite of the meal before her. "Ah've missed those lovely evenings when Henry and Ah would come down for dinner with you and Charles. And the way Ah feel today, Ah'd adore staying here forever."

"How do you feel today, Merribelle?" Beth honestly wanted to know. "Working on the League's fall activities must have kept you running this past month or so. Each one has so much pressure to be a huge success. You must be tired. . . . " Beth read all the signs. Merribelle had more on her mind than League, and she needed to let it spill out.

Tears welled in Merribelle's eyes, splashing down her cheeks, taking a smudge of black mascara with them. She seemed humiliated at her unusual show of emotion, but there was no turning back.

She sobbed, "Sweetie, this is so embarrassing to break down like this. Ah'm being a silly ole woman . . . do you realize Ah'm pushing sixty? And Ah'd like," she paused, eyes clamped tightly shut while tears flowed in a stream, "Ah'd like to run away from home, but there's nowhere to run to," she cried, as her head dropped against her heaving bosom.

Beth stood and bent down beside her, stroking her shoulder. "Let the tears come, Merribelle, cry them out. Almost everyone has had a time when they want to run away. What do you want to run away from, or to?"

For several moments she didn't move but steadily rubbed her friend's shoulders until Merribelle's sobs subsided. Tillie appeared to remove the dishes, but a shake of Beth's head turned her away. She shut the door behind her.

Sniffles replaced sobs, and Beth gently suggested, "Let's move over here into softer chairs." Merribelle dabbed at red, smudged eyes.

"Sit here, and let's talk." From counseling at the center, Beth knew the first step in trying to help a troubled heart is simply to listen.

"The part of mah life that nobody sees is a shambles, honey. Mah marriage is sheer disappointment. Not that Ah don't enjoy having beautiful clothes, and nice things, and a lovely house to live in, but we don't have a real home. Nobody's ever there.

"All Henry thinks about is money. 'Course that's a silly statement, since he does have almost the largest mortgage banking business in the city. But all, and I do mean *all*, he ever thinks about is work. Oh, Ah drag him off to our social affairs, and he loves hosting our big bash of a party for the opening of the opera, but he never *talks* to me!

"Ah don't feel we have a marriage but an 'arrangement' whereby we just look like a happily married, affluent couple. It's a sham. There's nothin' on the inside . . . nothin'." She started to cry again.

"You were happy early in your marriage, weren't you?"

"Ah've never breathed this to a living soul in our San Francisco circles, but honey. . . . "

Merribelle poured out her heart and her life to Beth. She'd come to San Francisco on money she'd saved from waitressing, then became a model at I. Magnin's. Henry used to come in to the "Invitation Only" fashion shows for men to help them shop for their wives. After his first wife was killed in an automobile accident, he turned his attention to the attractive Merribelle.

He had this darling little boy, who "wasn't so darling anymore," and Henry was lonely. They got married, but it never exactly sizzled.

"What about your first marriage?"

"Mah husband left my daughter and me without a penny. Ah've come a long way, baby, and Ah'm proud of it," she said with a resolute toss of her head.

Yet instantly, the pride left her voice, and just above a whisper, she added, "Would anyone think to look at mah life, that it's hollow inside? An' mah children," she went on, "when they came out of the hippie culture, Ah lost them. Especially when my daughter said we never cared about them, just dashed off a check instead of listening—remember that? That hurt!"

"Those awful times separated many families," Beth nodded.

She listened as Merribelle raved on. The son and daughter had gone from living in the park in dirty jeans to becoming obsessed with Rolex watches, BMWs and impressing people with their success. They'd gone from hippies to yuppies, and she seldom saw them anymore.

"Let me tell you, Beth, you ah fortunate indeed that you never had children to break your heart." She paused, realizing too late what she'd said. "Ah do know you've had your share of heartache though, hon," she said apologetically. "Honestly, Ah don't know what keeps you in one piece, considering the loved ones you've lost, especially in the last year. How do you 'keep your cool,' as the young people say?"

"I'd say it's not so much a matter of keeping my cool, Merribelle, dear," Beth replied, "as it is keeping my faith. So many years ago, when our baby died, and through the years of my dearest friend's suffering with cancer, and the death of Charles, it wasn't me who held myself up. It was my loving God.

"There isn't a single area of my life that He doesn't know about or care about, or want the best for me in. No doubt about it—life is plain brutal at times. But God can bring us out the other side of heartbreak so we can smell the roses again. If I didn't trust in Him to do that, I know I couldn't keep my cool or my sanity."

Merribelle interrupted. "Ah was afraid you were going to say something like that. You don't have to tell me about God. Honey, Ah was raised a Baptist, and there isn't anybody hears more about God than those folk—morning, noon and night, and twice on Sundays. My mama and daddy dragged me off to church 'til Ah thought Ah lived there. But Ah'm not sure God ever heard mah prayers.

"Mah mama and daddy were tenant peanut farmers, nothing in the world like our rich former president, Mr. Jimmy Carter. Ronald Reagan's rich, too, isn't he? Anyway, my folks were so poor, they had to believe in something. Right? Ah was never sure God was up there in the first place. But if religion works for you, honey, how come it doesn't work for me?"

A sympathetic smile swept Beth's face. "Merribelle, I think it's important to realize that total pagans have a religion. Christianity is about a personal relationship with Christ. . . . "

Merribelle interrupted, "Honey, personal relationships are where Ah'm having most of mah trouble!"

"You're not alone, and that's why Jesus came—so He could personally show people how deep and wide and immeasurable His love for us is. From there we're able to have loving relationships with one another. Help each other in times of trouble. Until you know that side of God's character, He doesn't feel real to a lot of people. And so it's easy to think He doesn't hear your prayers. But I know in my own life, He does."

"Ah haven't heard Him knocking at mah door lately."

"He'll never force His way in. He just waits until you're ready. It's sad that so many people put Him off. For them God's love doesn't become real until there's nowhere else to run to escape life's disappointments. That seems to be the way you feel right now."

"Well, Ah'm not that desperate, yet. Beth, honey, you're very sweet to listen to mah troubles. Being here with you makes me feel ten times better than when Ah go to mah $100 an hour therapist."

Beth smiled.

"That reminds me," Merribelle said, "Ah stopped into the center to see you one day, except you weren't there. Your other workers are certainly nice and friendly, just like you. But honey, Ah could never sit and listen to everyone's troubles."

Beth's heart ached. Often the people who came into the center were much more likely to find help than the Merribelles. They weren't wearing as many protective layers, or as many masks.

A thought flashed in her mind. "Everyone needs a friend to listen at times. It seems to me that if you've been seeing your psychologist for years, she's not been the answer. You said you'd like to stay here forever. I think that's because it seems to you, as it always has to me, a retreat from the hurts of the world.

"If there was a place like this, with friendly, qualified people like we have at the center, would you come and stay? A week, perhaps two, or even longer for counseling, and then possibly group therapy?"

"Oh honey, is there such a place? Ah'd love it!"

Beth's heart pounded with the birth of an idea. There were multitudes of people like Merribelle, spending fortunes on humanistic psychological therapists, going nowhere. Their focus often never got outside of self, or they focused on blaming others while failing to acknowledge that it's God's business to heal. The New Hope Center in the city was working because God's hand was in it.

Was it possible the very wealthy people could find new hope too, and in a setting such as Rosehaven's would open their minds to insight from Christian counseling? The thought of it made Beth tingle, especially as she saw her friend's face light up, waiting for an answer, for hope.

Beth smiled encouragingly, "At the moment, I don't know of any. But God only knows, maybe there will be, someday soon."

"Well, thank you, honey. Ah must toodle on back to the city. You know, Ah think mah pity party is because Ah'm tired—sick and tired if you must know—of always doing all the work for League." With a wry smile she added, "On the other hand, I suppose that it's one of the places Ah run to. Ah'm doing something good for others, and it does keep me out of trouble." Merribelle forced a laugh, and to Beth's ears, it was tragically devoid of humor.

The fall social season of 1986 looked different to Beth than ever before. For years she'd searched behind the outer glitter for the real people underneath. Among them, there were talented, brilliant, good and caring people. People for whom libraries of universities were named, or wings of hospitals.

Yet many confided to her alone that their sons and daughters were into drugs and alcohol, homosexuality, abortions. They were brokenhearted with their own problems as well. Where could they go for healing?

The humanistic therapists treated minds and wrote prescriptions for the body but knew little about the soul and spirit. She saw the glamor of the jet-setters, but also the ones so accustomed to making corporate decisions they'd lost touch with their feelings. Many focused so intently on attaining material success they were poverty-stricken in family relationships. Abortions, amphetamines and alcohol abuse were not limited to the masses. There were many more Merribelles and Henrys and dysfunctional families than met the average eye. There were those with everything money could buy—except happiness. There wasn't another Charles, anywhere. . . .

The seed of a dream took root in Beth's mind: *Rosehaven Retreat Center.* The name wouldn't include the byline with any connotation "for the rich and famous," nor would it be labeled a Christian retreat.

The desire of her heart was to provide a Christ-centered refuge with an opportunity to get in touch with God. Anything less would be like putting a Band-Aid on a broken back. Yet it seemed everyone with a hangup searched for their own identity, to get in touch with or find themselves.

The inspiration continued to germinate as Max drove her home from the city or from parties at some estate in the suburbs. In the privacy of her bedroom, she talked to Charles, listening and praying for God's leading. Everything she heard seemed to nurture new ideas. She'd sit quietly in the gardens, drinking in the fragrance of the last blooms on the roses, while a vision took shape.

She pictured people sitting peacefully in the acres of gardens, living in comfortable cottages that could be built on the other side of the tennis courts and swimming pool. The ballroom could be for large group lectures and concerts, perhaps open to the public. Smaller groups could meet in the galleries, with ample rooms in the 30,000-plus square foot mansion for private counseling. The resident administrative staff could live in the main wing.

The potential for lives to be enriched, turned around, possibly changed forever at Rosehaven stimulated every fiber of Beth's creativity. Her mind raced.

The courage of Betty Ford to acknowledge her problem with alcoholism provided a major breakthrough for celebrities and the wealthy to find help. It suddenly seemed to enhance the acceptability of counseling for chemical dependency when the lovely former First Lady made public that pressures in her life drove her to drink. Furthermore, she did something about it. Beth remembered the publicity and positive response to the center in the prestigious desert community of Palm Springs, California, about three years before.

Yes, Beth told herself, psychological therapy in the '80s was definitely the "in" thing. She thought of the headlines that had become familiar: Hostile conglomerate corporate takeovers, Ayatollah Khomeini's vicious revolution and terrorism, Americans taken hostage in Iran, assassination attempts on the Pope and the president, San Francisco gays and lesbians paraded the streets, AIDS ravaged not only the gay community but the nation as well. Such sickening events rolled on and on. Last year's earthquake in Mexico City had taken thousands of lives within minutes, but people constantly live with the aftershocks of culture shock. Small wonder the term, "sick society," had entered the vernacular of American speech.

The government and various agencies attempted to provide assistance for the poor, the homeless, the sick. Beth often thought of the up-up-up and outers, whose success, if one wanted to call it that, had driven them beyond their limits. Those whose education, dedication, hard work and intelligence had rewarded them with ultimate affluence and material luxuries, yet they were also among the lost. The very ones most qualified to build up our nation and model leadership for our youth were searching too. "What is real?" they asked their therapists.

Beth prayed they'd make that discovery—at Rosehaven. "Oh, Charles," she whispered. "If only you were here to help me."

Another letter from Josh arrived, dated October 15. This one had taken nearly three weeks in the mail.

Dear Beth,

You'd be as excited as I am with the amazing results here in Bangkok. People are accepting Christ in droves. Home churches are springing up throughout the city and in the villages.

However, I find our missionaries here aren't without their problems too. Guess my ears look big enough to hear them all, and they seek me out in my free time. I'm glad I'm able to help, and counseling my coworkers with their troubles makes me feel God brought me here for a dual purpose.

How lucky you are, though, to watch our Teddy developing a real personality. Kerry says he's more than made up for his slow start, gurgling, cooing, totally responsive at three months. I remember how adorable Kerry was. . . .

I'm thrilled about Bob being in such demand as a speaker for both youth programs and churches. When he finishes seminary next year, I'm not sure whether he's best suited to full-time pastoring, or full-time counseling, or a mix of both. He gives a concise, captivating message that holds an audience in the palm of his hand. It's a mystery to me how he ever got any studying done at home. There were always young people there after Bible studies, eager to learn more when the main group left, or just to talk. Interestingly, several of their parents came to him for counseling. He does have a gift—rather, several.

Kerry and I are closer than ever. I guess when you're far away from someone you love, you say things in letters you take for granted when you're near.

You are ever in my prayers. Have I told you I miss you? In everything I do, you are always in my thoughts. I love your letters— and live from one to the next.

Love always,
Josh

Beth carefully folded the letter and put it in her big box of precious things on the dresser.

She could see him now, standing above the heads of most other men. He'd grown up on a ranch in Montana before coming to San Jose State on a football scholarship, and even now hardly looked any older than his college picture on Kerry's dresser. In a very masculine sense, she thought of him as beautiful, with his most outstanding feature being that perpetually jovial smile. Thick straight hair, the color of cinnamon only slightly sugared with gray, hung above a smooth unwrinkled brow. The only creases on his face were the laugh lines around his warm brown eyes.

If he could be with her now, he'd know exactly how to set her dreams for Rosehaven in motion.

21

The singing of birds announced a new day with a chorus of various melodies, ranging from chirps to operatic trills. Somewhere among them, Beth imagined the song of the thrush that sang in the chestnut tree outside the window of her room in Hampstead when she was a child.

Quickly she flung back the satin sheets and slid into her jeans and sweater. In only moments, the sun would flood the landscape with a symphony of color, and she didn't want to miss even a moment of autumn's fiery splendor.

The crisp air gilded the grape arbors over the paths that framed the rich palette of color ahead. Beyond the rose gardens, the tea house and rambling English gardens, tennis courts and swimming pool, she walked the acres of grassy fields. She looked back up at Rosehaven, standing majestic on the knoll. Her heart quickened.

In England, so many of the stately mansions seemed to slumber in the past with a lost sense of time. They passed from generation to generation or served as Bed and Breakfasts, yet the focus centered on a bygone era.

Rosehaven, like a queen, had a vibrant future Beth prayed would overshadow all of its former self. With pad and pencil in hand she surveyed the possibilities for building residence cottages. She sketched from memory the small cottages of the Cotswolds, positioning their facsimiles this way and that on the paper. When the cottages were built, furnished and nestled in place, and landscaping complete, they would perhaps look like keepers' cottages around a manor house.

On this morning, as the lawns glittered with dew, her heart caressed the land, cherishing this idyllic setting. She paused by the scattered clumps of berry bushes, the delicate blush of the snowberry beside the fire thorn, ablaze in its most glorious cloak of scarlet. These and other mature, unabashed favorites that could not be replaced in a season or two were noted on her sketch pad.

A sudden bolt of pain pierced Beth's heart. In a not-too-far-off day, Rosehaven would no longer be her home. It would take months before the plans and permits were approved by the county, but the time would come. One day her life here would be finished, and she would leave Rosehaven for . . . she didn't know what. Tears stung her eyes at the thought of being separated from this beauty.

At the beginning of Rosehaven's finest hour, she would leave. She really wouldn't have to. After all, it was hers to make any provision she wished. It would just be best if she did. Soon she would contact her attorneys to draw up a perpetual trust and form a board of directors, on which she would always have a seat. Then they would search for psychological therapists, trained spiritual lay counselors, a resident pastor couple, and an administrator. Except for the latter two positions, she was almost certain she knew where to find the perfect personnel. It would be wonderful to also offer a Bible study.

But she saw her presence as intimidating. The staff would be reluctant to take ownership of the program if they imagined the founder there twenty-four hours a day, hovering, constantly the overseer. It simply wouldn't work. But her heart would always be here.

The rising sun bathed the masterpiece before her in a topaz glow as she visually gathered the rich jewels of autumn to store in her mind. Like the changing of the seasons, when the roses are past their blooming cycles and must yield to the gardener's pruning to await another spring, so must she one day yield her treasure. Also like the seasons, it was part of the plan—one could look ahead with expectancy. The heartbreakers came during those times of her life when it seemed to snow in August.

Beth's meandering now led her above the wedding garden to the crest of the knoll, and the bench where she and Charles had sat in twilight hours. The long broad corridor of yew trees and stretch of lawn ahead led back to the mansion. Her thoughts had come full circle. Now the morning ritual at the ballet barre, then her day at the center called. She quickened her steps and walked briskly to the house.

Beth's dream reverberated in her head and took shape on scratch paper. It wasn't ready for unveiling to anyone else or having holes shot through it by her lawyers quite yet. She wanted the details thoughtfully in place before laying it out for thorough professional scrutiny. How she wished Josh were here, but her first airing would be with Bob and Kerry. There was much to do, and she must get on with it.

Beth felt ridiculously self-conscious being chauffeured to the center. She would prefer to drive and made Max let her off down the block. He was part of their household, so she would never let him go. But he felt rather useless without Charles, and so she learned to make the best use of travel time, as Charles had. By the time Max dropped her on Market Street in the midst of San Francisco's congested traffic, she'd made numerous calls on the car phone and drawn up a long list of potential contacts. Rosehaven Retreat Center now captured her thoughts nearly every conscious moment. Everything seemed to relate to it, and she sought to pull the scattered pieces together into a clear, concise plan.

Throughout the weeks ahead, up to Thanksgiving and the beginning of the holidays, Beth fought off those moments when her mind was tempted to wander into grief. She tried not to think about how it would feel to sit down to their festive dinners with the three huge voids—actually four, with Josh out of the country. Thanksgiving would be hard to face, but it was only a day or two. Christmas was a whole season unto itself.

Remembering the verses in Ecclesiastes, "For everything there is an appointed season . . . a time to be born, a time to die, a time to plant, a time to uproot what is planted," Beth decided, *It's also not a time for focusing inward, but a time for reaching out.* She wasn't the only one who hurt.

Rather than the traditional Thanksgiving feast in the dining room, Beth transformed the ballroom into a banquet hall. She invited Annie and Ali, now grown and married with two children. Bob and Kerry were encouraged to invite every seminary student and their other friends who didn't have a family nearby. She sent an invitation to the pastor-couple of their church in San Jose, as well as the volunteers at the center. Families from the neighboring estates in the valley came. Jimmy was ecstatic to have his friend Shelly come with her son, Robby.

Tillie and Cookie enlisted three of the neighbors' cooks, and the kitchen fairly burst with delicious aromas for days. Max, under Tillie's tutelage, had become an expert shopper, and he kept busy with errands and trips to the supermarket. He was also superb at serving. The household staffs were included for the feast, as was the custom on holidays at Rosehaven.

Bob delivered a mini-sermon which led right into the blessing of the food, with everyone around the festively decorated room holding hands and singing, "Praise God from whom all blessings flow."

After dinner, many stood up and shared special things God had done in their lives that year—things they were thankful for. The neighbors who said they hadn't worshiped in a church for years, some never, enjoyed it so much that they were eager to drive down to the church in San Jose. In fact, several guests suggested that Kerry and Bob come up to Rosehaven sometimes and do just what they'd done today. "Except we aren't inviting ourselves to dinner," everyone laughed.

"What an absolutely fabulous day this has been!" Bob enfolded Beth in a crushing hug when the guests had left.

"I wanted to fill this day so full that the void would be crowded out. But I couldn't help thinking how our dear ones would have loved it. I felt their presence though, didn't you?" Beth asked Kerry with tears dancing in her eyes.

"Yes," Kerry agreed. "Mom would have sung beautiful solos, and Dad and Charles would have had a ball. I hope Dad calls tonight, then we can tell him what fun he missed," she laughed and then added soberly, "He probably felt lonely today. He's never been away from home on a holiday before." She choked up and turned away.

"That reminds me, Kerry," Beth reached out with a comforting hug, "please don't let me forget to ring up Mum in the morning. I couldn't get through earlier. I hope her cold is better. She'd have been here if she hadn't been so ill. She promised to come for Christmas though."

*　　*　　*

The week after Thanksgiving, Beth and Max began hauling the Christmas decorations out of storage. Volumes of burgundy velvet swags and golden cord sprawled over the hallways, waiting to suspend garlands of cedar and swaths of shimmering lamé.

Cookie hummed merrily while spicy scents of fruitcakes and a variety of cookies and tarts floated from the kitchen. Kerry came to help with special favorites to be sent in huge quantities for Josh and the missionaries. Extra treats were made for Beth to take to the center.

The weeks flew by, filled with the joy of doing for the days ahead. The activity crowded out thoughts of sorrow, leaving the loveliness of Christmases past and the hope of Christmas present and future.

Mum arrived just in time for the Christmas Ball. Moments before the party, Beth beamed with pride at her elegant mother, "You look regal as a queen."

Margaret wore a deep rose velvet gown frosted with embroidered lace and pearls at the high Victorian neckline, and opera length pearls. The pearl and diamond antique earrings were those Sean had given her on their fortieth wedding anniversary. Her shimmering silver hair was coiled high upon her head, held with priceless pearl combs of the sort antique shop owners cannot part with.

Giving her a tender hug, Beth smiled, "You're positively stunning, but I've never seen you any other way. And you look very distinguished with your gold-headed cane. When did you start using that, Mum?"

"When our English winters bring that bit of a nip in the air, my arthritis flares up," she admitted. "Joints get stiff and simply won't perform. But I'll bet you a biscuit I'll feel better here, my dear. You look marvelous, simply smashing, love. Have I seen that gown before?" Beth appeared regal herself in royal blue draped velvet trimmed in white mink, her eyes sparkling in the same deep blue. Her hair, too, had its strands of silver threads.

"Yes, though I haven't worn it in ages. I'm into nostalgia. It's the one Charles bought me on our honeymoon in Rome. I've kept it carefully wrapped in cold storage to keep the mink white. I could never bear to discard it."

"Well, you do look fabulous. Let's go have a ball, at the ball, as Charles would say." Margaret took Beth's hand to descend the stairs, a portrait of mother- and daughter-beauty equal to a Reynold's painting.

The halls, main rooms and the ballroom were dancing with thousands of twinkling lights. The lights reflected on delicate white branches dipped in silver and crushed crystals, complementing the theme, "Winter Dream."

Shimmering swirls of chiffon intertwined with the rich whites of Christmas roses and creamy poinsettias amidst leaves of burnished gold. The effect created a fantasy of white and gold, magnificent against the rich colours of Rosehaven's decor.

Beth drifted through the evening as if in a fantasy herself, forcing out the other years when she and Charles had waltzed and whirled about the ballroom. Mum's charm drew a constant circle of attentive admirers about her. She had never attended with her husband, so for her, it was an exciting diversion, especially after being ill.

Clouds of emptiness hung over Beth's "Winter Dream," bleak and lonely without Charles. Yet another dream waited in the wings, one she knew would greatly please him, and she saw his incredible blue eyes smiling at her once more.

*   *   *

Two days before Christmas, Kerry and Bob arrived with Teddy, excited about his first Christmas. God was so good to fill up empty spaces with new life, Beth praised as she fled out to the drive to meet them.

Mum had never been around any infant but Beth. She was always too occupied to flirt with one and encourage the possibility of Sean's wanting another child. But she became instantly enamored of Teddy's round brown eyes and his button nose so like his daddy's. As soon as she met the little charmer, she sat down and held him.

"He's a little love," Mum smiled. "Such a darling, gregarious child. Are you always so happy, hmm?" She tickled his cheek. "And how lovely you're not taken back with strangers."

She turned to Kerry and Bob and said, "This is positively splendid, to be with you again for Christmas."

A look of sadness passed over her smile. She'd previously written to express her condolences of Hope's passing. And she had also sent regrets that this Christmas would indeed be altered by not being with either of Kerry's parents, or Charles and her own dear husband. Somehow, face to face, she could never have managed to put such things into words. "We shall make every attempt to have a jolly time of it."

"Absolutely," Bob gave her a hug that said he understood.

Later that afternoon, Tillie announced to Beth that Europa Floral Fantasies had just delivered an enormous arrangement. Where would she like Max to place it?

The fabulous creations for the Christmas Ball seemed simple by comparison. Sitting on the large fringed tapestry-skirted table in the entry, was a magnificent woven willow basket. It contained an array of freshly misted cedar boughs and sprays of juniper with plump blue-gray berries. Spires of eucalyptus, peacock feathers and crystal-encrusted branches formed the background. The heart of the composition held gilded nuts, dried pomegranates, clusters of purple grapes and ruby red apples. Christmas roses caught up with flowing golden ribbons added the glorious finishing touch.

Beth had an immediate desire to set up her easel and paint the gorgeous still life, right where it sat. Everyone in the household gathered around to admire the work of living art.

"Where would you like me to take it, Miss Beth?" Max asked.

"It's perfectly scaled to the entry. I've never seen anything so fabulous! We'll leave it right there, thank you, Max."

"Who, pray tell, sent it?" Mum asked.

"I've been too awestruck to look. Let me see. . . . "

Beth blinked. The card read, "A happy Christmas, *Bella Rosa,* to you and yours. Roberto."

"Roberto?" Mum repeated. "Is he that Italian Count, Cabriollini or something? It seems he's sent such splendid arrangements before."

"He gave us an outrageously extravagant gift and came to our wedding, I remember that," Bob added.

"Just who is he, Bif?" Kerry asked, twisting the ring with the diamond he'd given her for her tenth birthday.

"He's an extremely generous person, with more wealth than he knows what to do with. And lonely, I think. An acquaintance from long ago."

Even Cookie had come to behold the extraordinary floral piece. The chimes of the gold and ebony clock in the entry hall struck four. "Tea time," she proclaimed. "It's set in the parlor."

*   *   *

Josh phoned on Christmas Eve, asking to speak to Kerry first, then to Bob, Beth and the others. Afterward Kerry cornered Bob and Beth.

"He sounds thrilled with all they're accomplishing there, don't you think? It's truly wonderful that in such an extremely different culture, thousands are looking for the one true God." Her lip quivered. "But under his jovial success stories of the mission there, I think I hear a very lonely man."

And they all understood because, though together, they were all lonely. Beth had anticipated the void they could never fill up, so she had invited those who came for Thanksgiving to come again on Christmas Day, following their more private Christmas Eve.

At both times, Bob presented a Christmas message. He spoke of the intimacy of the personal relationship with the Father, brought about by the human birth of His Son. "The gift of God's love and forgiveness that passes all human comprehension is the true beauty of Christmas," he said. Beside that ultimate realization, every other circumstance seemed insignificant. "Immanuel, God with us," they all sang.

Not only had her little family come through that one holiday of the year that can be so ultimately wonderful or dreadfully depressing, but Beth knew they'd each been blessed as well. Blessed by a heavenly Father who had foreseen and provided for all their needs, and beyond.

In the kitchen, when everyone had left and only the core of her own loyal and dear household staff remained, Tillie and Cookie, Max and Jimmy were cleaning up. Beth asked them to pause to allow her time to say thank you. She'd already given them beautifully wrapped personal gifts with the rest of the family. The housekeeping and gardening staffs had received their bonuses days before. Yet these were the nucleus of what made Rosehaven function. She wanted to present them with their annual bonus checks where they mostly lived, behind the scenes.

"Thank you for your kind hearts and loyalty," she said with tears in her eyes. "Each one of you is precious to me. You've worked hard today. Sleep in tomorrow. Do whatever you wish, and I'll take care of our little family. You all deserve a day off."

She passed Bob in the hallway, on the phone making arrangements to meet and counsel early the next morning with a family that was breaking up. Beth said a simple "thank You" to the Lord for bringing such a sensitive and caring son-in-law into their family.

Before saying goodnight, Beth hugged Mum and Kerry. "I'll make breakfast tea and coffee, and have rolls in my room in the morning," she invited. "Come in your robes when you feel like it. We'll not even care when we get dressed. We'll just sit and talk all day if we want to."

She and Kerry had always made time to do that, but she and Mum never had. Another new era, Beth hoped.

Kerry pulled Beth aside and whispered. "Mother, are you ever going to tell Mum the—the secret?" It was Beth's right to reveal or not to reveal the secret. But Beth knew in her heart that Kerry yearned to be an acknowledged granddaughter.

"Yes, honey, when the time is right—because I love you both with all my heart," Beth held her daughter close. "Merry Christmas, and good night, dear."

Of all the loss, the great gain this year was to have Kerry call her that most cherished of names—mother. Though she could only hear it in private, that was where it mattered.

"God," Beth whispered as the kettle boiled and coffee perked in the morning kitchen, closeted in the corner of her room, "after all these years, how am I going to tell Mum she has a granddaughter, and a great-grandson? Hope paved the way, so I owe them their rightful relationships, but how do I begin? What do I say?"

Mum rapped softly, opened the beautifully grained oak door a crack and called, "May I come in, love?"

Margaret Sheridan, the ballerina, the legendary mistress of the Commonwealth's most prestigious school of ballet, the poised, elegant, private person she'd always appeared to be, came with shining silver hair streaming down her back like a schoolgirl's at a slumber party. "Is our tea ready, love?" She crept in with twinkling eyes.

Beth, in a periwinkle blue velour robe, enveloped her in a cuddling embrace, leading her to the floral skirted table by the window, already set for breakfast.

"Isn't this fun?" Beth bubbled with delight. She had always longed for a cozy, unhurried time like this with Mum.

Another soft knock, and Kerry came in with Teddy, who tried to squirm right out of her arms. He lunged in Mum's direction, which pleased her to no end.

Beth's hand shook as she nervously poured Mum's tea and placed the silver roll basket, butter, jams and coffee pot on the pretty table. Then she joined them.

"I adore my new robe and slippers, and this luxurious silk nightie, Beth," Margaret ran her hand over their smooth surfaces. "I feel so decadently pampered. Sean bought me lovely things like this, but I never have for myself. I've been hopelessly spoiled, I'm afraid, by both of you."

"There's one more gift I've been holding back for a special moment. . . . "

Mum interrupted. "Oh my dear, there isn't another thing on earth money can buy that you could give me. The only thing most women adore and I've never had, probably never had time for except in my old age anyway, is a grandchild. But it is a wee bit late for that, now isn't it?" she smiled.

Beth's eyes widened in shock. Then she began to laugh, first in relief, then in amusement, and finally in appreciation for making it easier for her. No use pretending. Mum, for all her private thoughts, never pulled any punches once they were in the open. Years of teaching the precise art and timing of ballet had produced a very straightforward individual. By her tone and twinkling eye, the innuendo was unmistakable.

"Mum, you're incorrigible, an absolute rascal is what you are. You've known Kerry is really my own daughter, and your granddaughter, all along?" Beth laughed accusingly. "And yet, you never let on!"

Kerry closed her eyes, her slim young body vibrating with tears of relief and overflowing joy. Her luxuriant eyelashes, even thicker when damp, framed those immense brown eyes as she looked up between the faces of her mother and grandmother.

"Love, we knew she wasn't Charles's baby. She had to be conceived before then. But while you were studying in Paris, none of your letters made the slightest mention of a boyfriend. . . . "

Mum went on explaining to Kerry about the fears she'd written to Beth about, how Beth had come home to help, and then solved Sheridan's problems in San Francisco.

Mum continued, "She was absolutely marvelous. She grew up with the antique business. And with her art background, she was brilliant."

"You're sounding like a proud parent," Beth scolded.

"Nonsense, it's true," she went on. "I've never seen a child more anxious to do her best, so eager to give back. I never had a twit of business sense, thought it's simply amazing that such a young woman could get an antique and art gallery back in the black. Surely there was no time for a love affair then. Sean was terribly proud of her but worried that she'd work herself to bits and pieces."

Mum glowed with pride at her daughter, refilled her tea cup and went on, still directing the reconstruction of the past toward Kerry. "That's when her father put his foot down and insisted she take a leave and build up her strength."

Turning to Beth, she said, "Beth, you even took a little extra time, as I recall, and that's the only period when you could have had time to have a baby.

"Not too long after, you met Charles. Of your interest in him, you kept us very well informed! Your father and I were jolly well pleased at your choice of a husband, dear. What a love he was."

Beth had never heard her mother talk so much.

"So you see, I don't know when, or where, or how our precious Kerry came to be. But I know the look of love in a true mother's eyes, in everything she does for her child. Sean and I observed it several times, and became almost certain of it at Kerry and Bob's wedding. That was a wedding only a mother could give a daughter."

"And neither you nor Daddy ever let on," Beth shook her head in amazement. "I couldn't bring myself to tell you I was pregnant. It happened, very innocently on my part, in Paris. You and Daddy were so proper and perfect and such public figures. I didn't want to embarrass or disappoint you."

Mum frowned. "Forgive us, love. We sent you out into the world with a marvelous cultural background, but with nary a word about life. It wasn't fair. Small wonder you couldn't come to your parents. Years and years later, after the fact, when we were almost certain about Kerry, we thought if and when you wanted us to know, you'd tell us."

Mum had never cried, except the night her husband died. But she cried now, as the three generations stood in a hug ring.

"Beth, love, how could you be so unselfishly brave as to keep these secrets, to give up your child? I'm still so confused as to who told Kerry, and oh mercy, so many things.

"If I had been a different mother, not so tied up with the ballet, you could have come to us. Sean was ever so much more tender. You probably would have gone to him, but not me. Oh, pet, forgive me. Because of your love for us, you've suffered terribly, denied rightful relationships with awful hardships. But I love you. I really do love you. And Kerry, God was better to me than I deserve to give me such a sweet and beautiful granddaughter. And now we have Teddy . . . it's so wonderful!"

Tears mingled with joyful laughter, with the three of them kissing and dancing about together.

Kerry squeezed Mum tightly. "I've always felt left out because I never had a grandmother. Mom and Dad's parents all died young, when I was a baby. But ever since I was a little girl, I thought if I could choose a grandmother, it would be you."

"Really?" Mum seemed delightfully surprised. "I've never been very playful with children, except of course I've adored teaching them ballet. You were different, so beautiful with your dark hair and eyes, well-mannered and sweet. You stole my heart, and of course Sean always thought you were bully special.

"But Teddy . . . well now—I want to make up for all the fun I've missed on him! He's becoming so much of his own little person, isn't he?" Her laughter went up and down the scale as she clapped her hands at Teddy, and he laughed and clapped too.

Beth glanced at Kerry intuitively. This was the moment of truth from which there was no turning back. *Time to bite the bullet,* Beth thought. Bracing herself, she dared to ask, "You've been doing the listening, Kerry, but I can see the wheels turning. What are you thinking?"

"Almost more than I can sort out," she admitted. "It's changed my life to learn you're my birth mother because, unlike most other adopted children, you've always been there. I seem to discover some new insight every day as to what a sacrifice you've made to protect us all from hurt, and the extent of what you've given up for me.

"Ever since I can remember, I've wanted to be like you, Bif. As I grew up, you became the most intriguing woman I've ever known. You're so multi-talented in dancing and the arts and have lived in fascinating places, you attract fascinating people. . . . "

Beth let the tears flow. *It has been worth it all,* she thought.

"I've thought back," Kerry went on, "to my tenth birthday party . . . my wedding . . . the flowers sent to funerals . . . and I've wondered about the Italian Count, the sad and wistful look in his eyes and how he seems to have such a pulse on your life. And I've wondered . . . why? I know Charles admired his art collections and his graciousness at his villa on Lake Como. But there's something mysterious. Something more."

Tears ran down Beth's cheeks again. "And you want to know who he really is. . . . "

"Yes."

"He's your father."

Kerry went to her knees at Beth's feet and flung her arms around her neck.

The dam had burst. The pent-up tension of the deepest secret of all flowed forth. The relief was almost more than Beth could bear, and yet she held her breath, uncertain how Kerry felt about Roberto.

"I've often wondered," Kerry began, "I just couldn't believe how you, of all people, could fall in love with a man so irresponsible you wouldn't even tell him you were going to have his baby. But having met the Count, it makes more sense to me. Oh, Mother, I do understand."

Beth's heart melted in relief.

"I can't imagine calling the Count 'Papa,'" Kerry smiled. "He looks like a movie star, sort of unreal—not a daddy."

Beth couldn't even remember when she'd felt this lighthearted. "But I also see he's a man of integrity." Kerry added thoughtfully. "I'm glad I have something of him, his eyes. But even with all his material possessions, I feel very sad for him. I think he's still in love with you. A man doesn't send flowers like the ones downstairs just because it's Christmas . . . there's another message."

"I believe my granddaughter's a woman of insight," Mum put in. "Surely Roberto wishes he'd never let you go. Would you see him again?"

"Perhaps."

"Would you ever tell him I'm his daughter?" Kerry asked.

"Do you want me to? I've agonized over his right to know."

"Not necessarily," Kerry said slowly. "I feel the same way I did when you first gave me the opportunity to know who my birth father was. Sometimes the entanglement of secrets is beyond unraveling. You've gone a thousand miles past the second mile for me. If I want him to know, I'd like to be the one to tell him. Would that be all right?"

"That's more than fair. And Kerry, I'm a very grateful mother for the woman you have become."

Mum, so reticent to share deep feelings, took Beth's hand, then Kerry's. "And surely, you both must know, though I cannot express things the way the two of you do, I love you and cherish you. And I thank you for your love and understanding of me, with all my heart."

22

Later that afternoon Beth descended the stairs, refreshed from her long, luxurious shower. The roses in the stained-glass window across from the graceful curve of the staircase glowed more beautifully than ever before. They seemed to smile at her, and she smiled back. But she really smiled at Charles, who a misty lifetime ago commissioned her to design it before she knew this was to be her home.

She smiled again. She designed a window, which never ceased to bring her pleasure, but he designed the memory.

The burnished woods of the banister seemed richer, the colours everywhere lovelier, her heart lighter, as her eyes danced about the room. Within the last few hours her whole world had become brighter. The dearest secret under heaven could now be openly shared and doubly treasured with her own mother. She wished everyone could know she had a daughter and grandson. The tightly bound secrets were untangled as far as they could go, but that was enough. She would be eternally grateful.

Even Jimmy's secret, which would have died with her, had been told over and over to the glory of God by Jimmy himself. He led several Bible studies for high schoolers, one in the affluent neighborhood church and the other in the wretched area in the city where he had grown up. He contrasted his pitiful poverty and hopelessness as a young man, who in desperation set out to burglarize Rosehaven, with the riches he found in Jesus. Like the apostle Paul, he boasted, but not of his own success and recognized authority among rosarians. Rather, he boasted of God's love and forgiveness, "whose amazing grace saved even a wretch like me," he told the kids.

"God, You are so good," Beth whispered at the foot of the stairs.

Mum's melodious voice from the sofa trickled into her reverie, returning her to the present and future. "This is ever so lovely, dear, sitting here quietly relishing the new notion of being a real grandmother," she said contentedly. "I simply adore it. But I shall have to ask you to cart me into the city to shop and lavish Kerry and our darling Teddy with sweet surprises!"

"Better yet, Mum, why don't we all three go on a shopping spree? Tillie loves to watch Teddy."

"Super idea, love. And, dear girl," she added with a twinkle in her eye, "I've been thinking I shan't return to London quite as soon as I'd planned, if you don't mind. Too beastly chilly and damp. I feel marvelous here, and I've some catching up to do."

"Oh Mum, I'm delighted! I was afraid you'd go home right away. We'll ring in a new year together. It will be such a comfort for me. I dread the end of January, and the first anniversary of Charles's. . . . ." She didn't finish. Mum had been through it. She knew how hard it sometimes was to say the word—death.

January brought greater acceptance and results of her dreams and plans for Rosehaven Retreat than she had dared even hope for. Bob and Kerry were at first stunned, yet readily remarked that Beth and Charles's benevolence had always seemed without end. The seed of the concept grew in their minds as it had in Beth's. They too would awaken in the middle of the night, making notes to discuss with her. They'd write to Josh with an idea, he'd write back, weaving in embellishments of his own. Sometimes it took weeks in the mail, and Beth continually wished he was nearer. Every letter reminded her how much she missed his humor and strong, comforting arms. "But he's happy," she kept telling herself.

Beth, as controlling stockholder of Townsend Enterprises, held a seat on the board of directors. Since the day Charles died, she had come to share his respect for Richard, who had become president of the firm. His other close associate, Tim, was now vice-president of new project development. Beth knew Charles would be elated with their Christian leadership of the empire he had built.

It was Richard who had personally presented the proposed use and development of Rosehaven to the county planning commission. Then a miracle happened, unheard of among planning commissions—there was no opposition. On the contrary, being fully aware of the Townsends' benevolence, they welcomed the idea of Rosehaven as a retreat center, grateful for the additional prestige it would bring to their wealthy community.

The Board of Supervisors had acted with amazing dispatch. They quickly approved, with notifications of intent sent to surrounding property owners within a designated proximity. Barring opposition, a variation of the code and a site approval would be granted.

Also miraculously, since the estate was so set apart in the sprawling valley, the board found no negative impact on the community, and not one objection was raised. Rather, Beth's altruistic generosity was held in awe. Nonprofit foundations and trusts of this nature were more often designated for ulterior tax ramifications or in wills with no surviving family.

Beth was delighted that she could direct her legacy in her own lifetime. With the permits in process, Beth thought, *Surely this is one more sign of God's seal of approval. It could have taken years—or never happened.*

Several weeks later, Beth observed to her mother, "The weather's unusually warm for the end of January, and I'd like to spend it in Carmel. Could you break away from your grandchild and the baby and go with me?"

"Certainly I'll go with you, love," Mum was enthused. "That would be marvelous. I'll simply ring up Kerry and tell her we're taking a little holiday."

In the quiet of Carmel where Charles had known such contentment, Beth longed to recapture their last stolen moments together, just a year ago. While Mum took an afternoon nap, Beth gazed at the silvery green sea shimmering to the brink of the horizon.

"Charles," she imagined him beside her, "it's because of you, all that you were and did, that this year has been bearable without you.

"How I wish, darling, you could bounce Teddy around like you did Kerry. She's a wonderful mother, Charles, certainly the perfect wife to help Bob in his ministry, which looks so bright. Won't it be exciting to see where God will use them when Bob graduates from seminary? I wish you could read the invitations he's received to pastor young, growing churches. They've contacted the school for its best recommendations, and he's at the top of the list. He so lovingly gives of his time to counsel with people who pour out their hurts to him. I know he'll have an effective ministry.

"And Charles, Bob would be my number-one choice for a resident pastor for Rosehaven Retreat, even though he's young. All ages seem to respect his wisdom because it's right from the Bible and because he's so tender. Charles, I don't think I should directly ask him to do that, though, do you? He may feel too much of an obligation to me, and pass up an opportunity that would be better for him. I'll keep praying about that. I only wish I felt as confident about the other prospects we're considering.

"And Josh—his insight has been so helpful. Rosehaven's board of directors has a wealth of Christian businessmen, but we need a hands-on administrator. You always admired his organizational expertise, and he'd be ideal. Especially with his compassion for people and his gift of counseling. But I couldn't ask him to leave the mission field. Not after he's waited so very long to be there.

"You told me once, darling, sitting right here, that if you died before me, you wanted me to marry again and be happy. But I can't imagine that'll ever be. There's only one man with whom I could ever imagine sharing my life. He's been so precious and I do love him. But he's in love with something besides me." Beth sighed. "You were a love to last forever, dear Charles, and I shall be content with that."

Mum appeared from her nap, still lithe as a ballerina, stretching her trim figure with a yawn. "I say, love, naps are a luxury I've never indulged in until this rather indolent period of my life. They're lovely. May I pop on the kettle for tea? It's nearly four o'clock."

"Splendid, Mum," Beth came out of her thoughts, noticing how very much more British her tones sounded the longer Mum was with her.

Over tea and biscuits, with the wondrous beauty of sea and sky spread before them, Beth basked in how special this time with her mother had been—times she'd longed for in her youth.

They combed the baby boutiques of Carmel where Mum delighted in buying a white bear for Valentine's Day. No wonder—the red heart on its neck said, "I Love My Teddy."

In the evenings, spread on the table before the fire, Beth worked on fine-tuning plans for the Retreat Center with an enthusiasm Mum reluctantly attempted to share.

It was just too vast a concept for her to grasp. And she could never imagine an English man or woman being open enough about their personal problems to seek counseling. Baring one's soul to another seemed a drastic remedy. She tried her best not to be negative, but the two women talked little about it. At the end of the first week of February, Beth announced she had to get back to Rosehaven.

On their return, a letter from Josh was waiting. . . .

New Year's Eve, 1986

Dearest Beth,

Happy New Year! I wish you were here to begin it with me. It's been a year of changes for all of us, and in some ways, it may be easier for me because I'm not there to see the empty places. And thank God, when I close my eyes I don't see Hope's suffering anymore. I didn't realize how much grieving I'd already done, even before she died.

But being far away, what I do realize is how central you've always been, keeping us all together for the past twenty-five years. I miss Kerry and Bob and would love to play with our grandson.

The people, the country, the culture are so strangely different here. Our Christmas and New Year are barely visible. But it's more than being homesick during the holidays, Beth. I miss you with a deep aching in my heart, and I wish you were here. . . .

You probably can't imagine, as I could not, how strange it was to celebrate the holiday season in a basically Buddhist country. By contrast, the miracle birth of our Savior became even more precious. We shared the meaning of Christmas with the new Thai Christians who brought others. Every evening, informal meetings were held at the university. As we told the Christmas story, about ten people each night came to know Jesus. I was deeply touched and thanked God for each one of them. As they came forward, I often wished we could have such response to Christmas in our own country. Isn't it sad we're so focused on the tinsel instead of the real thing?

At the end of the week we were all pretty exhausted. About a dozen of us went to the Duse Thani Hotel, a golden building with lush gardens and a luxurious restaurant. Thai dancers in their traditional silk gowns, long, lacquered fingernails, and hair tied in golden threads were exotically beautiful. I kept wishing you were here. . . .

Please pray for God to show me the next step. My commitment to fill out the Regens' term will be over at the end of the month, and they will be returning. I could stay on. I've felt a fulfilling sense of accomplishment here, yet I'm also pulled to be evangelizing in the States. When I close my eyes I see the faces of lost and hurting people, but they're Americans. And truthfully, I miss my family— and you.

On the other hand, the call of the overseas missionary is to leave dear ones at home and tell the world about Jesus Christ. I keep vacillating, but suspect I shall stay here in Thailand. Only God knows. Would you consider coming to Bangkok?

I'm sorry—how could I forget about Rosehaven Retreat Center? Please keep me informed. Even the name has an inviting ring, and surely God has His hand upon it.

*You are always in my heart and prayers and have my love. Also
my regards to Margaret, Tillie, Cookie, Jimmy, Max, et al. . . .*

Josh

Beth breathed a heavy sigh and put the letter down. As she'd read, she
heard the deep rich tones of his voice, but what was he trying to say? They'd
loved each other as dear friends from the time they'd met, shared the bitter
with the sweet, but were they both now falling in love? She trembled as she
read again, "I miss you . . . wish you were here . . . you have my love . . .
would you come to Bangkok?"

Oh Josh, I miss you too, her heart cried, longing for his nearness. And
yes, only God knew where He wanted this extraordinary man to serve Him.
The need for him right here seemed so obvious to her, but until he saw and
wanted it more than the mission field, more than anything else, it was too
much to ask. "God, give him a clear answer and peace within himself," she
prayed.

Two days before Valentine's Day, dozens of red and white roses were
delivered by Europa Florists, and Beth knew even before reading the card—
they were from Roberto.

An ornate Valentine read, *"Bella Rosa Mia,* will you do me the honor
of having dinner with me in San Francisco, at the Cafe Majestic at eight
o'clock in the evening on February 14? I will be waiting—Roberto."

The very formal, courteous, proper, and absolute audacity of the bold
Italian made her smile. He'd had the good manners to observe a year of her
mourning for Charles. Now he was taking what he obviously perceived to be
the first respectable opportunity to come back into her life. The magnani-
mous flowers at Christmas were certainly a statement that he would not allow
her to forget him. And how like him to choose Valentine's Day! After all, it
began with the Romans, as a festival of romance and affection.

"I will be waiting. . . . " *Oh, Roberto,* she thought, *are you so sure of
yourself that you haven't considered the possibility I won't come? Or so hopeful
that it doesn't matter?* It was an incomprehensible distance for him to travel
on the chance she'd accept. And she had no way to reach him to decline.

His certainty that she would come rankled her. But, she finally decided,
she would have to go. Did this decision evolve out of courtesy, a sense of
obligation, or an acknowledgment that it was merely a matter of time before
she could no longer put him off? Possibly the old fascination drew her to

him. Roberto's maturity would only add to his glamor. Beth pictured him aging with style and grace, but no less persistent.

She thought, *Thank God, I'm not the same naive young girl I was at the Beaux Arts, or I might still not trust myself.* She knew she must see him, once and for all. Max would drive her in, she'd spend the night at the Towers suite, and take care of business downtown on the fifteenth.

Other thoughts jarred her. What if Roberto had more on his mind than merely a dinner date? Did he truly want to come back into her life? Exactly what did he hope for? Or had he suspected the truth and now burned to know if Kerry was his daughter?

This last question was her conscience speaking. It twisted and churned in her mind. Roberto deserved to know. She wrestled with the agreement she'd made with Kerry, though, and came to the conclusion that it wasn't her decision. But if Kerry consented, Roberto would have the most memorable February 14 of his life.

The restaurant in the Majestic Hotel, one of San Francisco's most exclusive and elegant, appeared especially romantic on this Valentine's evening. Candlelight bathed the walls in a soft glow as the maitre d' led the way to a discreet corner.

Roberto, waiting at an intimate table, stood when he saw Beth. His magnetic dark eyes swept over her appreciatively, as they had the first time he saw her on the sidewalk in Paris. Her shining black hair, falling loosely to her shoulders, shone with silvery strands on a black velvet dinner dress of conservative cut, with a crystal-encrusted white lace collar. The sway of pendulous diamond and pearl earrings caught the motion of her slim, graceful body gliding toward him.

Roberto wore an exquisitely tailored black suit, creamy silk shirt, deep red tie. All the distinguishing marks of the most elegant gentleman imaginable. Beth's heart skipped a beat as he took her hand in his and kissed it, in true Roberto fashion.

"*Bella Rosa Mia, buona sera. Si,* you are more bee-u-tiful than ever before. You make me the happiest man in the world. You did not disappoint Roberto. *Grazie.* "

She saw in his eyes that nothing existed but her. Everything else had blurred into oblivion since the moment she appeared. Still holding her hand, he again brushed its softness with his lips.

Suddenly he became aware that another beautiful woman, with eyes of deep brown velvet like his own, stood quietly to the side. Beth inwardly cringed at his expression of betrayal. His eyes darted between them to the romantically set table for two. Clearly, he was momentarily at a loss for words.

"The roses are gorgeous, Roberto, thank you. And I found your invitation quite irresistible," she smiled. Pulling back her hand, she gestured, "You've always been so extremely kind to Kerry. I invited her to come with me so you two could become acquainted."

Obviously he was stunned, but also delighted that Beth came at all. Like the gentleman he was, he graciously bowed to Kerry. *"Grazie, signora.* It is my pleasure to have two most lovely ladies to dine with. Your husband . . . you could not be with him on this night for lovers?"

"No, I'm afraid he had classes. We'll have to have our romantic evening some other time," she smiled.

Beth shifted the conversation back to Roberto as he seated them. "I was fascinated with *Architectural Digest's* article on Villa Cabriollini last October. Tell me about the paintings it mentioned in the estate collection of rare antiquities you recently purchased."

The tuxedoed waiter deftly began serving the epicurean starter courses Roberto had ordered.

"A toast to being together once again." He raised his glass and flashed a winsome smile. "We will speak of art later, *per favore.* I am interested only in you, *Bella Rosa.* It is so long ago that I looked into your eyes, bluer than the waters of Lake Como, across a dinner table. If you had not come, Roberto's heart would surely break."

For a moment Beth's careful determination wavered. Perhaps it was outrageously foolish to have brought Kerry along as a third party for the romantic evening he'd so carefully arranged. She immediately regretted being there. Then she took a firmer grip on her feelings. *You're not a schoolgirl anymore,* she reassured herself, and adroitly directed the dialogue back to the Villa.

Roberto acquiesced, entertaining them throughout each course of the lavish dinner. Ever the raconteur, he exaggerated the humorous antics of museum curators and other such unpredictable creatures, but never made light of the integrity of the art or artist. Kerry laughed until she cried at his fascinating tales. Beth eventually relaxed, but at the same time wondered how they would ultimately steer the conversation to their purpose.

"Roberto, this has truly been a delightful evening," Beth smiled over their cups of espresso.

"The night is still young," he smiled, very sure of himself.

From behind the flowers encircling the candle, he withdrew a box wrapped in gold foil with a red satin bow, and placed it before Beth. "For you, *Bella Rosa Mia,*" he smiled.

She eyed him nervously. "You are always so extravagantly thoughtful, Roberto. Whatever you've done, you shouldn't have." Her scolding was gentle, but never more sincere.

"Open it, you will see," he smiled.

She opened an aged black velvet box. An antique Venetian brooch, a tracery of gold filigree set with amethysts, pearls and diamonds, shimmered with the glow of the candle. Beth blinked, astonished. She couldn't possibly accept such a gift from him but could think of nothing to say at that moment, except, "This is truly the most beautiful brooch I have ever seen."

"It has a special story." He smiled with love shining in his eyes.

"Please tell me then," she said softly, setting the box aside.

"In a moment. First I must tell you what is in my heart." It didn't seem to matter that they weren't alone. He proceeded as though Kerry weren't there. He'd permit nothing or no one to alter his course.

"Many years ago, I tell you Roberto does not wish to fall in love, because love ruins everything. Remember, *Cara Mia?*"

Beth nodded with misty eyes.

"I tell you too that you are the only woman I could ever fall in love with. Beautiful, *si,* but also intelligent, and good. You are a woman of rare quality. And always since then, it is true. My love for you burns in my heart, Roberto's only true love. I also called you 'little fool.' But I am the fool, to ever let you go."

Tears glistened in his eyes. "The villa of my father's, the wealth, the honor, Count this and Count that, everyone trying to impress me—the Count. *Si,* I am the fool. It is all nothing. I have only what one can buy with money. Things. No children, and I would not have known how to be a father. No family. No one who loves Roberto, for Roberto. You are a beautiful woman because your heart is beautiful. It shines from inside of you.

"Charles Townsend, he was a great man, also one of much money, but I saw he knew how to love a woman like you. But he is gone, and I am so sorry."

Beth's heart went out to Roberto. He was truly a lonely man. "Now, I tell you the story of the brooch," Roberto smiled his enchanting smile. "It is in the personal collection of my father, which with his own hands he gives to me before he dies. He says to me, 'Give this only to the woman who is your wife, and be certain that it is inherited only by the wife of your first son, and so on.'

"It is very rare, very special. *Cara Mia,* Beth, I have foolishly squandered too many years without true love." He took her hand across the table, pleading, "I love you, and desire with all my heart for you to be my wife."

Beth swallowed the lump in her throat and grasped for words, grateful for the dim lighting.

"Roberto, dear Roberto." *God, help me to be gentle, to make him understand my heart, too,* she silently prayed. "You have never been out of my heart. You were my first love, but I was unprepared for life beyond the unrealistic romance of art and ballet. Please realize, you were the older, wiser man, the accomplished artist, my mentor, and we had such lovely times together. In a sense you were as naive as I, for how could you have known how sheltered, how totally inexperienced I was in the ways of life?

"But Roberto, I've discovered a truth far more important than the ways of the world. Charles came to know the shared reality of that truth with me. And that is, there's a love and forgiveness of all our mistakes, beyond our comprehension—the love of God through His Son, Jesus Christ. I hope that's the light you see within me.

"I love and treasure you in a very special way, but I can't return the love you hoped for. I cannot be your wife. I pray for your understanding. . . . "

Lines of anguish furrowed his brow. "You break my heart after all, *Bella Rosa Mia,*" he lamented. "But come to Lake Como with me, many rooms will be yours. I will be the perfect gentleman. Do not worry. We will begin again . . . " he added hopefully.

"Roberto," she smiled tenderly. "I cannot do that. Our lives remain worlds apart. But, please, know you are forever dear to my heart. Yet for a reason you've never known." She turned toward her daughter.

His dark eyes searched Kerry's. *"Che significa questo?"* He looked confused. *"Scusi,* I'm sorry. . . . What does she mean?"

Kerry reached out to touch his hand, "It means, Roberto, that at last it is time to share a secret with you. Beth is my mother, and you—you are my father."

Roberto looked at her incredulously. After a moment he picked up her hand, pressing it to his lips, then his cheek, as though he could not let it go. Tears glistened in his eyes.

"And all these years you cannot tell me because of what I say so long ago, *si?*" Roberto asked sadly. "I have looked at your eyes, and wondered, but always I am afraid to ask. My father, he was not a papa. He was occupied being a Count, an art connoisseur. I know nothing of being a papa. I have missed so much. Is it too late for me to try?"

"Not at all." Kerry leaned over and kissed his cheek. His repentent honesty had won her heart while his elegance melted into the shape of a daddy's yearning for his child to climb upon his lap.

"Someday you shall meet your grandson," Kerry said quietly. "His name is Teddy, and he could call you Papa, if you like."

"Oh, *si,* I like!" he beamed. "Tomorrow I have meeting and lunch in New York, and in two days, London. But soon, we must play—I think you say—'catch up,' *si?*"

In the next moments they were standing, and he reached out to Beth, then Kerry, for a parting embrace. Kissing Beth upon the cheek, he said, *"Bella Rosa,* I wished upon a star for a different answer tonight, but you . . . and our daughter . . . and to know I have a grandson, put new meaning to life in my heart. *Grazie,"* he said softly.

They left the almost empty restaurant together. Max sat waiting at the curb. In the lobby Roberto again brushed their cheeks with his lips. *"Arrivederci."*

"Arrivederci, Roberto," Beth said, freely returning the affectionate gesture, with no concern now of being misunderstood.

In the privacy of the Tower suite, Beth sighed wistfully. "He's quite a man, isn't he?" Yet she knew with all her heart she'd made the right decision.

"Roberto's a deeper, more sensitive person than I'd ever imagined," Kerry said. "I'm glad I decided to know who my real father is. I think, deep down, it's something every adopted child hungers for. And I think he really does care about me."

Beth was silent, immersed in a sense of tranquil relief. "But Mother," Kerry went on, "I've wanted to say this for a long time. I hope you will marry again, and I wish it could be Josh."

Beth look startled. "Really? You've thought about that? The first time I even heard that wonderful voice of his on the phone I easily understood how my best friend could fall in love with him. He's been so dear to me, but our lives just don't seem to fit together."

She drew Kerry close and kissed her forehead. "This is when I feel so blessed to have my daughter be my best friend." They talked until the clock struck 2:00 A.M.

"Honey, I'm exhausted. Aren't you?" Beth asked. "I think we've had enough emotion for one night. Sleep well, dear."

Tomorrow, there would be more documents to sign and the interview with the press. And the day after, the bomb would explode among high society when the papers hit the streets with the announcement about Rose-haven.

And now that day was here. At last, Beth's thoughts had come full circle. It seemed a lifetime ago, rather than just that morning, when she had welcomed the dawn in her bedroom alcove above the rose garden.

Leisurely, she'd wandered through every significant period that brought her to this moment. And only this morning she'd wondered if she'd have the courage to go back and live it again, endure the secrets only God and the roses had shared for so many years.

After today there would be no time to sift through the memories in the lace-covered box, to let go of the past, to end an era, slowly and gently as she'd done today. Rosehaven was more than stone and mortar, magnificent furnishings and gardens. It symbolized her whole life—a life of quality music, ballet, art. To possess the finest things was never her ambition, God just gave them to her. To be the best daughter, dancer, artist, mother, wife, friend, to be a person skilled in the art of living with a worthy purpose, and to give back in appreciation for all she'd been given—those had been her goals. She and Charles had shared this way of life together.

It would be too cruel for her to tear herself from it without first tucking away its precious moments, carefully, as one stores delicate crystal.

Charles, in his wisdom from Ecclesiastes, had often said that living only for material things is like chasing the wind—it doesn't satisfy. Great wealth could purpose great things. And she was very satisfied with Rosehaven's future. "Thank You, God," Beth said aloud. "I pray that troubled lives will lovingly be pruned back to fresh growth, and bud and bloom because of this place. And, Lord, if they have secrets to share with You and the roses, may they be easier to bear than my own."

In the cool of the morning she'd wound along the paths of the gardens, sought the shade of the friendly trees at midday, and now as the last ray of a pearl pink sunset faded, she whispered toward heaven, "God—life is fragile, but love is stronger than steel. Most of the ones I've loved who promised to be there always seem to go away or die. You are forever. As long as I keep my eyes on You, every good thing is possible!"

The long shadows melted into dusk, still she lingered with her thoughts. She'd stay here, hold the reins until the administrator and resident pastor couple were found, and as soon as the initial organizational wheels were running smoothly, she'd slip away.

She felt liberated—no longer expected to be the belle of the ball. She could lay down the burden of living life on high society's pedestal. Perhaps she'd live in the Tower suite for a time. Then find a home above the Bay, up by Coit Tower maybe, and paint, and work at the New Hope Center in the city, serve on the Rosehaven Board. "I've a full life ahead of me. Thank You again, God," she whispered.

The first star twinkled.

"Thank you too, dear Charles." Her last thought, a swirl of joy and sadness, centered on Josh, with a new awareness of her even deeper love for him since they'd been apart. She wished he could be with her now, to begin this new adventure. "Please bless him, Father, in that foreign land."

Beth walked briskly now toward the house in the chill evening breeze, startled at the welcoming lights glowing from the windows. Kerry and Teddy must have brought Mum home from her day with them.

She heard Bob's laughter, and "Shhh, here she comes."

"What's happening?" Beth called out, delighted to have her family about as she stepped out of the past.

Bob swept her up in a crushing hug. "Surprises!" He beamed. "Sit down. We've something important to tell you."

Teddy, half toddled, half crawled to greet her. "Come to Gammy Beth," she whispered. "All right, I've got my baby now. What's up?"

With mock seriousness, Bob cleared his throat, "Mrs. Townsend, I have a report to you, as founder, from the special meeting held by the other members of the board of directors of Rosehaven Retreat Center. Since all of you have reviewed the applicants for the position of Resident Pastor and Lay Counseling Coordinator, and found none upon whom all can agree, they have vetoed your objections to seek who—in their opinion—is the highest qualified. That candidate is eager to take this responsibility. I have been given the honor of informing you that Mr. Robert C. Daniels has accepted their unanimous appointment!"

"Oh, Bob!" she jumped up with Teddy still in her arms, tears flowing down her cheeks. She handed Teddy to Mum and cried, "You were always my number-one choice, but I wanted you to be absolutely certain it's what's best for you. You're sure?"

Kerry hugged her mother. "It's an answer to prayer for all of us. And I come with the package too. I'd love to offer Bible studies."

Beth felt choked with joy.

Bob interrupted, trying to look serious again. "There are, however, a few conditions."

Beth's smile faded. "What are they?"

"First, I wish to work with a certain individual who has my personal recommendation to be the administrator, as well as the unanimous vote of the other members of the board. I'd like you to meet with him."

"Of course. I'll do that as soon as it's convenient for you both," Beth answered, somewhat puzzled by his suppressed grin.

"He's waiting to see you in the library."

"Now?" she gasped. "I'm not presentable to be meeting an administrator, in jeans and this old sweater. And my eyes are all bleary!"

"Now," Bob was firm. "But I warn you, he has a condition of his own."

Smoothing her hair, Beth gingerly opened the library door. She stood stock still for what must have been a full minute before she screamed and flung her arms out.

"Josh!" She ran to him. "Oh, Josh, is it really you?" she cried.

He enfolded her in his great strong arms, holding her close against his massive chest. She choked back the tears, struggling to find words. "You're home. Is it true, you're going to be the administrator? You're giving up the mission field?"

"Yes, dear Beth. I'm home where I know I belong, with you and our family. I've loved you too long," he whispered softly into her hair. "We've shared too many of life's joys and sorrows to be on opposite sides of the world."

Looking into her eyes, he said, "I've always cherished you as a wonderful woman, but I hope you've read in my letters that my love has grown far deeper than friendship. I was afraid to even think we had a life together. I visualized dozens of wealthy men at your feet. But I love you with all my heart. I'm asking you to be my wife."

Beth's tears streamed down her cheeks as she looked up at him with a radiant smile.

"I guess I had to go to Thailand to discover what I'm meant to do in this season of our lives. I think we'd be a terrific team with the work at Rosehaven."

"And you really are the administrator I came in here to meet?"

"Only if you agree with Bob and the board of directors," he smiled. "They seem to think I'm the best qualified. At this moment I'm more interested in knowing if I qualify as a husband." He kissed her cheek. "I got so excited writing back and forth with you and Bob and Kerry, I couldn't stand to be left out. But Bob said you'd never ask me to leave the mission field, so he put me in touch with the board. And here I am!"

"Bob said you'd accept on one condition. What is it?"

"That we'll work side by side, breathe new purpose into Rosehaven, together."

Beth's eyes sparkled as he held her close, then he tilted her chin to look into their blue depths for an answer. Overwhelmed, she wondered if this was merely a ribbon of illusion tying her unspoken dreams together. But his lips upon hers were fervently sweet, real. She knew she loved him with her whole being. With a new love only God could have given her.

Tenderly he repeated, "Beth, will you marry me? Do you accept my condition?"

"I do—with all my heart."

The secrets of all the years had come together for good, beyond all she could ever ask or hope for. Yes, truly this was the end of an era—and the beginning of another.

About the Author

Lila Peiffer is a native Southern Californian. She and her husband, Rick, own and operate Bluebelle House Bed & Breakfast in the resort community of Lake Arrowhead. They retired from corporate life in 1983, where she wrote a publication for the firm for over twelve years. She has served in church leadership throughout her life, leads a weekly women's Bible study, and is also a public speaker.

Lila's love for travel and her background in interior design add richness to her writing, as does her love for family. She and Rick have four married children and eight grandchildren.

The Secrets of the Roses is her first novel.

Beth's Story Continues . . . Lila Peiffer's Sequel to *The Secrets of the Roses*

Rose-haven

A NOVEL

Brave, beautiful Elizabeth Townsend Sterling has rebuilt her life. Two years after the death of her first husband, Beth plans to open her magnificent mansion, Rosehaven, to the wounded and hurting.

But complications could postpone the opening of Rosehaven Retreat Center. And when it opens, how will it affect Beth's family? Will rich, spoiled Shelby Fairchild Harding recover from her attempted suicide? Does Roberto, Beth's first love, still harbor a secret passion? And will Beth find deeper faith as she faces another loss?

Rosehaven is the sequel to *The Secrets of the Roses*, continuing the stories of Beth, her daughter Kerry, and the men they love. An adult romance in the tradition of *The Shell Seekers, Rosehaven* follows wealthy Christians through tragedy and life's challenges.

From *Rosehaven*. . .

Awakened by a chorus of birds chirping across the sloping alpine meadows, Beth smiled at Josh, who reminded her of a sleeping giant, lying beside her. How could she ever have imagined, when they first met over twenty-five years ago, that they'd be here, today, together—honeymooning in Switzerland? Joy washed over her at the wonder of it all. . . .

Moving to the window, she saw the rugged majesty of the glacier towering almost straight up from the serenity of the valley to the pristine blue sky above the little chalet in Grindelwald. It was a storybook scene. If Heidi and Grandfather appeared up on the high meadow to the right, it would not have surprised Beth.

On tiptoe she slipped back under the puffy, down-filled duvet to savor the awesome view and snuggle against the warmth of her husband of three days.

Beth savored the luxurious reprieve from the plans, agendas, and names yet without faces that would soon enough consume their lives. They'd spent months focused on the complex details of transforming Rosehaven, the magnificent estate her beloved husband, Charles Townsend, had built for her as a bride. Perhaps the most brilliant achievement in the wealthy architect/entreprenuer's career had been his own home. The 30,000-square-foot mansion and its sixteen acres of grounds, rather than remain the center of San Francisco's elite benefit balls and garden parties, would soon open as Rosehaven Retreat Center.

Her whole world had changed when Charles died. Josh's did also when his wife Hope, Beth's precious friend since childhood, succumbed after years with cancer. The four of them had been close friends. She felt Charles and Hope were smiling at them from heaven, glad for their happiness and the purposeful new future for Rosehaven.

Psychological counseling and therapy in the '80s had become more than the "in" thing. People now searched in desperation for their "identity," to "get in touch with themselves," and find hope and solutions for dysfunctional families.

But the desire of Beth's heart reached deeper than this. Rosehaven would provide a Christ-centered refuge that offered opportunity to get in touch with God. And Josh would be beside her—just as he was now.

Beth pushed Rosehaven out of her thoughts. Josh and this moment mattered—nothing else. She gazed adoringly at her sleeping husband. She felt whole again, knit together with him as husband and wife. And it seemed as amazing a mystery of God as the grandeur of the Alps, framed like a painting by the window.

Beth's eyes misted at the incredible beauty. *Lord, it's too wonderful,* she thought, *that You, who created such magnificence, could also be mindful of me. Thank You for the husband You have given me.*

Josh threw a strong arm around her and drew her closer to his lean but massive body, peeking with half an eye. "Mm," he nuzzled sleepily, "please tell me I'm not dreaming. I haven't died and gone to heaven, have I?"

Awake now, propped on his elbow, he searched her violet-blue eyes, curling tendrils of a silver streak in her black hair around his fingers. "Aren't you glad we did this?"

"Glad we're married?" she teased, "or that we're here?"

He smiled, kissing her brow. "I mean, aren't you glad we listened to our family's persuasion and made a honeymoon trip out of my meeting in Geneva? We need this time for just the two of us."

Long moments passed. Josh gently kissed her lips. "You're staring at me," he smiled.

"I couldn't help thinking . . . we've shared so much of life together; our dreams, joys, and sorrows. We've laughed, cried, encouraged, consoled, and held each other up when no one else could begin to comprehend the depths of our needs. I'm happy I have you so completely now."

Josh cupped her face between his hands, "I can't even begin to put my feelings into words. I want to hold you, forever."

Beth had first loved Josh in a totally different way, since the first day she'd met him as Hope's husband. They'd married in San Francisco while Beth was living in London, studying ballet, just before she'd stunned her parents by announcing her desire to go to Paris to study art.

Beth pictured Josh as the young missionary pilot, a graduate from San Jose State, beside Hope, who worked with terminally ill children at Stanford's Medical Center. In their first year of marriage, they discovered Hope had cancer. Surgery followed, and with it the inability to have children.

Everyone loved Josh. A cheerful giant of a man, who looked younger than his fifty-three years. Laugh lines radiated around his warm brown eyes, and the only gray in his cinnamon-colored hair was sprinkled through like sugar. But his perpetually jovial smile and kindness of heart drew people to him.

They had both been lying quietly, dreaming with open eyes. "What are you thinking?" he asked, brushing her cheek with his lips.

"Just how much I love you, Josh," she breathed, slightly above a whisper. "This moment seems exquisitely fragile. I'm afraid it might explode in my hand like delicate crystal."

The love of her life had been snatched cruelly, suddenly, from her almost two years before by a massive heart attack. Josh had long ago set aside his own natural desires, robbed by the ravages of Hope's cancer.

"Surely life itself is fragile," he agreed. "But look at that rugged mountain. It just stands there, in all its majesty, eternally secure."

"Mm-hmm," she sighed, "it's like an ageless sentinel, appointed to restrict us from plunging too rapidly into the days ahead."

"So do you think that big ole mountain is trying to tell us something?" he smiled.

"I do. I hear a Voice saying, *Be still, and know that I am God.*"

"So do I . . . and in the next breath it's shouting, *put the rest of the world on hold.* Beth, this time belongs to us alone." They snuggled closer and dozed off again. She felt him slip out of bed a little later, but she burrowed deeper, savoring all the reasons why she loved him. . . .